FIENDS OF THE RISING SUN

THE SINISTER INVOLVEMENT of Japanese vampyr in the Pacific war is finally revealed! From the dramatic build-up to the devastating attack upon Pearl Harbour, to the American troops landing at Guadalcanal eight months later, follow the story of the US Marines as they battle against an enemy that would rather die than admit defeat. But in this war, death is where the hell truly begins...

FIENDS OF THE RISING SUN

DAVID BISHOP

BLACK FLAME

To Alison, for all her love and support.

Historical note:

This novel is a work of fiction set during the Second World War. As far as possible the historical details are accurate, but the story takes liberties with reality for narrative effect.

A Black Flame Publication
www.blackflame.com

First published in 2007 by BL Publishing, Games Workshop Ltd., Willow Road, Nottingham NG7 2WS, UK.

Distributed in the US by Simon & Schuster, 1230 Avenue of the Americas, New York, NY 10020, USA.

10 9 8 7 6 5 4 3 2 1

ISBN 13: 978 1 84416 494 3
ISBN 10: 1 84416 494 2

A CIP record for this book is available from the British Library.

PROLOGUE: September, 1940

"When he gets to Heaven,
To Saint Peter he'll tell,
Another marine reporting, sir,
I've served my time in Hell."
Anonymous

ADOLF HITLER SMILED. In little more than a year his Wehrmacht forces had stormed across Europe, using their lightning war tactics to sweep aside all who dared oppose the might of Germany. True, his plans to invade Britain had been postponed temporarily, but the Luftwaffe would soon pound Churchill and his stubborn nation of shopkeepers into submission. Stalin and the Bolsheviks remained yoked by a non-aggression pact, keeping Russian forces away from the battlefield. All of mainland Europe was under the Führer's control, just as it should be. Yes, he had good reason to smile, as all those around him knew well, and today's gathering only reinforced that.

Hitler sat at a long polished table inside the Chancellery, in the heart of Berlin. To his right sat two men he considered his inferiors. The closest of the pair was Benito Mussolini, Italy's fascist dictator. Mussolini was dressed in his typically elaborate and

self-aggrandising military garb, his barrel chest dripping with large, gaudy medals. Intelligence reports
suggested the man known as Il Duce had to wear a
whalebone corset beneath his uniform to conceal
his increasing corpulence. Hitler considered Mussolini to be a vainglorious and troublesome ally. Il
Duce's bulging waistline was a symptom of his bur-
geoning decadence, but the Italian forces still had
their uses, however limited they might soon
become.

Beyond Mussolini sat Saburo Kurusu, the
Japanese ambassador to Berlin. As with so many
Japanese diplomats, he dressed like an undertaker
in a black tailcoat and grey trousers. His dark hair
was slicked back close to the scalp, while a small
moustache perched above a weak mouth. Kurusu
wore glasses in public, a sign of weakness as far as
Hitler was concerned. Never advertise your flaws,
never let anyone see them; it gave others a reason to
believe they were better than you. Kurusu was weak
and timid, a willing puppet of the Japanese government. But a more powerful representative of that
nation was elsewhere in the room; General Tojo was
Japan's war minister for the moment, but the Führer
had little doubt that he would soon be second only
to the emperor in Japan's power structure. For now,
official protocol required that Kurusu sign the agreement that would bind Germany, Italy and Japan
together in a new axis of power.

Hitler put pen to paper, scribbling his name across
the Tripartite Pact. The three signatories exchanged
their copies of the document and continued the
signing ritual, finalising an agreement forged

through long and tense negotiations. The wording of the accord carried little importance for the Führer. For example, by signing the pact Japan accepted the hegemony of Germany and Italy in Europe, something few would dispute. In return the two European nations recognised Japan's right to organise what it called the Greater East-Asia Co-prosperity Sphere. In reality, the sphere was a metaphor for Japan's efforts to steal natural resources from neighbouring countries. Fine, let the Orientals do what they wanted in their own lands, Hitler decided. Japan had already been fighting a war in China for three years, so the land of the rising sun posed no threat to his grasp on Europe. More important was the fact that all three nations promised to maintain the status quo in their relations with the Soviet Union; that kept Stalin and his comrades in check, outside the fighting.

One statement in the pact was of interest to the Führer. Japan, Germany and Italy pledged to aide one another with all political, military and economic means available should any of them be attacked by a power not involved in the European war. Put simply, the statement was a warning shot at the United States of America. Eleven days ago, the US Senate had passed a bill introducing conscription for all citizens aged between 21 and 35. For a neutral country, it was a provocative act. The Tripartite Pact's message to President Roosevelt was clear: stay out of Europe and the United States of America would stay out of trouble.

While the final signatures were drying on the documents, Ambassador Kurusu was giving a long, hesitant speech about the historic significance of this unprecedented alliance. Hitler's thoughts were elsewhere, his eyes focused on one of the foreign dignitaries present at the signing ceremony. A lone figure with a haughty face and piercing eyes stood at the back of the chamber, making sure his likeness wasn't captured by any of the official photographers. Curious, the Führer thought. Most of the inconsequential delegates were only too eager to thrust themselves into the spotlight, but the man at the back did no such thing.

Hitler beckoned one of his men close enough to whisper a question in his ear. "That dignitary at the rear, in the blue uniform, who is he?"

"Lord Constanta, from the Rumanian province of Transylvania."

The Führer smiled. "Ah! I have heard of this individual, but doubted I would have the chance to meet him. Make sure he remains behind when the other observers depart."

"Of course, Führer."

Hitler watched as his messenger moved unnoticed through the throng to Constanta. The pair exchanged a few words before the Rumanian nodded his acceptance of the Führer's continued hospitality. The hint of a smile played about Constanta's lips, as if he had been expecting the invitation. No matter, Hitler decided. The Führer had listened to endless litanies from his deputy, Heinrich Himmler, about the rare power wielded by this Rumanian aristocrat. Now Hitler would have the chance to meet Constanta and judge for himself whether the man from Transylvania was as important as his reputation suggested.

Himmler believed having Constanta and his people fighting alongside the Wehrmacht against their mutual enemies could shorten the war by months, even years. Let's see if my deputy is correct, Hitler decided.

CHAMPAGNE WAS SERVED at a reception after the signing ceremony, but Hitler permitted himself only a glass of fruit juice. Let others indulge their vices and frailties; he preferred to keep his thoughts clear of all such impediments. When Constanta was brought forward to meet him, the Führer noted that his guest had also foregone offers of alcohol. Good. Hitler found it hard to trust any man whose will might be held in thrall by drink. "Lord Constanta, I presume?"

The Rumanian bowed low, his eyes humbly cast downwards. Better and better, thought the Führer. This man knows his place, unlike that drunken, belligerent buffoon Mussolini. Il Duce had the manners of a pig and the tastes of a philistine.

"Thank you for inviting me to remain behind," Constanta said in impeccable German, no trace of an accent audible in his words. "You do me a great honour."

"Not at all," Hitler replied, allowing himself a brief smile. "My Reichsführer has frequently made mention of you, and the rare abilities you possess. Himmler tells me you and your people would make valuable allies for my Wehrmacht."

"Again, your words honour me," Constanta said, nodding his thanks for the compliment. "Alas, Rumania is not yet part of your Axis forces."

"That day may not be so far away."

Constanta smiled, flashing his pronounced canine teeth at the Führer. "I'm glad to hear it. I cannot speak for all of Rumania, but the people of Transylvania are eager to spread their wings and become part of a larger empire, one that spans all parts of Europe, and lands even beyond this continent, perhaps."

"Of course," Hitler agreed. "My deputy indicated you had particular talents that would be a considerable asset to the Reich, but he remained rather vague about what those talents might be. Would you offer me a demonstration?"

The Rumanian's eyes narrowed. "Willingly, but it would be better if it took place under the gaze of a more discreet audience." His eyes glanced sideways to the boorish Mussolini, who was laughing loudly at one of his own jokes and slapping the back of an uncomfortable Ambassador Kurusu.

"Naturally," the Führer said. "What will you require for this demonstration?"

Constanta grinned. "A victim."

GUIDO FIORAVANTI WAS a minor functionary within Il Duce's travelling entourage. He had few illusions about his importance in the world, nor any belief that his status and rank within Mussolini's party would change soon. Guido helped the leader of all Italy dress each morning, but doubted Il Duce could recall his name. It did not matter, for Guido was devoted to his master. He loved the dictator, the flamboyant and outrageous politician. Il Duce was a true leader of men, capable of swaying people with the strength of his oratory, and able to put fire in the bellies of the most craven cowards. Guido had wept tears of joy upon first hearing Mussolini speak to the people of Italy, so swept up had he been in the power of those words.

It was Guido's job to travel everywhere with the great dictator and make sure Il Duce always looked his best. Others might write the words Mussolini spoke, some might negotiate on the great man's behalf, but it fell to little Guido Fioravanti to have the last word before Mussolini stepped out into the public gaze. He was the one who adjusted the shape of Mussolini's jacket, who ensured the dictator looked his best, who pulled the stays of Mussolini's corset tight to keep Il Duce's gut in check. Like his people, the Italian dictator loved his food, a fact that made Guido's tasks increasingly difficult. While others slept, Guido stayed up until dawn, secretly letting out the seams of jackets and trousers, making sure Il Duce kept his dignity, even if he couldn't keep to his diet.

Guido was happy to linger in the background at official ceremonies like the signing of the Tripartite Pact, ready to be called upon at a moment's notice if required. His presence was not strictly necessary, but he liked to be there, just in case. The one time in the past five years he'd taken a day off – to attend the funeral of his beloved mother at Cortona – Mussolini had split a pair of trousers and was left screaming at his staff, wondering why there was nobody present to make the invisible repairs. After that Guido had forbidden himself ever to leave Il Duce's side again. They needed each other, in their own ways.

"Excuse me, is your name Fioravanti?" a voice asked in impeccable Italian.

Guido turned to find he was being addressed by a tall, austere man in a handsomely cut, blue uniform. The speaker had a thin face with piercing eyes, the pupils dark as night. Fioravanti found himself staring into those eyes, drawn towards them, quite unable to resist the pull of those bleak, malevolent pupils. "Yes?"

"I understand you're Il Duce's dresser?" the stranger continued.

"Master of the Wardrobe," Guido replied, instinctively reciting the rather grand title he'd bestowed upon himself.

"Quite." The stranger gestured towards a nearby doorway. "The Führer asked if you would come with me, to participate in a demonstration."

Guido didn't understand. "Demonstration?"

"The Führer was admiring the cut of your leader's jacket and wondered if you might be persuaded to show his tailors how you achieve such finesse."

"I would be honoured, of course, but I should like to check with–"

The stranger stepped sideways, putting himself between Guido and the rest of the room. "We had a word with a senior official from the Italian delegation and he said you could be spared for an hour." He moved closer to Guido. "You would be doing the Führer a great service if you agreed."

Guido could feel those dark eyes boring into him, as if they were scouring his soul, searching for any sign of resistance and crushing it. He wanted to say no, that his place was at Il Duce's side, but his lips mumbled yes. "The honour would be all mine," he heard himself reply.

"Excellent. If you'll follow me?" The stranger strode out through the door and Guido trotted meekly after him, hurrying to keep pace with his escort's lengthy gait. They moved quickly through corridor after corridor, until the little dresser had lost all track of where they were or where they'd come from. Hopefully, one of the German tailors would help him find the way back.

After passing through a dizzying number of doorways the two men reached a spiral staircase, and hurried down the wrought iron steps, descending into the bowels of the Chancellery building. When Guido thought they could go no further without descending into hell itself, the staircase came to an end, terminating in a dimly lit corridor. His guide strode briskly onwards into the darkness, while Guido paused to look back up the steps. He could see no other souls, nobody around who might help reunite him with the rest of Mussolini's entourage. The dresser felt a cold shiver run up his spine at the idea of getting lost down here. It didn't bear thinking about. He thrust his hands into his waistcoat pockets, seeking the two things most familiar to him in the world: his rosary beads and his measuring tape. The nimble fingers of his right hand worked the beads while his left hand clutched the cold metal clasp on the end of the measuring tape. With these in his grasp, Guido had always felt nothing could harm him – until today.

"Hello?" he called out, his words trembling at the edge. "Is anyone there?"

This way, a cold voice crept into his mind.

Guido wanted to run back up the stairs, but found himself walking away from them instead, his feet involuntarily taking him into the darkness. *Closer*, the voice whispered in his thoughts, its sibilance grating and grinding at his will. Guido's body jerked and twitched, trying to fight against the force impelling him into the blackness, but the dresser was quite unable to resist. He stumbled on in the shadows, unable to see where he was going, his other senses just as useless.

Finally he saw a door in the distance. *Quicker*, the hissing voice snarled, and Guido's legs responded, taking him ever closer to the rectangle of light ahead. Beyond it he could see nothing but pure white. What was happening to him? Was this all some terrible dream? Yes, that must be it, he had fallen asleep and this was the nightmare that troubled his slumbering. Guido willed himself to wake, but to no avail. Even his fingers holding the rosary were beyond his control, unable to move from one bead to the next, denying him the reassurance of the holy catechism. He wanted to pray, but something, some force, stopped him. *Forget the Nazarene*, the voice whispered in Guido's mind. *He has forgotten you. He has left you in my power, little man.*

Guido stepped through the doorway into a cold concrete bunker, its grey cement walls and floor made brilliant by blazing white lights overhead. The dresser could see a hole, high up on one wall, an opening. Beyond that, he could make out the silhouette of somebody watching him, a lone figure with its arms folded.

"Begin the demonstration." The words drifted down to Guido from above, the voice that of the Führer. The dresser wanted to reply, wanted to say there must be some mistake, but he couldn't speak. Words caught in his throat, trapped in vocal chords tightened by terror.

He was aware of a presence in the room with him. A low, translucent mist floated above the floor. No, not floated, hovered. How was that possible? That question was forgotten as the mist coalesced, forming itself into a distinct shape. The mist became a pallid silhouette, the size of a man. A face formed within the fog, features emerging from the mist, dark eyes solidifying, their penetrating gaze rooting Guido to the spot, forbidding him to run. In another instant the mist was a man, the same man who'd lured Guido down into this forsaken chamber.

The dresser watched in bewilderment as the figure changed again, hunching down on all fours, trans-forming from a man into a wolf. Just as quickly the wolf was a bat, flapping its wings in the still, cool air. Then it was a man once more, all these transfig-urations taking place within a matter of moments. The man took three brisk strides closer, opening his mouth wide to reveal grossly enlarged canine teeth. Guido watched as they grew larger still, extending down from the upper jaws to form fangs. He whim-pered as the apparition buried his fangs in the side of his throat, pain lancing through his body as the skin was broken. Then came the suckling: an unearthly feeling that his life's blood was being drawn out from the carotid artery, accompanied by the hungry, wet sounds of an animal feeding.

Guido's eyelids fluttered and his limbs went limp, brutal terror undoing him. But the thing that was feasting at his throat would not let him go, not yet. Strong arms embraced him like a lover, and a searing warmth invaded the dresser's body, penetrating at the neck and spreading out through his bloodstream. He felt pleasure beyond anything he'd ever experienced, and a sense of excitement and wanting that he'd never known before. Yes, he thought, take my blood. Take it all. I give in to you willingly.

The Italian gave a sob of dismay as the fangs came away from his neck. The man sucking Guido's blood leaned back to meet the Führer's gaze. "Having taken the victim's blood, he is now utterly in my thrall, a slave willing to say or do anything I command. If I drain them, they can become like me, one of the undead, a vampyr, if I choose. They will possess much of my strength and abilities. They will be able to change their shape and survive on blood alone. Alternatively, I can take enough blood for the victim to die and remain dead. If needs be, I am able to resurrect the dead as cannon fodder, lifeless warriors for the battlefield."

Guido listened to all this with dispassionate annoyance. He wanted the suckling to continue, wanted to feel those twin fangs buried inside his body again. He knew he was dying, but he had never felt so alive.

"What is your wish, Führer?"

"Get rid of the victim, Lord Constanta; he's of no further use."

The vampyr bowed his head to Hitler before turning back to Guido. Constanta licked his lips, removing the last morsel of blood from them. His cold, leathery hands took hold of Guido's face, cradling it like a lover would.

"More," the dresser heard himself whisper. "Take more of me."

Constanta ripped the head sideways, bones inside the neck snapping like brittle twigs. Guido was dead before his broken body slumped to the floor.

ZENJI HITORI WISHED he was anywhere but in Berlin. Until two weeks ago, he had been fighting for the Imperial Japanese Army in China, leading a crack squad of warriors into battle. His grandfather had been a samurai in the days when that meant something, and the day Hitori first strapped on the sword once worn by his father's father had been among the most important of his young life. He was wearing the sword, as he stood in the Chancellery building, dutifully keeping watch over General Tojo. Adjutant to the minister of war, it was Hitori's task to keep the general safe from harm. There was great honour in dying to protect a man so important for the future of the Japanese Empire. Alas, Hitori felt the only danger to the general's life at this dry diplomatic reception was dying of boredom. The likes of Mussolini could talk anyone to death.

Not for the first time since arriving in Berlin, Hitori wished he was not fluent in Italian, German or English. Had his father not insisted young Zenji learn the languages of other nations and other peoples, the adjutant would have been able to occupy his thoughts more usefully at such functions. Instead the general insisted Hitori maintain a constant watch on what was being said. Once they were back in their own quarters, Tojo would expect a blow by blow account of everything that had been uttered within earshot. It did not matter that the Japanese embassy had provided a perfectly adequate translator. The general did not trust diplomats and certainly did not trust translators. So Hitori was required to listen and file away everything he heard for later regurgitation, no matter how dull.

He had noticed the Führer slip away from the champagne reception as soon as possible, and envied Hitler that freedom. As adjutant, Hitori was expected to stay alert and awake as long as his master did. He would have given anything for the chance to return to their quarters, rather than endure another hour or more of pitiless tedium at the hands of these sallow faced officials. I'm a soldier, Hitori thought. I should be on a battlefield, fighting for the good of the empire, not fighting to stay awake in some distant drinks reception!

But his boredom vanished the moment Hitler returned to the room, striding straight towards Tojo. The Führer invited the general out into the corridor, and Hitori followed them, determined not to be left behind if something interesting was going to happen. He noticed Mussolini was not honoured with an invitation to join them, something that left the Italian dictator visibly angry. Good, Hitori decided. The man stinks of wet pork and has all the manners of swine too. Let him stay in here and stew in his own fetid juices.

Once they were out in the corridor, Hitler waved away his own underlings, choosing to use Hitori as translator. The adjutant was surprised by the choice, but did his best not to let that show. The Führer focused his attention on Hitori, his eyes staring at the adjutant. "Tell the general there is someone he should meet, someone who might be useful to him in the future."

Hitori passed this on to Tojo, who merely nodded. The adjutant looked around, expecting to see someone else in the corridor, but it was empty. "Excuse me for asking, Führer, but where is this person?"

Hitler smiled. "Is that you asking, or the general?"

Another exchange of translations took place before Hitori replied, "Both."

"Allow me introduce you to Lord Constanta, from Rumania," Hitler said.

"It's an honour," another voice interjected from behind Hitori. A tall, upright figure strode past the Japanese delegates and stood beside the Führer. He bowed low, keeping his eyes cast down to the floor before straightening up. "May I say how much I admire the activities of your Black Dragon Society? It sets an example other nations would do well to follow."

Hitori was about to translate when he realised the newcomer was already speaking Japanese. Curious, since Hitler also seemed to understand everything that Constanta was saying to the general. Hitori risked a glance over his shoulder, trying to ascertain where the Rumanian had come from, but there were no doors close to them. It was almost as if Constanta had appeared from thin air – a ridiculous notion. The adjutant decided to focus his attention on what was happening here and now. The general was shaking hands with the new arrival, speaking with him as if they were old friends. No doubt it was praise for the Black Dragons that had smoothed the way. The society was a strident right-wing paramilitary group affiliated with the Japanese secret service. To get anywhere in the imperial government these days, you had to have connections with the Black Dragons. Fortunately for Hitori's career prospects, his father had been an active member between the wars. Still, the adjutant was surprised this outsider had even heard of the Black Dragons. They were a secretive society and few acknowledged their existence within Japan. How had this thin-faced, austere figure from Rumania come to know about them?

The general exchanged a few words with the Rumanian, asking him many of the same questions that had occurred to Hitori, but Constanta deftly avoided giving any direct or meaningful answers. "As yet my country is not part of the war that rages across much of Europe," the Rumanian said. "But I believe it will not be long before my people find themselves on the battlefield, fighting for what we believe in. Those of us who hail from the province of Transylvania have particular talents that will stand our allies in good stead. I have offered those talents to the Führer, once Rumania joins the Tripartite Pact. I make the same offer to you, general, as minister of war for Japan."

"You would do well to listen," the Führer added, a mischievous twinkle in his eyes. "I have seen what Constanta's kind can do. They offer the Axis a weapon against which our enemies can have little

defence. If you form an alliance with the Ruma-
nians, they can offer you that same weapon."

The general raised an eyebrow, intrigued by
Hitler's words. "And what is this weapon?" he asked
via Hitori. The adjutant sensed Constanta's gaze
upon him and felt an uncanny fight or flight urge
surging through his veins. The hairs on the back of
Hitori's neck stood up and his hand shifted to the
hilt of his grandfather's samurai sword, tensed and
ready to fend off an attack. Thinking back on the
meeting afterwards, Hitori couldn't explain, even to
himself, why he had suddenly felt so endangered.
There was just something behind Constanta's gaze,
a hunger that verged on the inhuman, like the stare
of a hungry predator.

The Rumanian laughed out loud, amused by the
young soldier's reaction. "Perhaps it would be better
if you spoke of this without the company of your
adjutant. He seems perturbed by my presence, general." Constanta's steely gaze shifted to Tojo, who
took a step back under its power. Overcoming his
fear, Hitori stepped between the two men and hissed
at the Rumanian in English.

"I go where the general goes, unless he tells me
otherwise."

Constanta smiled before replying, also in English,
"You show remarkable strength of will for one so
young. Most are too terrified to challenge me
directly, let alone intervene on behalf of others. You
intrigue me. What is your name?"

"Zenji Hitori."

"Very good, Zenji Hitori, I admire a man who can
control his fears and even confront their source. I

will remember your name for the future. Now, let your master and I speak; you need not worry on his account, he's quite safe."

The adjutant stared hard into Constanta's eyes before stepping aside. The Führer, Tojo and the Rumanian strolled away from Hitori along the corridor, Constanta acting as interpreter between the two allies. Twice, the unlikely trio stopped to look back at the adjutant, but he couldn't hear what they were saying. Whatever it was, Constanta seemed most interested in him. Hitori was not used to being looked at like that, as if he was an object, not a person. It left him feeling disquieted and filled with an unaccountable dread. The sooner he got the general back on the plane to Tokyo, the happier Hitori would be.

PART ONE: September 1941

FROM: Private Juan Martinez,
somewhere in the Pacific.
DATE: September 15, 1941

Dear Selma,
  We're well on our way to the Philippines. I have to admit, I never thought
I'd be writing that when we were growing
up on the farm, but life can take you to
funny places sometimes. Hard to believe
it's only five months since I got
drafted. Hard to believe it's only a few
years since I was playing ball at Field
High, dreaming about being a big league
hitter and seeing the world. Now I am
seeing the world, thanks to the Army!
  Sorry I haven't written before now, but
it's been a mad scramble since we

shipped out of El Paso and I wasn't sure where we were headed. Once we completed basic training, the Army could send us anywhere. Me and the other guys in our unit got put on a train headed west. After what felt like forever we ended up in San Francisco. Sis, you've never seen a place like it! Everywhere we went there were hills, and so many people! We saw the Golden Gate Bridge and these things they call trams and all kinds of crazy stuff. You wouldn't believe your eyes, honestly.

Anyways, they put us on barges and we went across the bay to a place called Angel Island. We had a week stationed at the Army camp there before a liner called the President Coolidge arrived to take us into the Pacific. I was kind of worried about being seasick and making a fool of myself, but I guess I must be a natural sailor or something because I haven't thrown up once. Some of the other guys haven't been so lucky. Poor Father Kelly, our priest, he's been looking green around the gills from the moment we got on board ship.

According to Buntz we'll probably stop in Hawaii on our way to the Philippines. He says we might get a day or two there before heading on. I don't know how long it'll take us to get where we're going, or what'll happen once we do. Some of the guys who work on the ship have been saying there's a war coming but I don't believe it. Sure, they're fighting over there in Europe, but that's got nothing to do with us, right?

Please write and tell me how Mom is doing, and give my best to Mack and everyone at the store. I hope you're all proud of me. I'll try and send you a photo of me in my uniform, once I get a uniform that fits properly! I'd better sign off now. I can hear the sergeant shouting and that usually means some-body's in trouble, one way or another. Please send me some news from home. It might take a while for your letter to find me, so don't worry if it takes a while for me to reply. Besides, you know I'm not big on writing and stuff, but I'll do my best.

Your brother,
Juan.

ONE

FATHER KELLY STEPPED off the gangplank onto dry land and made the sign of the cross, offering a silent prayer to heaven. *Thank you, oh Lord, for delivering us safely to our destination. Look after these young men as they run wild here in Hawaii. Keep them from harm and from harming others. Amen.* He pulled at his clerical collar, conscious of how closely it clung to his neck. Studying at the seminary in Chicago, where it seemed to be winter so many months of the year, the collar helped keep out the cold. Here in the stifling humidity of Hawaii, it felt like a vice around his throat.

The priest lifted a hand to shade his eyes from the dazzling sun and looked around, trying to get his bearings. Beyond the dock buildings were several multi-storey structures, but few stretched towards the sky. No, the dominant features on the horizon were the lush, green hills and mountains, to which

clumps of white cloud clung like scarves of mist.
The contrast between the jutting emerald behe-
moths and the brilliant azure sky overhead was
startling. Father Kelly wondered if the weather
would be so oppressive, so overwhelming when
they reach the Philippines. He hoped not, but it was
too late to change his mind.

All around him members of the 200th Coast
Artillery were whooping and hollering at each
other as they spilled on to the quayside, overjoyed
at being off the ship that had brought them from
San Francisco to this island in the middle of the
Pacific. The priest couldn't help smiling at their
joy. It was infectious, much like the social diseases
several of them were likely to contract over the
next twenty-four hours. Such was the reality of life
in the armed forces. Young men full of hormones
were on their way to some distant island where
female company could well be at a premium, the
sowing of wild oats en route was all but inevitable.
Father Kelly sighed. He had the same urges himself, of course, but his vow of chastity forbade
such indulgences. Besides, he had more pressing
problems.

"Father, are you going anywhere near a mailbox?"
an eager voice asked. The priest turned to see Private Martinez running towards him in a neatly
pressed uniform, an envelope clutched in one hand.
"It's just I promised my sister I'd write and I did, but
I know that if I don't get this in the mail today–"

"Don't worry," the priest cut in, smiling at the
young soldier. "I'd be happy to post it for you. This
is your first shore leave, isn't it?"

"Yes, father," Martinez grinned. He ran a hand across his close-cropped black curls. "I even got my hair cut."

"It suits you."

"What about the moustache?"

"Moustache?" The priest looked closer and noticed a few wisps of downy hair gathered on the soldier's upper lip. "Ah, yes, I see, very impressive."

Martinez shrugged. "I only started growing it a few days ago, but I think it makes me look older, don't you?"

"Definitely. You could be twenty."

Martinez's shoulders slumped a little. "Father, I am twenty."

"Ah! Well, I've never been very good at guessing anyone's age," the priest bluffed, adjusting his silver rimmed spectacles. "My eyesight leaves something to be desired, as well, if I'm being honest."

"Ah, who am I trying to kid?" the young soldier asked. "I'm still a baby face kid, like I've always been. My pop was the same. The Hawaiian women are gonna know I've never–" Martinez stopped, remembering who he was talking to. "Sorry, father, I didn't mean to... sorry."

"Don't worry, Juan. I may not be wise but I know a little of the world." The priest smiled. "I'm sure you'll be a hit with the ladies, but be careful, okay?"

Martinez grinned, his boyish enthusiasm resurfacing. "I've got two guides to show me around Honolulu, what could possibly go wrong?"

"Well, that depends. Who are your guides?"

"Buntz and Wierzbowski," the young soldier said, pointing at a pair of impatient soldiers waiting for him. One was overweight, with thinning hair and a cheesy moustache. Father Kelly had no trouble recognising the surly, self-serving slob, even at this distance. The other man was tall, sinewy and lean of face, with a stance that suggested he was itching for a fight. The priest had yet to encounter Wierzbowski, but it was only a matter of time. With a name like that he had to be of Polish descent and almost certainly a Catholic. Lapsed or otherwise, Wierzbowski would soon be in need of Father Kelly's services. Martinez waved to them before bidding the priest farewell. "I'll see you at mass tomorrow, father."

"Juan, the letter to your sister?"

Martinez blushed and handed over the envelope. "Selma will kill me if I don't write. Thanks for posting it, father."

The priest nodded, muttering a prayer under his breath for the safe return of Private Juan Martinez as the young soldier ran to join his brothers in arms. Father Kelly had heard Oahu was a vibrant and exciting island, with all manner of temptations on offer to unwary visitors. With Buntz and Wierzbowski as his guides, Martinez was going to need all the help he could get to make it back on board ship in time for tomorrow's sailing to the Philippines.

HITORI COULDN'T BELIEVE it when he stepped from the plane in Tokyo and found his oldest friend in the world waiting on the tarmac.

"Shiro? What on earth are you doing here?"

Suzuki's face split into a smile, softening his hooded eyes and cruel mouth. "Waiting for you, of

course!" The two men embraced, clapping each
other on the back and laughing at being reunited.
They had grown up in the same neighbourhood,
attended the same military academy and been given
their postings to Manchuria on the same day. Their
lives had diverged thereafter, Hitori becoming a
rising star in the imperial army while Suzuki worked
his way more steadily up through the ranks. Perhaps
it was Hitori's samurai ancestry that made him
stand out, drawing the attention of powerful men
like General Tojo.

Whatever the reason, Hitori had found himself
making less of an effort to keep in touch with his old
friend as the years went by. He had no wish to make
Suzuki lose face by flaunting his promotions at the
lower ranked officer. Now they were together again,
Hitori realised how much he had missed his friend.
Life in the army was tough enough, without for-
saking those who'd been close to you and
experienced the same horrors of the battlefield.

"It's good to see you," Hitori said, and he meant
it.

"You too," Suzuki agreed.

"So, what are you doing here?"

"Waiting for you. I'm to deliver you to the general
as a matter of urgency."

Hitori smiled. "Are you his new adjutant?"

"There was an opening after you got transferred
back to Manchuria. Tojo went through half a dozen
candidates in as many months before settling on me.
Apparently my name was on a list left behind by one
of my predecessors." Suzuki grinned. "I'm guessing
I have you to thank for that."

"It seemed like a good idea at the time."

"Well, thank you. It's the easiest job I've had since graduating from the academy, and my mother is much happier now that I'm no longer on the frontline." Suzuki gestured towards a staff car waiting nearby, a chauffeur stood obediently holding the passenger door open. "Your carriage awaits, Zenji!"

The two old friends got in the back of the sleek black vehicle. "Don't worry about your bags," Suzuki said. "I'm having them transferred directly to your new quarters at the Ministry of War."

"So my new posting is at the ministry?"

"Your orders didn't specify?"

Hitori shook his head. "Report back to Tokyo and await instructions."

"Typical! The sooner Tojo is prime minister, the better," Suzuki spat. He noticed the alarm on Hitori's face and laughed. "Don't worry; the driver is loyal to Tojo, so you need not fear anything he might tell others about our conversation."

"Fine, then what can you tell me about this new posting?"

"Not much," the new adjutant admitted. "It's top secret, but beyond that the general's been playing his cards very close to his chest. I did overhear something yesterday that made me wonder, though. Does the name Constanta mean anything to you?"

"Yes, it does. I met him once, at the Tripartite Pact signing in Berlin."

"I know your new posting involves him somehow. I believe Tojo wants you to head up a new covert operations unit, and Constanta has some involvement."

Hitori gazed out of the window at the cherry trees lining the boulevard. How he wished it was spring and the blossoms were out; they brought a delicate beauty to the ugliest of landscapes. But it was September and autumn was close.

"Who is this Constanta?" Suzuki asked. "His official file is all but empty, beyond stating his place of birth as Sighisoara in Rumania, the fact that he is considered part of the local aristocracy in a region called Transylvania, and that he's been sighted on numerous occasions along the battlefields of the Eastern Front."

"If you know all that, then you know more than I do," Hitori said. "All I can remember is how much his presence disturbed me in Berlin; that, and the fact that he could speak fluent Japanese, despite never having set foot in this country."

"Well, he's set foot in it now. Constanta's here in Tokyo!"

BUNTZ LED THE way into Honolulu, having been to the city once before with his family ten years earlier. His father was a commercial traveller, the sort of man who boasted he could sell refrigerators to Eskimos. A decade ago he'd won salesman of the year and the prize was a week's vacation for the whole family in Hawaii. Every night, fat fifteen-year-old Arnie watched his mother drink herself into a stupor, and his father sneak out of the hotel room. On their last night, Arnie had followed his father to a succession of nightclubs, bars and dives, each one rougher than the last. Eventually Buntz senior had retired for the night with a Japanese woman called Mai Ling. Arnie waited outside their room for an hour before he heard what sounded like a struggle. Worried the slant-eyed witch was trying to hurt his pop, Arnie had burst in and found the two of them having sex. Of course, Arnie had never told his mom about what he'd seen, but his pop became extra generous to fat little Arnie after that. Oh yeah, he'd all kinds of memories of his last time in Honolulu, and tonight he was going to see where they led him.

"We're starting at the pineapple factory," he announced as they strolled through the streets of Honolulu.

"The what factory?" Martinez asked, his dark brown eyes full of wonder at the exotic sights all around them.

"Pineapple, it's a kind of fruit," Buntz replied, "grows on trees here."

"I ain't had no pineapple before."

"Trust me, Juan, before this shore leave is over you'll experience a lot of things you've never had before. We'll be calling you Don Juan before tomorrow comes, ain't that right, Wierzbowski?"

The third member of the trio kept his own counsel, as usual. Some of the men had thought taking Wierzbowski out on the town might loosen his tongue, but there was scant evidence to confirm that theory so far. His staring, glaring eyes had frightened away three women and turned a passing military policeman a whiter shade of pale. Buntz was coming to the conclusion that bringing

Wierzbowski with him and Martinez had been an error of judgement. He gave up trying to engage the monosyllabic soldier in conversation and focused his attentions back on the wide-eyed Martinez.

"After you've made yourself sick on pineapple juice, we move on to the Squeeze Inn. That's a bar and grill I once went to, where they serve the best octopus on Oahu, fresh off the boat, seared over a blazing fire and sprinkled with lemon juice, salt and pepper. I tell you, Juan, that's some good eating."

"Octopus?"

"Yeah, mainly the tentacles."

"Tentacles?"

Buntz laughed as the young soldier's face shaded to green. "All that time on board and you never threw up. Now I get you on dry land and mention eating some tentacles, you look like you're gonna lose your lunch, Juan."

Martinez swallowed hard. "No, really, I'm fine."

"I mean, it's not like the tentacles are still squirming around!"

That did the trick. The raw recruit from New Mexico stumbled to the nearest gutter and emptied his stomach into a storm drain, retching violently, again and again. Buntz had managed to wipe the smile off his face by the time Martinez had straightened back up. "Feeling better?"

The youngest of the trio wiped the back of his hand across his mouth, cleaning away the final flecks of vomit. "Much better, thanks."

Buntz wrapped an arm around Martinez's shoulder. "That's what friends are for, Juan. That's what friends are for. Now, if my memory serves me correctly, the pineapple factory should be just around the next corner."

GENERAL TOJO STOOD by a tall window in his office at the Ministry of War in Tokyo, staring out at the city beyond the rectangular panes of glass. How long until that fool of a prime minister bowed to the inevitable and resigned? How long until the Japanese Empire attacked the Americans, those self-important adventurers who dared to impose a trade embargo on Japan's ability to import oil and other crucial resources? How long until the westerners realised they had a tiger by the tail when they tried to blockade ports to Japanese vessels and froze Japanese assets overseas? Did Roosevelt and his lackeys in Washington believe they could hold back the coming storm with their ill-chosen words and idle threats?

The general's face twisted into a scowl at the Americans' arrogance. Soon they would discover the folly of their presumptions. Soon they would learn to fear the power of the Japanese Empire. Soon they would know the true meaning of fear. It was not fear itself they should be afraid of, but those wielding it as a samurai wields his sword, with precision and economy and utter ruthlessness. When the killing blow came, the Americans would not know what hit them. They would be rocked back on their heels, shaken to the very core by the audacity and skill with which their forces had been undone. Then and only then would it be time for negotiations and diplomats, once the imperial navy and army had done their duty and all of south-east Asia was under Japanese control.

Tojo removed his wire framed glasses and used a cloth from his pocket to clean the small, circular lenses. All of that was still in the future. For now, he needed to secure a vital new weapon for the coming war, a thunderbolt to cast into the storm of battle, a dagger of stealth to strike terror into the hearts of the Americans and their allies in the Pacific. Putting his glasses back on, the general returned to his desk and opened the plain manila folder. Inside were reports from observers along the Eastern Front, the Ostfront as the Germans liked to call it. Each made mention of three words: vampyr, terrifying, powerful. In each case, Lord Constanta or one of his acolytes had been assisting the Wehrmacht, driving fear into the hearts of Red Army units.

The effect had been devastating. Combined with the blitzkrieg tactics that had served Germany so well in other parts of Europe, the Wehrmacht and its Rumanian allies had smashed through the Russian defences and penetrated deep into the Soviet interior. At the current rate of progress, Hitler's forces would be inside the Kremlin by December. When Moscow fell, Russian capitulation would be all but inevitable. The observation reports stressed the fact that Constanta and his vampyr forces were a small part of that success, but they had been a powerful insurgency force in key battles. Used well and used wisely, the same weapon could be even more effective in the battle for control of the Pacific.

Tojo stroked a hand across his bald pate, subconsciously enjoying the sensation of skin upon skin,

the sensuality of it. Very well, we shall make selec-
tive use of this weapon of terror, he decided. But the
Imperial Japanese Army did not need outsiders to
fight battles for it. If we Japanese are to embrace
what Constanta has to offer, it must be done on our
terms, Tojo determined, not for the benefit of this
inscrutable Rumanian. The general prided himself
on being a good judge of character, able to read
those around him, and instinctively know their
thoughts, fears and feelings, but Constanta was a
closed book, impenetrable to insight or interroga-
tion. It did not matter, Tojo was certain of that, but
he was still disquieted by it.

A knocking at his office door focused the general's
thoughts. He closed the file and slid it in a desk
drawer, turning an ornate brass key in the lock.

"Enter!"

His adjutant Suzuki opened the door and came in,
nodding to Tojo before stepping aside to allow
another figure in a crisp military uniform to enter.
The general smiled at the arrival of Hitori, one of the
most decorated soldiers in the interminable quest
for supremacy in Manchuria. "It is good to see you
again," the war minister said. "Come in and sit
down."

Hitori nodded and followed Tojo to the far end of
the office where a baroque table and chairs waited
in front of a fireplace, a delicate display of orchids
standing in a Ming vase on the table. The general
glanced at Suzuki, who remained waiting at the
door. "Bring us green tea and warm sake," he
ordered. The adjutant snapped his heels together
and bowed to acknowledge the command, before

withdrawing from the office, closing the door after him. Tojo sat in the chair with a clear view of the doorway, an old habit borne of too many years spent in dangerous situations where it was hard to know your friends well.

Hitori sat down opposite the general, easing himself into the padded chair. The general knew his former adjutant was only twenty-seven, but Hitori looked older than his years. Too long spent on foreign shores, fighting brutal battles in service of the emperor had left their marks on the young officer. Hitori bore no visible scars on his face or hands, but his eyes carried the haunted look of a man who had seen damnation done in this life and been responsible for much of it. His cool, calculating eyes and emotionless face made him almost as difficult to read as Constanta. Hitori gave the impression of being effortlessly able to lead others into certain death while remaining totally self-sufficient and contained. Admirable qualities in a warrior, Tojo thought, qualities he would need if all went according to plan. "There is much we have to catch up on, my boy."

FATHER KELLY STOOD outside the imposing white building in downtown Honolulu for the longest time, summoning the courage to go inside. People bustled by on foot, or drove past in their cars. A few tipped their hats or beeped their horns to acknowledge the priest's presence, but most were too busy going about their lives to pay him much heed. Besides, what was more natural than a man of god standing outside the Cathedral of Our Lady of

Peace? The coral stone church was one of the city's oldest buildings and a local landmark.

The priest took off his straw hat and wiped the sweat from his forehead. He hadn't expected Hawaii to be so humid, the air so close. It felt like a sauna. Father Kelly replaced his hat and took a deep breath. Enough was enough, he decided. I came here for a reason. The priest crossed the boulevard and strode into the cathedral. As soon as he stepped inside the air was cooler, the atmosphere calmer. The hubbub of the street outside was replaced by the gentle murmur of prayers from the faithful, sitting in pews or kneeling before burning candles. Father Kelly gave his eyes a moment to adjust, letting them get used to the gently lit interior.

By comparison to most cathedrals he'd been in, this was simple, almost stark. There was no gaudy gold leaf or elaborate trappings here. The walls were white, while a stark wooden altar stood at the far end of the church. Woven matting lined the aisle, soft underfoot. Even the pews were plain wood, roughly hewn, with no sign of the ornate carvings and curlicues commonly found in cathedrals stateside. The simplicity of the place pleased the priest. He had long felt uncomfortable preaching how difficult it was for a rich man to enter the kingdom of Heaven, while serving communion wine from a solid gold chalice; and asking poor parishioners to give generously while living rent free in a rich house seemed hypocritical, at best.

"Hello? Can I help you?" a young voice asked. The priest turned to find a Hawaiian child in the garb of an altar boy looking up at him. "Sorry, father, I didn't realise... I couldn't see your collar before."

Father Kelly smiled. "That's all right, my son, you weren't to know. I was looking for the confessional, actually."

The altar boy pointed to a corner of the cathedral, where three tall wooden cubicles stood side by side, red velvet curtains drawn across each entrance to shield the occupants from view.

"I was hoping there'd be someone to hear mine."

"Priests have to go to confession too?"

"None of us are perfect, my son, except the Holy Father in Rome."

The boy nodded. "You can wait in one of the pews. When a curtain is open, it means that confessional is available." He laughed and clapped a hand over his blushing face. "Sorry, father, you probably already knew that."

The priest shrugged. "Each place of worship has its own ways. Thank you for explaining to me what happens here." Father Kelly walked over to the pew nearest the cubicles, but didn't sit down. He waited for a few moments, biting his bottom lip. The priest was about to leave when one of the curtains was pulled aside and an old woman emerged, her head bowed. Once she had moved away, Father Kelly took her place inside the booth and pulled the curtain closed. He knelt down in front of a small wooden grill that masked a window between his booth and the centre cubicle. After a few moments, a ruddy face peered at him through the grill, while whisky soaked lips whispered the ritual greeting.

"Forgive me, father, for I have sinned," Father Kelly replied, making the sign of the cross before clasping his hands back together in prayer. "It has been three months since my last confession."

"Why so long, my son?"

"I was on board a troop ship that came here from San Francisco."

"Could you not have taken confession with your unit's chaplain?"

"I am the unit's chaplain."

"Ah, I see, difficult." The other priest considered these facts. "But the voyage from San Francisco doesn't take three months, does it?"

"No, father, it's..." Father Kelly didn't know how to continue. He had come this far, and now his courage was failing him, but to lie in the confessional was a sin, and he already had enough of those on his conscience.

"Go on, my son," the other priest urged.

Father Kelly took off his glasses and rubbed his nose between thumb and forefinger, massaging the indentations where his spectacles rested. "I find it hard to admit this, even to myself, let alone say it out loud."

"Whatever you have to confess, God can forgive. He is listening, my son."

"That's just it, I'm not sure he is listening. I'm not sure there even is a god, not anymore, not after what happened in my old parish." The troubled priest put his glasses back on and peered through the grill at his confessor. "Please, father, you've got to help me. I've... I've lost my faith."

"TELL ME, HOW goes the fighting in Manchuria?" Tojo gestured towards his desk. "I get the official reports, of course, but my generals only tell me what they think I want to hear. I can trust you to speak the truth."

Hitori took a deep breath and succinctly outlined the various battles being fought between China and the Imperial Japanese Army. He spoke dispassionately, confining himself predominantly to facts and figures, coloured with a few anecdotes. "In all honestly, we're winning most of our battles, but we're fighting a war that can never succeed. China is simply too vast to be conquered by one army, however brave and resourceful its warriors, no matter how superior their skills and weapons to the peasant militia."

The general nodded at the truth of these statements. "You sound tired."

His former adjutant smiled, for a moment. "More like exhausted. It's a long way back from Manchuria and your request for me to return sounded urgent."

"It was," Tojo replied. "It is." Suzuki returned with their drinks before the general could explain further. The general waited until the adjutant had left, before continuing. "Hitori, I must ask you some difficult questions. Be as honest with your answers as you have been with my previous questions."

"Of course, general."

"Many of our people believe the emperor is a living god, a deity in human form, sent to lead us to greatness. From birth, we Japanese are trained to believe in the divinity of our emperor, to trust in our inherent superiority to other races, and to know that we all share a collective destiny. No one of us is any more important than another, and all of us would lay down our lives in the service of the empire." Tojo poured each of them a cup of green tea. "Is that what you believe, Zenji?"

"Yes, of course, general."

"You would lay down your life for the emperor, if he asked?"

"Yes."

"Say it."

"Sir?"

"Say it out loud, so I can hear it for myself." The general leaned back in his chair, sipping the hot tea, his cold eyes fixed on Hitori's.

"I would willingly and happily give my life for the emperor, if he asked."

"I see, and what else would you sacrifice for the emperor?"

Hitori frowned. "I'm sorry, general, I don't understand the question."

Tojo put his tea back down on the table between them. "It's quite simple. What else would you sacrifice for the emperor?"

"Anything," the younger replied, "everything."

"Your life?"

"Yes, I've already said I'd–"

"Your wife?" Tojo interjected.

That stopped Hitori, giving him pause for thought. "Is there something the matter with Aiko, sir?"

"No, your wife is fine, as is your baby son."

"I have a son?"

The general smiled. "You didn't know?"

"Aiko was pregnant the last time we saw each other, but that was several months ago and letters from home rarely reach their destination in Manchuria."

"Of course. Forgive me for breaking news that I imagine your wife would rather you'd heard from her lips. Well, congratulations are due. You have a son, fit and healthy. His name is Noriyuki, I believe."

Hitori smiled. "In honour of my father."

"Quite so." Tojo poured a tumbler of warm sake for himself and another for his guest. "So, would you be willing to give up your wife and your son? Would you sacrifice your young family for the emperor, if he asked?"

"I... Yes, of course. If that was what the emperor asked of me."

"You hesitated before answering my question."

"It is difficult, being asked to sacrifice a son you have not met yet."

"It's better you do not know him. It may make the loss a little easier."

"Loss? But you said he was fit and healthy—"

"He is, as is your beautiful wife. I am not asking you to sacrifice their lives."

"Then what, sir?"

"Drink your sake first," the general suggested.

"Please, sir, I need to know—"

"Drink it," Tojo snarled.

Hitori snatched at the tumbler, raising it to his lips. Then he stopped to stare into the clear, colourless liquid, as if afraid the sake might contain some deadly substance. The general arched an eyebrow at his subordinate, and Hitori emptied the sake into his mouth, swallowing the warm liquid with a grimace. He put the porcelain tumbler back down on the table and waited, but nothing happened.

"Did you think I had poisoned you?" Tojo asked, laughter in his voice.

"I wasn't sure," Hitori admitted.

"But you drank it anyway. Very good, I like a man who can follow orders, even if he believes those orders may cost him his life." The general swallowed his own sake, licking his lips appreciatively at the taste. "It is not that I wish you to sacrifice your life for the emperor – quite the opposite in fact. But I'm sorry to say that you can never see your family again after today. They will be told you were killed in Manchuria, a warrior's death, of course. They will be well compensated for your loss and can be proud of your heroic sacrifice. But you will not die today, at least, not in any conventional sense."

The young officer shook his head. "You speak in riddles, general."

"I'd have thought you'd be used to them after so long in China."

"Be that as it may, please tell me what you wish."

"You said you would willingly give your life for the emperor, Hitori. Would you also willingly give up your soul?"

"My soul?"

Tojo rose from his chair and clapped his hands. "You can come in now," he called out. Hitori turned towards the double doors through which he had entered earlier, but nobody came in. Instead a thin white mist crept beneath the door, forming into a pale, translucent cloud inside the office. The mist solidified, slowly merging into the figure of a man. As the fog became flesh, a familiar face appeared within it: Lord Constanta of Rumania. He smiled at the young officer, making no effort to conceal the prominent fangs that protruded from his upper jaw. Hitori sprang up to put himself between the apparition and Tojo, protecting the general from the supernatural wraith. He spat a crude curse at the fearful visage as it coalesced before his amazed eyes.

"You need not fear our guest," Tojo said, moving across the room to stand beside the creature from Transylvania. The general smiled at Hitori like a kindly father. "I seem to recall you two have met before, in Berlin. Lord Constanta is what the Nazis call a vampyr, a blood drinker, a creature of the night, if you will."

"We prefer to think of ourselves as favoured sons of the Sire," the Rumanian interjected, plainly enjoying the fear and disbelief on Hitori's face.

The general clapped a hand on Constanta's right shoulder. "Take a good look at his lordship, Zenji. You will become like him. You are my first recruit for a new covert division. You will lead the Imperial Japanese Army Vampyr Unit."

REPORT ON U.S. READINESS FOR WAR

In accordance with orders, we have
infiltrated the island of Oahu and
established our presence within the
downtown sector of Honolulu city. Occu-
pation of the safe house has been
secured without incident and our new
identities as siblings went unquestioned
by the authorities. The cover story
about our 'uncle' was not challenged,
nor his abrupt disappearance. Both
Hawaiian natives and Americans from the
mainland have welcomed us as newcomers
to the community.

Our observations of the US servicemen
suggest a nation far from ready for war.
The vast majority of those we encounter

are drunkards and fools, lacking discipline or moral strength. Our clients include pilots, marines and soldiers passing through Hawaii en route to US military bases scattered across the Pacific. If these are the best America has to offer in the event of war, the conflict will be short and our victory a certainty. The enemy exhibits an arrogant belief in its superiority that stands no scrutiny.

We are beginning efforts to infiltrate America's armed forces bases. Enclose the latest reports on movements of troops, vessels and aircraft. As yet the US shows little indication it is making ready for a war in the Pacific and even less inclination of willingness to fight such a war. In view of these factors, we believe a swift and successful outcome to any such hostilities would be likely and, indeed, probable.

SOURCE: Agents TN and SN, Station H.

TWO

BENJAMIN H PAXTON of the United States Marine Corps had the perfect plan for his day off in Honolulu: get drunk, probably get into a fight and, hopefully, get laid. Since joining B Company at the marine barracks in Pearl Harbour he had walked in and stumbled out of almost every bar on the island of Oahu. Paxton could claim with some measure of authority to know the best places to attain at least two of his three goals within the next twelve hours. If he got lucky with the beautiful Kissy Nagara tonight, he might even hit the trifecta of happiness. Hell, was there a better way to kill another dull day and night in the middle of the Pacific Ocean?

The way Paxton saw it, Honolulu was a melting pot where red-blooded Americans like him could mingle happily with people from the Orient and the locals. Of course, Paxton's idea of cultural intermingling usually involved the exchange of bodily fluids, but that didn't make it any less effective as a way of breaking down boundaries between people of different origins. There was no better example of that philosophy than Tokyo Joe's Bar and Grill, a popular drinking hole in downtown Honolulu that often got so crowded that customers spilled out on to the sandy beach behind it. According to legend, the bar had once been called the Oahu Oasis, but that was too much of a tongue twister for most drunken US servicemen. Back then the owner was Mitsuo Nagara, a tiny, bespectacled man from Japan. He had soon been nicknamed Tokyo Joe and the title became so universal that Nagara adopted it for his business.

More refined establishments on Oahu didn't willingly welcome grunts like Paxton and his brothers in arms, fearful of what would happen if men from different services ran into each other while inebriated. There was little love lost between the navy flyboys and men from the corps, both sides considering the other to be inferior fighters. Tokyo Joe's Bar and Grill was one of the few places that allowed all comers from all services without question. In gratitude for this attitude, it was deemed neutral territory by all branches of the US armed forces, a sanctuary from their petty rivalries. Anyone who started a fight in Tokyo Joe's could mess that up for everyone. So, a simple rule was instituted: if you had a beef, you took it outside. Otherwise the military police were liable to take it out on everyone. Paxton had seen the MPs in action. They had truncheons and sidearms on their side, not to mention military law, so, one way or another, the MPs always won every battle.

Mitsuo Nagara had gone home to Japan in August, but before leaving he made certain his bar and grill didn't change its easygoing attitude towards servicemen. Management of Tokyo Joe's shifted to the old man's nephew Tetsuzo, and niece Kissy. The same open door policy remained in place for all the servicemen from Pearl Harbour and Hickam Field. As long as you had money to spend and the good sense to keep any fighting outside, you were always welcome at Tokyo Joe's. As far as Paxton was concerned, the bar and grill had gotten a whole lot friendlier with the arrival of Kissy Nagara. She was the sweetest little honey he had ever laid eyes on, and Paxton had known more than his fair share of ladies before joining the corps.

Hell, it was his love of the ladies that had landed the wisecracking Californian in the damned marines. He'd been making his living as a tennis pro in San Diego, helping the bored, neglected wives of wealthy naval officers improve their backhand, amongst other things. The wives were happy, he was having fun, and the tennis club appreciated the extra memberships his tutoring skills brought in. But one of the women got knocked up and pinned the blame on Paxton after suffering a messy miscarriage. He'd been given a simple choice: a long walk off a short pier or a voluntary enlistment with the marines. The husband in question had pulled a few strings to ensure Paxton got sent as far away from San Diego as possible on short notice. The unwilling marine had been rotting on Oahu ever since, wishing he'd had the forethought to take a few more precautions.

Paxton had liked to think of himself as a tomcat, romancing one woman after another, spreading his loving around as if it was a blessing. Kissy Nagara changed all that. She was the only woman who'd ever turned him down, explaining that her family back in Japan wouldn't approve of any relationship with an American soldier. Paxton kept asking her out and she kept refusing, until it became a game between the two of them. Then, one day the cocky marine had realised he was smitten, bewitched by the coy young woman with the warm brown eyes and cute-as-a-button smile. He woke up thinking of her, spent his day wondering what she was doing and fell asleep hoping to dream about being with her. If he didn't know better, Paxton would have said he was falling in love. But Paxton believed in loving one person before all others, and that was himself.

He strolled into Tokyo Joe's from the street and stood with both hands on his hips, striking a mock heroic pose. "Hi, honey, I'm home." A handful of customers propping up the bamboo bar glanced over at him before slumping back into their rum and pineapple drinks. Kissy was dutifully polishing glasses, while her brother swept the floor. She sneaked a smile at Paxton, but soon turned away, made bashful by a disapproving glare from Tetsuzo. Her brother was fighting a losing battle against the white sand traipsed inside by those who entered the bar from the beach instead of the crowded down-town street.

"We're not open yet," Tetsuzo growled as the marine strolled past him.

"Then who are your friends at the bar?"

"Still here from last night. They never leave."

"Lucky them." Paxton found an empty stool and sat on it. "Don't worry, I only came in to savour your sister's gorgeous face."

Kissy blushed and giggled, hooking an errant strand of long, black hair behind one ear. She stole another glance at Paxton, the two of them sharing a secret smile before Tetsuzo interceded. "How many times we tell you? My sister is not interested in marrying an American. She already has husband waiting for her back in Tokyo. She is marrying him next summer."

"Well, she ain't married yet. Besides, I'm only looking, 'Suzo."

"My name is Tetsuzo!"

"Whatever you say, kemosabe." Paxton glanced at his wristwatch. "You open at midday, don't you?" The red-faced Tetsuzo nodded. "Then I'll have a pineapple juice, and make sure it comes in one of those hollowed out coconut shells, with a paper umbrella on top. I just love those little bitty paper umbrellas you guys have in the drinks here."

Tetsuzo stomped his way behind the bar, hissing angrily in Japanese at his sister. She fastened the buttons on her blue silk blouse up to the neck before taking charge of the broom. Paxton waited until her surly brother was distracted before whispering into Kissy's ear, "Don't you worry about Tetsuzo. He's just trying to look after you. Anything that keeps you safe is fine by me."

Kissy smiled at him. "How long until you have to go back to barracks?"

"Not 'til midnight. Got me a day pass and I'm spending it here with you."

"Hey, Paxton, there you are!" a voice shouted. A diminutive man of Japanese descent stood in the street doorway, dressed in a colourful Hawaiian shirt and khaki trousers. Behind him lurked a nervous teenager with a painfully thin face, round framed glasses and a crop of acne across his cheeks.

"Pat!" Paxton called back, waving for the new arrivals to come over and join him. "You took your sweet time getting here, didn't you?"

The newcomers strolled over, the younger man straggling along behind his more confident companion. "I had to persuade Walton here of the wisdom that could be found at the bottom of a Hawaiian fruit punch."

"There's no alcohol in one of those, is there?" the timid youth asked.

"Not so as you'd notice," Paxton laughed. He watched Pat admiring the beautiful young woman with the broom. "Kissy, this is an old friend of mine, Toshikazu Maeda, but everyone in the corps calls him Pat. We did basic together. Pat's just transferred in from Stateside."

Maeda bowed to Kissy, his hands together as if in prayer. She returned the gesture before asking a question. "You are Japanese, but in the Marines?"

He smiled. "If I had a buck for every time somebody's asked me that."

"So sorry, I did not mean to—"

"No, no, it's fine. My parents are from Japan originally. They travelled to America in 1919. I was born and raised in San Francisco. I joined up when war broke out in Europe, figured it was my duty. Who knew we'd still be sitting on the sidelines after all this time, eh Paxton? Two years later and I'm still waiting to see some action." He jerked a thumb towards the fretful youth at his side. "As for this extrovert, his name is David Walton and he's from Virginia."

"Hey, how you doing, Flinch?" Paxton asked. "I didn't notice you there."

"Why you call him Flinch?" Kissy asked. "I thought his name was Walton."

"It is, but our young friend here startles easily, don't you, Flinch?" Walton shook his head, but still jumped when Paxton suddenly shouted, "Boo!"

Kissy punched her would-be suitor in the arm. "You leave him alone, Paxton, he done nothing to you," she remonstrated.

"Yeah, yeah, whatever," Paxton replied. "You run along and ask your brother to make two more of those pineapple juices. I want to buy my brothers in arms here a drink. Reckon we all deserve it, right boys?"

"Now you're talking," Maeda replied, grinning from ear to ear.

HITORI STARED AT the Rumanian, uncertain what to make of this demon. He had heard rumours about monsters stalking the battlefields where the Wehrmacht was crushing the Red Army, creatures that emerged at night and fed on the enemy as if they were carrion. Some said the demons sucked the blood from their victims, others claimed the fiends consumed the souls of the fallen. Hitori had believed such reports were merely ghost stories, the kind of legends one would tell a child to frighten him.

Fables about demons and supernatural monsters had been among his favourites as a child, but he had put away such childish things when he became a man. Now General Tojo was asking him to believe this grinning Rumanian standing opposite was just such a monster. Hitori could not deny what he had seen with his own eyes, but he still tried to convince himself it was a trick of the light, or perhaps a hallucination brought on by something in the tea or sake.

"You're wondering if I'm real," Constanta said in Japanese. "You're trying to tell yourself all of this is some dream or nightmare, the imaginings of a poisoned mind perhaps, an illusion. I may not conform to any of your native legends, but I am real, Zenji Hitori. I am the most real thing you have ever seen."

"Prove it."

The Rumanian smiled to himself.

"Very well." He snapped his fingers and the double doors to Tojo's office swung inwards. Suzuki ushered in a Chinese soldier in a tattered uniform, the prisoner's hands tied behind his back, bruises on his face and forearms mute evidence of the struggle he had endured. Suzuki gave his old friend a look – what's going on in here? – but Hitori could offer only the slightest shake of his head in reply.

"That will be all," Tojo told his adjutant, and Suzuki withdrew, closing the doors after him. The general moved to his desk and sat down behind it. "You will find this demonstration... illuminating," he said to Hitori.

Constanta waited for a nod from Tojo before approaching the prisoner. He grabbed the Chinese soldier by the throat and lifted him bodily off the floor. The Rumanian tossed the prisoner against the double doors, throwing the soldier as if he weighed no more than a rag doll. The Chinaman sank to the floor, all the breath knocked out of his body. Constanta glanced over his shoulder at Hitori.

"Many of the world's oldest cultures have tales about my kind and our abilities. They have tried to portray us as monsters, parasites and creatures of darkness. Nothing could be further from the truth, of course, but mortals are fond of their lies. I have made a limited study of your nation's literature, its myths and legends. Until a few years ago, when foreign cultures insinuated themselves into your literature, the word vampyr did not exist in your language. Together, we shall change that."

He advanced on the prisoner. "Stand up," he commanded. When he did not move, Constanta snarled at him in a Chinese dialect that Hitori recognised from Manchuria. The captive soldier clambered to his feet, terror all too evident on his features.

"Become like me and you can command mortal men, hold them in your thrall simply by the force of your will," Constanta said in Japanese. He turned back to the prisoner, locking eyes with him. At first the enemy soldier's fear remained, his breath coming in short gasps, his eyes betraying his fear. But soon his expression softened, his shoulders relaxed and his breathing became more regular, more controlled. In less than a minute he was placid, almost smiling, staring lovingly into

Constanta's eyes. "You see? He is utterly in my power. He will do anything I ask. That makes him a valuable tool, an insurgent we can turn against his own kind, a weapon against your enemies."

"Incredible," Hitori whispered.

"Keep watching," Tojo commanded, "there's more."

Constanta spat a two word command at the prisoner. He moved closer to the vampyr, tilting his head aside to expose his neck and throat. The Rumanian smiled at Hitori. "This is how you will feed. Once you become like me, the hunger will be strong within you, a creature that must be sated with blood from a living human. You must feed, otherwise you will die; it is one of the few ways our kind can perish. You will have no choice in the matter. Feeding to us is like breathing for mortals, a matter of instinct. It will come naturally to you."

He rested one hand against the prisoner's face, tilting the head still further away. The Chinaman did not object. Constanta drew back his lips, revealing the length of his twin fangs, before clamping his open mouth against the prisoner's neck. A look of panic and pain crossed the Chinese soldier's face, but still he did not pull away, did not fight back. Hitori found himself urging the prisoner to strike out, to defend himself, but the prisoner remained docile even as a trickle of blood escaped from the side of Constanta's sucking mouth.

The Rumanian ripped his face away from the prisoner's neck, his lips stained crimson with fresh, wet blood, his eyes alive with animal hunger. "How long you feed decides whether your meal lives or dies," he hissed, licking his lips to get every last drop of blood off them. "Take a little and they will survive, ready to provide further sustenance, eager to succumb to your will. Our saliva leaves a coagulant film across their wounds, to prevent them bleeding to death needlessly. Take too much and you will kill your victim, but that has its uses. In extreme circumstances you can resurrect them from the grave, to act as an undead army on your behalf. Such warriors are cannon fodder at best, their value deriving from the dread and horror they instil in your enemy. Few mortals enjoy killing their dead comrades." Constanta pushed the prisoner across to Hitori. "Taste his blood."

Hitori caught the soldier and held him up, stopping the weakened Chinaman from collapsing. He stared at the two puncture wounds on the prisoner's neck and could see blood inside them, pulsing below the surface. Hitori swallowed and looked away, unable to contemplate what was being asked of him.

"I can't."

"Can't, or won't?" Tojo asked, a chill of disappointment in his voice. He rose from his seat and stalked around the desk. "There is someone else waiting to meet you, Hitori, in the next room. Perhaps he will be able to persuade you." The general marched to a side door and held it open. "You will come with me, now!" Hitori did as he was told, not daring to look Tojo in the eye. The general ushered him through the door, before glancing back at Constanta. "Feel free to get rid of that as you see fit," he said, gesturing dismissively at the prisoner.

"You're too kind," the Rumanian replied. As Tojo followed Hitori through the side door, the Chinese captive screamed for mercy. The cry was cut short, replaced by the sound of hungry sucking and slurping.

Hitori found himself in a narrow passageway. The general pushed past him and strode along the corridor, towards another door, Hitori following close behind. When they reached the door, Tojo stopped his former adjutant and stared into his eyes. "It saddens me that I was not able to convince you of the wisdom of accepting what Lord Constanta has to offer. But I'm certain you will not be able to refuse the person who waits beyond this door. Now, in you go."

Hitori reached for the door handle, aware that his whole body was trembling. He opened the door and stepped through it into an ornately furnished room. A single, gold framed chair stood in the centre of the chamber, facing away from Hitori, its high back shielding whoever was sitting in it from view. He watched as the occupant stood up, pulling on the hem of his jacket. He walked around the tall chair and faced Hitori, who dropped to one knee and bowed his head. He was in the presence of Emperor Hirohito, living god and leader of all Japan.

FATHER KELLY SAT in the cathedral sacristy, sipping a cup of coffee. "I'm sorry we haven't anything stronger," the other priest said, "but I keep the communion wine under lock and key these days. One of the new altar boys is rather too fond of sampling it away from the altar."

"Coffee's fine," Kelly replied, deciding not to mention the scent of whisky on his confessor's breath. The two of them had retired to the sacristy where they could talk face to face, rather than continue discussing the visiting priest's problems in a confession box as if they were simply another litany of misdeeds to be admitted and forgiven. Father Kelly had been startled to emerge from the confessional to find he was facing Bishop Sweeney, leader of the Catholic faith for all of the Hawaiian Islands. The bishop was well over fifty, but had the burly physique of a former prize fighter, with a pugnacious face to match and a crop of unruly silver hair. He was an imposing figure, not at all what Kelly had been expecting. The visiting priest waited until they were in the quiet seclusion of the sacristy before asking why the bishop was hearing confession in the cathedral.

"I like to keep my hand in," Sweeney quipped. "The higher you go within the church, the easier it becomes to forget about your flock, their daily woes and troubles. They need a confessor and I'm as well qualified for that as any of my parish priests. Besides, it makes me feel like I'm doing some good."

"Making a difference, helping people," Kelly replied.

"Exactly. That's why I became a priest, to help people." Sweeney finished taking off the last of his vestments and sat down. "Why did you become a priest, father?"

"Kelly, Shamus Kelly."

The bishop smiled. "There's a good Irish Catholic name. Where do you hail from originally, Chicago?"

"Yes, the south side." Kelly took another sip of his drink, giving himself time to think. "I guess I was like you; I wanted to make a difference."

"You don't have to take the sacraments to do that. I've known plenty of good Chicago Catholics who became policemen, fire fighters, even soldiers."

Kelly nodded. "To be honest, everybody expected my brother Dermot would be the boy from our family who took the cloth. My sister Marie is a nun back in Chicago, but most people had me pegged for something other than the priesthood, for anything other than the priesthood, if I'm honest."

"And your brother died, before he was ordained?"

"How did you know?"

"I've seen it before," the bishop cut in. "You're not the first person to find himself filling another person's shoes, and you won't be the last. Families can put terrible pressure on young men."

"The thing is, I wanted to be a priest," Kelly insisted. "I believed in the sacraments, I still do. But when I got my first parish, something happened and…" His voice trailed off as he was overcome by the press of memories and regrets.

"You began to doubt yourself, your vocation… your faith."

"Yes." Kelly looked down at the tired rug on the floor, ashamed of his admission. "There was a young woman in my parish, little more than a girl."

The bishop sighed. "How old was she?"

"Fifteen, when she died." Kelly realised what his confessor was thinking and hurried to explain. "We never… I mean, I didn't–" He stopped, shaking his head as it all came flooding back. "Her name was

Catherine. She fell in love with me. I thought it was just a schoolgirl crush, something she'd grow out of. I considered going to my bishop, asking to be transferred, but running away from the problem felt wrong. I believed I could handle the situation."

"Did you love her?"

"I cared about her, in the same way I cared for all of my parishioners. I tried to explain to her that we could never be together, that she had to put all thought of me as a man out of her mind. She promised to try, but..." Father Kelly was crying, bitter tears rolling down his face. "The last time I saw her alive, she seemed happy, at peace with herself. I thought it was a good sign, that she'd turned a corner, that things would get better."

The bishop leaned back in his chair. "She killed herself, didn't she?"

Father Kelly nodded. "I returned to my sacristy after saying mass one Friday and found her hanging from a curtain rail, naked, with the sign of the cross carved into both her wrists. Her face was blue and the blood was–" He broke down, overwhelmed by his memories of that terrible day, by what he had witnessed in the little room off the main body of the church.

His confessor waited until the tears subsided before speaking again. "What did the girl's family do afterwards?"

"That was the worst part," Father Kelly said. "They forgave me. It seems they knew about their daughter's imbalance, her obsessions, but they were too ashamed to get her the help she needed. They didn't blame me at all."

"You wanted to be blamed?"

"It was my fault, wasn't it?"

"Not if what you've told me is true. This girl needed help and you tried to give it. We can't save everyone, Father Kelly. We can only do our best."

"I know, but..." The priest sighed, brushing the blond hair from his eyes. "I couldn't understand how God could have abandoned that girl. If she was made in his image, how could she be so troubled as to take her own life? Where was God when she was hurting herself, when she was killing herself? How can her death be what God intended? Why did she have to die? Why?"

The bishop stood and went to a stack of Bibles beneath a window. He selected one and opened it, retrieving a small bottle of whisky from within. "When I have too many questions, I give myself a sip of Ireland's finest export," he announced, pouring a liberal jolt of whisky into Father Kelly's coffee cup. "It doesn't provide any answers, but sometimes it helps numb the pain of knowing how little I do know, and how much less I understand."

"Drink your way to happiness?"

"Would that I could, I'd be the happiest man in the world by now," the bishop replied. "It's no surprise you had a crisis of faith after what happened, but how did you end up a chaplain in the army?"

Father Kelly shrugged. "I wanted to be somewhere the same thing couldn't happen again. The army seemed like the safest place."

"Hmm, I'm not sure I've ever heard the army described as a safe place," the bishop said, a wry smile on his lips. "Besides, there's more than one kind of love, no matter what the Bible may have to say on the subject."

"I'll take my chances."

The bishop returned the whisky bottle to its hiding place. "It's obvious you're still haunted by what happened in your parish. Running away from that won't change the past, and it won't get the image of that dead girl out of your thoughts, or your nightmares, either."

"How did you know?"

"The black rings under your eyes are something of a giveaway in someone so young. It's obvious you haven't been sleeping well lately."

"No," Father Kelly admitted, "but what can I do?"

"I can't offer any easy answers. All priests must face the same questions, the same uncertainty at some point. We get hurt and we see hurts done to other people when we're helpless to intervene. Over time those wounds will heal and become scar tissue. Eventually, you start to wonder if you're nothing but scar tissue. Your particular wounds are an extreme example, but most men who take the cloth face such dilemmas in their lives."

"You haven't answered my question. What can I do? What should I do? How can I find my faith again?"

"I'm sorry, but you'll have to find that answer for yourself." The bishop rested a comforting hand on Father Kelly's shoulder. "When you do, write and let me know. In the meantime, I'll keep you in my prayers."

"You may stand," Emperor Hirohito said in a quiet, humble voice. Hitori rose from his knees, but kept his eyes fixed on the ornate rug covering the floor.

"Forgive me, my lord, I did not–"

"You have done nothing that needs my forgiveness," the emperor said. "But our conversation will be much easer if you look me in the eye."

"Yes, my lord, of course." Summoning all his strength of will, Hitori lifted his eyes up to gaze upon Japan's supreme ruler. He was surprised to see how small the emperor was, slight of build and unremarkable of appearance. When a man is worshipped as a living god, you expect him to have the stature of a deity. But Hirohito reminded the soldier of his father, with kind, concerned eyes and a small mouth. "It is an honour to be in your presence, my lord."

The emperor waved the remarks away. "My minister of war asked me here so we might talk. You have met the Rumanian?"

"Lord Constanta? Yes, my lord."

"And you know what he is."

Hitori nodded.

The emperor clasped his hands together, staring down at the interlinked fingers. "The power this creature possesses, the abilities Constanta is willing to share with us – it is a kind of weapon, we suppose, albeit a weapon of merciless savagery. We fear we shall have need of such weapons in the months to come."

"For our war with the Americans," Hitori said.

"It is not yet certain we will go to war with the Americans," the emperor insisted. "We know the likes of Tojo and his friends within the Black Dragon would have us attack as soon as possible, but we believe we should continue to negotiate until the last. Our battles in Manchuria have been costly enough. To go to war with the Americans, it may be a battle too far, even for us."

Hitori acknowledged the wisdom of these words with a nod, not trusting himself to say more in such august company. Yes, he had fought in China, but merely as one soldier in a much larger army. To stand in the presence of the emperor and have him talk with such candour, it made Hitori dizzy. He felt some small inkling of how the weight of history and the expectations of a nation must bear down upon the narrow shoulders of the man standing opposite. What price divinity in such circumstances? He realised the emperor was looking at him, waiting for an answer to a question Hitori hadn't heard. "I'm sorry, my lord, I was too busy thinking about what Lord Constanta is offering."

"Indeed," Hirohito said, his brow furrowing. "We asked what you thought of our prospects in a war with the Americans."

"In truth, I know little about them as a nation. From this distance they seem scattered, lacking in unity, a people without the sense of community or collective purpose to be found here in Japan. I've heard it said the Americans lack the stomach for war; otherwise they would have come to the aid of Europe long before now. If we strike a great enough blow against them, I believe it will cause one of two reactions. Either they will retreat in shock, or they will strike back with a force ten times as strong as the injury they suffered."

"We fear the latter will probably be the case," the emperor sighed. "The United States is a young nation, but a proud people. We'll need all possible weapons against them if a war is our collective destiny. That is why we're asking you to surrender yourself to Constanta, to sacrifice yourself for the greater good of the empire. It is not an order, Hitori, but it is the wish of your emperor. Will you do this terrible thing, in the hope it may turn the tide of war?"

Hitori bowed his head, picturing the face of his young wife, trying to imagine what his infant son must look like. He would weep for them another day. "Yes, my lord, I will do it, for my family, my country and for you."

"Thank you. Few will ever know the truth of the sacrifice you are making, but we believe it is for a higher cause and all will be well." The emperor took a deep breath, his shoulders slumping. "It is good that you enter into this devilish pact of your own will, with the best of intentions. Remember that in the dark times that lie ahead. You do this for the noblest of reasons."

"Yes, my lord."

"There is one more thing we must ask you to do for us."

"Yes, my lord?"

"Always remember where your true loyalties lie. No matter what this monster says to you, no matter what temptations Constanta may offer, always remember you are one of us. Zenji Hitori is a true servant of the Japanese Empire, and he always will be. Constanta may lay claim to your soul, but we own your heart."

FROM: Military Police Sergeant
J. M. Hook, Honolulu City Station.
RE: Incident at Tokyo Joe's Bar
and Grill.

Multiple reports detailing a disturbance
of the peace at the above-named establishment were received at around eighteen
hundred hours. Due to the number of
reports received and the suggested level
of disturbance indicated by these reports,
it was decided prudent to send all available MPs to the scene. Upon arrival, the
nature of the disturbance was ascertained.
It proved to be a free-for-all within the
establishment, involving men of all ranks
and services. A brief assessment of the
situation adjudged there to be significant
property damage in addition to the violent

conduct, and swift action was deemed necessary.

Half the detail of MPs was despatched
to the south side of the establishment
and entered from the beach, while the
rest of the men entered from the street.
Upon securing both access points, those
engaged in violent activity were given
ample warning to cease and desist all
such activity. This warning went
unheeded and direct action was required.

Appended is a listing of all those
arrested at the scene of the affray, along
with notes about the nature of their individual offences. When possible, specific
culprits were singled out as ringleaders.
They were subdued with all necessary
force. A list of those still receiving
medical treatment is appended, as is a
summary of the injuries sustained by MPs
in the course of this action.

It is suggested that all servicemen be
banned from this establishment for the
next few weeks, to allow tempers to
cool. It seems the incident stemmed from
a dispute between marines stationed on
Oahu and men of the visiting 200th Coast
Artillery. In the view of the fact the
latter company is due to depart Honolulu
tomorrow, it is believed reprisals are
unlikely in the future, but all precautions are being undertaken.

End.

THREE

WALTON WASN'T SURE who threw the first punch that transformed Tokyo Joe's from a peaceful establishment into a miniature warzone, but he suspected Paxton had something to do with it. The two of them and Maeda had stayed in the bar all afternoon, sampling almost every kind of food and drink available. For the first time since joining the marines, Walton found he was relaxing. The sound of waves lapping on the nearby beach blended with the strumming of the resident Hawaiian band in one corner of the bar provided a gentle underscore to the hubbub of happy customers.

Walton knew he could never keep up with Maeda and Paxton's intakes. They were older than him, and knew far more about the ways of the world. So he persuaded Kissy to make sure every second drink he got was unadulterated juice; fruit punch without the punch, so to speak. But his legs still felt as if they'd been replaced by rubber bands when the complaints of his bladder became so urgent they required immediate relief. The young marine got up and staggered, lurching sideways into a neighbouring table where three army recruits were sitting. The nearest of them was a bloated, red-faced slob with thinning hair and a greasy moustache. He sprang to his feet, anger in his eyes and spittle flecking his lips. "Hey, you gonna watch where you're going, or do I have to rip you a new one?"

"Sorry, I'm sorry," Walton slurred, struggling to keep from giggling.

"What, you think this is funny?" his belligerent accuser demanded. The two soldiers with him tried to persuade their angry comrade to calm down. A young Hispanic trooper with a friendly face tugged at his colleague's sleeve.

"Hey, Buntz, there's no need to get mad; he apologised, okay?"

"No, it's not okay, Martinez! And keep your nose out of my business!"

Martinez held his hands in the air, as if surrendering. "Have it your own way if you want, Buntz. I was just saying the kid's said he was sorry."

"That's right," Walton slurred, unable to get the sloppy grin off his face.

"I notice you keep smiling at me. You think I'm funny?"

"No, not at all."

"You better not, or else I'll teach you what is funny!"

"Absolutely," Walton agreed, nodding slowly. By now his brothers in arms had noticed the argument brewing and decided to get involved. Paxton was up and out of his chair, his hands clenching into fists, while Maeda was also rising from his seat, ready to step in if required.

"Hey, Flinch, is that guy giving you a hard time?" Paxton growled.

"Not at all," the young marine replied. "He's been a perfect gentleman." Walton staggered away, squinting his eyes in the hope of getting his blurred surroundings into some sort of focus. He bumped into a surly Japanese man emerging from a side door bearing the word HEAD. "'Cuse me, is that the way to the bathroom?" The man didn't reply, just nodded wearily before walking away towards the bar. "Thank you," Walton called after him.

The youthful marine emerged several minutes later to find a massive brawl in progress. A bamboo stool flew past his face and smashed against the nearest wall, splintering apart on impact. "Did I miss something?" he asked nobody in particular. "I thought we weren't supposed to fight in here."

Maeda appeared beside him, grinning cheerfully. "Hey kid, there you are, thought I'd lost you!" He ducked beneath a swinging right hook from a snarling soldier and deftly kicked his attacker in the groin. The unhappy soldier went down with a groan and stayed down, nursing his crushed pride.

"What happened?" Walton asked. In front of him sailors, marines and soldiers were beating seven kinds of hell out of each other, using tables, chairs and stools as weapons to supplement their fists, foreheads and feet.

"That guy you bumped into tried to kiss Kissy," Maeda replied. "Paxton's kinda sweet on her and, well, you can probably guess the rest. Never get between a man and the woman he lusts after, that's my advice." An unfamiliar marine flew between the two of them and smacked into the wall. He slumped to the sandy floor, out cold long before his body had stopped moving.

"What should I do?" Walton wondered.

"Punch anybody that tries to punch you," Maeda said with a grin, "but try to punch them first." He rubbed his hands with glee. "You ready for action?"

"I guess so."

"Then pick your partner and let's get started!" Maeda jumped on top of the nearest table and dived straight into the middle of the carnage, taking several men down with him in the process. Within moments he was gone, swallowed by the chaos, another body battling for supremacy in the middle of the mayhem and madness.

Walton was about to follow Maeda's example when a strong hand clasped his arm. "I wouldn't if I was you," a deep voice whispered in his ear. The young marine twisted around to see three men leaning against the wall nearby, all dressed in naval pilot's uniforms, content to watch the brawl without getting dragged into it.

"But my buddies are in there," Walton said, gesturing at the mass of flying fists and bruised flesh, "somewhere."

"Trust me, the MPs will be here any minute. Once that happens, you don't want to be in the middle of that mess," the nearest pilot advised. His jaw line was so chiselled and his eyes so blue that he looked like he'd stepped off a navy recruiting poster. The pilot offered to shake Walton's hand. "My name's Richards, by the way, Lieutenant Charles Richards, but everyone calls me Chuck."

"Err, Walton," the marine mumbled, "David Walton. Everybody calls me... David Walton, I guess, except for Paxton, he keeps calling me Flinch." Another body went flying past, startling Walton.

"I can see where you got that nickname," Richards laughed, before jerking a thumb at his fellow pilots. "This is Ensign Ramon Marquez and Lieutenant Peter Taylor, but we call 'em Skid and Bravo. We're all off the *Enterprise*."

"How come you're not fighting?" Walton wondered.

"Captain's orders," Marquez replied. He had a drooping moustache, black hair slicked back, and a pock marked face. "We get caught fighting again and we're grounded, no flying for a week."

"I'm not losing my privileges for anyone," Taylor sneered. He had dark hair, brooding eyes.

"Bravo is our team player," Marquez quipped.

Before Walton could reply, a cacophony of harsh, penetrating whistles cut through the chaos, bringing a halt to the bar brawl. Everyone inside Tokyo Joe's stopped hitting each other and turned to look for the source of the ear-piercing sound. A phalanx of grim faced military policemen were standing at both entrances to the bar, a dozen blocking the way out to the street and another dozen cutting off any escape to the beach. One of the MPs stepped forward, his face cherry red with anger. "This is over! Each and every one of you is under arrest! You've brought disgrace on our units, disgrace on your country and disgrace on yourselves. You've got thirty seconds to–"

He never finished the sentence. A bamboo stool, thrown by unseen hands, smacked into the side of his head. That brought a roar of approval from the heart of the brawl. Within moments the fighting resumed, but now the unruly warriors had a new target: the MPs. All those who had been busy beating each other senseless joined together to attack their common enemy. If such a thing was possible, the first brawl had been almost benign, the chance to let off some steam. This fight was serious. The MPs waded into battle, using their truncheons to bludgeon a way through those nearest to them. In less than a minute, the floor was awash with blood and teeth, as skulls were cracked and bones broken.

Walton saw his friend Maeda knocked senseless by a military policeman with sergeant's stripes. But the MP kept beating Maeda even after the marine was out cold.

"Hey, you can't do that!" Walton shouted.

The sergeant grinned at the young marine. "You want some too?"

Richards stepped between them, putting one hand on Walton's chest to hold the youth back. "This guy's innocent, sergeant. I've been in here since before the brawl started and he hasn't thrown a single punch, okay?"

"If you were in here before the fighting started, why didn't you stop it?"

The pilot laughed. "Are you serious?"

The MP advanced on Richards, slapping his bloody truncheon in the palm of one hand. "You bet I'm serious, flyboy. It was your duty to stop this."

"Yeah, right!" Richards looked over his shoulder at Marquez and Taylor. "Can you believe this goon? He actually believes–" The rest of his words were cut off by the MP's truncheon smacking across his face. By the time Richards hit the floor, Walton and Marquez were laying into the sergeant, raining blows down on him. The last thing the young marine could recall was hearing a high-pitched whistle behind him. When he turned to see the source of it, a fist flew into his face. After that there was only pain and darkness.

FATHER KELLY WAS lost. Since leaving the cathedral he'd been wandering around downtown Honolulu, failing to find a way back to the docks. It was embarrassing, getting lost in a city so small compared with his native Chicago. In truth, he wasn't trying that hard, as his mind was still replaying the conversation with Bishop Sweeney. The priest was so deep in thought he came close to being run down by a convoy of jeeps transporting MPs. Father Kelly realised his jeopardy at the last moment and threw himself out of harm's way as the vehicles sped past. The men inside them looked grim faced and ready for war, making the priest grateful he was not their target.

A thought occurred to him, sending a shudder up his spine. Private Martinez was out on the town with Wierzbowski and that disreputable slob Buntz. Those two could start a fight in an empty field, and Father Kelly had little doubt that Martinez's feelings of loyalty to the regiment would drag the young soldier into the melee. He strode off in the direction the jeeps had taken, though they were long gone by now, swallowed by the press of traffic and pedestrians. Fortunately, the MPs did not go much further before abandoning their vehicles and racing into a bar and grill near the beach.

The priest found the jeeps a few minutes later, outside a ramshackle building bearing the name TOKYO JOE'S. He didn't bother going inside to see what was happening, it was all too evident from the sound of fists on flesh and the cries of men being hurt. Father Kelly made the sign of the cross and offered a silent prayer heavenwards that Martinez had the good sense not to get involved with senseless brawling. Moments later Martinez appeared in front of him, having been thrown out of a grease smeared window, on to the street. The private scrambled to his feet, brushed himself down and made as if to go back inside.

"Oh no you don't!" the priest insisted, grabbing the young soldier's arm.

"Father? What are you doing here?"

"I could ask you the same question, my son."

"Buntz and Wierzbowski are still in there. They need my help!"

"I see, and how many MPs did you see enter that bar?"

Martinez shrugged. "I don't know, ten, maybe a dozen?"

"I counted at least twenty, if not more."

"Then Buntz and Wierzbowski definitely need my help."

"They'll be fine without you. One man more or less won't make any difference. Besides, even I know fighting MPs is fighting a losing battle."

"You can say that again!" Martinez agreed. "Those guys fight dirty."

"They have right as well as might on their side, Juan. You go back in there and you'll find yourself under arrest. Do you want to spend the rest of the voyage to the Philippines confined to your cabin or stuck in the brig?"

"No, but I–"

"No buts, you're staying here, with me."

A surly MP emerged from the bar, a bloody truncheon in his right fist. He saw glass from the broken window in front of Martinez and marched straight towards the private. "You! You're the one I threw out of that window!"

Father Kelly raised a hand in protest. "Actually, I believe you may be mistaken about that, my son."

The MP glared at the priest, his snarl softening a little when he saw the ecclesiastical collar. "Stay out of this, father; it's between me and the boy."

"You're not suggesting I'm lying, are you, my son?"

"Well, no, but I saw–"

"You called me father before. That tells me you were raised a Catholic."

"Yes, but that's–"

"So you must know a priest would never lie, would he?"

"No, of course not, but–"

"So I must be telling the truth, mustn't I?"

The MP's mouth flapped soundlessly, unable to formulate an answer.

"Therefore, this young man cannot be the soldier you threw out of the window, can he?" Father Kelly gave Martinez a sly wink, unseen by the MP.

"But he's got glass in his hair."

"I beg your pardon?" the priest stammered.

The MP walked across to Martinez and pulled two fragments of broken glass from the private's curls. "See? How could he have glass in his hair unless he was the person I threw through that window?"

"I was sitting under the window when another soldier came through it," Martinez volunteered when Father Kelly had no answer to the question. "Some of the glass must have fallen on me, but I didn't notice because–"

"Because another soldier had just been thrown out of the window above you," the priest said, completing the sentence. "I did see somebody in uniform running off before. Sadly, I didn't get a good look at his face."

The MP rested his fists on his hips, glaring first at Martinez and then at Father Kelly. "That's the story you're sticking to, is it?"

"It's not a story, it's the truth," Martinez replied. "You wouldn't call our company chaplain a liar, would you?"

More MPs emerged from Tokyo Joe's, shoving semi-conscious prisoners ahead of them. The sounds of fighting in the bar had subsided and the mopping up was underway. One of the military policemen called for help from the MP standing staring at a priest and a private. That was enough for their accuser, who admitted defeat. "I'll be watching you," he warned Martinez.

"And the good Lord will be watching over you," Father Kelly replied.

The MP stomped away, muttering obscenities under his breath.

"Thanks, father, you're a lifesaver," Martinez whispered.

"I wish that were true," the priest said. "Still, I hope you'll take a lesson from this. Buntz and Wierzbowski may be older and more experienced than you, but that doesn't automatically make them any the wiser. Right now they're probably under arrest and no doubt nursing a few bruises."

As if to prove Father Kelly's point, another MP came out of the bar and grill, pushing a battered Buntz ahead of him. Moments later four burly MPs burst out into the street, each of them holding on to one of Wierzbowski's flailing limbs. He was still fighting, still raging against them. It took the intervention of two more military policemen to bring him down, clubbing the soldier over and over with their truncheons until he crumpled on the sidewalk.

"I see what you mean, father," Martinez said. "But won't lying to that MP get you in trouble with the big guy upstairs?"

"Having to confess twice in one day won't kill me," the priest sighed.

CONSTANTA MADE HITORI wait until nightfall before allowing him to surrender his soul. "Go outside, walk in the daylight, be among your people," the vampyr advised. "All being well, you will remember this day for a long, long time to come. Savour your humanity while you still have it. Most vampyrs have their souls torn from them by hungry predators. Few are given the choice about whether or not they wish to embrace immortality. Consider yourself fortunate."

Hitori did as he was told, walking out from the Ministry of War's building into Tokyo, letting himself mingle with the throngs of ordinary people, all of them hurrying to complete the rituals and minutiae of their daily lives. He found a square set aside as parkland and lay down on the moist grass, savouring the autumn sun on his skin and the soft, gentle breeze that wafted through the air. Last but not least, he found a small stationery store and bought paper, pen and ink to write a letter to his beloved wife. Hitori could not conceive ever forgetting how much he adored her, how much she meant to him, but nor could he imagine what effect sacrificing his soul to a vampyr would have upon that love. He wanted to express all the feelings in his heart but could not find the words, the eloquence to say them. Let no hint of my sadness, my loss creep into my words, Hitori decided. Let her have this last, happy letter to treasure, and leave it at that.

He returned to the park and wrote four pages, his hand hurried by the knowledge that the sun was sinking towards the horizon and his last moments of humanity were accompanying it into the darkness. As people in apartments overlooking the square of park lit lanterns for the evening ahead, he walked back to the ministry building, his feet trudging every step of the way. Suzuki was waiting at the door to let him in, the other workers having already gone home for the evening. "Zenji, what is it? What's going on? The general told me to wait down here for you, but has forbidden me to ask any questions."

Hitori could not help smiling, despite the hollow numbness he felt deep inside his chest. "The general forbade you, and still you ask your questions."

Suzuki shrugged. "You know me; I've always been the curious one."

"Be careful it does not get you killed one day." He handed his oldest friend the envelope, addressed to Aiko. "This has to be sent to my wife from Manchuria, she has to believe I died there. Can you do that for me, Shiro?"

"Of course, but–"

"No more questions, please." Hitori pushed past his friend into the building, but Suzuki followed him inside.

"Okay, okay, I won't ask you any more questions."

"Good."

"But that doesn't mean I can't speculate. If I guess right, I'll see the truth in your face. You always were a terrible liar when we were young, and even worse at bluffing." Hitori walked on, doing his best to ignore Suzuki. "Obviously, this has something to do with that Rumanian. If your wife has to believe you died in Manchuria, it means you're going on some kind of covert operation, and you're not expected to make it back alive. Am I right?"

"I thought you weren't going to ask any more questions?"

"Hmm, good point." Suzuki peered at Hitori's face as they walked along a corridor towards Tojo's private office. "I am right! But what kind of suicide mission would the general send you to undertake that involved a Rumanian officer? I mean, I screen all the intelligence reports that come in and the only mentions I've seen made about a Rumanian are those wild stories about–" Suzuki stopped, realisation and horror competing for dominion over his face. "Constanta, he's one of those creatures, isn't he? Red Army troops on the eastern front have been telling Moscow for weeks about a cadre of bloodsucking fiends fighting alongside the Wehrmacht. Lord Constanta, he's one of them, isn't he?" Suzuki's mind was racing, putting together the pieces far faster than Hitori had done. "The general's ordered you to form an alliance with this monster."

"Keep your voice down," Hitori hissed. They were standing outside the general's office and he had no wish to involve Suzuki any further in this. "He didn't order me to do anything, Shiro. I volunteered."

"Why?"

"The emperor asked me, and I would do anything for the emperor."

Suzuki staggered back a step, still reeling at the reality of it. He looked down at the sealed envelope, understanding why Hitori considered it important. "You're giving up everything to become like Constanta?"

"Yes."

"Then let me take your place."

"No. You don't know what you're suggesting, Shiro."

"I don't have a wife or a family like you do. The army is my life. If doing this spares you from losing what you love, it's a sacrifice worth making."

"No. I told the emperor I would do this," Hitori insisted. "I gave my word of honour. I cannot renounce that. It is too late for me."

"Then let me do this thing with you," Suzuki urged. "I have nothing to lose."

"You don't know what you're asking."

"Explain it to me."

"I don't have time," Hitori sighed. He knocked on the office door and it swung open to reveal Tojo and Constanta waiting for him inside. "Please, just make sure the letter gets sent to my wife from Manchuria, as you promised."

"I will," Suzuki said.

Hitori embraced him for one last time. "Goodbye, old friend." Then he walked into the office and closed the door, leaving Suzuki outside.

CONSTANTA TOOK HITORI out on a terrace near the top of the ministry building. It offered a stunning view of Tokyo as dusk settled over the city, but neither of them paid the vista any attention. Instead Constanta gestured to a group of figures held in an enclosure below, half a dozen men clustered around a pitiful paper lantern. "Once you are a vampyr, you will hunger. You must feed at once; gorge yourself on the blood of living humans. The general has arranged your first meal, a party of Chinese prisoners to do with as you wish."

Hitori remembered his earlier revulsion when Constanta had offered him the chance to drink the blood of a captive. "I'm not sure if I can go through with this. I will not dishonour my emperor, my unit, my family name by breaking my word, but to sup on another man's blood…"

The Rumanian rested a leather-gloved hand on Hitori's shoulder. "Before, in the general's office, I made you that offer as a test. You were still human then. When you are one of us, one of the everlasting, your hunger will overcome all other considerations. Your need to feed will command you."

Hitori took a deep breath. "How do I become like you?"

"Firstly, I must drink your blood. It is part of the price you must pay in exchange for immortality. Don't be afraid, it is a necessary step."

The Japanese soldier undid the collar of his uniform and pulled it aside, exposing the throat. He tilted his head to one side, all too aware of the jugular pulsing against his skin. "Do it, before I change my mind."

Constanta smiled, his lips slowly drawing back to reveal his fangs, like a predator unsheathing its claws. He took a firm grip on Hitori before rearing his head back. The Japanese soldier closed his eyes and tried to picture the face of his beautiful young wife, tried to imagine what their son must look like. Then he felt two sharp stabbing pains driving down into his neck, and a gush of warmth as liquid spilled from the twin wounds. Hitori smelled his own blood, the metallic scent clogging his nostrils, and he tasted the bitter tang of adrenaline in his mouth.

Slowly, gradually, the pain eased. In its place was the uneasy feeling of something being sucked out of his body, the disturbing sense that his life's blood was being pulled away. Hitori's heart pumped faster, trying to compensate for the loss, pushing his remaining blood around his body. He wanted to tear himself away from this monster, this fiend supping at his throat. The fight or flight impulse was close to overwhelming him, but he used every last ounce of his remaining willpower to resist that most primal of urges. He surrendered himself utterly, his old life ebbing away with his blood, giving in to the darkness and damnation.

Hitori felt disappointed when Constanta pulled his fangs away. It was as if the vampyr's presence had become the most important thing in the world, the sole reason to live or die. The Rumanian licked his lips lasciviously, savouring every morsel of crimson liquid. "Delicious, quite delicious," he hissed. "It seems a shame not to take the rest, but I made a promise to Tojo and to the Führer, back in Berlin." He undid the right sleeve of his uniform and pushed the fabric up his thin, pale arm. Two old puncture holes were visible in the fold of his elbow. Constanta dug into the wounds with his long, sharp fingernails, tearing back the scar tissue to reopen them. Two trickles of blood so dark it was almost black dripped down from the holes.

"Now it is your turn," Constanta said, his voice a bleak rasp. "By taking your blood, but leaving you enough to survive, I have remade you in my image. If you feed before the next sunrise, you will become a vampyr, but a vampyr of little power or status. You will discover there is a strict hierarchy to our kind, and your place within that is defined by your strength and abilities. Greatest of us all is the Sire, who sleeps beneath the lake of blood hidden deep inside Transylvania, awaiting the day when he will rise up and claim dominion over the world for all vampyrs. He was my blood sire, resurrecting me in his image. I have been blood sire for a select few, endowing them with much of my power and abilities. In turn, they have sired the next generation of vampyrs, imbuing them with part of their status and strength, and so it goes, on and on, generation after generation.

"It is rare that I sire a new vampyr," the Rumanian said. "According to tradition each of us can sire only ten new vampyrs. Alas, I lost one of my kin on the eastern front in recent weeks. But that is fortunate for you, as it means there is a gap in my family and I can endow you with far greater powers than you might otherwise have gained. You will need these to create the cadre of samurai vampyrs that Tojo wants as his secret weapon in the coming war."

"How?" Hitori asked, swaying in the cool twilight breeze, his legs weakened by the substantial loss of blood. "How do I attain these powers?"

"You must feed. You must drink my blood." Constanta held out his arm so it was level with Hitori's face. "Close your mouth over my wounds and nature will take its course. Forever more, part of my blood will be part of your body, augmenting your senses and your abilities. You will become one of my creatures, one of my übervampyrs!"

Still Hitori hesitated, his old self repulsed by the thought of drinking another creature's blood. But something else was stirring deep inside him, an insatiable need, a hunger that grew until it became a torrent, a storm of wanting and anger, of violence and need. An animal instinct was overtaking him, until he could hold it back no longer. Red mist descended upon his reason and he gave in to it, pulling back his lips with a hiss of triumph. Hitori sank his teeth deep into Constanta's cold, sallow flesh and drank of the liquid within. He felt the warmth of it smearing his chin, running down his neck and staining the front of this uniform, but he didn't care. He wanted to suckle those wounds forever, to bury himself in that black and crimson moisture; he wanted to feed upon the source until it ran dry.

"Enough," Constanta commanded, trying to pull his arm free.

"More," Hitori replied, his voice as guttural as some base animal's.

"Enough!" The Romanian ripped Hitori from his arm, throwing the Japanese soldier across the terrace. Hitori's body thundered into the stone balustrade, but he was up on his feet within moments, licking his lips and advancing on Constanta. The Rumanian rolled his sleeve back down, hiding away the wounds that had become irresistible to Hitori. "You tried to drain me."

"I was hungry," the Japanese soldier smiled.

"You want to keep feeding?" Constanta pointed at the prisoners waiting below. "There's your next meal. Feed on them."

"Cattle," Hitori spat. "None will taste as sweet as you."

Constanta folded his arms and glared at what he had created. "Be that as it may, you took more than enough to assure your future as one of my kinsmen. But I still control you, Zenji Hitori; you will be ever in my thrall."

"We'll see about that," the Japanese soldier snarled and hurled himself at the Rumanian. Constanta smashed him aside, as if swatting away a gnat.

"Do not try my patience," the vampyr lord warned. "Yes, I have made you powerful, more powerful even than my faithful Gorgo, but I still have your measure, Hitori. I can resurrect myself from the smallest speck of dusk. You remain vulnerable, you can still be killed. You are immortal, but only up to a point. Do not make the mistake of believing yourself unbeatable."

"How?" Hitori demanded. "How can I be killed?"

"I will tell you as dawn approaches tomorrow morning. For now, you should go and feed. Discover your abilities, what you can do, the powers that you have. Return here before the next sunrise and I shall complete your education." Still scowling, Hitori moved to the door that led inside. "You need not go that way anymore," Constanta said. "You are a vampyr. Fly and be free!"

"I can fly?"

The Rumanian grinned. "There is little you can no longer do, kinsman."

"But how?"

"Leap from this terrace and your new instincts will do the rest."

Hitori stared at his benefactor, as if trying to see into his thoughts. "How do I know I can trust you?"

"Would I let you drink my blood and then suggest jumping to your death?" Constanta gestured at the vast cityscape splayed out before them. "This is all yours now, take it! Enjoy your new freedom, your new abilities. Embrace them. Become one with the night."

Hitori looked down at his hands, studying them as if they were newly grown. He opened his mouth and ran a finger across his fangs, freshly emerged from within his upper jaw. He grinned, a grin that turned to laughter. "So be it," the Japanese vampyr said, before throwing himself off the terrace.

FROM: Lieutenant Hitori,
      Manchuria
DATE: September, 1941

My dearest Aiko,

By the time you get this letter, I imagine you will have already had the baby. Is it a boy or a girl, I wonder? If our child is a girl, I hope she has your beauty and your serenity, your patience and your compassion. If our child is a boy, I hope he has your courage and your faith in human nature, your openness and your smile. I wish I could have been with you at the birth, but know that your parents and mine will have done all they can to help you.

As always, there is little I can tell you about our situation here, in case

this letter should fall into the wrong
hands. I can't wait until the day we are
reunited, so that I can tell you in
person how much I love you and our child,
how much both of you mean to me. Be
assured that your devoted, loving husband is fighting bravely and as well as
he can for the empire. Our enemies are
many and our resources finite, but the
men show great courage and I am proud to
lead them into battle.

Outside the sun is setting and I can
smell jasmine on the breeze. It makes me
long for our little home, to be drinking
green tea with you and sharing the story
of our day, to be sharing our love for
each other, as husband and wife. I would
give anything in the world for this war
not to have taken me away from you, but
such wishes are beyond my power to
grant, sadly. I must put such fancies
from my mind and concentrate instead on
the happy day when we are all reunited.
Know that my thoughts and feelings will
be with you, always.

  Your loving husband,
  Zenji.

FOUR

SERGEANT EMERY LEE Hicks had never seen such a pathetic, useless, despicable and craven collection of marines in his life and he wasn't afraid to say so. More than a dozen men from B Company had been arrested for fighting at Tokyo Joe's the previous night. All of them sported bruises and bandages, several had black eyes, and a few displayed broken noses. It was embarrassing for the corps and especially so for Hicks. B Company was responsible for policing and security within the navy yard, yet his men had been starting brawls with other divisions of the service in downtown Honolulu. Hicks gave the twelve unhappy marines an ear bashing that would have made a battleship blanch. After shouting himself all but hoarse, he announced that each man would be confined to barracks for a fortnight and that they could expect no privileges for a month. He dismissed most of the marines, but kept

back the trio accused by the bar manager of having
started the brawl: Paxton, Maeda and Walton.

Walton had two black eyes and a swollen jaw from
the blows that had knocked him unconscious.
Maeda's head was swathed in bandages and his left
arm was in a sling, due to a dislocated shoulder he'd
suffered while trapped on the floor of the bar.
Despite having thrown the first punch, Paxton had
gotten off lightly. A split lip was all the evidence he
bore of his involvement, having taken shelter
behind the bamboo bar with Kissy as soon as the
brawl got out of hand. He'd emerged grinning afterwards, as usual.

The sergeant glared at the men identified as ringleaders. All of them had been standing in the
blazing sun for more than an hour, and their uniforms were soaked with sweat. "You three disgust
me," Hicks snarled, his words thick with venomous
hatred. "You disgrace the good name of the corps
with your antics, turning a perfectly respectable bar
into a battleground for your petty squabbles and
rivalries. You pick a fight with navy pilots and any
passing grunts that happen to be inside Tokyo Joe's,
when everybody in uniform knows that place is neutral territory! You attack the military police when
they arrive, ensuring that everyone in this unit is a
marked man in future. But you know what makes
me most ashamed, what chills the blood in my
veins, what makes me sick to my stomach?"

Walton opened his mouth to reply, but thought
better of it and stayed silent.

Hicks spat on the parade ground tarmac, his face
twisted by rage. "It's the fact that you three didn't

win your fight before the damned MPs arrived! In my day we would have beaten the living snot out of everybody in the bar, before using their ugly faces to wipe the floor clean of blood. My god, we're talking about raw recruits and navy pilots! If you can't beat those pantywaists, what hope have you got against a real enemy? The three of you are a disgrace to the corps!" The sergeant marched straight at Walton, not stopping until their noses were touching. "Well, Flinch, what have you got to say for yourself?"

"I... I was in the head when the fighting started, so I–"

"You were what?"

"I was relieving myself, sergeant."

"Is that a fact?"

"Yes, sergeant. When I came out, I saw one of the MPs attacking Maeda, even though Pat was already unconscious on the floor."

"So you intervened, is that it?"

"Yes, sergeant."

"A likely story." Hicks moved along to Paxton, who was grinning from ear to ear at Walton's discomfort. "What's so damned funny?"

"Nothing, sergeant," Paxton replied, forcing the smirk from his features.

"I should hope not," Hicks snorted. "Way I hear it, all of this started over some little Japanese whore at the bar that you've been chasing for months."

"Kissy's no–"

"Did I ask for your opinion, numb-nuts?"

"No, sergeant," Paxton muttered.

"I can't hear you!"

"No, sergeant!"

"That's better." The sergeant clamped a meaty fist around Paxton's groin and squeezed, until the marine's eyes were watering. "You want to sow your wild oats, that's fine by me, but I suggest you chase a skirt that's worth catching. Everybody knows these Oriental types will stab you in the back as soon as look at you. Count yourself lucky she didn't cut your privates off and feed them back to you." Hicks released his grip, and Paxton let out a pathetic whimper of relief. The sergeant moved on to Maeda, last of the unfortunate trio. "Well, what have you got to say for yourself, my slant-eyed little friend?"

"Nothing, sergeant."

"So you agree with my assessment of Paxton's taste in squeezes?" Maeda didn't reply. "I'm guessing your mother was just the same, another Oriental whore who got her kicks jumping the bones of good, honest, red-blooded Americans. How many fathers have you got, or don't you know?"

Still Maeda kept his counsel, refusing to rise to the bait.

"God forbid we ever have to fight a war," the sergeant sneered, his spittle spattering Maeda's bruised face, "with slant eyed, traitorous scum like you in the corps. You'll probably knife us in our beds when we're still asleep. That's how you under-handed, sneaky little Oriental devils operate, isn't it?" Hicks glared at Maeda, willing him to fight back. "What's that? Got nothing to say to me? Is it because I'm only speaking the truth, or is it more likely you're too damned yellow to stand up for yourself and your family? That's it, isn't it? You're too damned yellow, like the rest of your slant eyed friends, as cowardly as the colour of your damned skin. You make me sick!"

Maeda reached a hand up to his face, making Hicks step back in anticipation of a blow. Instead the marine wiped the sergeant's spittle from his eyes and flicked it on to the tarmac, before standing to attention once more.

Hicks shook his head and retreated a few steps so he could glare at all three of them simultaneously. "Since the exact and precise circumstances of this brawl are unclear, the captain's given me permission to determine how those involved get punished. Paxton and Walton, I'm satisfied you were led astray by Maeda here, who was no doubt endeavouring to undermine the strength and integrity of this unit. So, you two will–"

"I'm sorry, sergeant, but that's wrong," Walton interrupted.

"What did you say?" Hicks demanded.

"Shut up," Paxton hissed out the side of his mouth at the young marine.

"Maeda didn't start the fight and he didn't lead me astray," Walton said.

"Shut your mouth, you'll drop all of us in it!" Paxton warned.

The sergeant smiled. "You should listen to your colleague, he knows what he's talking about. Paxton, you will serve the same punishment as the men already dismissed. Walton, your punishment will be doubled. You're hereby confined to barracks for a month and denied privileges for two months."

"But, sergeant–"

"But nothing!" Hicks snarled, any trace of sympathy ripped from his taciturn features. "Last but not least, Maeda. You will spend the next four weeks incarcerated in the hope that you will have time to consider the error of your ways. After that you can expect to spend the next month confined to barracks. You're to be denied any and all privileges indefinitely, until you prove yourself worthy of the Marine Corps. Now, does anybody have any questions?" The sergeant glared at Walton. "Any further statements or excuses they'd like to say in their defence or on behalf of their friends?"

Walton bit his bottom lip, his hands clenching into fists behind his back.

"I thought not," Hicks said, triumph in his voice. "See, Maeda? These two don't care enough about you to speak out on your behalf. I think that speaks volumes about your place in this unit, don't you?"

Maeda didn't reply.

"I'll take that as a yes," the sergeant announced. "Paxton and Walton, you two can escort Maeda to his new home for the next month. Dismissed!"

HITORI RETURNED TO the Ministry of War building as dawn neared Tokyo, furling his vampyr wings as he descended to the open terrace. He was still amazed by the massive spans of skin and sinew that had burst from his back when he had leapt from the terrace the previous night. He had plummeted to the concrete walkway below, screaming in terror as it rushed towards him. Suddenly he heard a ripping sound and felt the back of his uniform split apart. Moments later he was flying, two mighty wings beating at the air, lifting him up into the sky. He could hear Constanta yelling his approval from the terrace, urging him on. Hitori was flying, against all logic or sense, against everything his learning and intelligence told him. He was flying and he loved it.

But the hunger soon overtook that sensation, laying claim to his thoughts and gnawing at his soul. He looked down and saw the six Chinese prisoners cowering in their enclosure, several of them pointing up at him in amazement. Instinct took over once more and he spiralled down towards the men, feeling the variations in the night air as it passed across his wings, savouring the smells of people cooking their evening meals nearby. Would he ever consume anything but blood in future? That was a question for tomorrow and his sire. For now all he wanted was to feed, to gorge himself on the crimson liquid pulsing inside every living human.

When all six prisoners were dead, he could still hear their screams of terror in his mind. They had spoken in several different dialects, some from northern Manchuria while others had been born on the coast, yet he had understood them all. Not only could he comprehend their words, he knew a little of their thoughts and sensed their innermost terrors. It must be another of my new abilities, Hitori realised, being able to look inside the minds of mortals, to insinuate myself into their hearts. I wonder what other talents I have acquired in exchange for my soul?

He had spent the rest of the night exploring the dark corners of Tokyo, seeing how the city lived after sunset, witnessing all the decadence and horrors that usually remained hidden in the shadows. Now he was at one with the shadows and the darkness embraced him, recognising him as a fellow traveller on the road to hell. He saw sad-eyed prostitutes wearily servicing businessmen in alleyways, watched husbands beat wives, and witnessed corrupt policemen taking fistfuls of cash from dens of gambling and vice to ignore the transgressions. Once these scenes would have appalled and outraged him, but now they were merely evidence of how little mankind cared for one another, for the weak and for the truth. There was no justice to be found here, Hitori decided. The empire's underworld was a sickening realm of secrets and lies. Strange, he thought, how it took the intervention of a monster to make me see this harsh and brutal reality.

"You see the truth now," a familiar voice said atop the terrace at the Ministry of War, interrupting Hitori's thoughts. "It is part of our curse."

He swivelled around to find Constanta at his shoulder. "What curse?"

The Rumanian held out his hands and smiled. "Immortality is a blessing and damnation, in its way. You can live forever, but you will see those you once knew and loved die. You may walk in eternity, but the price of admission is to watch civilisations rise and fall, entire empires eventually, inevitably, crumbling into dust. You are apart from the world that you once knew, a stranger in your own land. But it is the fate you have chosen for yourself. The sooner you learn to accept the truth and take comfort from it, the better."

"You speak like the monks in Shinto temples."

"I'm not that inscrutable, am I?" Constanta asked disingenuously.

"You promised to tell me of my weaknesses, now that I am like you."

"And so I shall, Zenji. You can live forever, but you are not truly immortal, not to the extent that I am. You can be killed. Silver can be fatal to our kind, in certain circumstances."

"How?" Hitori asked.

"An ordinary bullet or blade cannot harm you, not in the way it once would. But a silver bullet or a blade coated in silver will harm you in the same way an ordinary bullet or blade harms a human."

"What else?"

"Holy water can burn your flesh, if you were a believer in a Christian god. There has never been a Japanese vampyr before and I know little of your faith, so I cannot predict what other beliefs you once held that will make you vulnerable. Often it is the faith of the person holding an emblem that imbues it with the power to harm. As a Christian with a cross can use it to burn your flesh, so a Jew with a Star of David can cause pain, or a Russian communist with a hammer and sickle on their badge. Beware symbols of faith, they can cause the most exquisite of agonies, but perhaps you enjoy such torments?"

Hitori ignored the question to ask another of his own. "What else?"

"Sunlight is our greatest enemy. If that touches your unprotected flesh it burns. If you are trapped in sunlight, you will suffer a most excruciating death."

Hitori shook his head, quite bewildered by it all. "So many ways we can die, it's a wonder any of our kind survive at all."

"You wanted to know the weaknesses of the vampyr, but becoming one of us has given you powers beyond the imaginings of mere mortals. You can fly, change your shape at will, understand the languages of others, and bend their wills to your own. You need never eat or drink again, except the blood of living humans. You do not even need to breathe, so you cannot be drowned. You are more than human: you are stronger, more powerful and far more important. Becoming a vampyr heightens latent abilities you already possess, gifts of which you may be unaware. It is not unknown for those made undead to discover they can sense when danger is approaching. That is a rare quality, manifested by perhaps one in a thousand vampyrs, but it is precious. If you find one among your recruits has that ability, nurture him."

Hitori filed that away in his mind. He had a more pressing matter he wanted to raise. "You haven't told me why the vampyrs are getting involved with the war. Surely these battles are irrelevant to us?"

Constanta nodded. "True, but when you become all but immortal, you have to take the long view. At present the humans number into their billions. For now, we are few, but our numbers are growing. The war in Europe will spread. Your own government cannot wait to accelerate that process. Soon the conflicts will involve almost every country, every continent on the planet. When the war of the humans is over, the vampyr nation will rise up to start a new war: the war of blood, a crimson conflict to decide the future of this world. We shall take our rightful place as the dominant species. Humans will be to us as cattle are to humans: fodder, nothing more, nothing less."

"That's why you came to Japan," Hitori realised, "to plant the seeds for your future empire. That's why you've made me like you, so I can be an agent for your kind, an insurgent against my own people."

"The Japanese are no longer your people. The empire you once served has forsaken you, just as you have forsaken it. This city is no longer your home, Hitori. You are a vampyr now. You are one of us."

"I made an oath to the emperor that I would serve him and Japan first."

Constanta smiled. "You may follow the will of your leaders, for now. You may fight their battles and strike at the Americans on their behalf. But there will come a day when I shall lay claim to your allegiance, and to all those you turn to our ways. When the war of blood begins, I will want you by my side, fighting for the vampyr nation. This war among humans is merely a prelude to a far greater conflict. Remember that, remember it well!" The Rumanian turned to go, but Hitori grabbed him by the arm.

"You're leaving?"

"I have done what I came to do. The rest is up to you. My part in the humans' war for control of the Pacific is over."

"But what do I do next?"

"You are a soldier, a brave and skilful one, or so I've been told. Use your natural talents and the powers I have given you to do what you do best. Find and recruit a cadre of men to serve as your seconds. Drink their blood and let them feed upon yours. The more you give to them, the closer in strength they will be to you. These seconds will go out and recruit their own lieutenants, form their own cadres of vampyr insurgents. You and your acolytes have the potential to become the emperor's ultimate weapon, an army of undead samurai warriors. After that, well..." Constanta's features became translucent as his body changed into a cloud of mist, floating in the air. "The rest is up to you." His devilish smile was last to vanish, fading away to leave but a memory of the vampyr's presence.

Zenji Hitori was left behind on the terrace overlooking Tokyo, more alone than he had ever been before in his twenty-seven years of life.

FATHER KELLY STOOD by the railings on deck as the *President Coolidge* sailed away from Hawaii. He held a traditional floral garland in his hands, given to him by a native girl as he had boarded the ship. Against all the odds, every member of the 200th had found his way back to the vessel in time and it was now bound for the Philippines and an uncertain future for those on board. All those who'd been caught up in the brawl at Tokyo Joe's faced a voyage filled with no end of punishments and absolutely no privileges. Martinez had escaped the commander's wrath, thanks to Father Kelly's intervention in Honolulu. The young soldier found his saviour staring wistfully at the lush green island of Oahu, holding the lei as if it were a set of rosary beads.

"Father, are you planning to throw that or pray with it?" Martinez asked.

"Sorry?" Father Kelly said, shaken from his private thoughts.

"I was asking if you planned to throw that in the water. I got talking to one of the locals, back on the island. She said if you throw a lei into the water when you sail and it goes back towards the island, that means you'll return one day, but if it floats out to sea, you won't ever come back to Hawaii."

"Oh, I see," the priest replied. "Well, by rights, all vessels coming back from the Philippines usually make a stop at these islands. Let's find out, shall we?" He tossed the lei away from the boat and it landed with a gentle splash on the churning blue and white waters. Both men watched the floral necklace intently. Slowly, gradually, the currents took the lei away from the islands.

Martinez frowned, a bitter thought occurring to him. "Well, it's just an old wives' tale. I'm sure it doesn't mean anything really. The propellers on the boat probably pushed your lei the wrong way, that's all."

Father Kelly smiled politely. "I'm sure you're right, Juan." He turned his back on the ocean. "How are your tour guides faring?"

"Wierzbowski and Buntz? They both got arrested by the MPs. The commander threw the book at them, no mercy. I was lucky you didn't let me go back inside." The young soldier shook his head at the memory of what had happened at Tokyo Joe's. "Of course, Wierzbowski ain't complaining, since he never complains about anything. But Buntz? He's been bellyaching twenty to the dozen, saying I should have caught as much flak as he did for what happened. I tried telling Buntz that if he hadn't been hitting on the Japanese serving girl, none of it would have happened, but…"

"He doesn't want to hear that?"

"Pretty much. I don't know how long it's gonna take him to get over it. I ain't holding my breath, let's put it that way."

"A wise course of action," the priest agreed.

"Anyways…" Martinez said. His nostrils flared at the smell of hot food leaking out from the nearest doorway. "They're serving lunch, if you want it."

"That's very kind, Juan, but I'll stay here. Your sea legs are better than mine, so I tend not to eat the first day of a voyage."

"Okay, father. Well, it was good talking to you."

"You too, Juan." Father Kelly turned back around and stared out across the ocean to the receding profile of the Hawaiian Islands. Martinez looked at the priest for a moment before going inside to eat lunch. He wanted to get that sad image of the lei floating away from Oahu out of his head. When they left port he had thought of the floral garland as a happy, cheerful tradition. But the garland Father Kelly had thrown into the water looked more like a funeral wreath, and there was nothing happy or cheerful about that.

HITORI REMAINED ON the balcony after Constanta had gone, watching the horizon as dawn crept nearer, the imminent sunrise already lightening the distant sky. Night was becoming day once more. For most people, that was something to be celebrated, but Hitori knew it would be fatal for him if he remained out on the terrace. Perhaps that would be for the best, Hitori mused, a kind of vampyr ritual suicide, seppuku for the undead. He had drained the blood from six people in the night, had drunk their life as if it were water, had feasted on their essences. What kind of monster did that make him? What right did he have to take their lives to sustain his own?

Killing on the battlefield was regrettable, but that was the nature of war. Trainee soldiers were told that it was not murder, but killing in the furtherance of a greater cause. Hitori grimaced. Did he believe that anymore? Had he ever believed it? No matter. The past was irrelevant. He had a decision to make, here and now: embrace the future as a creature of the night, or sacrifice himself to the daylight. The latter choice might keep the vampyr taint away from Japan for a while longer, but there was little doubt Constanta would return and offer the same opportunity to another soldier. No, if anyone had to carry this burden, it had better be me, Hitori decided. I will serve the empire as best I can and for as long as I can, until the hunger undoes me.

He walked inside as the first beams of sunlight stabbed through the clouds to illuminate the morning. General Tojo was waiting for Hitori, his face betraying nothing. "Well? How do you feel? Has this Rumanian made you stronger, more powerful?"

"Yes, general," Hitori conceded.

"Excellent. Word of your demise in Manchuria has already been posted and I sent my adjutant to break the news to your beautiful young wife, Aiko."

"Thank you, sir."

Tojo took a piece of paper from his desk and handed the document to Hitori. It was marked with the emperor's seal. "This gives you power to requisition anyone and anything you need to further your cause. War with the Americans is imminent and you will play a vital part in ensuring our first strike is an effective one. The greater the surprise, the deadlier our blow will be." A knock at the office door interrupted them. "Come!" the general snapped.

Suzuki entered and bowed low to both men. "Aiko Hitori has been told of her husband's unfortunate demise," he reported.

"Very good," Tojo said. "There is no turning back for you, Zenji. Your future is bound up in the inevitable war to come. The same will soon be true for all of Japan, all of the empire. I have much to do in preparation for that glorious day, and so do you. Dismissed." The general returned to his desk and sat down, doing his best to ignore the others.

Hitori let his friend usher him out. But the vampyr paused to look back over his shoulder at one of Japan's most powerful men. Tojo was trying to drink from a steaming cup of green tea, but his right hand was shaking too much. The general was forced to use both hands to hold the cup steady, his fingers visibly trembling. He's terrified, Hitori realised, terrified of me. The Minister of War for Japan is afraid of me.

Suzuki closed the office door. "I'm sorry, Zenji, he made me tell Aiko about you dying in Manchuria. She's... She didn't take the news well." Suzuki waited, but his friend did not react. "Zenji, did you hear what I said?" He grabbed Hitori by the arm. "Zenji!"

Hitori frowned. "Don't touch me," he warned.

"But you were–"

"It doesn't matter, not anymore."

"What about Aiko?"

"I can't think about her, not now." Hitori looked along the corridor in both directions. From his time as Tojo's adjutant, he knew that this early in the morning most of the building was still empty. "Your office, is it still by the stairs?"

"Y-Yes… Why do you ask?"

"I need your undivided attention and I don't want us to be disturbed."

The two friends strode to Suzuki's office, locking the door once they were inside. Hitori was careful to keep away from the window, where sunlight was already flooding into the chamber. "Yesterday, you offered to take my place. Would you still do that?"

"Of course."

"Would you give up everything and everyone you know if I asked?"

"Zenji, you know I would."

"Good," Hitori said, a smile curling his lips. "Then you will become my lieutenant, my second in command for the dark days that lie ahead."

"Whatever you want of me, it's yours to take," Suzuki replied.

"You have access to all the efficiency reports, citations for bravery and valour in combat, yes? You can identify the best of the best among all of our sol-

diers, pilots and sailors, the men who would sacrifice anything and everything if they believed it was
in service of the emperor?"

The adjutant gestured at filing cabinets behind his
desk. "It's all in there. Anything else you need I can
summon from records."

"Excellent," Hitori said. "Those men will be our
weapons, bringing terror to the skies, seas and soils
of the Pacific. They will become like us."

"Like us?"

"Yes, like us. Loosen your collar, Shiro, I'm going
to drink your blood, before letting you drink a little
of mine. After that we shall be bonded together for
eternity, our fates intertwined for all time. What
more could any friend ask?"

TO: Sister Marie Kelly, Our Lady
of the Sacred Heart Convent,
Chicago

Dear Sis,

Well, we're due into the Philippines
tomorrow and I can't tell you how much
I'm looking forward to being off this
boat. I knew becoming an army chaplain
would have its hardships, but thought
the vocation we've both chosen would
leave me well prepared for such things.
I hadn't grasped the need to spend so
long in such uncomfortable conditions. A
natural sailor I am not, as you'll
recall from that time we went out on the
boating pond. Sadly, my sea legs have
not improved over the years.

As chaplain, I've been fortunate enough to be afforded a little more privacy than most of the men. They're a good group, earthy and likeable, although that applies more to some than others, of course. Young Juan Martinez is a wonderful fellow, kind and generous to a fault, always willing to come to the aid of his fellow recruits. At the other end of the scale is Arnold Buntz, who would steal the pennies from a dead man's eyes. I know that sounds harsh, but Buntz has all the morals of a sewer rat, and none of the charm. My silver crucifix, the one you gave me last Christmas, went missing on the first day of our voyage.

Martinez returned it to me a week later. At first he wouldn't say how or where he found it, but I later discovered Buntz was responsible for the theft. He may not have taken it himself - Buntz rarely gets his own hands dirty - but it came to rest in his possession. As a result, I've taken to locking my tiny cabin each time I leave. A priest should be able to trust his parishioners, but I suppose Buntz would argue he's not among my flock, no matter how many times I invite him to mass. Yes, I know Sis, I should consider him a challenge. Something tells me I'll have challenges enough in the weeks and months ahead.

Well, I can hear the other men making their way to the mess for our evening meal, so I'd better finish this if I want to eat tonight. Please write with all the news from home. I miss it and all of you terribly.

All my love,

Shamus.

FIVE

"MAKE NO MISTAKE, men, you have not come to the Philippines for a holiday!" Douglas MacArthur was standing on a raised dais, hands on his hips, a pipe clenched in the corner of his mouth. The commanding general of the United States Army Forces in the Far East looked out over the assembled ranks of the 200th Coast Artillery, all of whom were standing at attention in the blazing, midday heat. "You have not been sent to this place to work on your tan or to fraternise with the locals. You are stationed here as America's first line of defence against the threat posed to our great nation from the Orient. The politicians back home will tell you that America has no interest in starting a war, and that is how it should be. But if someone picks a fight with us, I'd like to think we'd be damn well ready to fight back!"

Buntz, Wierzbowski and Martinez were standing shoulder to shoulder at the back of the assembled troops, under the watchful gaze of Sergeant Aimes. The stone-faced disciplinarian had been on their backs since the incident in Honolulu, berating Wierzbowski and Buntz for their part in the brawl at Tokyo Joe's and for disgracing the good name of the regiment. Martinez had escaped punishment for his part, but not the sergeant's suspicion. "I'm keeping my eye on you," Aimes snarled once a day at the young private, "my good eye!" The sergeant had lost one of his eyes in a regimental boxing match ten years earlier and the glass eye that replaced it was slightly too large, bulging grotesquely from the socket.

"Make no mistake, we're in harm's way here," MacArthur continued. "I believe we will be at war within a year, maybe sooner. The Imperial Japanese Navy has been aggressively rearming itself for the best part of a decade. It is one of the few armies in the world with practical fighting experience, thanks to four years of battling the Chinese in Manchuria. You may think of them as little slant-eyed, yellow-skinned cowards, but I believe they pose the greatest possible threat to our position within the Pacific. All the negotiations in the world won't change the fact that war in this region is inevitable. When that war comes, and, by God, it will come, you men will see all the action you ever wanted and more. We need to get you ready for that action. We need to defend these islands with our hearts, our minds, our weapons and our lives!"

Buntz snorted. "No way I'm putting my ass on the line for some two-bit rock in the middle of nowhere, not me. Hell, if the Japs want to come around my old neighbourhood and start something, they'll find plenty of people there spoiling for a fight."

"Put a sock in it, Buntz," the sergeant hissed.

The general pulled the pipe from his mouth and used it to gesticulate at his troops. "I have confidence in all of you. You've already proven yourselves in non-combat situations. Each of you has undergone eight months of hard, rigorous training at Fort Bliss in Texas. It was due to the quality of your efforts during training that you were selected for this assignment. Hell, the 200th is officially the best anti-aircraft regiment in the entire US armed forces, regular or otherwise. That takes some doing. I am confident that with men of your calibre we'll defend these islands with honour, with strength and with precision!"

"Three cheers for the general!" Aimes bellowed. The assembled troops replied in unison, some two thousand of them cheering their new commander.

MacArthur smiled, accepting the honour with a nod. He waited until the cheers had died down before continuing with his address. "Now, I know you're all tired from the long voyage and no doubt eager to get to your new postings. I won't keep you out in this sweltering sun any longer than I have to, you'll be glad to hear. But I believe we should all pray for the success of your mission here. Would the regimental chaplain please join me on the dais?"

Father Kelly was standing near the back of the assembly, his thoughts elsewhere. It took a nudge from behind by Martinez to get his attention. "Hey, father, the general's calling for you!"

The priest looked around and realised everyone was staring at him. "Father, would you join me up here on stage?" the general asked. "That's if you're not too busy." That got a laugh from the men, further embarrassing the priest. Blushing to his blond roots, Father Kelly fell out of line and hurried towards the dais. He almost stumbled on the stairs before reaching MacArthur. The general shook him by the hand and welcomed the nervous priest to the Philippines. "The men and I would certainly appreciate it if you could lead us all in a prayer of thanks for their safe voyage, and of hope for the future."

"It would be my honour," Kelly replied.

"Good. We'll have need of your faith in the weeks and months to come," MacArthur said. He stepped aside so the priest could address the men.

"Let us pray," Kelly said, endeavouring to make his voice loud enough to be heard by everyone. The soldiers lowered their heads, ready to receive his blessing. "Heavenly father, we ask that you look after these young men, sent here to defend these islands. We ask that you give them the gift of faith: faith to believe in themselves and each other, faith to do what's best."

At the back of the assembled troops Martinez and Wierzbowski both had their heads bowed forward, listening to the priest's words, but Buntz was too busy smirking to pay much attention to the prayer. "Hey, Wierzbowski," he hissed out of the side of his mouth. "You hear what MacArthur called his little boy? Arthur MacArthur! What kind of name is that for a kid?"

"Buntz, shut up!" Martinez whispered.

"I wasn't talking to you, Sancho. I was talking to my buddy here."

"If you don't want to hear the father's prayer, at least shut up so the rest of us can listen to it, okay?" Martinez hissed, aware of the sergeant's gaze.

"Don't tell me what to do," Buntz growled. "I spent every day since we left Hawaii getting punished for that brawl and you got off scot free. You don't got the right to tell Arnold Buntz what to do, you little 'spic!"

"What did you call me?" Martinez demanded.

"Don't get your panties in a bunch, Sancho. I only called you a 'spic, it's short for Hispanic, okay?"

"No, it's not okay. And stop calling me Sancho! My name is Juan."

The smirking Buntz made an obscene, sacrilegious suggestion and got a punch in the nose from Wierzbowski. The overweight soldier responded by flinging himself at the taciturn recruit. Within moments the two of them were grappling on the ground, fingers trying to gouge out eyes, fists pounding flesh. Buntz had a weight advantage over his opponent but little else, and soon found himself pinned to the dirt, Wierzbowski giving him a pasting.

"Amen," Father Kelly said at the front of the assembly.

"Amen," the general echoed. "Thank you all for being so patient with me. Hopefully I'll get to know some of you a little better in the days to come." His gaze shifted to the altercation at the back of the assembly. MacArthur suppressed a rueful smile. "I see some of you are eager to practise your hand to hand combat techniques. Such enthusiasm is to be applauded, but let's not leave our best game in the locker room, okay boys? That's all, dismissed."

The sergeant waited until MacArthur had left the dais before ripping Buntz and Wierzbowski apart. Aimes concentrated his attentions on Buntz while Martinez stopped Wierzbowski from going back for more. "Why'd you do that? Buntz was insulting me, not you. I could've dealt with him myself."

His comrade shrugged. "I've been wanting to wipe that smirk off his face since San Francisco. He just gave me a good excuse."

Buntz was busy arguing with the sergeant, protesting at being held back. "Let me at him! I could take that ape, anytime, any place!"

"Yeah, sure," Aimes replied, "and my sister-in-law's ass isn't the size of Nebraska. Well now, the two of you just earned yourselves a month without privileges for that display. Count yourself lucky the general decided not to get involved, otherwise you'd both be facing a court martial. Now get your sorry asses out of my sight, before I double your punishments. Move!"

VICE-ADMIRAL CHUICHI Nagumo's face split into a sneer. "This fool wants what?" He snapped his fingers until one of his men handed across a handwritten list detailing pilots and planes being requisitioned from the aircraft carrier Akagi. Nagumo was commander of the Imperial Japanese Navy's 1st Air Fleet, and notorious for the shortness of his temper. The vice-admiral's narrow, steely eyes slid down the document, his nostrils flaring.

"Outrageous! On what authority does this upstart expect to take my best men and machines? Bring him in here, now!"

The officer who had delivered the list stepped out of the bridge for a few moments before returning with a younger man. Nagumo glared at the new-comer, committing his features to memory. I will make an example of this whelp, he decided. I want to be able to describe his face well when I tell others the story of how I crushed him. Nagumo doubted the man standing opposite was more than thirty, and probably much less. The newcomer had a cruel mouth and a wry, questioning aspect to his demeanour, as if he had a secret advantage over everyone else in the room. His eyes were hooded, revealing no trace of fear or misgiving. Everything about this upstart screamed of insolence, his casual stance, the refusal to acknowledge the ritual bows when he entered, even the way he looked Nagumo up and down.

The vice-admiral had expected this messenger to be humbled, even petrified, standing on the bridge of an imperial aircraft carrier. Instead he found his own will weakening, and his desire to see this worm humiliated melting away like the snow on Mount Fuji during summer. Nagumo broke eye contact with the visitor, determined not to give in. He chose to study the arrogant arrival's uniform. It bore the emperor's insignia, suggesting the wearer was drawn from Hirohito's personal guard. But there was another emblem visible on the collar, the peaked cap and over the left breast of the new-comer's tunic. Nagumo squinted, finding it difficult to make out the emblem's detail. The symbol was sculpted from black metal, so the insignia blended into the black tunic and cap band on which it rested.

"It's a bat with wings unfurled, clutching the rising sun in its claws," the newcomer said, his voice thick with disdain for the vice-admiral.

"I can see what it is," Nagumo snapped.

"You seemed to be having a few problems making it out. Still, not that surprising at your age. I'm surprised the IJN chose you for this command."

The vice-admiral's nostrils flared. "You insolent pup! How dare you address me in that manner! Do you have any conception of how many ways I could destroy you for that remark?"

"I'm guessing... none."

Nagumo stepped closer to the newcomer. "What is your name?"

"Why should I tell you?"

"It would be helpful to know for when I notify your next of kin."

"Is that a threat?"

"Consider it a promise."

"Don't make promises you can't keep, Chuichi." The other officers on the bridge gasped in shock at hearing a stranger use the vice-admiral's first name so casually, as if the two men were old friends. Nagumo drew back a hand to strike the sneering, smirking upstart, but it never reached its target. The fist flailed at thin air, the newcomer evading the blow with contemptuous ease, as if Nagumo's attack was slower than that of an infant. When the vice-admiral had recovered his composure, he found the upstart standing behind him, yet he hadn't seen the man move. How was this possible?

"My name is Suzuki, Shiro Suzuki, and as much as I enjoy goading pompous old men like you, I don't have time to play any more games today."

"You will pay for this with your life!" Nagumo raged.

"I think not." Suzuki produced a sheet of parchment and handed it to the vice-admiral. Nagumo's eyes raced across the text, and then widened in dismay. "As you can see, I have full authority from the emperor to do and say whatever I please. You have no choice but to obey my every whim. Had I the time, I'd make you and your men dance around this aircraft carrier like little girls, but I've wasted enough energy on your petulance. You will furnish me with the pilots and planes I have requested, or suffer the consequences."

"Of course, sir," Nagumo replied, bowing as low as he could to Suzuki. "All will be as you ask, but when will my men and machines be returned?"

"They are my men and machines now. That's all you need to know."

"Of course. Forgive my impertinence in asking."

"Perhaps. In the meantime, I want my men sent to the officers' mess. I will be telling them about their new mission and I don't wish to be disturbed. While I am... teaching them about the future, you will have all the aircraft I've requested repainted to these specifications." Suzuki produced a piece of parchment with a diagram of a plane upon it. The aircraft was jet black, including the glass of its canopy. The only emblems visible on the fuselage were the red circle of the rising sun, and a bat with its wings unfurled. The nose of the plane had a mouth painted on it, with a red interior and pronounced, white canine teeth. To Nagumo's eyes, they looked like fangs. "The details on the nose are optional," Suzuki added with a smirk.

The vice-admiral knew better than to question the orders, having read how much power the emperor had placed in this impetuous young man's hands. Nagumo nodded in agreement before bowing once more, gesturing for the rest of his officers to follow suit. Suzuki moved to leave the bridge, but Nagumo remained standing between his visitor and the way out.

"Excuse me for asking, but how did you get on to this ship? We have not put into port for the past two days, and it is close to midnight. Getting on board an aircraft carrier without being noticed should be impossible."

"Yes, it should, shouldn't it?" Suzuki agreed. "You'd best do something to improve your security for what lies ahead, Chuichi. If I can get on board, what's to stop the enemy from achieving the same thing, hmm?" He arched an eyebrow at the vice-admiral, who stepped aside. Suzuki retrieved his letter of authority and marched from the bridge.

AIKO HITORI HAD the strangest feeling she was being haunted. Ever since hearing of her husband's death in Manchuria, Aiko had felt as if her beloved Zenji was close by, watching. Perhaps it was his spirit standing guard over her and baby Noriyuki. The child was still less than a month old, but she could

see the boy had his father's eyes and that same
determined chin. When little Noriyuki made his
mind up to stay awake or cry or smile, nothing could
persuade him to stop, not mother's milk, not
pleading, not laughing. The child had a mind of his
own. Sometimes, Aiko felt as if she and the boy
were not alone in their modest home on the out-
skirts of Tokyo. Sometimes, she felt as if Zenji were
still there with them, his spirit, his essence, his love.

Aiko had tried talking to the local Shinto priest
about her feelings, but he would only smile and
nod. Her mother would not listen to talk of spirits
and ghosts, but her mother had never liked Zenji.
No, that was unfair, her mother hated wars and soldiers. Aiko's father had been a soldier, had been
taken away by war and never came back. When
Aiko said she was marrying a soldier, her mother
had cried for a week and thereafter always
expressed doubts that Zenji would be alive long
enough to sire a son and continue the family line. At
least he had proved her wrong, in part; Noriyuki
was the proof of that.

Aiko, a voice whispered.

The beautiful young woman dropped the teapot she
was carrying into the modest kitchen. Fortunately, it
did not break, the matting underfoot protecting the
porcelain from harm, but warm green tea did spill
across the floor. Aiko ignored the mess, her eyes
searching for some sign of her dead husband's presence, her ears listening for some sound that might
reveal him to her. She knew Zenji was gone, but still
struggled to accept the cold, hard facts that his friend
Suzuki had presented to her. Zenji died a hero, but he

died in another country, blown apart by an enemy shell. There was nothing left to bury, only his old uniform. Perhaps it was the fact that she never saw his body, never got a chance to honour his remains as she would have wished that left her troubled, unable to believe he was truly gone.

Aiko, the voice whispered again.

She spun around, convinced that Zenji was standing behind her. Instead she found only a bamboo curtain, the canes sliding back and forth across an open window. A fog was rolling in on the evening breeze and wisps of its mist drifted in through the window. Aiko shivered, not sure if there was a sudden chill in the air or whether someone had walked over her grave in some future time. No, don't be so foolish, she told herself. It's a cool wind, that's all. She went to the window and pulled it shut, before drawing the silk kimono closer around her voluptuous figure. Zenji had always teased her for being so slender, so slight. He would have enjoyed the extra curves left by the pregnancy and the way nursing little Noriyuki had swollen her breasts. He would have caressed her belly and kissed her lips and–

A gurgle of happiness from the baby brought Aiko back to the present. She pushed away thoughts of his dead father and walked into the bedroom where the infant boy was lying in his crib. The baby was playing with a soft toy, a delicately sewn replica of a panda sent over from Manchuria by Zenji a few weeks before his death. Aiko frowned. She could have sworn the panda was lying on her bed before, not in the cot with the baby. It was not important.

Noriyuki was happy and that was what mattered to her most now.

Aiko sat down on the bed and a scent caught in her nostrils, a scent she knew so well. It was warm and masculine, a musky aroma she recalled from when Zenji made love to her. She had buried her nose in his chest, savouring the scent of him, drawing it deep inside her lungs, wanting him to invade every part of her, wanting the two of them to be joined together forever. The war with China had ripped that away, but still his scent lingered on in her imagination. She let herself fall backwards on to their bed and closed her eyes, willing him to be with her once more, trying to remember and relive their last time together in this bed.

Zenji had known his orders to cross the Sea of Japan were imminent, as Suzuki had tipped him off. So her clever husband had swapped shifts with a colleague and arranged to race home, for one last night in bed with his wife. Both of them knew how dangerous the war in Manchuria was, despite the lies and propaganda published by the Imperial Japanese Army about its successes. Every time Zenji went to that accursed place, his chances of coming back became fewer. So they had made love as if it were the last time, because it could well have been the last time, and, for once, they were proved right. At least their last time had also given her little Noriyuki, so she would always have a part of Zenji to treasure. Aiko felt the tears welling up in her eyes once more, grief getting the better of her. She hated herself for crying so often and so much, but she was helpless to stop it.

You shouldn't weep for me, her dead husband's voice whispered in her mind. *My spirit has been freed. I am one with the winds now, one with the stars.*

"Zenji!" Aiko wanted to look at him but found she couldn't.

Don't try to open your eyes, he said. *I am but a ghost, a spirit from beyond this life, sent to say goodbye to you one last time. Open your eyes and you will see nothing. Keep your eyes closed and let your other senses show you what your eyes cannot. Feel my lips against your lips, my skin against your skin. Hear my words and be happy that we have this one last chance to be together.*

"I will," Aiko whispered. "I am... but how can this be?"

Don't question it, the voice said, soothing away her worries. *Just surrender yourself to the moment and we shall be one once more.*

SUZUKI SAT IN the officers' mess of the Akagi, watching the navy pilots file in. He had hand-picked them personally, choosing the best of the best that this vessel had to offer, men who had proven themselves in combat. But there had been other criteria too, stipulations laid down by Hitori about who could and who couldn't be offered the chance to join the vampyr samurai, a unit known to Japanese military authorities as the kyuuketsuki. None of the men could be married and none of them could have children. Suzuki had argued long and hard against these restrictions, knowing how many experienced and superior flyers it would eliminate from consideration, but his commander had been adamant.

"I sacrificed everything to become the first of the kyuuketsuki," Hitori had said to his oldest friend. "We ask enough when we ask the men to give up their lives and their souls for the greater good of the empire. I will not have their minds fogged by thoughts of the wives and children they've left behind."

So Suzuki had begun the long sift through every military personnel file of the Imperial Japanese Navy and Army, eliminating those with dependent families. Now he was travelling from base to base and ship to ship, carrying a list of those he wanted to recruit for the kyuuketsuki. Not all had taken the chance when it was offered, either fearful for their own lives or none too eager to join a fledgling unit with a vague and apparently suicidal future ahead of it. Suzuki had learned to judge in advance those who would jump at the chance and those who would shy away. He discovered Hitori had been right to restrict the offer to unmarried, childless men. They were more likely to accept this chance and more willing to sacrifice everything they held dear for the empire.

Once all the pilots were gathered in the mess, Suzuki barked at them to be seated. They responded at once, all well trained and disciplined by Vice-Admiral Nagumo. Excellent, the vampyr thought. That will make my task easier. He rose to his feet and addressed the men, strolling around the mess, moving between them as he talked. Suzuki spoke in generalities, outlining the challenges inherent in joining the kyuuketsuki: they could never see their families again, their lives were forfeit and considered expendable, their names would be erased from all military records and their exploits would never be celebrated or mentioned in despatches. For all intents and purposes, they would cease to exist, and become part of an invisible unit known only in whispers.

But the news was not all bad. The kyuuketsuki were guaranteed the best planes, the best equipment, and the best mechanics. They would be at the forefront of every battle, leading the charge as the Japanese Empire rose like the sun to attain its rightful place as ruler of the south-east Pacific. They all knew war with the Americans was imminent; join the kyuuketsuki and you would be a crucial part of that war, a first strike weapon spreading fear and terror among the empire's enemies. They would become gods of the skies.

"Soon, I will ask those of you who still wish to join the kyuuketsuki to come with me. You will not have time to say goodbye to your shipmates, you will not even have time to go back to your bunks for any personal possessions you might treasure. I will expect you to leave everything behind, to walk away from your old life and embrace your new existence without help or hindrance. But before you can do that, you need to answer these two questions. If you hesitate before saying yes to either of these questions, don't bother following me when I walk out of this door. Where I am going, you cannot. Is that clear?"

The pilots murmured a dutiful response, some nodding more eagerly than others. Suzuki let those gathered fall silent before continuing with his speech. He had made this address more than a dozen times and suspected he already knew how many of these men would follow him into hell. But the formalities had to be met, the rituals followed, as ordered by Hitori. The kyuuketsuki leader did not want any man in his ranks who did not wish to be there with every fibre of his being. There was too much at stake to risk the fate of the war on those without the courage of their convictions.

"There are two questions you must answer before my kinsmen can accept you," Suzuki continued. "They are the same two questions our leader had to answer, before he became the first of the kyuuketsuki. Think long and hard before you reply. Firstly, would you sacrifice your life for the emperor?"

"Yes, sir!" the pilots replied in unison.

"Good. I should expect nothing less of you all," Suzuki said. "It is the second question that decides your future. I will stand by the doorway and whisper the question in your ear as you file past me, one by one. If I decide your answer is an instant and unequivocal yes, I will tap you on the shoulder. Upon leaving the mess you should turn left and wait in the corridor outside. If I am not satisfied with your answer, I will shake my head and you will leave, never to see my face again." He nodded to the man nearest him, beckoning the flyer over. When the perspiring pilot was close enough, Suzuki leaned in to whisper his interlinked questions. "Would you sacrifice your soul for the emperor? Would you make a deal with the devil himself to become one of the kyuuketsuki?"

The first pilot frowned, hesitating too long for Suzuki's satisfaction. He shook his head and the flyer stumbled from the room, turning right and walking out of sight. The second man was already waiting to be asked, his eyes gleaming in anticipation. Suzuki asked his questions and the flyer did not pause for a moment before nodding in agreement, a broad smile evident on his features. Suzuki tapped the pilot's shoulder and moved to the next man.

Within twenty minutes he had selected eleven recruits. Once the last of the eleven was selected and the final failure sent away, Suzuki summoned his chosen few back into the mess. He congratulated them on their courage and bravery, but said those qualities were about to be tested further. Suzuki shut and bolted the door into the officers' mess. "What I'm about to show you is highly classified, a secret more closely guarded than any other secret in the empire. You will be transformed into the ultimate weapons of war, creatures that will tear apart the souls of our enemies and feast on their blood. You will become immortal warriors, vampyr samurai."

Suzuki gritted his teeth and willed his wings to unfurl, the mighty spans of skin, bone and sinew bursting out from the back of his uniform. The pilots were startled but, to their credit, they did not scream as some had done before them. Suzuki grinned, letting his lips slide back from his teeth to reveal the massive, elongated fangs jutting down from his upper jaw. "Tonight I shall feast on your blood and allow you to sup on mine. I shall make you all my kinsmen, my kyuuketsuki, my brothers in blood. Let the feasting begin!"

HITORI LEFT HIS wife sleeping in bed, still murmuring his name and sighing with pleasure. The vampyr knew he could not risk coming back here again. Aiko had long believed in ghosts and spirits, so he had used that belief and his new abilities to disarm her. He had hoped the experience would sate his hunger for Aiko, and give him the chance to say goodbye properly. Instead he stumbled away from their home, feeling as if a fresh hole had been torn in his chest. To be with her again and have to leave was the worst torture of all, reminding him of what he had sacrificed to become a vampyr. But perhaps it was worth all the pain, just to see his son once.

Whatever the truth, he could not go back there again, couldn't trust himself not to tell Aiko the truth. She would want to be with him, no matter the cost to her soul, and he could not steal that away from her. Aiko and Noriyuki were the purest things left in his life. He would not corrupt them any further with his taint. He must stay away from his family. He was dead to them and he must stay that way. Better to sate his hunger with blood and terror and warfare, than destroy the only two people he had ever loved without question or hesitation.

Besides, his elite cadre had less than eight weeks until the point of no return, the moment when war with the Americans became inevitable. Hitori had been briefed on the plan of attack. The US Navy's Pacific base of operations in Hawaii was the key target, but Japanese forces would be striking in many other places at the same time. He had to have his vampyr samurai trained and ready, able to operate without his direct supervision when the time came. If all went to plan, these multiple strikes would cripple the enemy and leave the rest of the region wide open for invasion and conquest. It all depended on what happened at a place Hitori had never heard of before his intelligence briefing, a place known to the US Navy by a simple, two-word name: Pearl Harbour.

PART TWO: December 1941

FITNESS REPORT: Buntz, Arnold.
DATE OF ASSESSMENT:
December, 1941.

Private Buntz was sent for an assessment
of his physical fitness for duty, following repeated spells in the sick bay
complaining about dizziness, nausea and
shortness of breath. His sergeant noted
that each incident of illness coincided
with Buntz being assigned to more physical
duties, such as digging latrines, heavy
lifting and other instances of hard manual
labour. The sergeant also noted that the
symptoms reported by Buntz were all non-
specific, difficult to refute and easy to
imitate. The purpose of this fitness
report is to ascertain whether Buntz is,

143

indeed, as ill as he suggests or, as
Sergeant Grant believes, merely malin-
gering.

The subject is twenty-five years of
age, but has the physique of a man ten
years older. He is overweight by at
least forty pounds, and could soon be
approaching clinical obesity if his tendency to gain weight continues at its
current rate. His urine is discoloured
and his stool is remarkably small, both
indicators of dietary problems and
intestinal difficulties. His pallor on
the appointed day for testing was ashen
and his uniform was soaked with perspiration, suggesting Buntz is a prime
candidate for cardiac arrest.

However, a discolouration was also
noted in his mouth and the subject was
kept overnight for observation, permitted
neither food nor drink. He complained
long and loudly about these deprivations
and asked to be returned to his posting
in the stores depot at Fort Stotsenberg.
The doctor who had first examined Buntz
caught the subject eating a small piece
of cordite the next morning. It is well
known among certain soldiers that con-
sumption of cordite produces symptoms
easily mistaken for those of a far more
serious condition. When Buntz was kept
without food and drink for another twelve
hours, his symptoms soon desisted.

In conclusion, the physical wellbeing of the subject is compromised by his poor diet and lack of exercise. If he put half as much care and effort into his physique as he does into avoiding exertion, Private Buntz would be one of the fittest and strongest men in the regiment. While his weight stays at a dangerously high level, he will continue to be at risk from the usual conditions and maladies associated with obesity: fatigue, bad breath, heart disease and diabetes. The subject's health makes him a liability to his unit and efforts should be made to enhance his physical fitness. Whether such efforts can have any hope of success is another matter.

ONE

COMMANDER NISHINO KOZO stood alone in the conning tower of his submarine, designated I-17 by the Imperial Japanese Navy. It was less than a year since the vessel had been commissioned from Yokosuka Navy Yard, and the submarine was on its first offensive mission, bound for the island of Oahu. The final destination remained a closely guarded secret, known only to a handful of officers on board. Fewer still knew the true reason why their commander had been obliged to surrender his private quarters for the two strangers that joined I-17 shortly before it left Japanese territorial waters.

Kozo pressed a pair of binoculars to his eyes, the magnifying lenses enabling him to better study the ocean ahead for enemy craft. They were still several days from the target and it was imperative that I-17's approach did not become known to the Americans. Representatives of the Japanese Empire and the US government remained locked in negotiations at Washington DC, searching for a way beyond the impasse that separated the two nations. The discovery of a Japanese submarine en route to America's naval stronghold in the Pacific would be problematic. The fact that it had a midget submarine strapped to the aft deck would be even harder to explain. Both governments knew war between them was fast becoming inevitable, but it was unlikely the Americans expected Japanese forces to launch an attack against Pearl Harbour. The submarine had already been forced to take evasive action to avoid a US Navy battle group headed towards Wake Island.

The commander felt a cold shiver run up his spine as one of the unwelcome passengers joined him in the conning tower, climbing up the metal steps into the open air. It was night and the moon overhead was almost full, casting a pale blue hue across the dark sea. But it was not the cool evening breeze that chilled Kozo's blood. The submarine had left Japan in the middle of November for its journey halfway across the Pacific. The vessel maintained radio silence all the way, but the I-17 didn't submerge until it neared the US controlled Wake Island at the end of the month. In all that time, neither of the passengers had ventured into the conning tower during the hours of daylight.

Since passing Wake Island the submarine had stayed underwater by day and surfaced only at night, as was procedure. The passengers had used the long hours of submersion to test their midget sub, charging all of the 192 two-cell batteries that would power its electric motor. The rest of the time the duo stayed in their borrowed quarters, speaking to nobody except the commander and refusing to acknowledge anything said to them by other members of the crew. Kozo knew how much this disquieted the ninety-three men serving under him, thanks to reports from his executive officer, Itami.

The fact that neither of the passengers ate in the officers' mess was common knowledge after this long at sea. It was assumed by most that the strangers had brought their own provisions, something to which Kozo could well attest. When word spread about the commander surrendering his own quarters to the outsiders, Kozo had felt forced to address his crew about the matter, in an effort to quell any unrest. It was better they never know the truth about the unwelcome guests. If their real identity was discovered, a bloody mutiny would certainly follow, and Kozo could not imagine the consequences of that.

"Good evening, commander," the passenger said, his voice as flat and calm as the sea around them. "We continue to make good speed, yes?"

"Yes sir," Kozo replied. It hurt the commander's pride to call a guest on his vessel "sir", but the orders sent by General Tojo left no doubt who was in charge of this mission. The I-17 and its crew were expendable, their sole purpose to deliver the midget sub and its passengers successfully to Oahu.

"And we're still on schedule to reach our destination?"

"Yes sir," Kozo said through gritted teeth, keeping the binoculars pressed to his face, trying and failing to conceal his anger.

"Call me Zenji, if it will irritate you less," Hitori said. "We are all on the same side, and I've no wish to pull rank."

"I'd prefer to maintain the formalities," the commander replied, lowering his binoculars. "After what happened earlier, you'll understand why I don't want to be on friendlier terms with you or your... associate."

"I must apologise for Kimura. He's among my most promising recruits, but he is also the most bloodthirsty of the kyuuketsuki. His hunger got the better of him. It is not easy for us to withstand such confinement. Unlike your crew, we have not had years of training to cope with life in a submarine."

"My crew would tear you and your associate limb from limb if they knew what had happened earlier," Kozo spat, unable to contain his fury any longer.

"Your crew could try to hurt us, but their lives would be forfeit."

"Is that a threat?"

"Consider it a statement of fact," Hitori said, his voice empty of emotion.

The commander glared at his passenger, searching Hitori's features for some hint of remorse or regret. The other man's face was austere, impossible to read, his hooded eyes like slits of darkness beneath a shock of short, black hair. "The crew will notice when Itami doesn't emerge from my cabin sooner or later. You can't keep his body there indefinitely."

"Kimura will put the corpse overboard, once he has finished removing the head. You must ensure the crew is kept well away from the gangways between your quarters and the conning tower at midnight. That should give Kimura ample time to dispose of the carcass."

"Carcass? That's my second in command you're talking about!"

"Tell your crew Itami's death was a tragic accident. He saw the cables holding our midget sub were coming undone. The executive officer risked his life to fix the cables, but was swept away soon after by a freak wave."

"Nobody will believe that," Kozo insisted. He felt Hitori's gaze boring into him, as if it were burrowing into his very soul.

"You will convince them."

"I will convince them," the commander heard himself say, though the words were not of his own making. Hitori smiled and looked up at the moon.

"In a few days we'll reach the target and depart in our midget sub, leaving your vessel and its crew in peace. Until then, the responsibility for concealing this unfortunate incident falls on you. Consider it a necessary evil."

"A necessary evil," Kozo muttered. Now that Hitori was no longer staring at him, the commander could feel his willpower returning. "Is that what you and Kimura are, a necessary evil?" Hitori did not reply, but Kozo could have sworn he saw a shadow of doubt pass across the other man's face. "Why remove Itami's head before you dispose of his body? Hasn't he suffered enough at your hands? Must you desecrate his remains too?"

Hitori did not speak.

"Answer me, damn you!"

The passenger laughed at this comment, but there was no humour in his voice, only bitterness. "There's little point in damning one whose soul has already been surrendered," Hitori murmured.

The commander shuddered, his mind still struggling to cope with what he'd witnessed earlier. Itami had been curious to discover what Hitori and his associate were doing for food, since they had taken no meals while on board the submarine. The executive officer waited until both passengers were busy with the midget sub before venturing into the commander's quarters. Itami left a message for Kozo with one of his crew, in case something went wrong.

It was an hour before Kozo was given the note. He went straight to his quarters and found the executive officer's pale, lifeless body inside, sprawled awkwardly on the floor. Two smears of crimson ran down the side of Itami's neck, stark red against the pale, wan skin. Kimura was hunched in a corner, licking blood from his fingers like a predator savouring its latest kill. Kozo shook his head. Kimura had not been acting like a predator; the passenger was a predator, a monster that had sucked the lifeblood from Itami's body. There were two other corpses in the cabin, both Chinese prisoners of war.

A third POW was shackled to the wall, his face frozen in terror. At first Kozo had thought the prisoner had been struck dumb by the horrors they'd witnessed, but when he examined the two Chinese corpses, he found that their tongues had been plucked out. A cursory examination of the survivor showed he had suffered the same violation. Without tongues, the prisoners couldn't cry out or beg for mercy. Hitori and Kimura had brought three oblong crates with them when they boarded the I-17. The commander now realised that each crate contained a living food supply.

"When this mission is over," Kozo told Hitori, "I have to write a letter to Itami's wife explaining why her husband is not coming home, why their children will have to grow up without a father. I can't tell them the truth, but at least you can explain to me why they can't have his body to bury."

"Would you condemn your executive officer to the same fate as I?" Hitori asked. He drew back his lips to reveal two fearsome fangs. "He has been killed by a vampyr. By severing his head we stop him becoming like us."

"Then... it is an act of mercy," Kozo whispered.

Hitori nodded. "It is the least we can do."

MARTINEZ ARRIVED AT Fort Stotsenberg's Stores Depot as Buntz was padlocking the front door for the night. "Hey, Arnie, what's the big idea? I thought you were meant to stay open another half hour?"

"You got a problem with me knocking off early?" Buntz sneered.

"The sarge sent me over to collect some blankets, if we've got any going spare. The nurses at the army hospital are running short."

The overweight soldier snorted. "Aimes sent you, or you volunteered? I swear you spend more time with those nurses than you do at firing practice."

Martinez shrugged and grinned. "What can I say? The nurses are a whole lot prettier than Sergeant Aimes."

"My butt's a whole lot prettier than Sergeant Aimes," Buntz observed.

"I'll take your word for it, Arnie. So, you gonna re-open? I promised Nurse Baker that I'd–"

"So, it's Nurse Baker who wants the blankets, is it? Not the sarge?"

Martinez grimaced. "Well, she didn't exactly ask for the blankets, but I heard her saying how few they've got left over at the hospital and–"

"And you thought a quick raid on Stores would get you into her good books, maybe even inside her uniform, if you catch my drift."

"It's not like that. Angela and me, we're just good–"

"Now it's Angela. I didn't know you two were on first-name terms."

"We're getting along all right. Look, Arnie, you gonna help me or not?"

"What's in it for me?"

Martinez sighed. "Does everything have to be for the benefit of Arnie Buntz? Can't you do something out of the goodness of your heart, just once?"

"Nope, ain't no profit in it."

"But I'm tapped out, and we don't get paid until Monday."

"That's too bad," Buntz said as he walked away, twirling the keys to the stores around one of his fingers. Martinez scurried after him.

"Arnie, this could be for your benefit. You know all the brass have been expecting a Japanese attack. What happens if you get injured and end up in the hospital? Wouldn't you want to have a blanket on your bed?"

"Ain't gonna happen," Buntz said. "First sign of a Jap plane, I'll be taking cover faster than you can say New Mexico. You want to impress the lovely Nurse Baker, you're gonna have to find another way, loverboy." He strolled off towards the barracks, leaving a deflated Martinez behind. But the prospect of seeing Angela soon restored the young soldier's spirits as he made his way across the base to the small army hospital.

The 200th Coast Artillery had been stationed at Fort Stotsenberg since September, moving to the facility soon after arriving in the Philippines. The base was some seventy-five miles north of Manila, adjacent to Clark Field where several US Army Air Force squadrons were based, mostly bombers. Ten weeks had passed since the regiment's arrival, ten weeks of settling in, unpacking artillery equipment and getting the guns into position. Aimes had the men in Martinez's battery running firing drills and mock target practice every day, but their guns remained unfired. There was no target ammunition available and the ammunition held in reserve for an enemy strike was as old as some of the recruits. God help us if the Japs do attack, Aimes often swore.

Martinez quickened his pace as he approached the hospital entrance, the concrete building a stark silhouette against the green mountains beyond it. He had met Nurse Baker, Angela, after Wierzbowski dislocated a knee in a game of gridiron. The big man had gone down like a wounded animal, and Martinez had stayed with his friend all the way to the base hospital. It was Angela who put Wierzbowski's knee back into position and bandaged the ruptured

joint. She had flame red hair, a smattering of freckles
across her cheeks and the cutest smile Martinez had
ever seen.

After that he went back and visited Wierzbowski
in hospital every day, twice a day if he could find a
good excuse. Martinez was heartbroken when his
friend recovered enough to be discharged. The private went back to the hospital anyway, on some
feeble pretext, and stammered out to Angela how he
felt about her. The nurse laughed when Martinez
offered to marry her. "Don't you think we should
have a few dates first, see if we've got anything in
common?"

"Sure," Martinez agreed. "Then we get married."

"One thing at a time, tiger," she had replied,
smiling her infectious smile.

So they dated, taking walks under the moonlight
after Angela finished her shift, or talking for hours
about their lives before the Philippines. The pair
shared war stories about growing up Catholic, the
thrashings they'd gotten from convent nuns keen to
instil discipline and a fear of god. Both came from
large families where money was scarce and hand-
me-down clothes the way of the world. Angela
laughed as she recalled spending her first pay packet
on buying a brassiere of her own, after years of
making do with lingerie inherited from her many
sisters.

The two of them made out like teenagers when
nobody was around, but they had an unspoken
agreement; they had both been saving themselves
for marriage and they both had to respect that. But
Martinez had decided that tonight was the night.

Tonight he was asking Angela to marry him, as soon as they could. He couldn't wait any longer to be with her. Besides, if war was as close as everyone said, he didn't want to risk getting shipped out to another station and being separated from her. Martinez closed his eyes to offer up a silent prayer before entering the hospital: Please, God, let her say 'yes'.

THE AIRCRAFT CARRIER USS *Enterprise* sailed west across the Pacific towards Wake Island, a tiny rock in the middle of nowhere that was home to an American detachment. But the ship designated CV-6 was not alone in the ocean. A US Navy battle group shadowed the vessel, with three heavy cruisers and six destroyers keeping the *Enterprise* company on its voyage. Marine Fighting Squadron 211 was on board the Big E, as many of the crew liked to call her. These dozen planes were to be stationed on Wake Island, and the *Enterprise* was delivering them to their new home. The notion of such a massive ship acting as a delivery service amused Ensign Ramon Marquez. Sure, the name "aircraft carrier" kind of implied the *Enterprise* should be doing just that, carrying aircraft, but he always thought of her as a fighting ship, a metal warrior slicing across vast seas and oceans in search of combat.

So far, the only combat Marquez had seen was at Tokyo Joe's back in Hawaii. Like Chuck and Bravo, he had been determined to stay out of the bar brawl, not wanting to lose a week's flying privileges, but then that MP had started causing trouble and Chuck had gone down bleeding, leaving Marquez little

choice but to step in. Bravo had remained on the
sidelines, not getting involved until someone had
taken a swing at him. That rattled his cage, and
Bravo had come out fighting, abandoning his usual
policy of non-intervention unless it helped his own
cause. When the dust had finally settled, all three of
them were hauled before their commander for a rol-
licking and not one, not two, but three weeks
without flying privileges. Marquez still wasn't sure
which irked the commander more, the fact they'd
been fighting in public, or the fact they hadn't won.
Pride was important on board the Big E.

It was a relief when October came and they could
finally get back in the air. Marquez loved to fly more
than anything else in the world. Growing up dirt
poor, he'd never have believed he stood a chance of
becoming a pilot. His mother was a cleaner at the
nearby training school for naval aviators. Marquez
often thought a mop and a bucket was the closest
he'd ever get to a cockpit. But a tutor at the school
had taken the youngster under his wing, arranging
scholarships and nurturing little Ramon's ambitions.
The day Marquez made his first solo flight had been
among the proudest of his life, and also one of the
scariest. The undercarriage on his plane had collapsed during takeoff, leaving the young pilot
without any way of making a regulation landing. His
mentor was summoned to the control tower and had
talked Marquez down, persuading the terrified flyer
to attempt an emergency landing. The young pilot
had belly-flopped his plane onto the grass beside the
runway and slid all the way to safety. After walking
away from that without a scratch, there was only

one nickname he was ever likely to have in his flying career: Skid Marquez.

Now he was a fully fledged navy pilot, in charge of an SBD Dauntless on the USS *Enterprise*. According to the navy, the initials SBD stood for the words Ship Borne Dive-Bomber. According to the pilots, the letters actually represented Slow But Deadly. Marquez couldn't care less about his plane's flaws. Sometimes he felt like pinching himself to make sure being a pilot wasn't a dream. Each day he went to look at his plane to make certain it was real. He ran his hands over the fuselage, feeling every curve and rivet of his beautiful sky chariot. He climbed into the pilot's seat and closed his eyes, imagining himself in aerial combat, his fingertips poised over the controls. He envisaged enemy aircraft crossing in front of him and saw himself opening fire with his twin .30 machine guns. The targets exploded into flaming shards of–

"Hey, Skid, you planning to start the war early?" Marquez opened his eyes and saw Chuck standing by his own plane, waving. The young pilot waved back, embarrassed at having been caught pretending. Chuck gestured for him to come over, so Marquez clambered out of the cockpit and jumped down to the floor, his boots landing with a heavy clump on the metal surface. He strode across to Chuck's plane. "You seen Bravo?"

"Not this morning," Marquez replied. He was still getting to know the other pilots and Bravo, Lieutenant Taylor, had done little to acknowledge his presence on board yet. "We're not exactly the best of friends."

Chuck laughed out loud. "Bravo's only friends are himself and his reflection. Did you know I once caught him staring at himself in a mirror? Most men would be embarrassed, but not Bravo. He went right back to staring at that mirror. Said he was picturing the enemy in his sights, imagining the moment of the kill. Claimed visualising the moment would make it happen."

"Really?" Marquez asked, too embarrassed to admit he had been doing much the same, just without the mirror. "Why are you looking for him?"

"Actually, I was looking for both of you. Bravo left a message on my bunk, said he wanted to meet both of us down here."

"Why?"

"No idea. He said it was a matter of importance, that's all."

"Oh, right." Marquez looked around but could see no sign of the other pilot. "Then I guess we should wait."

Chuck consulted his watch. "I'll give him three minutes. After that I'm due up on deck for a briefing about Thursday."

"Thursday?"

"When the fighters are launched for Wake Island?"

"Oh, yeah, right." Marquez grinned. "I got confused after we crossed the international dateline yesterday. Now I can't remember if today's Tuesday or Wednesday. I've never been over no dateline before."

"It's Tuesday on board, but it's still Monday back in Pearl. That makes it today here and yesterday there, as far as we're concerned, or tomorrow here and today there as far as the people in Pearl are concerned. Does that help?"

"Not really," the ensign admitted. "All this waiting around, it's driving me crazy. Halsey said we were on a war footing when we left Pearl last week, but nothing's happened since. I'm ready for action, you know?"

"Don't be so eager," Chuck said, laughing at his colleague. "If there is a war, you can guarantee there'll be plenty of it to go around."

"You said 'if there's a war'. You don't think it'll happen?"

The lieutenant shrugged. "The Japanese starting a whole new war in the Pacific doesn't make sense to me. Congress may be doing its best to keep us out of the war in Europe, but even they won't let the Japs take over the Philippines and places like that. As soon as they attack an American base, we're going to strike back, and hard. We'll crush 'em in weeks."

"I guess so," Marquez murmured.

"Hey, you two, over here!" The two pilots swung around to see Bravo standing in front of his Dauntless, pointing proudly at the fuselage beneath his cockpit. As Marquez and Chuck got closer, they could see a crude image painted on the side of the plane, depicting General Tojo as a slant eyed cartoon figure with a target on his forehead. Beneath that was the legend, "Tokyo or Bust". "What do you think about my work of art?"

"You painted that yourself?" Chuck asked.

"Paid one of the ground crew to do it. Granberg was a sign writer back in Minnesota before he got drafted. So, what do you think?"

"I thought the CAG forbade painting emblems on planes," Marquez said.

"The commander of the Air Group has got a big old stick up his butt the size of a flagpole," Bravo replied. "I'm amazed he can get in his cockpit." The sneering pilot produced three cigars from a breast pocket. "I've decided the three of us should place a little wager on the outcome of each sortie. Whoever brings down the most enemy planes collects a buck from the other two at the end of each day. Obviously, I intend to be the best flying ace in the Pacific, so I understand if you two are scared of taking my action–"

"I'm in!" Marquez blurted.

Bravo arched an eyebrow at the young ensign. "Very good, but try not to lose every day, otherwise you won't have any money left to send home to your poor mom. What about you, Richards, you up for a challenge?"

Chuck smiled. "I'm more worried about the state of your finances. Nobody's ever seen you open your wallet, Bravo. You sure the moths haven't eaten all your millions by now?"

"My finances are fine," Bravo retorted. "Are you in too, or do I have to ask one of the other incompetents to take your place in our little wager?"

"I'm in, all right, wouldn't miss it for the world, in fact."

Bravo nodded. "Glad to hear it." He handed each man a cigar. "As a gesture of goodwill, I thought we could share these, before the contest starts."

"Don't mind if I do," Chuck said, accepting the gift. Marquez followed his example, mimicking the others as they lit up. He'd never smoked a cigar before and within moments the ensign was choking and gasping for air. Chuck clapped a heavy hand on his back. "Don't worry, Skid. Everybody coughs the first time they smoke a cigar."

"R-right," Marquez coughed. He looked at Bravo through the cloud of pale blue cigar fumes. "Why choose us for your contest?"

"Plainly, I'm the best pilot on this ship," Bravo replied. "You two are about the only competition I've got on board, though that's damning you both with faint praise, frankly. I'll take what I can get."

"Charming as always," Chuck commented. "Good cigar, too."

"Only the best, that's my motto: only the best."

"In that case, may the best man win," Marquez said.

"Oh, I will," Bravo replied, "I certainly will."

Suzuki waited until the last rays of sunshine had disappeared well below the horizon before climbing from the cockpit of his Mitsubishi Type O aircraft. The Zero fighter was jet black from nose to tail, its sole distinguishing marks the red circle symbol of the rising sun and the kyuuketsuki insignia. Even the glass of its canopy was tinted black, as he had specified when requisitioning the plane from the Akagi. Six near identical Zeros had stopped behind his plane on the runway, arranged in a V-formation. At a signal from Suzuki, the pilots all opened their canopies and climbed out.

The aerial kyuuketsuki unit had been training diligently for more than two months in anticipation of the coming conflict. Suzuki had chosen dozens of men from among the Imperial Japanese Navy's best pilots, and from these selected the six pilots who would accompany him in the first attack wave. He had sired them personally, to make certain of their complete and utter loyalty. He had moulded them in his own image, to be as ruthless and bloodthirsty as he was, utterly merciless when the time came. In the heat of battle, Suzuki needed his kyuuketsuki flyers to think with one mind.

While he was training them in the ways of the vampyr, they were teaching Suzuki to fly the Zero as if he had been born in the cockpit. He had crashed three times, but emerged from each impact unharmed, grateful for the strength and resilience that being undead gave him. It took time, far longer than he had expected, but Suzuki was mastering his single engine fighter. He was good enough to lead the formation as it landed in Taiwan, though his landings still left a lot to be desired. No doubt his second in command, Otomo, would tease him about that later, as was the young pilot's way.

A sleek black sedan raced towards the seven Zeros, flanked by a covered truck and a refuelling rig, their headlines gleaming in the twilight. The sedan stopped close by and an officer emerged from the driver's seat. He strode over to Suzuki and bowed low, humbling himself before the new arrivals. "Captain Juzo Yoshihiro at your service. Forgive us for not being here when you landed," the officer said, a tremble of fear audible in his voice. "News of your coming reached me only as your planes were touching down. Had Tokyo given us more notice–"

"The short notification was my idea," Suzuki snapped, a curt flick of his left hand waving away the apology. "I wanted to see how soon your facilities could be ready for our particular needs. Once hostilities begin, you will need to be far quicker and more efficient in your response to surprises. From all I've heard, the conflict in Manchuria rarely runs to a schedule."

"Yes, sir, of course," the officer agreed, his eyes still downcast. "If I may be bold enough to ask, how long will you be gracing us with your presence?"

"My kyuuketsuki and I will be here until the eighth, when our first true mission begins. Have you prepared quarters for my pilots?"

"Yes, as specified. The windows have been blacked out and all the surrounding buildings vacated. You and your men will not be disturbed." For the first time, the officer risked raising his eyes to look at Suzuki's face. "You also asked for the provision of a dozen comfort women. We have taken them from the native population, but some are... more comfortable than others."

Suzuki heard a snigger behind him, and recognised it as Otomo. "Comfort woman" was the official term for a female forced to be the sex slave of Japanese servicemen. The practise had become popular in Manchuria where local women were plentiful and soldiers were away from their wives for months at a time. But Suzuki and his kyuuketsuki lusted for blood, not just any pleasures of the flesh. "The beauty and age of these women matters little to my men. They don't need these unfortunates for their looks."

The officer could not disguise a shudder at this, but his face remained impassive. He gestured to the covered truck. "If your pilots would get inside, they will be transported to their quarters. I will take you in my car."

The vampyr leader shook his head. "I go where my kyuuketsuki go. We fly as one and we travel as one. That is how we will conquer our enemies."

MARTINEZ FOUND NURSE Baker hunched over her desk in the main ward, writing on the charts for her few patients. The base hospital didn't see many serious injuries. Most were the result of accident rather than conflict, and anything life-threatening was soon transferred to a military hospital in Manila with superior facilities. As a consequence it was rare for more than one nurse to be on duty at a time in Fort Stotsenberg. A shift change was due within the hour, offering Martinez his chance to pop the question. He realised his hands were sweating and wiped them dry on his trousers before approaching Angela.

"Hey, how you doing?" he asked, trying to keep his voice cool and calm.

She jumped, not having heard his approach on the smooth floor. "Juan! You shouldn't sneak up on people; you almost gave me a heart attack."

He looked around and smiled. "Least you'd be in the right place for that."

Angela nodded, unable to stay angry at him for long. "I've got to finish these reports before Ruth arrives to cover the night shift."

"No problem," Martinez agreed. But he stayed where he was, reaching out a hand to stroke her back between the shoulder blades. Angela tried shrugging him off but he persisted until she gave in, surrendering her task.

"What is it?" she demanded, an angry tone in her voice that Martinez hadn't encountered before. He looked at her eyes and noticed how red they were, and recognised telltale blotchiness on her freckled cheeks.

"You've been crying. What's wrong?"

"Nothing," Angela said before turning away, unable to hold his gaze.

Martinez crouched down on one knee beside her. "I can tell when a woman's been crying, I saw it with my mother often enough. What is it?" She didn't reply, only shaking her head. "Look, if it's about the extra blankets, I tried my best but Buntz shut down Stores early today. I'll try again tomorrow, I promise." A fresh tear trickled down Angela's cheek and splashed on the medical chart beneath her face. "Please, tell me, maybe I can help."

"You can't," she said, her voice close to breaking, "nobody can."

"You can't be certain of that."

"Yes, I can! There's nothing either of us can do about this." Angela wiped the tears from her face. "I got a new posting today. I'm being transferred back to the military hospital at Manila. They think we're overstaffed here."

Martinez felt as if he'd been punched in the gut. "When do you go?"

"Monday. I'm to hitch a ride on the dawn transport, and start my new posting in Manila the next day, December ninth." She managed a weak smile.

"Never thought I'd be sorry to see the back of Fort Stotsenberg."

"You can't go," Martinez said.

"My orders say otherwise, Juan." Angela rested a tender hand against his face. "We always knew this would happen one day. I just didn't think that day would come so soon. I'm going to miss you."

He took a deep breath and looked into her eyes. "Marry me."

She smiled. "You're only saying that because I'm leaving."

"No, that's what I came here to ask you, once your shift was over. I want you to be my wife, Angela Baker." Martinez smiled at her. "I'm down on one knee and everything. Please, at least tell me you'll think about it?"

Angela frowned and shook her head. "I don't need to think about it."

"You mean..." But Martinez couldn't finish the sentence, a sudden fear clutching at his throat and stealing away his words.

"I've already made my mind up," she continued. "Yes, I will marry you."

"You will? But I thought... You're sure you want to marry me?"

Angela nodded, fresh tears running down her face, but these were tears of joy, not sorrow. "Yes, Juan, I do."

Martinez threw his arms around her, kissing her sweet lips over and over. It was only the arrival of Ruth for the night shift that stopped things getting out of hand. She cleared her throat several times before they noticed.

"You two ought to get a room," the nurse commented.

"We will, on our honeymoon," Martinez replied, his voice full of joy.

"You're getting married?" Ruth asked. Angela nodded. "When?"

"Before I get shipped back to Manila next week, I guess." She looked at Martinez. "If that's okay with you, Juan?"

He grinned. "The sooner, the better. How about this Saturday?"

"Not so fast, loverboy," Ruth cut in. "We've got an inspection on Saturday, all the nurses will be run off their feet until then. After that, you'll be fine."

"Sunday it is, then. We'll have the wedding on December the seventh."

From the diary of Angela Baker,
            Fort Stotsenberg
          - December 5th, 1941

I can hardly believe I'm writing these
words, but it's true, I'm getting married on Sunday. Juan asked me after I
got my transfer papers. The corps
decided Sternberg General Hospital
needs more nurses and so I'm going back
to Manila next Monday. The idea of
leaving Fort Stotsenberg meant little
to me, compared to the thought of never
seeing Juan again. Sure, he might get a
posting to Manila in time, but it'll be
months before we see each other. Imagining that left me hollow inside, as if
someone had stuck a cold ice-cream

scoop in my chest and ripped out my heart.

I guess Juan must have felt the same way because he asked me to be his wife as soon as he heard about my transfer. I said yes before I'd even had time to think. I want to be with him so badly. I want to spend every minute I can with him. Juan's not like all the other recruits on the base. Most of them just want what they can get from the nurses, and to hell with the consequences. Give in to them and you're easy, refuse them and you're called all kinds of names. At times, being part of the Army Nurses Corps here is like being back in high school, except the ratio of men to women is a hundred to one. I always swore I'd never get involved with a soldier. Then there was Juan.

He makes me laugh. I think that's what I like the most about him. He's sweet and kind and gentle with me. He doesn't try to push me into doing anything I don't want, and I know he cares about me, I can see it in his eyes. That's not to say he isn't all man. There are times I want to rip his clothes off and... Well, you can guess the rest! Just thinking about him like that makes me blush, but it makes me wish he was here, too. I don't know much about being with a man, not like some of the other nurses, but I know

being with Juan will be something I'll
never forget. Let's hope we can keep our
hands to ourselves until the wedding
night!

The thing is, I'm excited but kind of
scared too. How do I know this is the
right thing to do? How do I know Juan is
the right man for me? We feel so comfortable together, but what if that
changes? There's the war to think about,
too. We aren't fighting it yet, but
everyone seems to think that it's a
matter of when, not if. I'm still getting to know Juan. How would I cope if I
lost him? I don't want to be a widow
before I'm 25.

Then there's my transfer. That's still
going ahead, no matter whether we get
married or not. We'll have one night
together and then months apart, keeping
in touch by letter and a few phone calls.
We might get leave at the same time, but
I doubt that. The army tends to set its
own schedules, and married couples in
the ranks just have to cope.

At the back of my mind, I can't help
thinking we're rushing into this. I
always imagined I'd have a big white
wedding, with all my family there.
Instead I'll be getting married in a
makeshift chapel, wearing whatever the
other nurses can find for me between now
and Sunday, with none of my family

beside me. They probably won't get my
telegram until after I've become Mrs
Juan Martinez. How are they going to
react to the news? All these questions
are going round and round in my head, and
it's starting to drive me crazy. Putting
my thoughts down on paper in this diary
helps a little, but I need to talk with
someone about all of this, and I think I
know just the person.

TWO

I-17 SLOWED ITS engines as the submarine came within range of the Hawaiian island of Oahu. The submerged vessel waited until day became night before surfacing briefly beneath the full moon. Commander Kozo went up into the conning tower to see the American territory for himself. He was close enough to hear music drifting out from the bars of Waikiki, and neon lights were visible in the distance. Several years before, he had commanded a Japanese tanker that took on crude oil at the Ellwood refinery north of Santa Barbara. He had slipped while walking to a welcoming ceremony and fallen into a prickly-pear cactus. His face still flushed an angry red at the memory of workers on the nearby rig laughing at his discomfort. Kozo was looking forward to the war, and reclaiming his honour from those hyenas. Satisfied with the submarine's positioning, he went below and ordered a descent to periscope depth.

As midnight passed, an American minesweeper on its way back into Pearl Harbour approached the I-17. This was the opportunity Hitori and Kimura had been waiting for. The US Navy had anti-submarine nets stretched across the harbour entrance, but they were retracted to allow the coming and going of surface vessels. The lumbering minesweeper would be the perfect decoy, clearing a path through the nets and churning the water to such an extent that the midget sub could follow it in, unseen.

The commander went to his private quarters where both passengers were waiting. They'd been unwelcome guests on board before Itami's tragic loss, but in the days since the executive officer's disappearance, wild rumours had circulated among the crew about Hitori and Kimura. Some claimed they were Black Dragon agents on a covert mission to infiltrate American naval defences at Pearl Harbour. Others believed they were actually spying on the crew before reporting back to Tokyo. One tale suggested the passengers had killed Itami because he discovered the truth about them, and now they were blackmailing the commander into following their orders.

Kozo kept his own counsel, knowing almost all the rumours had an element of truth, but that none of them told the whole story. If the crew had discovered the real nature of these blood-drinking parasites, he shuddered to think what the consequences could have been. Now, at least, he could get these monsters off his vessel. That couldn't happen soon enough for him.

He'd learned what to expect on entering his quarters, but still could not disguise his revulsion.

Kimura had disposed of the two dead POWs at the same time as Itami, but the final prisoner was still alive. Hitori and his murderous associate had been slowly draining their captive of blood until he was close to death, before giving him a day's respite. By this method the passengers had sustained themselves and their food source. Kozo walked in to find Kimura supping at the prisoner's throat, a wet splash of crimson on the POW's uniform all too obvious amid the many older, drier stains.

"It's time," the commander announced, keeping his gaze fixed on Hitori.

"How long do we have?"

"The minesweeper will take an hour to reach the anti-submarine nets. That's long enough for us to surface and get you into the midget sub. Once you're ready, we submerge again and release the cables before starting the engine. You get behind the minesweeper and follow it all the way in."

"Good," Hitori agreed. He nodded to Kimura. The other vampyr finished drinking from its victim before snapping the prisoner's head sideways. The POW died, a pool of yellow liquid spilling out of the corpse and mingling with old and new blood on the floor. Kozo felt certain he'd have to scrub the room for weeks to remove every trace of the horrors perpetrated in here, not least the slaughter of his executive officer.

"Once the minesweeper is inside the harbour, the anti-submarine nets will be reinstated," the commander said. "You'll be trapping yourselves within Pearl Harbour, and the midget sub's batteries have a limited lifespan. It cannot stay submerged indefinitely. Besides, you'll run out of air long before that happens."

"Don't worry on our account," Kimura replied, baring his still bloody fangs at Kozo. "We don't need to breathe. We only need to feed."

Hitori said something to his associate, but the words were spoken too quickly for the commander to catch them. Whatever they were, they sent Kimura back to the prisoner's corpse. He resumed twisting the dead man's head, as if he was unscrewing the lid from a bottle. Kozo could hear the ligaments and other connective tissue within snapping and ripping apart. Kimura tore at the neck in frustration with his fangs and talons, tearing through skin and sinew. At last the head came off, rolling unevenly across the floor before coming to rest by the commander's boots. Kozo swallowed hard to stop the bile rising in his throat from becoming a stream of vomit. He glared at the smirking Kimura.

"I don't know what kind of monsters you are, but a Japanese warrior would never torture and debase his captives like that."

"You'd be surprised at how savage people can be," Hitori replied.

Kozo gestured at the decapitated head by his boots. "Nothing human could have done that."

"True, but you're talking about brute strength, not force of will. I saw our soldiers commit atrocities in Manchuria that defied belief: murder, rape and wanton butchery. Why should my kyuuketsuki be any different?" Hitori nodded to Kimura, who trod on the dead prisoner's chest as he walked out. Hitori followed, pausing at the doorway. "I apologise for leaving this mess behind, but our mission must take precedence. Have a good war, commander."

FATHER KELLY SAT at the back of his makeshift chapel and sighed. Business had not been brisk since he arrived at Fort Stotsenberg with the 200th Artillery, if you could call saving souls and offering spiritual counselling a business. At most services he considered himself fortunate to get more than a handful of worshippers, those hardy few who kept faith with their beliefs this far from home. Sundays were his busiest day of the week, naturally, but even then there was no guarantee of more than a dozen people in the congregation.

Tomorrow would be different, the priest told himself. Tomorrow he was performing the wedding ceremony for Private Martinez and Nurse Baker. That was guaranteed to draw a crowd and, with a little luck, some of them might be moved into making the Lord a more regular visitor into their lives. If only I can find the right words to persuade them, Father Kelly thought, and discover the way into their hearts and minds. He had been sitting at the back of the chapel for more than an hour, a pencil and paper in his hand, waiting for inspiration. He had prayed for guidance, offering novena after novena to Heaven in exchange for the hope of inspiration, but no angel whispered in his ear, no vision told the priest what he wanted to hear. His page remained blank, his faith bankrupt.

The trouble comes from lies, Father Kelly realised. I've been living with my lies for so long that I've started to believe they might be true. I've even lied in the confessional. It's the most holy place I know, and I broke the commandments to conceal my shame. I betrayed you, my Lord, and I betrayed my vows. Is it any wonder my soul is so barren, my heart so empty?

The priest put the pencil and paper aside before dropping to his knees. He clasped his hands together and closed his eyes, determined to renounce all the falsehoods and confess the truth to the only being that truly mattered. "Forgive me, oh heavenly father, for I have sinned," Father Kelly began, his voice a hoarse whisper of fear and guilt. "It's been three months since my last confession." He stopped, thinking back to what he had said on Oahu, the lies he'd told then. "No, it's been much longer than that. I can't remember when I last told you the truth, the whole truth. I know you see into my heart and already know all of my sins, but I must confess them to be worthy of your redemption. I must acknowledge my sins and show remorse. I must."

Father Kelly opened his eyes and saw the crucifix atop the cloth-covered trestle table that served as his altar. The silver representation of Jesus on the cross seemed to be staring at him, daring the priest to admit the dark secret that gnawed at him like some malignant cancer of the soul. Father Kelly looked away, unable to stand the unspoken accusation. He wanted to repent his sins, but the shame of what had happened, the shame of what he–

"Father? Father Kelly?"

The priest spun around to see Nurse Baker in the chapel doorway. "My, you startled me, Angela! How long have you been standing there?"

"Only for a few moments, father. It looked like you were praying. I can come back later, if that's more convenient for you."

"No, no, this is as good a time as any," Father Kelly replied as he got up. He brushed the dust off the knees of his trousers before walking over to the nervous nurse. "How can I help you, my child?"

Angela forced a smile. "It's about the wedding, father. I'm not sure I can go through with it. I'm not sure how much I love Juan Martinez."

HITORI PEERED AT US battleships through the midget sub's periscope. Kimura had navigated their way into Pearl Harbour, stalking the minesweeper past the American defences, just as Commander Kozo had suggested. Now the midget sub was lying off the docks, studying the positions and strength of the enemy's vessels. The battleships were moored in pairs, one beside the other. It was the early hours of Friday, the fifth of December, and Hitori knew Japan's strike force was two days away. Judging by the lack of action on board the battleships, the approaching attack remained unseen and unde-tected by the US Navy. There must be at least half a dozen battleships moored in close proximity, a per-fect target for torpedoes and dive-bombers. Hitori smiled. The Imperial Japanese Navy would wreak havoc in this harbour come Sunday, all being well.

Hitori's mission was to help ensure that the attack remained undetected, it was the reason that he and Kimura had travelled halfway across the Pacific to this place. He could have entrusted the mission to Suzuki and one of his other lieutenants, but the kyuuketsuki leader wanted to be there. He wanted to be part of the moment when the world changed irrevocably. He wanted to be a witness to history in the making. Most of all, he wanted to show his cadre of vampyr samurai that he would always lead them from the front, that he'd never ask his kyuuketsuki to do anything that he was unwilling to do.

"It's time." Kimura sat below him, gripping the vessel's wheel. "If we're to scuttle the sub and make it to shore before sunrise, it's time."

Hitori nodded. "Take us to the deepest part of the harbour. We'll open the hatches and let the water have her."

Once they were in position, Kimura turned off the engines and released all the air from their tanks. As the midget sub sank into the watery depths, Hitori opened the hatch atop the small conning tower. He had to use every ounce of his inhuman strength to force it open, the weight of water threatening to defeat him. Once he succeeded, his reward was a crushing wall of water forcing him and Kimura down inside the tiny compartment. Panic took Hitori for a moment, a lifetime of breathing making him gasp for the air his vampyr body no longer needed. But once the pressure inside the midget sub had equalised, he was able to stand upright again. Pulling Kimura behind him, Hitori swam up towards the moon shimmering overhead.

They broke the surface, both panting from the effort of escaping the midget sub, happy to have eluded the iron coffin. The two kyuuketsuki trod water while they looked around the harbour, searching for anyone who might have noticed the sudden appearance of two Japanese men in the water. But the harbour was quiet, with no sign of movement nearby. They were at least half a mile from the nearest stretch of shoreline.

"How's your swimming?" Hitori asked his disciple.

"Not my best feature," Kimura admitted. "You chose me for my record as a foot soldier, not as a fish, remember?" A wicked smile spread across his features. "We could always fly to our destination," he suggested.

"This is a covert mission. The less we draw attention to ourselves, the better. Revealing the presence of Japanese vampyrs on US territory would jeopardise our forces' surprise attack."

"GETTING COLD FEET before a wedding is perfectly natural," Father Kelly said. "Marriage is a lifelong commitment, and not something to rush into. You wouldn't be human if you didn't have doubts, Angela, but that doesn't mean getting married is a mistake for you, either. Tell me, what's brought this on? Have your feelings for Juan changed?"

"No, father, I want to be with him."

"Well, then, that's a good thing–"

"No, father, you don't understand," Angela cut in. "I want to be with him. I want us to be together, as man and woman, if you know what I mean."

"Ah," the priest said.

"I want him more than I ever wanted anything in my life. I was brought up to believe that should only happen inside marriage. That's why I said yes when he asked me to be his wife. But now…"

"You're worried that you're in lust with Juan, not in love." The nurse nodded, her freckled cheeks blushing bright red. Father Kelly took her hands in his. "I've seen the two of you together, Angela. I've seen how you look at each other, how much both of you care for each other. You have much more than the simple animal longings of two creatures that find one another attractive. What you two have is better than that. I believe you love each other, and you can make that love last a lifetime. But it doesn't matter what I believe."

Angela looked him in the eyes. "I have to believe it."

"And so does Juan."

She nodded. "You're right. It's all happened so suddenly, and with my transfer orders coming through I was worried we were rushing into this for the wrong reasons. But I don't want to lose him, father."

"Then go to him. Tell him how you feel, and look into his eyes as you just looked into mine. You'll find all the answers you need there."

The nurse smiled. "Thanks, father. I don't know what I would have done if you hadn't been here." She gave him a quick kiss on the cheek and hurried from the chapel, leaving the priest alone again.

Father Kelly turned to the altar and saw the crucifix, the image of Jesus on the cross staring back at him. "I told her what she wanted to hear," he said. "If we do go to war soon, what are the chances that both of them will survive? What gives me the right to deny them a little happiness now, while they still have that chance? Didn't Catherine–"

He stopped, biting back the rest of his words. The priest could feel his emotions churning inside, wracked by guilt and shame over what had happened to Catherine. He could have sworn the crudely moulded replica of Jesus was laughing at him, sneering at his pain. Father Kelly snatched a hymnal from the bench where he'd been sitting and threw it at the crucifix. The book thudded against the altar but the crucifix didn't budge. "Damn you! Damn you to hell!" The priest burst into tears, unsure if he'd been cursing his saviour or himself.

TETSUZO NAGARA PROPELLED the last drunken GI from Tokyo Joe's with a kick to the backside. "And stay out!" he shouted at the soldier as they staggered away into the early hours of the morning. Nagara muttered curses under his breath. The sooner his countrymen came and bombed this island, the better. He couldn't wait to get home to Japan and his own people, instead of acting as barman and confidant to a nation of drunkards without dignity or honour.

A shimmer of darkness in the night caught Nagara's eye. He peered at the alley where the movement had been, trying to make out what was there. The moon was full overhead, casting heavy shadows in the night and bleaching everything else a cold, metallic blue. Nagara shivered as the hairs on the back of his neck stood up, his instincts sensing what his eyes could not see in the darkness. "Is somebody there?" he asked, aware that his voice was trembling. "We're closed now, no more drinking tonight!"

Closer, a voice whispered in his thoughts. *Come closer.*

The Japanese barkeep had no intention of getting close to whatever was lurking in the shadows, but his feet and legs had taken on a mind of their own. No matter how much he willed them to stop, they sent him staggering towards the alleyway, his pace quickening with each step.

Closer still. Come into the darkness with us.

"No, please!" Nagara whimpered. His voice was still his own, but control of anything else was beyond him. His body felt as if it was possessed, drawn ever nearer to some malevolent presence in the alley. He could see a pair of terrifying eyes there, glinting in the night.

Be one with us. Become like us. Together we'll climb Mount Niitaka!

Nagara realised the voice in his head was Japanese, speaking in a Tokyo accent. He relaxed a little, remembering a message he'd received the previous day from Kohichi Seki. Officially, Seki was treasurer at the Japanese consulate in Hawaii. In reality, he was one of several spies stationed on Oahu. The decrypted message from Tokyo had said two friends from home would be visiting before Sunday. Black Dragon agents were required to acknowledge the authority of naval intelligence spies at the consulate, but Nagara's first loyalty was to his masters in Tokyo. Mount Niitaka was a favourite code of the Black Dragons, a recognition phrase designed to identify fellow members.

But as Nagara got closer to the shadows, he could see that the creatures waiting for him in the dark were monsters, not spies. Their hands stretched out elongated fingers, their nails like the talons of a predator. Their features were more like savage masks of hunger than faces, inhuman eyes aglow in the darkness, skin stretched taut over bulging bones. Worst of all were their mouths, black tongues licking dry lips, while razor sharp fangs protruded from their jaws. "What are you?" Nagara whispered.

Destiny, desire... and death!

The Japanese spy opened his mouth to scream but the cry for help never came. One slash of those talons severed his vocal chords, slicing open his throat and exposing the sinews within. Blood gushed from the wound and the two creatures dived forwards, lapping at the dying man's neck with their grotesque tongues, sucking and licking every morsel from his bleeding arteries. Nagara sank to his knees, still bewildered by the voices in his head.

Feed us, they hissed, *sustain us, all in the name of the emperor.*

MARTINEZ WAS SHARING a drink with Wierzbowski when Angela found him. The two soldiers were sitting outside their quarters, each sipping from a bottle of beer that Wierzbowski had bullied out of Buntz. The suds were warm and sticky, much like the humid air in the Philippines, but that didn't diminish the novelty of having a beer. Buntz considered the stores his own private domain. Rumour had it that he'd been diverting supplies that went "missing" en route to the base.

Some said he was selling the lost items on the black market, while others claimed Buntz was squirreling away the lost items into caches around the island, in anticipation of a Japanese attack. Whatever the reality, anyone at Fort Stotsenberg who wanted contraband went to Buntz first. Most soldiers had to make it worth his while, or leave empty-handed. Wierzbowski was the exception, his imposing physique and malevolent gaze enough to erode even Buntz's cocky arrogance. So it had been with the bottles of beer.

"Can't believe I'm getting married on Sunday," Martinez said. "I thought I was coming over here to defend peace and democracy, not find a wife." He glanced at the big man by his side who shared so little. "What about you, Wierzbowski? You ever think about getting hitched?"

The other soldier shook his head. "I'm not the marrying type."

"Don't say that. You never know when some little angel of love's waiting around the corner." Angela appeared from the far side of the base. "Speaking of angels, here comes mine now." Martinez drained his beer and stood up as the nurse got closer. "Welcome to our humble abode, Nurse Baker. And how can we help you, this fine evening?"

"Juan, I want to ask you something," she replied.

"Ask away."

Angela's eyes flickered towards Wierzbowski. "It's important."

"Oh. Right." Martinez turned to his comrade. "Umm, Wierzbowski…"

The other man drained his beer and stood up. "No problem. I've been thinking it's a good night for a walk anyway, so…" He nodded and smiled to

Angela before strolling away, whistling something jaunty and tuneless.

"He's a good guy," Martinez whispered once Wierzbowski was out of earshot. "Most of the others are scared of him, but I'd rather have him by my side when the shooting starts than somewhere else."

"Why?"

"He's a bigger target than me." The private laughed at his own joke, before noticing the look on his fiancée's face. "Hey, what is it? What's wrong?"

"I need to tell you something and I need you to listen. No jokes, no teasing and no interrupting me, okay?"

"Okay," Martinez agreed.

"I think I'm in love with you," she began.

"Just as well, since we're getting–"

"No interruptions, Juan."

"Sorry!" He pretended to pull a zipper across his mouth, turned an imaginary key to lock his lips shut and throw it over his shoulder. Angela smiled at the elaborate mime before resuming her speech.

"I think I'm in love with you, but I'm not sure, not a hundred per cent. I know I want to be with you all the time, want to share my bed with you, share my body with you. But I'm worried we're rushing into the wedding because of my new posting and everybody talking about how war is coming anytime now. So I need you to answer a question for me. By the time you finish, I'm hoping I'll know what we should do. Is that okay?"

Martinez nodded.

"Why do you want to marry me, Juan?" He pointed at his mouth, the lips still pressed together. Angela laughed. "It's okay, you can talk now."

He smiled. "Why do I want to marry you? That's easy. I want to spend the rest of my life with you. I want to have children and grandchildren with you. I want to grow old with you and be with you, always. I love you, Angela, like I've never loved anybody before. Yeah, I know we're both young and maybe we haven't seen a lot of the world – I sure haven't, not yet – but I've seen enough to know you're the one for me. I've known that from the moment I met you."

Through all of this Angela stared into her fiancé's warm, brown eyes, searching for the answers Father Kelly had promised would be there. She waited until Juan had finished before turning away, her feelings threatening to get the better of her. "Well?" he asked. "Do you know what we should do now?"

"Yes, I do," Angela replied. She flung herself at Juan, kissing him as if they'd never have the chance to kiss again. Her hands clawed at the buttons on his uniform, scrabbling at the fastenings, desperate to undo them. Martinez grabbed her by the wrists.

"What do you think you're doing, Angela?"

"I want you, now!" she replied, her voice brooking no opposition.

"But I thought you wanted to wait until our honeymoon?"

"If I'm spending the rest of my life with you, soldier, I want to make sure all the goods are in full working order." She slid a hand down his chest, past the belt of his trousers until her fingers were cupping his–

"Oh boy," Martinez gasped. "What say we take this inside? I happen to know the sergeant's off base tonight and his bed is empty."

"Lead the way," Angela smiled.

PRIVATE JEFFREY DORN had a drinking problem. He knew it, his sergeant knew it, hell, everybody knew it. As far as the world was concerned, Dorn was an alcoholic, drinking his way to an early grave. As far as Dorn was concerned, his only problem was finding enough to drink on a regular basis. His daddy had been a drinker, and his granddaddy before him. Drinking ran in the family, in fact it was about the only talent his granddaddy had left him. He sure as hell didn't leave any money or much of anything in the brains department to his son. The private had hated every minute of high school. He couldn't enlist fast enough when an army recruiting officer came around offering free trips to exotic locations and all the chow you could eat. That had sounded like Dorn's idea of heaven. All the army needed to do was make sure the booze didn't flow like mud and it'd be the perfect life for him.

He'd spent most of Thursday night and a good part of Friday's early hours aggressively pickling his innards at a variety of tropical taverns around downtown Honolulu. A run of luck at a friendly gambling den had provided him with more than enough funds to keep drinking until dawn, but eventually his binge had come to a halt in Tokyo Joe's. Play your cards right and that cute little Oriental girl behind the bar might let you pass out there for the night, or so the story went. But Dorn never did have much luck when it came to the ladies, and that night was no different. Kissy was missing in action, leaving her less delicious brother in charge of the bar and grill.

Dorn's copious behind was still smarting from the vicious boot that had propelled him out of Tokyo Joe's not long ago. He had staggered away, grumbling to himself, trying to remember where he'd parked the colonel's jeep. No doubt the colonel would expect the vehicle to be present and correct in its appointed parking place come reveille, and that meant driving the damned thing back to base, soused or sober. Of course, driving it back would be that bit easier if Dorn could find the keys. He was almost certain he had remembered to remove them from the jeep before abandoning it outside the cathedral – that's where he'd left it, the cathedral! Well remembered that man, the private thought, somebody give him a cigar. Now all that was required was the keys and he'd be home free, give or take a few miles of weaving and swerving along the roads of Oahu.

Dorn patted the pockets of his uniform, searching for the keys. Last place he could remember having them was in Tokyo Joe's. He'd put them down on the bar while searching for a dollar bill. He had no memory of picking them back up, but then he couldn't remember much of the last few hours. There was only one thing for it: he'd have to go back and reclaim his keys. Otherwise it was going to be his ass in a sling come sunrise, and he was planning on spending the morning nursing a hangover that could kill an MP.

The drunken soldier made an about face and lurched back towards the bar and grill, staggering along empty streets. Ahead he could see a painted sign for the bar and two dark figures outside the door, looking at something on the pavement. Dorn squinted, trying to get the scene in focus, but his state of inebriation was making that well nigh impossible. Whatever the case, both figures were startled when he called out, his words as wayward as his progress.

"Hey! Has either of you seen my keys?" he shouted. "I think I left them on the bar." As Dorn staggered closer, the two figures moved apart and moonlight fell on the shape at their feet. It was the sour-faced manager, the same slant eyed SOB that had kicked Dorn out earlier. At least, that's what it looked like to the private, but the body's ruptured neck and blood flecked face made it hard to be certain. "Whoa," the soldier slurred, "what happened to old misery guts Tetsuzo?"

"He had an accident," one of the men replied, his face cast in shadow.

"I'll say! Looks like somebody cut his throat!"

"Yes, we did."

Dorn frowned. He didn't have much sympathy for the murdered man, but that was no way to die, even for the likes of Nagara. "W-why'd you do that? He kick you out of the bar, too?"

"Not exactly."

A hand flashed through the moonlight and two long fingers buried themselves in Dorn's skull, stabbing straight through his eyeballs. He wanted to scream but fear froze his voice. A childlike croaking was all that escaped his dry, parched lips. The two fingers lifted him into the air, his legs kicking at nothing as his body went into a death spasm. Then he was flying sideways across the street, the early morning breeze cool across his skin and the scent of hibiscus flowers heavy in the air. The last name to pass through Dorn's mind was that of a deity to whom he had long since stopped praying. God, he thought in the last moments of his wasted life, I need a drink.

KIMURA STOOD OVER the corpse, his nose wrinkling in protest at the stench of warm urine and cheap liquor that rose from Dorn. "I still hunger, but I'm not sure I can bring myself to feed upon this."

"We drink blood from the living, not the dead, no matter how fresh the kill," Hitori said. "Corpses are carrion, not fit for our needs. His blood would taste like squid ink, pickled in alcohol." Hitori opened the door into Tokyo Joe's. "Bring the body here. We need to conceal both these corpses so they're not found until after Sunday. Once the attack begins, it matters little."

Kimura picked up Dorn's remains with contemptuous ease and carried them to the entrance. Hitori followed him, bringing Nagara's remains. Inside the bar chairs were balanced atop circular tables and row upon row of glasses had been stacked along the bamboo bar, waiting to be washed. "No obvious hiding places in here," Kimura observed.

"Strip the corpses and remove their identification," Hitori commanded. He marched across the sand-strewn floor to the other doorway. The sound of the waves crashing on the nearby beach testified to how close they were to water. "We could make it look as if they drowned. If we weigh down the bodies, it'll be days before either of them surfaces."

"And by then we'll be long gone." Kimura found a wallet choked with American currency in the dead soldier's back pocket. "There's enough here to buy half of Honolulu a drink."

"Good," Hitori said, returning to kneel by the corpses. "These Americans are slaves to their vices. We can use that against them. Now, help me rip the limbs off. The fewer body parts there are to identify, the longer it will take the authorities to realise what's happened." The vampyrs set about their task with clinical efficiency, removing the appendages as if plucking a chicken. Kimura asked questions while they worked, keeping his head tilted away from Dorn's corpse so as not to inhale its foul fumes.

"You still haven't told me the specifics of our mission on Oahu, sir."

Hitori pulled Nagara's head off as if removing the cork from a bottle of champagne. "You will replace this Black Dragon agent as manager of the bar and grill. Work alongside his partner on the night shift, and gather all available intelligence from the American servicemen that frequent this bar about the state of combat readiness. The more we know about the strength of their defences, the easier it will be to disable them on Sunday. I will contact you each dusk and dawn, so we can collate intelligence and plan our next movements. I have other objectives to pursue before the attack comes. Your task is here, gleaning intelligence from the enemy and Nagara's associate."

Kimura did not look impressed by his assignment. "Is this the best use of my abilities? We are kyuuketsuki. We could terrorise the Americans, make them afraid of their own shadows–"

"No," Hitori cut in, his voice low and menacing. "The time for that will come, but not yet. Our presence here, our very existence must remain a secret. In years to come the kyuuketsuki will be recognised as the empire's greatest weapon in this war. For now, we must work covertly." His expression softened as he rested a hand on Kimura's shoulder. "I know you are eager to spread your wings, to prove yourself in battle as a vampyr. Before we leave this island, you'll have that chance, I promise. You will bathe in American blood!"

Extract from the personal journal of
Lieutenant Charles Richards:

December 1st, 1941.
Well, it feels as if the waiting may
soon be over. All my life I've dreamed
about flying, and joining the navy made
that dream into a reality. But I always
knew there could be a price to pay for
that: war. When the fighting broke out
in Europe, it seemed inevitable that the
United States would get involved. Hell,
Pop fought in the Great War, as he liked
to call it, the war to end all wars,
that's what he believed. Guess I should
be glad he's not alive to see how wrong
that belief was, but I'd rather he was
still alive and disappointed. I wish he

could have beaten the cancer long enough
to see me graduate and get my wings, but
it wasn't to be.

Two years and the best part of three
months have passed since Great Britain
declared war against Hitler and his
damned Nazis. In that time the Germans
have marched all over Europe in their
jackboots and only the Brits have stood
up to them. Watching the newsreel footage
of how places like London have suffered
from German bombing raids makes for
pretty sobering viewing. I can't imagine
the same thing happening to LA or the Big
Apple, but I suppose it's possible,
thanks to aircraft carriers and sub-
marines. You never know what horrors the
future holds, what curveballs life has in
store.

As a navy flier, it could well be my job
to bomb the hell out of some other country
one day, to help flatten a city. I'll have
to do that knowing there are civilians
below me, innocent women and children cowering in shelters, praying not to get
blown to kingdom come. Is that just, is
that right? Dropping bombs on innocent
people because their leaders choose to go
to war over oil or rubber or whatever
other natural resources they crave? I sure
as hell didn't vote for Roosevelt but he's
our president, our commander in chief, and
if he commits us to war, I'll do my best

on his behalf. Strange the roads democracy can take you down.

Halsey's had us on a war footing since last week. Scuttlebutt on the Big E says he got a telegram from Washington suggesting the Japs are getting ready for war. A first strike is expected soon in the Philippines, maybe Singapore too. That's a long way away from Pearl but Halsey's got us jumping through hoops anyway, running drills and preparing for the worst. If the Japs do hit one of our bases in the Pacific, I know Halsey will be itching to hit back, and our SBDs will be right there at the front of the queue.

In the meantime I'm doing my best to keep the rest of the pilots and their gunners ready, but not too ready. We don't need anybody going off half-cocked and starting something nobody's ready to finish. If we are going to war in the Pacific, the other side has to fire the first shot. Even then, I'm not sure America has the stomach for war, not so soon after the last war, the Great War, the war that Pop thought would end all wars. I guess we wouldn't still have a navy or an army or an air force if it had ended all wars. We wouldn't need them anymore and I'd be out of a job, unable to fly. Strange the way life takes you sometimes, the paths it finds for you to walk, or fly, very strange.

THREE

SERGEANT HARVEY AIMES knew something was amiss when he found a brassiere hanging from the door handle of his private quarters. It was white with lace cups, and utterly incongruous in the barracks of an artillery regiment. The presence of lingerie inside the building was unwelcome, but the sergeant had known soldiers who liked to keep souvenirs of their conquests, all their conquests. Such men were not welcomed by Aimes and soon learned the error of their ways. The last thing his men needed was a distraction. Hell, if the sergeant had his way, there wouldn't be any women anywhere in the armed forces, and that included the nursing staff. Male medics were good enough for combat zones and they ought to be good enough for military hospitals, too.

Aimes knew for a fact that none of the men under his command had any female undergarments in their possession. He undertook snap inspections at least once a week, and secretly searched the recruits' lockers while they were eating their chow or taking showers. So, that left one simple explanation for the brassiere coiled around his door handle: there was a topless nurse inside the sergeant's room. Aimes grimaced. He'd been away from Fort Stotsenberg overnight, overseeing a work detail to improve the road south to Manila. Aimes had pushed the men hard and they'd finished early, so he'd marched back to camp in the early hours, arriving not long before reveille. The sergeant had wanted to get a shower and shave. Now he had other priorities.

Aimes removed the offending garment and opened the door. It was still dark inside the room, a single bunk and an army locker the only furniture. In normal circumstances the sergeant's quarters were immaculate, not a thread or speck of dirt to be found within. But these were not normal circumstances, and the dawn's early light revealed a floor strewn with discarded clothing: a nurse's blouse and skirt, along with the fatigues of a private. There was no mystery in determining who had left their uniforms on his floor, as the two culprits were asleep on the bed, snuggled together between the covers.

"Martinez!" Aimes bellowed. "What the hell do you think you're doing in my bed, private? I'm away from the barracks for one night and I come back to find you in here with one of the nurses! Or perhaps her name is Goldilocks?"

His words and their volume had the desired effect. Martinez was so startled he fell out of bed, his naked butt bouncing on the floor. The nurse

shrieked in horror or shame or embarrassment –
frankly, Aimes couldn't care less which – before
pulling the covers up over her head. But the
woman's evasive manoeuvres were not quick
enough to prevent the sergeant from getting a good
look at her flame red hair. "There's no use trying to
hide, Nurse Baker," he snarled. "I know perfectly
well that's you under there." She lowered the covers
to look at Aimes. "Getting a head start on the honeymoon, were we?".

"Sergeant, I can explain–" Martinez began.

"You can?" Aimes folded his arms and smiled.
"This I have to hear." The private opened his mouth
to speak but nothing came out.

"Actually…" Martinez began, "no, I can't. You
were right first time."

"My aim's always accurate," the sergeant said,
"even with a glass eye."

"We didn't mean any harm," Baker offered.

"Let me guess, you just got carried away, is that
it?"

The embarrassed twosome looked at each other
and nodded.

"And my bed was nearest?"

That got another sheepish nod from the guilty
pair.

Aimes sighed. "Remind me, when's the wedding?"

"Sunday," Martinez said.

"Just after midday," the nurse added.

"Then you two can consider this an early present.
I'm not going to report your conduct, Baker. I see no
reason to besmirch your record with this sordid incident. But if I ever catch you within twenty feet of my

barracks again, I'll take great pleasure in telling your superiors every detail of your excursion into enlisted territory. Once I leave the room you'll get dressed and vacate these barracks as soon as humanly possible. After that you're not to set eyes on loverboy until the wedding. Is that quite clear?"

"Yes, sergeant," she replied.

"Good. Martinez?"

"Yes, sergeant?"

"Stand up when I'm talking to you, soldier!"

The private leapt to his feet and snapped to attention. Baker giggled at the effect this had on his groin, until a glare from Aimes silenced her.

"Permission to put on my underwear," the blushing Martinez asked.

"Permission denied," the sergeant replied. "If I ever catch you pulling a stunt like this again, I'll have you cleaning latrines with your tongue for the rest of your life. Since you like misusing the beds of others, you'll be responsible for stripping and making every bed in this barracks for the next three months. You can start by boiling my sheets and finding a fresh mattress for my bed."

"Yes, sergeant!" the private responded.

"Since you seem so eager to engage in test firing your own weapon, I'm putting you in charge of artillery drills. You'll run a drill every hour of daylight, on the hour, from now until your wedding ceremony."

"Yes, sergeant!"

"Any questions?" Aimes asked.

"No, sergeant," the pair replied in unison.

"I should hope not. Dismissed!"

Martinez scrambled around the floor, picking up the discarded clothes and throwing Baker's garments over to her. She got dressed under the covers while Martinez hurriedly did the same in a corner. Still shaking his head, Aimes went to the door and opened it. All the other recruits were outside in the corridor, laughter frozen on their faces. "Get the hell out of here," the sergeant snarled, "otherwise you'll all be on report. Move!" They got out of his sight as quickly as possible, eager to escape his piercing gaze.

He was still standing in the doorway when he heard a voice behind him. "Excuse me, sergeant, could I have my brassiere back?" Aimes looked down and found he was still holding the piece of lingerie, his battle scarred fingers gripping the lace cups. He threw it over his right shoulder before stomping away to the main bunkroom. "Thank you!" Baker called after him.

Women, Aimes thought, more damned trouble than they're worth.

Kissy Nagara hadn't been feeling well on Thursday and stayed home while Tetsuzo worked at Tokyo Joe's. As far as the customers knew, the two of them were the nephew and niece of the original owner, Tokyo Joe Nagara. In fact they were husband and wife, sent by the Black Dragon Society to be its spies on Oahu. The two of them had laughed at the American sailors and soldiers who fell for Kissy and tried to spirit her away from an over-protective brother. She had been most effective at getting precious secrets out of her drunken customers, especially

those who believed they had a good chance of bed-
ding the apparently innocent young woman from
Japan.

There was nothing unusual in Tetsuzo not getting
home by midnight, as the bar rarely managed to
clear its more drunken patrons before then. But
when he wasn't back by three on Friday morning,
she started to worry. When dawn came and there
was still no sign of him, Kissy got a taxi from their
home in the hills to downtown Honolulu. She found
the bar and grill closed, its windows shuttered and
all entrances securely locked. Kissy hammered on
the front door, but got no response. She tried asking
the staff at nearby stores and passers-by, but nobody
could recall seeing Tetsuzo since Thursday.

Some suggested he might have gotten into a fight
with a sailor. He was probably sleeping it off in a
gutter somewhere, with a black eye and a throbbing
headache for his troubles. Others speculated that he
had found himself a woman. They said Kissy should
be happy, since it was long past time her angry,
over-protective brother settled down and stopped
worrying about her. She knew they were all wrong,
but couldn't explain why. Tetsuzo knew better than
to pick a fight and attract unwanted attention from
the authorities, and he certainly wouldn't endanger
their marriage or their mission.

She spent the afternoon across the road from
Tokyo Joe's at a cafe, waiting and hoping for Tetsuzo
to reappear, safe and sound. At sunset the bar's
bamboo shutters were pushed back and the front
door opened, but the Japanese man who emerged
was not Tetsuzo. Kissy did not recognise him, yet he

seemed to know her. The stranger smiled at her from across the street, gesturing for Kissy to join him inside the bar. Not sure what to expect, she crossed the road and walked into Tokyo Joe's. She had come to know every inch of the bar, having spent most of her waking hours inside it these past few months. She had swept sand back out on to the beach and washed away the vomit left by servicemen too drunk to reach the toilets before retching. Now, as she walked inside, the familiar interior felt strange, foreign, as if she was entering a different world. This place belonged to someone else now, no, not someone... something.

The front door swung shut to reveal the stranger standing behind it. "You must be Kissy Nagara, I recognised you from our intelligence files. I have to say the photo we possess doesn't do you justice."

"Who are you? Where's my brother?"

The stranger frowned. "There's no need to maintain the pretence of being siblings with me, I know Tetsuzo Nagara is your husband. Your controller told us all we needed to know."

"What do you know?"

"Climb Mount Niitaka!"

Kissy gasped, shocked to hear the Black Dragon recognition code spoken aloud. That morning she'd received a message from Tokyo, saying the code would be used to signal the Japanese attack on Pearl Harbour, setting in motion events that would change the world. The moment that phrase was transmitted, Kissy and her husband faced arrest, imprisonment and even execution. To hear those words spoken aloud sent a chill down her spine. It was not merely the words that scared her, but the way this stranger had said them. He spoke with arrogant ease, unafraid of anything or anyone. That same arrogance was evident in his face: the gleaming, hairless scalp, the cruel twist of a mouth, those dark, hooded eyes.

He wore a loud, colourful Hawaiian shirt over grey trousers and sandals, his toenails curling forwards like a bird of prey's talons. He stood at ease, but the ramrod straightness of his spine suggested years of military training. He spoke perfect Japanese, but his English was clear, precise and clinical, without accent or affectation. The way he looked at her, the way his eyes slid over her body... Kissy shuddered. She was nothing to this stranger, irrelevant, unimportant.

"We're forbidden to say those words out loud."

He laughed at her caution. "Not for much longer. Soon the whole world will know our power, will recognise our empire for its strength and courage."

"You still haven't told me where my bro– Where Tetsuzo is."

"Probably on his way back to Tokyo by now."

"Impossible!" Kissy exclaimed. "He wouldn't leave without me."

"I was sent here to replace him temporarily. Once the attack comes, this operation will have served its purpose," he said, gesturing at their surroundings. "I've come to close down the facility."

"But why would Tetsuzo leave without me?"

"He didn't have much choice in the matter. When the call comes, we are all required to obey. He told me you were unwell, too ill to travel. You will return to Tokyo with me on Sunday."

"How are we getting back? The Americans will be on full alert then."

"The same way as Tetsuzo. He was collected by the midget sub that brought me to Oahu last night." The stranger stepped closer to Kissy. "Why all the questions? Don't you believe me?"

"I don't even know your name," she said as he moved closer still, his left hand reaching out to brush her long, dark hair back over one shoulder, exposing the side of her neck. Kissy shivered as the stranger brushed a finger up and down her throat, stroking her skin as if they were lovers.

"Nabuko," he whispered in her ear. "My name is Nabuko Kimura." He leaned against her, their bodies pressing together, his breath hot against her neck. "And you will believe me, won't you, Kissy?"

She wanted to scream no, but her lips said, "Yes, I believe you."

"That's my girl," Kimura smiled. "You'll tell anyone who asks that Tetsuzo had a family emergency. Your uncle fell ill back in Tokyo."

"A family emergency…"

"You're hoping he'll be back in time for Christmas."

"Yes."

"That's good, that's very good." Kimura leaned closer still and licked the side of her neck. Kissy could feel his teeth dragging along her skin. An urge to cry out for help was growing inside her, but something stronger than Kissy's will made her submit to this stranger. She realised she wanted him, more than any man she'd ever wanted, wanted him so much the need threatened to consume her. She wanted to feel him inside her, wanted this charismatic stranger to bury himself in her flesh and–

Two sailors stumbled into the bar, laughing at some private joke. Their sudden entrance startled Kimura, who stepped backwards and turned to smile at the new arrivals. "Welcome to Tokyo Joe's Bar and Grill, gentlemen! Have you been here before?" Within moments he was escorting them to the bar, playing the role of dutiful host, his English now not so accomplished, matching his choice of words to the expectations of the two Americans.

Kissy watched him go, her need to be possessed by him fading as Kimura busied himself with the customers. She staggered, her legs suddenly so weary she had to sit down. What had taken control of her? Never in her young life had she felt such hunger, such all-consuming passion. It terrified Kissy to think how much Kimura's closeness had consumed her will and excited her senses, making her lose all control.

If those sailors hadn't walked in, what would have happened? She caught Kimura glancing across at her, his eyes narrowing. Something was terribly wrong about the new agent, though she couldn't put her finger on what it was about him that disturbed her so. Kissy resolved to keep as far away from him as possible for the rest of the night. She didn't trust him and, worse still, she couldn't trust herself while she was near him. Better to keep her distance, keep away from the seductive lure of temptation.

SHIRO SUZUKI WAS hungry. The need to feed was buried deep in his belly, its yearning like some mewling infant crying out for attention, always demanding fresh blood. He could sate himself until he was bloated, and it only quelled the hunger for a while, the yearnings abated, but not for long. All too soon they were back, gnawing away at him. He could still remember the adrenaline rush his first kill had given him, the supernatural high of draining every drop of blood from a victim, the raw power and majesty he felt surging through his body. The thrill was so exquisite, so absolute, Suzuki believed it could never end.

But the high did end, all too soon, and every feeding since had been that little bit less delicious. He still felt the excitement of the kill, the joyous anticipation of that moment before plunging his fangs into the veins and arteries of his prey. He learned to savour the terror in his victims' eyes, see their horror and witness his animal savagery in the reflection of their pupils. But the sensations were fading, losing their attraction. The hunger was still there, that never went away, but the ecstasy of killing was gone now.

Part of it came from the creatures he was sucking dry, Suzuki was sure of that. A true vampyr was a predator, hunting its prey before claiming the kill and savouring the spoils. But Hitori had forbidden the kyuuketsuki from hunting until war was declared with the Americans. Even after the opening salvoes of war, their leader had placed explicit restrictions on when, where and whom they could kill. For now the existence of the kyuuketsuki had to remain a secret from the enemy. If the Americans realised how far the empire was willing to go, what

212 DAVID BISHOP

weapons living and undead the empire was prepared to employ, it was impossible to know how they would respond. A wise warrior did not reveal all the weapons in his arsenal at the first skirmish.

Denied their supernatural tendency to hunt for fresh victims, the vampyr samurai were forced to feed on prisoners and unwitting volunteers. So it was on the airbase at Taiwan. Suzuki and his fellow kyuuketsuki pilots had been restricted to their quarters during the hours of daylight. When darkness fell on the Japanese military facility, Suzuki led his men to a nearby aircraft hangar where a fresh cluster of Taiwanese prisoners was left at sunset, locked in a barbed wire cage. The first night the hungry pilots had been content to gorge themselves. The blood of their victims had a different taste to what the fliers were used to, perhaps a reflection of the prisoners' diet.

By the end of the second night Suzuki could tell that his men were bored. They had been training for months in anticipation of the coming conflict. All of them were eager and ready to go into battle, using their enhanced vampyr abilities against the Americans. Instead they were stuck here in Taiwan, with a few terrified comfort women in a cage as prey. It wasn't enough. They needed to spread their wings, to hunt and catch and kill. They needed to be true to their nature, no matter how supernatural that might be. They hungered for it.

An hour before dawn Captain Yoshihiro entered the aircraft hangar. Suzuki knew the captain was under orders to provide the kyuuketsuki with anything and everything they needed. The leader of the vampyr pilots could not help smirking as a wicked notion occurred to him. Yes, Captain Yoshihiro would provide exactly what the kyuuketsuki needed: a target that would put up a fight, a victim that forced them to use all their skill if they wanted to feed.

Yoshihiro kept his eyes averted from the bloodless corpses littering the barbed wire enclosure, preferring to concentrate on Suzuki. "I trust everything was to your satisfaction, sir?"

"No, it wasn't."

"I'm sorry to hear that, sir. Did you mean more... fodder?"

"We're not cattle," Suzuki snapped. "You can't satisfy us so easily."

The captain blinked, his composure shattered by the violence of this reply. The other vampyr turned to observe the confrontation, intrigued by their commander's opening gambit. "I'm sorry, sir," Yoshihiro said. "I didn't mean–"

"I don't care what you meant," Suzuki hissed. "Your meaning and your opinion are as insignificant to me as the lice on our last meal."

"Forgive me, if I offended–"

"Enough!" the kyuuketsuki commander snarled. "We require sport."

The captain frowned, confusion in his eyes. "Sport?"

"We are predators. We live to hunt, and hunt to live."

"I see."

"You will provide us with a quarry, a creature of cunning who knows the surrounding terrain better than us, a victim with a sporting chance of escaping our best hunters. It is an hour until sunrise, yes?"

Yoshihiro checked his watch. "Yes, about that."

"Then it is settled. My men will hunt their quarry for the next hour. If the target eludes them, it lives for another day. But if they find the target…" Suzuki let his voice trail away, but his head tilted towards the leftovers splayed across the floor behind him. "Then the victim's blood, the victim's life is forfeit."

The captain nodded. "As you command, and who is to be the target?"

Suzuki smiled. "You are, of course. I give you sixty seconds to run."

"No, you can't!" Yoshihiro protested.

"You've seen my orders. You know I can do anything I want. I would start running, if I were you. There are now less than fifty seconds before I let slip my kyuuketsuki to hunt you down. They've never pursued a target in the wild before. You do want to give them good sport, don't you?"

The captain's mouth fell open. His gaze slid around the hangar, taking in the ravenous expressions on Suzuki's pilots. They best resembled savage dogs, feral animals ready to pounce on their prey. There was no sympathy, no help to be found in their eyes, only blazing hunger. Realising any pleas for mercy would fall on deaf ears, Yoshihiro turned and ran from the pitiless hangar, drawing a service pistol from the holster on his hip as he fled.

Otomo approached Suzuki, flanked by the others. "Is it true?"

"Yes, he's all yours. Consider it thanks for all your efforts these past months, becoming kyuuketsuki and teaching me how to fly a Zero. We shall achieve great and terrible things together. For now, enjoy yourselves. You all know the drill: be back by sunrise or suffer the consequences. Go!"

KISSY SPENT THE rest of Friday night keeping busy with the customers and staying away from Kimura. It wasn't difficult, Friday being the second most popular night of the week. Servicemen on 48-hour furloughs and those with overnight passes flooded into downtown Honolulu looking for drinks, love and a good time, Tokyo Joe's specialised in two of those. But anyone looking for love had better look elsewhere, as one sailor discovered not long after midnight. He grabbed Kissy and sat her down on his lap, determined she would kiss him before he let her go. A peck on the cheek wasn't enough; he wanted to put his tongue down her throat and his hand up her silk skirt. She squirmed and struggled, trying to get away from his iron grip without success.

If Tetsuzo had been there, the incident would never have happened. He kept a close eye on her to make sure she stayed out of trouble. But Kissy's efforts to keep away from Kimura were almost her downfall. When the soldier grabbed her, she called out for help but none of the men at nearby tables came to her aid. Those who bothered to look around cheered her assailant, whistling and applauding. All that stopped when Kimura appeared as if from thin air, standing next to the drunken sailor. Kimura grabbed the American's wrist and squeezed, until the sailor let go of Kissy. She got herself to safety, but Kimura kept hold of the sailor.

"Touch her again, you never use this hand again, yes?" Kimura asked. He clenched his fist tighter, until the bones in the sailor's wrist were grinding together. "You understand?" The sailor nodded, his ugly face contorted by pain. "You leave now," Kimura commanded, his voice like gravel and thunder mixed together. He released the sailor and turned away.

The humiliated serviceman looked at the others around his table. All were nodding and gesturing for him to go after Kimura. The sailor got up from his seat and hurled himself at Kimura. "No, don't!" Kissy shouted. She was trying to stop the sailor, not warn Kimura, but she was too late.

Kimura spun around and slammed the base of his hand up into the sailor's face, snapping his attacker's head back. Blood spurted from the sailor's nostrils as he flew through the air to land atop the table he had just vacated. It shattered beneath his weight, collapsing to the floor and scattering the others around it. Total silence fell on the bar, as everyone stopped to see what had happened, even the Hawaiian band in one corner stopped playing.

"Touch her again and you all need ambulance to get home," Kimura warned the sailors. "You want girls who love you long time, go down street to Madame Cho," he added.

The sailor's friends carried their insensible colleague from the bar, and several more tables nearby emptied, the customers unhappy at seeing one of their own felled by a single blow from a Japanese barman. But the empty seats were soon taken by other customers, eager to take the weight off. "Thanks for the warning," Kimura said as he walked past Kissy on his way to the bar. His mouth was smiling but his eyes remained cold, devoid of life. They reminded Kissy of a shark's eyes, empty and chilling.

JUZO YOSHIHIRO WAS running for his life. Dawn was still thirty minutes away, but the sky was softening from black to blue, like a bruise changing colour. As sunrise got nearer, so it became easier to see where he was going, to find his footing in the dense undergrowth. But the captain was all too aware that this also worked against him; if he could see better, so it was easier for the hunters to see him. His survival was all a matter of time: could he avoid the kyuuketsuki long enough to see another dawn, or would they find him first?

Thus far he had been lucky, using his local knowledge of the dense jungle around the airstrip to his advantage. Yoshihiro was fond of getting away from the stresses of his job by taking extended walks beyond the base's boundaries. He found the exercise enervating, and the chance to stretch his legs also gave him the opportunity to get some perspective on whatever was troubling him. He'd never thought that those long, brisk hikes might one day save his life, had never imagined he'd be using those same tracks and byways to avoid the fangs and talons of blood-drinking monsters.

Twice he'd been close to disaster, when the creatures had swooped low above him, scouring the jungle for his presence. To look upwards and see something that looked human flying overhead, a pair of massive wings of skin and bone beating the air, it beggared belief. Then there was the sound those wings made, a mighty thunderclap that chilled the soul. Yoshihiro had flung himself into the shadows, using whatever foliage was close at hand to hide.

The second time one of the vampyrs came close, it spiralled down to the ground and landed nimbly on its feet, less than a stone's throw from where the captain was cowering beneath a fragrant jasmine vine. The creature sniffed at the air, inhaling its surroundings, filling its lungs time and again as it turned in a slow circle. Yoshihiro felt certain the stench of his fear would give him away. He gripped his pistol in both hands, hoping that might steady his aim, as the kyuuketsuki's gaze swept towards his hiding place.

The captain could see the face of his hunter. It was the pilot called Otomo, whose chubby features usually gave his face a friendly, childlike aspect. There was nothing friendly or childlike about the creature standing in the midst of the jungle. The face was stretched and distended, the jaw line unnaturally elongated. The brow bulged and furrowed, while Otomo's eyes were black slits of malice. Two fangs jutted from the mouth like twin daggers. Everything about this creature was terrifying and brutal.

Otomo's nostrils flared as he caught a whiff of something on the early morning breeze. He stopped and stared at the shadows where Yoshihiro was hiding. Convinced he had been discovered, the captain closed a finger around the trigger of his pistol. He didn't know if bullets could harm these monsters, but it was better to die fighting than to surrender himself and his honour. Yoshihiro offered a silent prayer to the heavens and willed himself to shoot. But his fear was too great, the malevolent gaze of those eyes too terrifying.

Otomo dropped into a crouch, his muscles tensing. This is it, the captain thought. This is the moment when I die. Instead the vampyr leapt up into the sky and flew off, leaving a mystified Yoshihiro cowering in the shadows. When the sound of beating wings had died away, he stood up and jasmine brushed across his face. The pungent aroma filled his nostrils, blocking out any other scent. Of course, Yoshihiro realised, the fragrance of the flowers must have concealed my odour! He tore handfuls of jasmine down and strung them in a garland around his neck. If it had worked once, it might work again. Any defence was better than nothing against these fiends.

Yoshihiro knew his luck could not last forever. The vampyrs had chosen to hunt for him individually, their greed overcoming their common sense. Once they tired of that, the monsters would realise a co-ordinated search of the jungle would be far more effective. Working together, the six of them could drive him into the open and then his downfall would be assured. Yoshihiro decided to take matters into his own hands. Running and hiding would not save him; he needed to go on the offensive.

The captain circled back towards the aircraft hangar, keeping under cover until he had the smallest possible distance of open ground to cover between it and the jungle. He waited and listened, watching the brightening sky for signs of the creatures hunting him. When he was satisfied it was safe to break cover, Yoshihiro tore across the open field, certain that he would be attacked at any moment. He was surprised to reach the aircraft hangar unscathed and flung himself through the door, gasping for breath. It was empty, except for the remains of the dead prisoners. Suzuki must have gone to check on the progress of his pilots, the captain thought. He'd made it, against all the odds he'd made it. But his relief was all too short-lived.

"Clever," a mocking voice said. "You led my kyuuketsuki out into a fruitless search of the jungle before returning here, knowing it's the last place they would think of looking for you, very clever indeed."

Yoshihiro twisted around, unable to understand from where the voice was coming. He watched in disbelief as a cloud of mist formed in the air close by, solidifying into the silhouette of a man. A face appeared in the mist, its snarling features a menacing mask of hunger and hatred.

"I suppose I shouldn't be surprised," Suzuki said. "My men trained as pilots, not predators. They are used to having maps to find their targets. Their chosen battlefield is the air, not the jungle. It seems they still have much to learn about their new lives as kyuuketsuki. Thank you, captain; your cunning has given my vampyrs a valuable lesson." He arched an eyebrow at the garland around Yoshihiro's neck. "Why do you wear those flowers?"

"The scent, it masks my own."

Suzuki sniffed the air, inhaling deeply. "So it does, fascinating. You're even more resourceful than I'd realised. It seems a shame to kill you."

"Please," Yoshihiro whimpered, ashamed to hear himself begging but unable to stop. "I don't want to die, not like this."

"You don't have to die."

"I don't?"

Suzuki shook his head. "There is an alternative. You've shown skill and cunning in evading my kyuuketsuki, along with a talent for thinking on your feet. We have need of men like you. Become like us and you need never grow old and never die. You can become all but immortal, with powers and abilities far beyond those of ordinary soldiers."

Yoshihiro glanced over at the remains of the prisoners, the scraps of flesh and skin where living people had once been, before turning back to face his tormentor. "You're offering me the chance to be like you, to survive by drinking the blood of other humans?"

"Yes."

The captain looked down and realised he was still holding the pistol. But his hands were not trembling anymore. His terror had been replaced by a cool, calm certainty. "Then my decision is simple," Yoshihiro said. He stuck the pistol inside his mouth and blew the top of his head off.

PSYCHIATRIC REPORT:
Wierzbowski, Russell.
DATE OF ASSESSMENT: Unknown.

The subject was brought for pre-sentencing
assessment, having been found guilty of
manslaughter after beating a man to death
in an argument outsider a diner. The subject stayed mostly silent and
uncooperative throughout the course of the
interview, refusing to offer more than
monosyllabic answers to questions. This
appears to be a primitive defence mechanism, employed by the subject's
subconscious mind to protect it from
attack. When challenged to explain his
violent behaviour, the subject offered
this chilling explanation of his deadly

tendencies: "I get angry sometimes, and I see red." The subject has twice been convicted of violent offences in the past, each one worse than the last. It is all too obvious to this observer that the subject is on an escalator of behaviour that will ultimately lead to murder.

An investigation of the subject's familial background found few simple solutions for what might have created these dangerous tendencies. The father was a farmhand who died after falling from a horse twelve years ago, when the subject was eleven. The mother died of cancer five years later, but the subject did not begin to exhibit violent tendencies for another twenty-seven months after her demise. As the subject is an only child [and, indeed, now an orphan] there are no siblings to offer any further insight.

It seems clear the subject suffers from both violent and homicidal tendencies. Left unchecked, these inherent traits will worsen until an unknown number of deaths are caused as a consequence. The subject is a powder keg with a short fuse. The presiding judge's suggestion that the subject be entrusted to the army in lieu of imprisonment is, while novel, highly dangerous. The subject's murderous urges may prove useful in the services, but that does not make him a suitable soldier. It is the recommendation of this observer that the subject be held at a maximum security psychiatric facility indefinitely, pending further study.

Failing that, if the court is determined to transfer this problem into the hands of the army, it is suggested the subject be posted as far away from large population areas as possible, ideally as far from the United States as possible. Be under no illusions: Russell Wierzbowski will kill and kill again. He may find his true metier in war, but the resultant slaughter could be unstoppable. Turning the subject loose with a loaded weapon is akin to letting a genie escape from its bottle. Once the monster is out, there's no guarantee it can ever be put away again.

In summary, Russell Wierzbowski is a dangerous individual with a history of violence and mental instability. Turn him into a legitimate killer and the consequences could be truly terrifying. Imagine what would happen if he were to survive his time in the army? Is the presiding judge suggesting we create this monster and subsequently let it free to roam the countryside in peacetime? Wierzbowski is a killing machine, waiting to be unleashed. God help us all if we add training and skill to the murderous intent that burns inside this monster.

FOUR

TOKYO JOE'S STAYED open until sunrise on Saturday morning, business at the bar and grill was so good. Kissy felt grateful because it delayed the moment she would be alone with Kimura. She didn't trust him, and she didn't trust herself to be alone with him, knowing how easily she had succumbed to Kimura the previous evening. But as dawn approached and the last few drinkers were stumbling out of the door, Kissy realised Kimura had disappeared. One moment he had been behind the bar, staring at her with those forbidding eyes, and the next, he was gone, like the night vanishing before the first rays of morning sun. She searched the bar inside and out, but could find no trace of him.

Perplexed but relieved, Kissy ejected the final customer and locked the doors before counting the cash. Japanese-run businesses were considered fair game in parts of Oahu, especially with tensions rising between the empire and the US government. Kissy counted the bills twice and separated them into bundles before carrying the night's takings into the storeroom. The safe was buried beneath the building, its sole access via a hidden panel in the floor, under an old icebox. But when she tried to shove the icebox to one side, it would not budge, as if there was a dead weight inside.

Kissy had moved the metal casket often enough without help. Perhaps Kimura had stored something heavy inside it before he vanished? If so, she would have to remove it before being able to get into the safe. She tugged at the lid, but it remained stubbornly shut, as if something inside was keeping it closed. Impossible, Kissy thought, wiping a film of perspiration from her forehead. The rising sun was beating down on her through a skylight in the ceiling, and the storeroom was heating up rapidly. Kissy had another attempt and wrenched the lid open. What was within would haunt the rest of her days.

Kimura was inside the icebox, arms folded across his chest. Resting beside his head was another, that of Tetsuzo. The dead man's neck had been ripped apart, flaps of bloodstained skin hanging from beneath the jaw line. His dead eyes stared at Kissy glassily, like a doll's eyes. Worse was his mouth, the lips pulled back from the teeth, as if caught in time somewhere between a smile and a scream. Dried blood flecked his features, dark and red.

Kissy screamed, and Kimura's eyes snapped open. He reached a hand up from inside the icebox towards

Kissy, his mouth hissing vile curses, but Kissy was standing beneath the skylight, bathed in the sun's warming rays. As Kimura's hand stretched for her Kissy backed away, and sunlight fell upon the icebox's interior. Kimura's screams sundered the air, and Kissy's nostrils were filled by the acrid stench of burning pork. She clamped her hands over both ears to block out the cacophony of Kimura's pain. His burning hand pulled the icebox lid shut, the slam of it choking the storeroom with more fumes.

She stumbled out into the main bar area, gagging on the aroma of burning flesh. Struggling with her keys, Kissy unlocked the door leading to the beach. She flung herself out on to the sand, retching and retching until her stomach had nothing left to expel. The image of that monster, resting inside the icebox as if it were a bed or a coffin was bad enough. The smell of it burning, she didn't know if she would ever get that stench out of her lungs, her hair, her clothes. But it was the sight of her husband's decapitated head that was burned deepest into her brain, imprinting itself on her imagination, the grisly revelation repeating itself over and over in her mind's eye.

WIERZBOWSKI WAS NOT feeling good. Like all the men from his barracks, he'd been doing artillery drills from dawn till dusk ever since Aimes had caught Martinez and Nurse Baker in bed. Normally that wouldn't be a problem for Wierzbowski. He had the biggest and strongest physique of any man in the barracks and he welcomed physical exertion. The sinewy recruit always felt at his best being pushed to the physical limit, where every ounce of his mind and spirit had to be focused on the task in hand. It stopped him thinking about the carnal urges he got, the murderous rage that gripped his very soul.

Wierzbowski hadn't felt right for days. Recurrent waves of nausea and dizziness kept surging over him, and he'd been running a temperature for a week. At first he'd put it down to the ever-present humidity of the Philippines, a sweltering blanket of oppressive heat. But none of the other recruits in his barracks seemed to be suffering as badly, and Wierzbowski had always been among the strongest. Now he felt as weak as a kitten, hardly able to stand up, let along keep going. He kept pushing himself, nevertheless, determined to finish what he'd started. The collective punishment ended when Martinez and Baker got married, in less than an hour. One more set of drills and they could all relax.

Wierzbowski had the exacting, exhausting task of raising and lowering the barrel of a three-inch anti-aircraft gun. The battery worked in tandem with two nearby devices, the height finder and the director. The director was a large metal box atop a wheeled tripod. Those manning it used tracking scopes to identify a target, calculating the elevation and azimuth of the enemy. That data was passed to the height finder, a long metal tube atop another tripod stand. This determined the range to the target and converted it to an altitude. From that the director could accurately predict the target's location, so those aiming the gun could fire at the right spot in the sky.

It sounded complex but after weeks of drilling, the battery crew had become slick and assured, confident they could shoot seabirds out of the air. Of course, any enemy fighters or bombers would be moving a lot faster than any wildlife. More worrying was the fact that all the ammunition had powder train fuses effective up to only 20,000 feet. Anything flying at a higher altitude would be able to attack the base and neighbouring airfield with impunity.

Aimes came out to observe the final drill before the wedding, making sure they did everything by the book and didn't cut any corners. Martinez ran the drill with ruthless efficiency, not letting any of the men slacken off for a moment. Wierzbowski had another reason not to let the others know about his illness. His presence was the only reason the others hadn't sought revenge against Martinez for all these extra drills. Everyone knew the two men were friends, and everybody in the barracks was afraid of Wierzbowski. He'd never lost a fight since joining the army, either in the boxing ring or elsewhere. Hell, even at the bar brawl back in Honolulu, he'd beaten half a dozen MPs to a standstill before letting himself be arrested.

When the drill was finally completed, Martinez had the recruits stand at attention so the sergeant could offer his assessment of their latest efforts. "You're tired," Aimes began. "I know you're tired. You've been drilling on this gun from sunrise to sunset since yesterday morning. That explains your physical exhaustion and your lack of speed. It doesn't explain the sloppy way you finished that last exercise. I've seen more precision in the mess hall!

I've a good mind to keep all of you out here drilling until tomorrow night."

A collective groan escaped from the recruits, their uniforms soaked with perspiration, their hands made red by blisters. Wierzbowski felt another wave of dizziness sweeping over him. His legs had the strength of melting rubber, and Aimes seemed to swim and sway before Wierzbowski's gaze, the sergeant's figure shimmering in the midday heat haze. The recruit blinked repeatedly, trying to focus on Aimes, but a bout of shivering overtook him. Wierzbowski hugged himself, desperate for warmth in the searing heat.

"Wierzbowski! What the hell's the matter with you?" the sergeant yelled.

"I'm c-cold, s-sergeant."

"Cold? It's boiling out here! How in God's good name can you be cold?"

"I j-just am, s-sergeant," the recruit said, perspiration rolling his face.

"If you're so damned cold, why are you sweating like a pig?"

"I d-don't know, s-sergeant." Wierzbowski's legs gave way beneath him and he sank to the ground, the side of his head thudding into the edge of the metal platform supporting the anti-aircraft gun. Blackness took him, but not before he heard the concerned voice of Martinez in the distance.

"Quick, somebody run to the hospital, get a stretcher and a nurse!"

Koнichi Seki was destroying files in his office at the Japanese consulate on Oahu. He didn't notice the

cloud of mist seeping beneath his door. His official
title was treasurer, but Seki had spent much of the
past nine months assisting Takeo Yoshikama,
another operative for the empire's naval intelligence.
The pair of them monitored American readiness for
war, hiring small planes for sight-seeing flights over
Pearl Harbour and even travelling on a US Navy tug
to eavesdrop conversations between sailors.

Now it was late on Saturday afternoon and war
was imminent. He'd received a message from Tokyo
instructing all agents on American soil to destroy
their covert materials. Once fighting began, it would
not be long before the US authorities moved in to
arrest any and all Japanese suspects. Seki's first pri-
ority was to break down the machine that had been
sending and receiving communications with Japan,
using the Purple cipher system. Once that was
irreparable, he had to burn any and all incriminating
files. As long as the Federal Bureau of Investigation
believed he was merely a treasurer for the consulate,
Seki stood a chance of being included in some future
prisoner exchange. If he was accused of spying, he
could face a firing squad.

"Good," a silky voice said behind the spy. Seki
spun around to find a stranger inside his office. The
features were Japanese, but there was something
else about this intruder that perturbed Seki, an
uneasy quality that set his nerves on edge. "I see
you have the good sense to cover your tracks."

"Who are you? How did you get in?" Seki
demanded, reaching for the pistol he'd left atop his
desk. But the blotter was empty, the weapon
missing.

The stranger held up the weapon. "Looking for this?"

"Yes, and you haven't answered my questions!"

"Nor will I. It's enough you hear these words: climb Mount Niitaka!"

Seki gasped. He had not been honoured with membership in the Black Dragons, but he knew the recognition phrase and its meaning. "Forgive me."

The stranger waved away all apologies. "Tell me what you've learned in the past two weeks. It took some time to get here from the homeland and I've been out of contact with the latest intelligence about US military movements."

Seki nodded, years of discipline and indoctrination informing his meek obedience to the commands of the intruder. He knew better than to question his superiors, especially one as disquieting as this mysterious arrival. Seki spread a hand-drawn map of Oahu across his desk and gave a status report. As he outlined which vessels were moored within Pearl Harbour and which were out at sea, the spy risked a few glances at his interrogator.

The intruder was tall and slim, but possessed a personal magnetism that Seki found bewitching. Beneath the slicked back, black hair was a patrician face with hooded eyes and narrow lips. Twice Seki thought he saw fangs inside the newcomer's mouth, but the covert agent dismissed that as whimsy. The stranger still had questions, even after the briefing was concluded.

"What about the Americans' attitude? They obviously believe we are ready to go to war, but are they ready for an attack on US soil?"

"I've heard that Admiral Kimmel doesn't believe the empire would dare move against Hawaii. His greatest worry for the bases here is saboteurs among the Japanese American population on the islands. They represent two out of every five workers. If mobilised against the US, the saboteur threat could devastate the naval facilities, not to mention the local economy."

The stranger laughed. "Kimmel does not believe we would dare start a war with his people. He will learn the error of his ways soon enough." Seki nodded, but added no further opinions. It was not his place. This appeared to amuse the stranger. "You're wondering how I got into the consulate on a Saturday afternoon, aren't you?"

"Yes. The outer doors are locked, as was the door to my office."

"Locks and keys are no barrier to my kind," the stranger replied. He grinned at Seki, a mesmerising gleam in his eyes. "Once I've gone, you will return to your task. Make sure nothing remains that could alert the Americans to any and all covert activities on the island."

"Make sure nothing remains," Seki echoed, his will no longer his own.

"If you make it back to Tokyo, ask for Zenji Hitori at the Ministry of War. I might have a place for you within my cadre. For now, close your eyes."

Seki did as he was bid. When nothing had happened after a minute, he dared to open his eyes again. He was standing by the filing cabinet once more, though he had no memory of having returned there. Seki almost wondered if he'd imagined the whole incident, until he noticed the map of Oahu still spread out on his desk. Atop the map lay a card with an insignia etched across it in blood red ink: a bat with wings unfurled, holding the rising sun symbol of the empire in its talons. Seki's fingers trembled as he picked up the card. He turned it over and found six words on the reverse, written by a spidery hand in red ink: Remember the symbol, burn the card.

NURSE BAKER'S WEDDING outfit was covered in blood by the time Wierzbowski reached the base hospital at Fort Stotsenberg. The brief engagement made it impossible to find her a dress, so she had borrowed a clean white blouse and matching skirt from one of the other nurses, and a veil had been fashioned from a lace curtain. Baker had been waiting in the entrance for Sergeant Aimes, who was supposed to give her away. Instead she found herself summoned to treat a collapsed soldier. She'd responded without a second thought, flinging the veil aside when it got in her way.

Wierzbowski was still bleeding freely when she arrived, and the crimson mess was soon all over her blouse and skirt. Once the wound was staunched, she had him transported by stretcher to the hospital. Baker questioned her fiancé about his friend's collapse as they hurried after the stretcher-bearers. It didn't take many symptoms for Baker to identify the likely cause. She briefed the doctor on duty as soon as Wierzbowski was carried inside the hospital. "Patient collapsed after several hours of strenuous exertion outside, but he'd already been running a temperature while exhibiting tiredness and muscle pain for several days. Witnesses say he started shivering shortly before the collapse, and seemed confused when questioned."

"Where'd all the blood come from?"

"Cracked his head open on the edge of a metal gun platform. I stopped the bleeding at the scene before moving him. I'd say he's got malaria."

The doctor gave Wierzbowski a cursory examination before nodding. "I'll take him to the ward, get some fluids back into him and start treatment. If he makes it through the next forty-eight hours, he'll be okay." The doctor led the stretcher-bearers away, leaving Baker alone with Martinez.

"It's supposed to be bad luck, a groom seeing his bride before the ceremony on their wedding day," she said.

He frowned. "I thought it was bad luck to see you in your dress."

"This is what I'm wearing to get married in," Baker replied.

"You sure about that?" Martinez asked. The nurse looked down and saw that her clothes were more crimson than white. "I think you look beautiful in anything," Martinez continued, "but that's a lot of blood."

"You're not kidding," she agreed as Sergeant Aimes walked in. "I look like I've been playing catch in an abattoir!"

"Well, you two ready?"

"Not quite," Baker said. "Give me five minutes." She kissed Martinez on the lips before sprinting for the door. "Tell Father Kelly I'll be right there!"

MAEDA WAS EXPERIMENTING with his thick black hair. After two months of being confined to barracks, he had finally earned himself a pass off base. It was Saturday night and he intended to have some fun in Honolulu. Hicks had been riding him ever since the brawl at Tokyo Joe's, apparently determined to make the young marine quit. But Maeda had stood his ground, refusing to give in. No matter how hard Hicks goaded him, Maeda kept his temper. No matter how many times he wanted to smash that smirk off the sergeant's face, the marine from San Francisco had held back, turned the other cheek. Now, at long last, he was getting his reward: a night on the town.

Determined to look his best, Maeda had gotten a haircut and borrowed a colourful Hawaiian shirt from one of the other marines. Now the only thing to be resolved was which side he should part his hair. Mostly he swept his hair across to the right, letting the fringe fall forward like a black comma above one eye, but tonight he favoured a change. He balanced a small mirror on a windowsill, crouching to see his reflection. He tried parting his hair on one side before shifting it back to the other. No matter what he did, it wouldn't sit properly. Maeda sighed. Maybe getting it cut had been the mistake.

Before he could decide, his hair was invaded by Paxton's fingers. The dirty digits turned the carefully brushed locks into a tousled mess in moments. "Hey!" Maeda protested, swatting his fellow marine. They slept in neighbouring bunks and Paxton was perpetually making a nuisance of himself.

"Don't worry about it, Pat, none of the ladies will be looking at you tonight, not when Captain Catnip is out on the prowl," Paxton grinned.

"Since when did you become a captain?" Maeda laughed.

"It's an honorary title, in recognition of my services to the many, many women of these islands," he replied before flopping down on his bunk.

"I'm surprised they haven't had you deported to the mainland."

"They know a good thing when they see one."

Maeda went back to brushing his hair, deciding his usual parting was the best choice. Stick with what you know and it would look after you, that had always been his father's attitude. Joining the marines was a way of rebelling against the stifling conservatism of the family home. Maeda once tried arguing with his father, pointing out the move from Japan to America in 1919 was not exactly the act of a man who stuck with what he knew. Maeda's father would not listen, saying that was different, but refusing to explain any further. So the American youth with the Oriental looks had enlisted with the Marine Corps. Perhaps his father would forgive him for that one day, perhaps.

"Hey, Pat, you listening to me?" Paxton demanded.

"Sorry, I was thinking about my father."

"Yeah, well I was thinking about that honey at Tokyo Joe's and what I'm gonna do with her. Tonight's the night, Pat, tonight is most definitely the night."

"You've been saying that since September."

"Well, one of these nights I'll be right, won't I?"

"Maybe." Maeda gave up on his hair, returning the brush and mirror to his locker. "Hey, how can tonight be the night? Hicks put you on sentry duty."

"I traded with Walton," Paxton replied, grinning from ear to ear.

"The sarge doesn't like anyone to trade duties, you know that."

"Sure, but Flinch doesn't."

"You should stop calling him that. The boy's got a name, y'know."

"Fine, have it your way, but Private David Walton hasn't got a clue what the sarge allows and doesn't allow. That boy's greener than a dollar bill."

"Who's greener than a dollar bill?" Walton asked as he walked in.

"You are, according to Paxton," Maeda replied. "Do you know how much trouble you'll be in if Hicks finds out you're covering for Paxton?"

Walton stopped, his face falling. "But we only swapped shifts."

"The sergeant'll have you spit-roasted at a luau if he catches Paxton going off-base when he's meant to be on sentry duty. Hicks hates that."

The youth pointed a finger at Paxton. "You never told me!"

"Stop your fretting, Flinch," he replied. "Nobody's gonna find out."

"I'm not taking the chance. You can do your own sentry duty."

Paxton was up off his bunk within moments. "Now wait a minute, boy. We made a deal, you and me. Back out of it now and I'll make sure everybody in the unit knows you welsh on your agreements. Nobody'll trust you after that. Hell, I'll make sure the whole damned corps knows about you."

"That's not fair," Walton complained. "I'd never have agreed if I'd–"

"Life's not fair," Paxton snarled, getting in the eighteen-year-old's face. "You wanna complain to somebody; go take it up with the almighty. In the meantime, I've got a date with little Miss Kissy Nagara tonight and I ain't missing out on account of you, Flinch."

Walton was about to protest, but Paxton feigned a punch, duping the young marine into jerking his head away. "Made you jump," Paxton sneered. "Now, you gonna keep your end of the bargain, or I do turn your name into a six-letter word for mud around these parts, hmm?" The youth looked to Maeda for support, but the other marine refused to intervene.

"All right, I'll do it," Walton conceded.

Paxton wrapped a beefy arm around his replacement's shoulders and slapped Walton lightly on the face. "That's my boy! See, that wasn't so hard now, was it? And you know I'll do the same for you, in the unlikely event you ever find a woman willing to give you more than the time of day."

"Thanks," Walton sighed. "You're all heart."

Paxton released him and swaggered back to his own bunk. "No, I'm all man, least that's what Kissy keeps telling me. The two of us are planning to put that to the test tonight, make no mistake about it." He pulled a bottle of blue liquid from beneath his pillow and emptied a few drops into the palm of one hand. Once the bottle was safely hidden away again, Paxton rubbed his hands together before slapping them on his cheeks.

Maeda sniffed the air. "What's that smell, formaldehyde?" Walton sniggered at the suggestion until a glare from Paxton silenced him.

"It's aftershave," the bully announced. "I bought it last time I was at the market. The guy selling it said this stuff is guaranteed to excite any female."

"A female dog, maybe, you smell like you're on heat."

"You're just jealous because you're not gonna see any action tonight," Paxton sneered at Maeda. "Kissy loves the smell of my aftershave."

"If you say so." Maeda finished lacing his boots and stood up. "Well, you ready to go, loverboy? Don't want to keep Kissy waiting, do you?"

"Ready? Hell, I was born ready!" Paxton marched out of the bunkroom, giving Walton a cocky salute as he passed. Maeda followed him, but paused to have a word with the browbeaten youth.

"Don't worry about Hicks," he said. "If Paxton does get caught, I'll tell the sarge you didn't know any better. You won't catch any flak for this."

KISSY COULDN'T EXPLAIN what made her return to the bar on Saturday. She knew Kimura would be waiting for her, but felt irresistibly drawn back to Tokyo Joe's. The horrific image of her husband's head next to Kimura in the old icebox kept returning to her thoughts, telling her not to go back. But something else was calling to her, a yearning to be with Kimura, a whisper on the wind that she couldn't ignore. She wanted him, wanted to be with him, to feel his skin on her skin, surrender herself to him, utterly and completely. The thought of him touching her, penetrating her with his body created a shiver of disgust and excitement she couldn't ignore. No matter how hard she fought the urge, her feet kept walking back towards the bar, inexorably, inevitably.

She entered as the sun set over Oahu. The place was half full with sailors, pilots and marines, all of them ready for a night of drinking and debauchery. Kimura stood behind the bamboo bar mixing a cocktail, one of his hands wrapped in a bandage. He saw Kissy come in and smirked, as if he had been expecting her to arrive. I didn't imagine that voice in my mind, she realised, that whisper in the wind. He was calling me here, like a master calls his pet. He called and I came, unable to help myself. She felt ashamed of her weakness, of betraying her husband with the man that had doubtless murdered him, and that shame only increased her excitement.

Kissy walked over to the bar and reached behind the counter for a waitress's apron. Kimura grabbed her wrist and twisted, making her wince in pain. "You hurt me this morning," he hissed. "When this shift is over, I'm going to hurt you back." Kimura stared into her eyes. "You'd like that, wouldn't you?"

"Yes," she admitted, her face flushing red at what she was saying.

"From now on, you'll call me your master. I can make you come and go at my will, that makes you no better than a dog, doesn't it?"

"Yes," she whispered, not daring to look him in the eye.

"Yes, what?" he snarled, twisting her arm still further.

"Yes, master!" she squeaked, her pretty face contorting.

"That's better." Kimura smiled and let her go. "Now, go and do your job while I decide how best to punish you." He pulled out an apron and threw it in her face before turning away, his attention already shifting to a thirsty soldier. "Yes, private, what can I get for you?"

Kissy stumbled away, concentrating on tying the apron around her waist, not wanting the customers to see her shame. Kimura was a monster, but he was also right, she was his plaything now, to be used and discarded as he saw fit. He had slaughtered Tetsuzo, she was certain of that. There were less than twelve hours until the attack came. Once that happened, she would be as dispensable as her husband had been. Kimura would do to her whatever he had done to Tetsuzo, unless she found some way to escape. The worst part was that she didn't even want to leave. She found her heart racing at the thought of what he was going to do to her. Kissy was completely in his power.

HITORI SAT IN the back of the taxi, careful to keep the collar of his long coat turned up to stop his skin being exposed to the last rays from the setting sun. Saturday was fading away, and soon it would be the seventh of December, a date with destiny for the Japanese Empire. At times it had felt as if this day would never come, during the many months since Hitori had become a vampyr. Assembling a fighting force of kyuuketsuki had taken longer than anticipated, and training them how best to use their abilities was just as time consuming. But the preparations were at an end. History was about to happen.

Hitori's last stop had been at Takeo Yoshikawa's second floor apartment, overlooking Pearl Harbour. To the US authorities this unassuming man was Tadashi Morimura, Japan's vice-consul in Hawaii. In fact this was an elaborate cover. Like Seki, Yoshikawa was an agent for naval intelligence, using diplomatic status to observe and report on US military preparations. Hitori made certain Yoshikawa had destroyed all documents that might betray the identity of any imperial operatives on Oahu.

There was no telling how long it would take the Americans to detain Japanese diplomats on the island once the attack had begun; it could be hours, it could be days. Hitori was determined to safeguard the coming storm from detection. Should Yoshikawa or Seki be arrested and interrogated, they knew enough to endanger the attacks. For the empire's war against the Americans to have any chance, this first strike must be devastating. Destroy the Pacific fleet while it was still in port and that might give the US pause for thought, might persuade President Roosevelt and his government to open a dialogue with Tokyo. Hitori knew this was a long shot, at best. He felt certain the attack was the first step on a long road to hell, but the decision had been taken and everyone had to fight this war to its inevitable, bitter conclusion.

The taxi paused near the gatehouse that guarded the navy yard by Pearl Harbour. "You getting out here as well, bub?" the driver asked. He'd been ferrying Hitori around Oahu all afternoon, thanks to a crisp twenty dollar bill and a psychic nudge from the passenger. Hitori peered out of the window at the gatehouse and buildings beyond.

"No, not here, not yet. How well do you know downtown Honolulu?"

"Better than any other cab driver on the island."

"Good. I wish to visit a bar called Tokyo Joe's."

Extract from encrypted message
sent to Japanese diplomats in
the US:

"I do not wish you to give the impression
that the negotiations are broken off.
Merely say to them that you are awaiting
instructions and that, although the opinions of your government are not clear to
you, to your own way of thinking the imperial government has always made just
claims and has borne great sacrifices for
the sake of peace in the Pacific."

Extract from a speech delivered
by President Roosevelt to a
joint session of Congress on
December 8, 1941:

"The United States was at peace with
that nation and, at the solicitation of

Japan, was still in conversation with its government and its Emperor looking toward the maintenance of peace in the Pacific. Indeed, one hour after Japanese air squadrons had commenced bombing in Oahu, the Japanese Ambassador to the United States and his colleagues delivered to the Secretary of State a formal reply to a recent American message. While this reply stated that it seemed useless to continue the existing diplomatic negotiations, it contained no threat or hint of war or armed attack."

FIVE

PAXTON WAITED OUTSIDE the barracks, despairing of his friend's fondness for Flinch. Sure, the youngster would be okay once he loosened up, but 'til then Walton was a first class pain in the butt. Maeda eventually emerged, hurrying to catch Paxton. "Don't worry, I didn't leave without you," the surly marine said.

"Why not?" Maeda asked, surprise evident in his voice. "I thought you were eager to get into the loving arms of Kissy?"

"Well, I might need your help getting off base."

"I don't see why. You've swapped duties with Walton, so now all you need's a–" Maeda stopped, realising the problem. "You have got a pass, haven't you, Paxton?"

"Not exactly."

"Not exactly? You leave without a pass and you're going AWOL. Hicks will fry you alive if he finds out. That's begging for a court martial!"

"Yeah, yeah, absent without leave, what's the big deal? It's not as if we're at war or anything. This is the middle of the damned Pacific Ocean, what's likely to go wrong if one marine takes off for a night with his lady? Nothing, that's what! Don't I deserve a night off just once this month?"

"Yeah, but–"

"But nothing! I've had it with this base, with Hicks getting in my face, and with doing like I'm told. Pat, I'm going crazy as a henhouse staying cooped up here, it's not natural. A man's got certain urges, if you know what I mean? Well, my urges are more urgent than most, let me tell you. There's a sweet little honey waiting for me in downtown Honolulu and I intend to leave her well satisfied by the morning, if you catch my drift."

"Enough, enough," Maeda said, waving his friend's words away, "no more, please! I do not want to know the sordid details of your love life, okay?"

"So you'll help me?" Paxton asked, trying to keep the desperation from his voice and not having any great success.

"Yeah, I'll help," the other marine replied, shaking his head in dismay, "but I've gotta be insane to let you talk me into this."

"Cool," Paxton grinned. "Let's get moving. Hicks will be back on base soon and I don't want to take any more chances than I have to."

The two of them emerged from the barracks a minute later and marched across the parade ground to the nearest gatehouse. A taxi was driving away from the gatehouse as they approached. Paxton tried to wave it down, but his efforts went unnoticed by the driver. As the vehicle departed the marine saw that there was already a passenger in the back.

"We'll just have to walk to Tokyo Joe's," Maeda said.

At the gatehouse, a sentry challenged them to hand over their papers. Private Piper's sour expression was obvious proof he'd rather not be spending Saturday night standing guard at the base. "You lucky dogs," he said while casting an eye across Maeda's pass. "What you got planned for the night? Dancing, drinking, a little hanky panky with the locals?"

"All three with a bit of luck," Paxton replied. "Now, can we get going?"

"Sure, sure, once you show me your pass, hotshot."

"You already looked at my pass."

"Like hell I did," Piper retorted. "Hand it over, Paxton!"

"Why? You stamped it once. You wanna stamp it again?"

"Prove to me I already stamped it and you can leave."

Paxton noticed a solitary figure marching along the road towards the gatehouse, keeping a brisk double time. "Look, Piper, you're right, I ain't got me a pass. But if I don't get out of here tonight, I'm afraid certain parts of my anatomy are liable to explode with frustration."

"Take a cold shower like the rest of us, lover boy," the sentry smirked.

"He'll make it worth your while if you turn a blind eye," Maeda offered.

"I will?" Paxton spluttered.

"Of course you will!"

"How much of my while will it be worth?" Piper asked, his gravelly voice a rasp amid the sounds of crickets and cicadas in the early evening air.

"Whatever you want," Paxton hissed, all too aware of the approaching figure. He had a horrible feeling he knew who it was. "Anything, just name it!"

"Boy, you've got it bad for this dame, ain't ya?"

"What dame?"

"Nobody gets that excited unless there's a dame involved."

"Just tell me what you want to let me through, okay?"

The sentry stroked his chin. "Gee, it's hard to say. I mean how often do I get an opportunity like this? How often does a humble solider like me get the chance to put the screws on an arrogant jerk like you? Not that often."

Paxton glanced once more at the approaching figure, and what he saw made him curse in despair. "It's him," he hissed to Maeda.

"Who?" The other marine followed his gaze. Maeda saw Hicks twenty yards away and closing fast. "Oh no, that's just what we need!"

OUTSIDE THE MAKESHIFT chapel at Fort Stotsenberg, Father Kelly waved farewell to the happy couple, their friends and colleagues. It was too long since the priest had conducted a wedding service and his rustiness was obvious to the small congregation, but that hadn't mattered. All eyes were on the blushing bride and her proud groom. Father Kelly thought it odd that Nurse Baker chose to get married in her uniform, but he had few illusions a white dress would have made any difference to her purity; the base was rife with rumours about Sergeant Aimes catching the two lovers in bed. Despite her garb, Baker was still beautiful and as radiant as any bride the priest had seen.

Once the wedding party had gone, Father Kelly went back inside his chapel and removed his vestments. He went through the same ritual after every service, cleaning the communion plate and chalice that had borne the wine and wafer, the body and blood of Christ on Earth. As he went through the rituals made familiar by thousands of repetitions, his mind wandered to something that had been nagging at him during the service. No, the feeling had haunted him for longer than that, ever since Nurse Baker had come to see him a few days earlier. Of course, he realised. It was her radiance, the glow in her eyes and the smattering of freckles across her cheeks. Seen from the right angle, she had an uncanny resemblance to his beloved Catherine.

Father Kelly was still weeping bitter tears of grief when Buntz bustled into the chapel, a small notebook in one hand and a stub of pencil in the other. "Hey, padre, I was wondering if you were interested in making a little wager. I know the church and the turf are friends of old, so I figured you wouldn't be averse to a little flutter…" Buntz's voice trailed away as he noticed the priest wiping away tears. "Oh. Sorry. I didn't… I can come back later."

The priest shook his head. "No, it's fine. I was overcome by the emotion of the day, that's all. What were you asking me, Arnold?"

"It's Arnie, if you don't mind, padre."

"Of course, Arnie, forgive me, and it's Father Kelly, if you don't mind."

Buntz arched an eyebrow at the priest. "Yeah, right." He licked the tip of his pencil. "So, like I was saying, I'm running a kind of sweepstake and I was wondering if you wanted to get in on the action."

"Well, I don't really approve of gambling, as such–"

"This isn't gambling, padre. It's more in the way of a game of chance."

"And how is that not gambling?"

Buntz sighed. "Did you want in or not, Father Kelly?"

The priest smiled. "Why not? What are the stakes?"

"Winner takes half the pot."

"And the rest of the money?"

"I've got expenses to meet, certain administration costs to defray."

"I see. And what's the wager?"

"We were going to bet on how long Martinez lasted in the sack with his blushing bride, but since the two of them have already done the dirty deed, that kind of took the novelty element away. Besides, getting exact verification of the result would be tricky, to put it mildly."

"I'm glad to hear that saner heads prevailed," Father Kelly replied.

"Instead we're betting on how many enemy planes our boys here on base can shoot down the first day we're attacked by the Japs." Buntz's hand hovered expectantly over his notebook. "I can offer you five, 11 or 22, everything else between none and forty has already been taken."

"But we're not at war with the Japanese," the priest said.

"Not yet, true, but I figure it's only a matter of time. Look at it this way: we're the biggest US airfield between Tokyo and Hawaii, right? Even the Japs wouldn't be crazy enough to attack Pearl, so it stands to reason that when the war starts – and it will happen, you can trust me on that, padre – our little yellow friends are gonna come here first and bomb the crap out of us."

"You're taking wagers on how many lives our batteries will end?"

"Yep. Think of it as a kind of incentive scheme. Not that I figure anyone will need much incentive once the Japs attack, but it keeps people interested while we wait for the inevitable. So, what do you want, five, 11 or 22?"

"I'm not interested in placing a wager on murder," Father Kelly scowled.

"It'll be war, not murder, padre. Don't the church think killing's all right during a time of war? I mean, if it didn't, would they send you here with us?"

"My job is to provide spiritual comfort, that's all."

"Tell the Japs. I reckon they'll shoot just as happily as the rest of us."

"Nevertheless, I will not gamble on the taking of lives."

Buntz stuck the worn down stub of pencil behind one ear and shoved the notebook into a pocket. "For a man who just married the two happiest people on the base, you sure don't seem happy, padre. Try lightening up!" He stomped out of the chapel, leaving Father Kelly alone with his thoughts.

The priest sank back down on the nearest pew. "I wish I could," he murmured, his thoughts still full of Catherine's joyous face, the memory intermingled with an image of her blue, bloated features after death. Would he never be free of the guilt? Would he never be rid of that thorn in his soul?

"WHAT'S THE DAMN problem here?" Hicks bellowed. He marched up to the gatehouse and stamped to attention, glaring at the trio standing across the entrance. "Well? Is somebody going to tell me, or do I have to guess?"

The sentry swallowed hard before replied. "Sorry, sergeant, I didn't see you coming. I was telling these two they needed a pass before I could let them off the base, but Paxton here wouldn't listen to reason."

"You lying bastard!" Paxton spat. "Sarge, this ass-hole was soliciting a bribe to let me pass. If anybody's in trouble here, it should be him."

"Is that a fact?" Hicks enquired, before his gaze moved inexorably to the third man standing at the gatehouse. "And what have we here? Private Maeda, I should have known. Wherever there's trouble, that's where I'll find you, won't I, Maeda? I swear you must go looking for it."

"He didn't have anything to do with this," Paxton insisted.

"Was I asking for your opinion?" the sergeant snarled.

"No, sergeant, but Pat–"

"This slant-eyed, yellow-skinned SOB has been lousing up my unit from the day he arrived," Hicks sneered. "Don't tell me he's got nothing to do with this! I know a traitor and a coward when I see one, and Private Maeda here has got a streak of yellow a mile wide running down his back."

"Actually, Paxton's right," the sentry chipped in. "I've already stamped Maeda's papers, he's free to go into Honolulu."

"You think so, do you?" Hicks snapped his fingers for Piper to hand over Maeda's pass. The sergeant glanced over the paperwork before slowly, methodically tearing it in half, then into quarters and finally into eights. "That's what I think of your pass, Maeda. What have you got to say about that?"

"I thought it was an offence to destroy official documents, sergeant."

"Smart guy, huh? Think you're so clever, so much more intelligent than the rest of us, is that it?" Hicks leaned so close to Maeda's face that their noses were touching, their eyeballs only a few inches apart. Every time he spoke the sergeant's spittle flecked the private's face. "Well, I've got a news flash for you, my Oriental friend. You might have a smart mouth but you sure as hell haven't got anything of any value in that skull of yours, otherwise you'd have known better than to enlist in the corps. We want real soldiers, not a bad case of the yellow peril. Have you got that, Toshikazu?"

"Yes, sergeant, loud and clear," Maeda replied before smiling.

"What the hell are you grinning about, boy?"

"Nothing, sergeant. Just like I'm looking at nothing, nothing at all."

"You're looking at me, boy, and that means you ain't looking at nothing. You're staring at a sergeant major in the United States Marine Corps!"

"Still looks like nothing to me," Maeda murmured.

"What did you say?" Hicks bellowed, his voice close to a scream.

"Hey, sarge, leave him," Paxton interjected. "Pat's done nothing wrong."

"Keep out of this," the sergeant warned, "you're in enough trouble."

"Yeah and that's my own stupid fault, but Pat's done nothing wrong." Paxton reached out a hand to pull Hicks away from Maeda. The sergeant whirled around and grabbed Paxton by the arm.

"You try laying hands on me again and I'll break your damned wrist!"

"Is that a fact?" Paxton snarled at Hicks, his temper fast evaporating.

"You better believe it, boy!"

"Oh, yeah? Well, try believing this, asshole!" Paxton smashed a fist into Hicks's face, the sergeant's nose breaking with a satisfying crack. Hicks stumbled backwards, utter disbelief crowding his features. His feet got tangled with each other and the sergeant tripped over backwards, falling towards the guardhouse. The back of his skull smacked hard against the concrete slab of a step, the impact making a noise like an egg cracking. A gasp escaped Hicks's lungs, but that was all. He didn't speak, didn't move, or do anything.

Piper crouched beside the body, searching for any signs of life. After a moment he rested back on his haunches and looked up at Paxton. "Sweet Jesus... I think you've killed him!"

MIKE DANNER STOPPED his taxi outside Tokyo Joe's in downtown Honolulu, all too aware of the malevolent presence sitting in the back seat. The Japanese passenger was paying him well for the privilege of being driven around Oahu, but Danner couldn't shake a feeling of dread lurking in his gut. After five years of driving a cab on the island, he'd learned to trust his instincts about such things. He knew when a passenger had drunk too much and was gonna throw up; marines were the worst, they always overdid it, in his experience. He knew when a passenger didn't have the money to pay for their fare by the twitchy way they kept looking at the door handle in the back. And he knew when somebody had violence in mind from their posture, the way they caressed their knuckles or kept one hand buried inside a bulging pocket.

But the Japanese passenger was a blank, a void, and that made his presence in the back seat all the more perturbing. His posture gave off no signals, and both hands rested comfortably in his lap. His sole distinguishing characteristic was to sit in the shadows, keeping out of direct sunlight at all times. Now the sun had set, the passenger appeared a little more relaxed, as if he no longer had any worries. Danner didn't know why this was significant, and his fare certainly wasn't volunteering any information. The cabbie had made a few attempts at conversation, but they were met by a stony silence from the back seat. He soon learned to shut up and drive.

Danner pulled on the handbrake and twisted around to look at his passenger. "Well, this is it, Tokyo Joe's Bar and Grill, the end of the line."

The Japanese man produced two twenty dollar bills and offered them to the driver, more than three times the required amount to settle the fare.

"That's too much," Danner said. "I can't accept that much from you."

His passenger frowned. "Why not?"

"I was just doing my job. Pay me the going rate and a tip if you want, but I can't accept that much. It wouldn't be right."

"You show great honour. I did not expect that."

"Like I said, I'm just doing my job."

"Very well." The passenger considered the two notes in his hand. "One of my countrymen or I may have need of your services later. Will you accept this money as advance payment to remain here until required?"

"Well, sure, but–"

Then we have an agreement, a voice whispered in the cabbie's mind.

"I guess we've got a deal," Danner said, accepting the twenties. "But if you or your friends don't get in my cab before midnight, I'm heading home."

"So be it." The passenger got out of the cab and shut the door.

"Hey!" the cabbie called out. "Nearly half the people on Oahu look Japanese. I need a name, otherwise I could give the wrong person your ride."

"Hitori or Kimura," the passenger said before entering the bar. *Stay*.

Danner decided he'd stay, and wrote the two names in pencil on one of the greenbacks. Maybe he'd been wrong about the passenger. Anybody who was willing to tip you more than twenty bucks couldn't be all bad, could he?

PAXTON STARED AT the fallen sergeant, his mouth moving, but no words coming out. It was Maeda who came to the sergeant's aid, crouching down on the opposite side from Piper. He leaned over the body, one hand resting on the ground beside the head, listening for any sound from Hicks. "He's... It's okay, I can hear something... He's still breathing!" Maeda pointed to the gatehouse. "Piper, get on the phone and call for a medic. Do it!"

"Your hand," the sentry said.

Maeda looked at his palm, the one that had been on the ground. It was covered in blood, crimson dripping from his fingers. Using his clean hand, Maeda tipped the sergeant's head to one side. There was a pool of blood underneath it. "Call a damned medic, Piper, now!"

The sentry hurried into the guardhouse, his frantic voice echoing within the small structure as he shouted into a telephone for help. Paxton knelt down on the other side of Hicks, his face still stricken by the shock of what had happened. "Pat, what should I do? Tell me what I should do!"

Maeda frowned. "They're gonna throw the book at you no matter what happens, whether Hicks makes it or not."

"You think he could die?"

"The sergeant's got blood pouring out of the back of his head, Paxton. You heard what it sounded like when he hit the edge of the step. That noise, I think it was his skull cracking open. God only knows what'll happen to him."

Paxton licked his lips, trying to focus and think. "All I did was punch him. I've punched a dozen guys before and none of them ever…"

"We'll all tell them that, you, Piper and me," Maeda said. "We'll tell them it was an accident. Yeah, you meant to hit him, but that was all; you didn't mean this." Maeda looked at his bloody hand and wiped it dry on his khaki trousers, staining them crimson. "You'll still face charges, but it'll be okay as long as—"

"As long as he doesn't die?" Paxton cut in.

Maeda nodded.

"I can't take that chance," Paxton decided, getting back to his feet. "If I stay here and he dies, that's it, my life is over too."

"Well, what's the alternative?"

Paxton looked over his shoulder to the world beyond the gatehouse. "I take off, lose myself somewhere on the island until this all blows over. If Hicks dies, it'll be in the papers, I'll know not to come out of hiding. If he makes it, leave me a message with Kissy and I'll come back, face the music."

Maeda stood up. "That's crazy! You'll be going AWOL, that only makes you look more guilty. Run now and you'll spend the rest of your life looking over your shoulder until they catch you, and they will catch you. Oahu's not a big place, and there're not enough places for you to hide. They'll find you, eventually."

"Maybe," Paxton conceded, "but if I'm going to spend the rest of my damned life rotting in a cell somewhere, I want one night in heaven first!" He turned and strode away from the gatehouse, away from the base.

"Don't do this!" Maeda called after him, but got no response.

Piper emerged from the gatehouse, drawing a pistol from his holster. "I told the MPs what happened. They say I've got to keep Paxton here until they arrive." The sentry glanced around, mystified until he spotted the marine striding away from him. "Hey, Paxton, come back!"

Still the fugitive didn't reply, his pace quickening until he was running away from the base. "I said come back here!" Piper yelled. "Otherwise I open fire."

Paxton was sprinting, running for his life.

The sentry raised his pistol and took aim at the receding figure. "Don't shoot," Maeda pleaded. "You know it was an accident."

"I've got my orders," the sentry said, hands trembling as his finger moved to pull the trigger. Maeda stepped over the prone sergeant and shoulder charged Piper so his shot flew harmlessly into the air. By the time the sentry had recovered from the attack, Paxton was out of sight. "Damn you!" Piper hissed at Maeda. "I'd have got him if you hadn't interfered."

"I doubt it; your hands were shaking too much."

The sentry swung his pistol around and aimed at Maeda, preparing to shoot the unarmed marine from point blank range. "Yeah, well, I think even I could hit you from this distance if I tried hard enough."

"Piper, I didn't do anything," Maeda protested.

"You aided and abetted the escape of an attempted murderer."

"What? All I did was bump into you, and Paxton didn't try to kill the sarge, he just punched him in the face. The rest was an accident and you know it!"

"Right now that's your word against mine."

"Fine! Shoot me if you want," Maeda snapped, kneeling back down beside the fallen man. "But killing me while I try to stop Sergeant Hicks from bleeding to death won't look good on your service record, will it?"

SUZUKI AND HIS cadre of kyuuketsuki sat at the back of the briefing as the assembled pilots were given their targets for the next day. More than 250 planes would fly from Taiwan to the Philippines where they were to attack Clark Field and Fort Stotsenberg. Two-thirds of the aerial armada would be bombers, with close to a hundred Zeros as escort. Once the bombers had finished pounding the US facilities, the fighters would swoop down and strafe anything that had escaped the high altitude bombardment. The goal was simple: to destroy the US Army Air Force in the Philippines, eliminating any American aerial counter-strike against Japanese forces.

The briefing officer was succinct and fierce. "Due to the time difference between here and Hawaii, our attack on Pearl Harbour will start before we reach the Philippines. We will not have the element of surprise on our side, so we'll need all our skill and courage to defeat the enemy. Dismissed!"

Suzuki kept his kyuuketsuki back while the other pilots filed out of the briefing. A few of those leaving risked a glance at the vampyr pilots, but most of the fliers didn't acknowledge their presence at the back of the room. Once the room had emptied, Suzuki stood to address his vampyr cadre.

"It will not have escaped your attention that our countrymen keep away from us. Like all mortals, they fear the unknown, so they fear us. Remember that well, my brethren. When the attack commences tomorrow, the seven of us will fly as a separate unit from the others. They have strategic objectives to fulfil. Our goal is to bring fear and terror to the Americans. That is why our fighters are painted black from nose to tail, to mark us out as different, a force to be feared. Our capabilities are unknown. Tomorrow we shall change that. Tomorrow our wrath shall become the stuff of legends and nightmares."

WALTON APPROACHED THE gatehouse expecting another dull night of watching other marines coming and going. They'd leave the navy yard reeking of aftershave and hormones, ready to spend their hard earned dollars in the city. Around midnight the survivors would stagger back to their barracks, stinking of beer and tobacco, usually in pairs to stop one another from collapsing. Those that didn't make it back under their own steam would reappear later, slumped over in the back of

MPs' jeeps, cuts and bruises telling their own story about what had happened.

After the brawl at Tokyo Joe's in September, Walton had little enthusiasm for similar bouts of debauchery. He was a simple country boy from a farming community, the eldest of half a dozen siblings. Aside from a few sips of hooch from an illicit still back home, he rarely drank and usually found himself regretting the consequences when he did. So, whenever Walton felt the urge to paint the town red, the young marine would volunteer for a night of sentry duty at the gatehouse. Seeing the effect demon drink had on his fellow recruits was more than enough to convince him that staying sober was the safer option.

But the night was still young when he reached the gatehouse to relieve Piper and already somebody was flat out on the ground. From a distance he looked dead drunk. When Walton got closer, the fallen figure just looked dead. He was shocked to realise that it was Sergeant Hicks, a pool of blood spreading out from beneath his skull. Maeda and Piper were standing over the sergeant arguing, the sentry shoving a pistol in Maeda's face.

"What the hell's going on?" Walton demanded.

"Thank god you're here," Maeda replied, relief all too evident on the marine's face. "Did you bring a medical bag or a first aid kit?"

"I'm just here to relieve Piper. What happened to the sarge?"

"Paxton attacked him and ran off, aided and abetted by an accomplice," the sentry said, pointing his pistol at Maeda, "him."

"That's crap and you know it!"

"That's what is going in my report, you slant-eyed SOB," Piper snarled. "Walton, put Maeda under arrest and escort him to the captain's office."

"Why? Pat says—"

Piper turned his pistol towards Walton. "I don't care what your yellow friend here says, I'm in charge now! Do what I tell you or else I'll have you brought up on charges as well. Is that clear enough for you?"

Walton stared at the end of the pistol. Nobody had ever pointed a gun at him before and the experience was frightening. All his life Walton had been fighting a constant battle with his terrors, fearful that someone would discover he was a coward. The smallest thing could scare him: spiders, heights, even the dark. He startled too easily, making him an easy target for bullies like Paxton. Walton had thought that joining the marines would force him to confront his demons and help him overcome his fears. There was no place for cowards in the corps, the recruiting officer had said. Guess I'm the exception that proves the rule, Walton decided. He swallowed hard and took a step towards the sentry.

"Now come on, Piper, you're not gonna shoot me, are you? I'm on your side, remember? Besides, I only just got here, didn't I?" Walton asked. He was close enough to touch the pistol now. The frightened soldier reached out a hand and wrapped it around the handgun. "Why don't you give me that weapon and then we can talk about what happened sensibly, okay?" He slowly, delicately, slid the pistol out of

Piper's trembling hands. "That's it, that's the way. No need for guns, we're all friends here, aren't we?"

Piper's hands fell to his sides while his head nodded a numb agreement.

"That's right," Walton agreed, pocketing the weapon. "Look, why don't you go back inside the gatehouse and call the medics? They should have been here by now, shouldn't they? You go and put a rocket up them. Go on."

Piper walked into the gatehouse, his face ashen, hands still trembling. After a few moments Walton heard his colleague talking to the base infirmary. Maeda came over and shook Walton by the hand. "Thank god you got here when you did, Walton. I honestly thought he was going to shoot me."

"How's Hicks?"

Maeda frowned. "Not so good. I put a cloth under his head to staunch the bleeding, but he's been unconscious since the accident." Maeda looked around, searching for any sign of an ambulance or medics approaching. "Why aren't they here yet? The sarge'll die unless he gets proper medical attention soon."

"What happened?"

"Pretty much what Piper said, but less exaggerated. Paxton was trying to talk his way off base without a pass when the sarge arrived. Paxton punched Hicks in the face and the sarge fell over, hitting his head on that step. He hasn't moved since." At last the wail of sirens could be heard, getting louder and closer. "Paxton made a run for it and Piper was going to shoot him."

"So you stopped him?"

Maeda shrugged, embarrassed. "I just gave him a nudge, put his aim off. It was nothing, really. Any of us would have done the same."

"I wouldn't," Walton replied. "Paxton struck someone of superior rank; he's got to be punished for that. If what happened next was an accident, he should have stayed to face the consequences—"

"That's what I told him," Maeda cut in.

"Running away makes him look more guilty, not less. Piper was within his rights to shoot." Walton undid the catch holding his sidearm in place and let his hand rest on the grip. "You shouldn't have intervened, Pat."

"I couldn't let Piper shoot Paxton!"

"That wasn't your decision to make. I'm going to have to place you under arrest, until all of this can be sorted out."

"What?"

Walton frowned. "Please, Pat, don't make this any harder than it is."

Maeda glanced over his shoulder at the road to Honolulu, the same road Paxton had used to flee. But he wasn't Paxton and he never would be. Sighing, Maeda turned back to Walton. "Fine, arrest me, but as least let me stay here until the medics arrive, so I can explain to them what happened."

To: Mrs Irma Paxton, San Diego,
        California.

Dear Momma,
  I don't know how to tell you this so
I'm just gonna write it down in a
letter and decide whether or not to
mail this to you later. I think I
killed a man an hour ago. I won't go
into the details - that'll be for my
court martial to decide, if it comes to
that - but I want you to know I didn't
mean to kill him. His name was Lee
Hicks and he was our sergeant major at
the base on Oahu. He's been ragging on
my buddy Pat for months and I decided
to step in. It seemed the right thing
to do at the time.

We got into a tussle, well, I guess you could call it that. Truth is, I punched him in the nose and he went down. He cracked his head something fierce on a concrete step and then there was blood everywhere. After that I ran. Didn't know where I was running to, just what I was running from. I guess if you could talk to me, you'd say I'm always running away from trouble: the trouble I caused at home, the trouble I caused with that officer's wife at San Diego. You name it, I've made a mess of it.

I thought the corps might be something I could get right for once, do some good, make a difference in the world. Everybody says war is coming. I figured that'd be my chance to redeem myself. Now I'm not even gonna get the chance to do that. I've screwed up again and this time I can't see any way around what I've done, no wriggling out of my responsibility on this one. I'm to blame and that's all there is to it, plain and simple.

I'm writing this on a park bench, outside the cathedral. It's a beautiful building, Momma; I think you sure would like it a lot. All of Oahu is beautiful. I was kinda hoping that one day I could bring you here and you could see it for yourself, but I guess that ain't gonna happen. Now I've got a choice to make.

I'm gonna go inside the cathedral and make my confession, tell the priests what I've done and ask for absolution. Then no matter what else happens, I'll know I've got God's forgiveness. If He can forgive me, then maybe I can forgive myself. That's the first step.

After that I plan on getting blind drunk. I know, I know, you don't like me drinking and I guess you certainly don't want to read a letter from me telling you about my drinking. I know Daddy drank himself into an early grave and maybe I'll end up doing the same, but I'd like to think I've learnt a few things from his mistakes, just a few, mind. So, while I'm waiting for the MPs to come find me and drag my sorry butt back to face the music, I figure I might as well get myself good and liquored up. I ain't no great shakes at facing the music, never having done it before, and I certainly don't want to start while I'm sober.

Once I'm drunk, I'm going to ask a beautiful young woman called Kissy to marry me. She's got the prettiest eyes you ever did see, Momma, and a smile that makes your heart sing. I love her almost as much as I love you, and if she says yes to me, it'll make everything else that little bit easier to take. Wish me luck, Momma, because I think I'm gonna need it.

Well, I've run out of paper and I've still got so much I wanted to say - ain't that just typical? Still, I can tell you how much I love you, Momma, and how much I appreciate everything you done to try and bring me up right. I'm sorry to turn out such a disappointment to you, and I hope and pray that one day you'll forgive me.

Your loving son,
Benjamin.

SIX

PAXTON WAS DRUNK and getting drunker by the minute. He'd been sitting at the bar in Tokyo Joe's for less than an hour, expecting the MPs to burst in any minute to drag his ass back to the navy yard. After that there would be questions, recriminations and accusations, with no doubt a court martial to follow, and, if Hicks died as a result of what had happened, the prospect of a long stretch in a military prison somewhere. Paxton figured that by the time he got out, he'd be too old to enjoy much of anything anymore. So he was downing drinks with alacrity, determined to savour his final minutes of freedom.

He'd been pleasantly surprised by how warm a welcome Kissy gave him when he arrived. Paxton talked a lot about his aspirations for the Oriental girl and how sweet she was on him, but he knew most of it was bravado. He hadn't been in the bar for weeks, giving her plenty of time to forget him and transfer any genuine affection she had to some other grunt with a fat wallet and an empty heart. Hell, he wouldn't have been surprised if Kissy hadn't remembered him at all. Instead he walked in to a hero's welcome from the beautiful young woman. She wrapped herself around him like a silk kimono, eager to feel the warmth and protection of his embrace. Eventually the new manager told her to get back to work serving the other customers.

So Paxton had taken up residence on one of the bar stools and ordered a row of drinks, all with tiny paper umbrellas. More than anything else, that was what he'd recall most about his sojourn in the Hawaiian Islands: paper umbrellas in drinks and the smell of hibiscus flowers, accompanied by the soft, soothing sounds of ukulele music and crashing waves. Never mind the humidity, the way your sweat made every shirt stick to your back in under a minute, or the constant threat of rainstorms and war. Oahu was a lush green tropical paradise and Paxton was sure as hell gonna miss it. He leaned over the bar and tugged on the manager's florid shirt. "I ain't seen you in here before, have I? What's your name, pal?"

The manager scowled at Paxton. "Nabuko Kimura... pal."

"What happened to Kissy's brother, 'Suzo?"

"Tetsuzo had to go back to Tokyo, family emergency."

"Is that right?" Paxton looked over his shoulder at Kissy. She smiled and gave him a little wave. "Funny, because Kissy doesn't seem upset about any family emergency that I can see, and she's 'Suzo's sister."

Kimura's eyes narrowed. "You know family well?"

Paxton turned back to the new manager. "Not really. I've always been kinda sweet on Kissy, but her brother didn't approve of us two."

"I'm not surprised."

"I figured if he was out of the way, I might have a chance with Kissy."

"All things are possible."

"You said a mouthful there, pal." Paxton pulled another dollar bill from his pocket and slapped it down on the bar. "Give me another of those drinks with the umbrellas, and have one for yourself out of the change."

"I prefer not to drink while I'm working," Kimura replied.

"Didn't anybody ever tell you the customer's always right?" Paxton slurred. "Go on, have a drink, one drink, it can't kill you."

The manager smiled. "Not me, but others might not be so fortunate."

"Suit yourself, Tojo."

Kimura's good humour faded. "My name is Nabuko Kimura, not Tojo."

"Whatever you say, pal!" Paxton picked up his drink and staggered over to where Kissy was wiping a table. A Japanese man was sitting there, his face sour as curdled coconut milk. Paxton ignored the customer to snake an arm around Kissy's comely waist. "Hey, doll, how's about you and me going back to your place for a private party? I hear your brother's away, so we shouldn't be disturbed. What d'you say, Kissy? Is it a date?"

She looked past him to the glowering figure behind the bar, terror in her eyes. "He told you what happened to Tetsuzo?"

Paxton nodded. "Said your brother's headed back to Tokyo, some kinda family emergency." He winked at her and nearly fell, his balance badly compromised by drinking so much alcohol in so little time. "So, you want to blow this pop stand and come with me? I can show you a good time, Kissy."

"I don't know. Kimura will be angry if I leave."

"That jerk? Don't worry about him. I'll protect you," Paxton promised.

"She does not want to go with you," the nearby customer said.

"Is that a fact, Jack?" the marine slurred.

"My name is Hitori, not Jack."

"I don't care if you're Emperor Hirohito," Paxton smirked. "The lady's with me and that's all you need to know."

Hitori stood up, his eyes ablaze with anger. "You dare use the name of a living god, you drunken dolt!"

"Hey, he may be a god to you, but he means nothing to me."

"You will pay for your blasphemy with your life," Hitori promised.

"Oh, yeah? And who's gonna make me pay, Tojo?"

"It will be my honour."

Paxton laughed. "You and whose army, pal?"

Kissy got between the two men, her face blanched white by fear. "Paxton, you drunk, you don't know what you saying–"

"I may be drunk but I don't need this jerk telling me what to do."

She leaned closer to him. "He can hurt you, Paxton. He can kill."

"So can I, darling – that's my job. I'm one lean, mean, killing machine. Hell, I've already laid out one man tonight, what difference is another gonna make, right? I'll be rotting in a cell from now on, might as well go out in a blaze of glory, know what I'm saying?"

"You said you would protect me," Kissy whispered, her voice trembling.

"Of course I will! Marines are the best trained fighters in the world."

Hitori hissed something at Kissy in Japanese. She looked at him and nodded her obedience before stepping aside. Once she was out of the way, Hitori moved closer to Paxton. "If you had any honour, you would apologise for abusing our emperor's name. If you do not, the consequences will be pain."

"I ain't apologising for nothing!" Paxton shouted. He twisted around to the sailors and soldiers at other tables nearby. "Did you hear that, boys? Our little, yellow friend here expects me to say sorry for just mentioning his emperor's damned name!" There were murmurs of dissent from the crowd inside Tokyo Joe's. Paxton nodded his agreement before turning back to face Hitori. "I ain't doing it, Tojo. You want to see some pain? I'll give you pain all right!"

Hitori's lips slid back into a snarl of hatred, revealing his vicious fangs.

"Sweet baby Jesus," Paxton whispered. A moment later he was flying through the air, propelled by a mighty punch in the chest delivered by Hitori. The drunken marine thudded heavily into the bar, splintering the bamboo cladding, before slumping to the floor. "What happened? What hit me?"

"I did," Hitori replied, his voice a savage growl of fury. He strode towards the stricken, helpless Paxton. "Prepare to meet your death!" But two marines attacked Hitori before he could reach his target, their size and strength enough to knock him over. Within moments three sailors had joined in, throwing themselves at the Japanese who dared attack a US marine. Hitori howled like a caged animal and smashed two of them away with a single blow. They staggered backwards, blood gushing from their wounds.

One of the sailors clutched at his neck, where a razor-sharp talon had severed his carotid artery. "I think the yellow bastard's killed me!" he gasped.

Hitori sprang to his feet, tossing aside the remaining attackers as if they were rag dolls. "It was my pleasure," he hissed, licking fresh blood from his fingernails. Everything inside the bar and grill stopped, as if frozen in a single moment of horror and disbelief. Hitori twisted around, studying the faces of the sailors, soldiers and pilots around him, savouring their fear and anger. A vicious brawl was about to turn into a massacre. He looked at Kimura behind the bar and smiled. "Lock the doors, Nabuko. It's time for us to feed."

KISSY DIVED UNDER a table when the killing began, so she didn't see the full horror of what happened. But within a minute the floor around her resembled that of a slaughterhouse, awash with blood, chunks of severed flesh and discarded flaps of skin. She heard men shouting in anger and screaming in fear, their cries like those of wounded animals. She watched as the dead and the dying were flung aside by two murderous figures standing near the bar. Most had their necks ripped open, by tooth or claw she couldn't tell, but the butchery was just as effective either way. Beyond the corpses Kissy could see Paxton slumped on the floor, his clothes stained crimson by blood sprays and splatters. His head was tilted awkwardly to one side, but his chest was rising and falling, so he must still be alive.

Paxton had promised to protect her from these monsters, though he did not realise what that meant at the time. If she could get him out of this makeshift abattoir, perhaps there was a chance they could escape the wrath of Kimura and his associate. Kissy waited until another cluster of American servicemen plucked up the courage to hurl themselves at the two fiends in the centre of the bar. Once they'd passed her hiding place, she crawled towards the bar on all fours. As Kissy traversed the corpse strewn floor, she did not dare look up to see how the bloody battle was progressing. The cries of pain and howls of anguish from the latest victims told her everything she needed to know.

To her amazement, Kissy reached Paxton's side unscathed. She tried to move him, but he was a dead weight, far too heavy for her to shift unaided. I have to wake him up, she realised, it's our only chance. Kissy clamped her thumb and forefinger over Paxton's nostrils, pinching his nose shut. That got his attention, as his eyelids fluttered open, revealing bloodshot eyes within. "Ssssh," Kissy whispered in his left ear. "We have to get out of here!"

Paxton looked past her to what she had avoided seeing. His eyes widened in disbelief and his mouth opened to cry out. Kissy shoved her fist inside his lips to silence him. "Say anything and they'll notice us, understand?"

Paxton nodded, tears welling up in his eyes at what he was witnessing.

"We have to go," Kissy urged, "now!" She slowly withdrew her hand from inside his mouth, before crawling away towards the door that led out on to the beach. Paxton followed, keeping low to the scarlet smeared floor. As they neared the exit a corpse flew past them and slammed into the door. The force of the impact shattered the lock, and the door opened a crack, revealing the empty beach beyond. Paxton shoved the corpse to one side and put his shoulder to the door, forcing it further open so they could escape.

He fell out through the gap, leaving Kissy alone inside. She followed him, but the buttons of her dress got caught on the doorframe's splintered wood, as if the building didn't want her to escape from the massacre within. Kissy tore at her dress, trying to rip it free, but that only made the snags worse. She didn't want to look back, but she had no choice. When Kissy twisted her head around, it was all she could do to stop herself from screaming.

Kimura and Hitori had slaughtered more than fifty customers inside five minutes. The two monsters stood in the centre of the room, surrounded by a ring of corpses, many of them torn limb from limb. All the victims had been attacked at the neck, some so savagely that the throats had been completely ripped asunder. Lifeless eyes stared from an untidy pile of decapitated heads, while the floor, ceiling and some of the walls were awash with fresh blood. The creatures responsible for the carnage were supping on their final victims, both bloated by feeding, stomachs distended by all they'd consumed.

Kimura tossed aside the sailor whose blood he'd been drinking, the body landing with a sickening *splutch* among the other corpses. He belched and licked his bloodstained lips, idly picking a scrap of pink flesh from between his teeth. Kimura glanced around in search of survivors and his gaze fell upon Kissy, still trapped in the doorway. He hissed at her, nudging Hitori with an elbow to get his associate's attention.

Kissy looked away, concentrating all her energies on trying to get free. She ripped and clawed at the splintered doorframe, all too aware of the two monsters moving towards her, whispering guttural threats and curses. Despairing of her plight, she wrenched herself free, her dress tearing apart as she fell on to the beach, the sand still warm from the day's sun. Kissy scrambled to her feet and ran to Paxton, who was staggering towards the surf. "Not that way!" she shouted. "We have to get away! They come for us!"

The marine whirled around, his eyes wide with fear. "Where can we go?"

"My home," Kissy said, "up in the hills. We safe there!" She grabbed his arm and dragged him to a narrow alley that ran between Tokyo Joe's and the neighbouring warehouse. As they passed the doorway to the bar and grill, a hand shot out from within and tore at Kissy, its talons slicing her left arm to the bone. She cried out in pain but kept going, shoving Paxton ahead of her.

They stumbled out on to the street in front of Tokyo Joe's. Kissy couldn't believe her luck when she saw a cab waiting outside, its motor already running. She ran to the vehicle and wrenched open the back door for Paxton to climb in. "Please, you must get us out of here!"

"No can do, this taxi is reserved, missy," the driver replied.

"My name is Kissy, not Missy!"

"I don't care who you are. Unless your name's one of the two I've been given, you can't ride with me tonight."

Kissy looked around, expecting Kimura or Hitori to burst from the bar and grill at any moment. Both men were drenched in blood, so they might think twice before coming out into the open, but they'd had no qualms about slaughtering a bar full of servicemen, so she couldn't depend on that stopping them. "Please, we have to go. We have to get out of here, now!"

"I told you, I need a name first."

"My name is Kissy Nagara!"

"That's not one of the names on my list, miss."

She paused to think. Who would pay a taxi to wait outside a bar all night, unless... "Kimura! My husband's name is Kimura!"

The driver smiled. "Why didn't you say so before? Let's get going!"

Kissy finished getting Paxton into the back seat and climbed in after him, slamming the door shut. "Take us up into the hills."

"Anywhere specific?"

"I give you address on way. Just go, now!"

"Your wish is my command." The cab rolled away from Tokyo Joe's with agonising slowness, before gently accelerating away into the night. Kissy looked back over her shoulder at the bar's entrance, expecting the two monsters to emerge at any moment. But the front door remained shut until she couldn't see it. Kissy looked at the drunken marine slumped on the seat beside her, unable to believe they'd escaped the massacre.

"We made it, Paxton," she said. "We're safe."

"Told you I'd protect you," he murmured before falling asleep.

KIMURA SAW THE taxi drive away, watching through a window tinted red by congealing blood. "We should go after them. If they alert the authorities–"

"A drunken soldier and a Japanese waitress, claiming a bar full of US servicemen was massacred by two vampyrs? Nobody will believe them." Hitori remained in the centre of the room, surveying the carnage around him, "Not if we destroy the evidence first. We must burn this building to the ground."

"Agreed. There's a drum of gasoline in the storeroom, we can spread that around before starting the fire to make sure all the corpses are incinerated."

Hitori nodded. "I'll help you finish decapitating them. After that, my orders take me elsewhere. Can you find the fugitives before the attack?"

"I heard the girl mention the hills. She and her husband rent a house up there, according to the papers in his office. She'll take the American there. Kissy Nagara has no living allies on the island, and nowhere else to go."

"Do what you want with them, but make certain you reach Hickam Field before the attack ends, otherwise you could be trapped on the island." Hitori walked over to his colleague and rested a hand on Kimura's shoulder. "You've done well on this mission, Nabuko. You will not go unrewarded."

Kimura smiled. "Thank you, sir. It hasn't been easy, putting up with these Americans. The sooner we go to war, the better."

Hitori looked at a clock above the bar. "Then you don't have long to wait. Our planes will be overhead within twelve hours."

WIERZBOWSKI OPENED HIS eyes and winced. There was a throbbing pain in his head so severe that it felt as if somebody had been using his skull for a baseball. He wasn't nearly as hot as before, but the surroundings were still a shimmer of movement and light. The recruit closed his eyes, giving himself a chance to prepare before reopening them. This time the shock wasn't so bad and things were more in focus. The last thing Wierzbowski could remember was being outside in the blazing sun, Sergeant Aimes berating their poor performance. Now the soldier was indoors, a pale cream ceiling overhead with a rotating fan suspended from it. He could smell coarse disinfectant, and that came from only one place: the base hospital. Something strange was digging into his left arm. Wierzbowski reached across to scratch it.

"You'll get better quicker if you leave that in," a woman's voice said. "That intravenous drip helped save your life earlier."

"Nurse Baker?" Wierzbowski asked. He tried to sit up, but a wave of nausea persuaded him against that. Instead he bent his head forward to see who was at the end of the bed. Martinez was standing to one side, while his bride was reading Wierzbowski's chart. "Did I miss the wedding?"

"Afraid so, big guy," Martinez replied. "We'd have kept you a slice of cake, but we didn't have a cake. Sorry about that."

"We were doing battery drills—"

"And you passed out. Smacked your head against the gun platform, blood everywhere. We had to stretcher you over here, took six guys."

Wierzbowski nodded at his chart in Baker's hands. "How am I doing?"

"Better," she said. "We're re-hydrating you, though that isn't finished yet, and the doctor's put you on anti-malaria drugs. Survive the next two days and you'll pass the worse of it. Right now, the best thing you can do is rest."

"I had malaria?"

"You still do. We don't think it's falciparum malaria, that's the most dangerous type, so you should make a good recovery."

"That's good," Wierzbowski agreed.

Martinez laughed. "You'd do anything to get out of being best man, eh?"

The patient shook his head for a moment before stopping, pain lancing across his skull. "I didn't mean to, honest."

"Don't worry, I'm only teasing you."

"Oh, okay."

Baker moved closer for a better look at Wierzbowski's head, swathed in bandages. "How's your skull feeling?"

"Sore."

"Count yourself lucky that's all it is. That impact would have killed or severely concussed most men. By rights you should have a fractured skull, but it looks like all you suffered was some blunt force trauma. You must have a skull like an anvil. You'll have a lump there for a while, but nothing more."

"Good, thanks." Wierzbowski frowned. "What's the time?"

Martinez stepped aside so the patient could see the setting sun out of a window. "It's nearly dark. Why do you ask?"

"Well," Wierzbowski said, blushing a little. "Shouldn't you two be enjoying your honeymoon by now?

The nurse smiled at her husband. "We will be after this, but we both wanted to see that you were all right before retiring for the night."

"You dislocating a knee was what brought the two of us together," Martinez said. "It felt like there was a kind of symmetry to seeing you in here again, before we spent our first night together as man and wife."

"Husband and wife," Baker corrected him.

Martinez smiled. "Husband and wife."

"That's better."

He grinned at the patient. "She's already house-training me!"

"You two should go," Wierzbowski said. "I'm in safe hands here, and you've got better things to do than hang around, keeping me company."

"Is there anything we can get you?" Baker asked.

"Some peace and quiet," he replied. "Go!"

"That sounds like an order," Martinez observed. He sidled over to Baker and slid an arm around her waist. "What say we take our friend's advice and retire to bed? I'm looking forward to a night away from the barracks."

She smacked his hand as it crept up from her waist. "Patience, Juan!"

"That's not one of my virtues," he admitted, "but I have got a few other things I'd like to show you." Baker giggled and let him lead her away. The two lovers waved to Wierzbowski as they left. "We'll see you in the morning."

IN THE MONTHS since surrendering himself to Constanta and becoming a vampyr, Hitori had experimented with the different shapes he could assume. Being a feral wolf gave him speed and a savagery that terrified victims. If he wanted to fly, he could maintain his human torso while extruding wings from his back, like some demonic angel, swooping and soaring across the sky. Alternatively, he could abandon his human form and become a bat, far less conspicuous and much more stealthy. In that form he could fly for hours on end undetected, invisible to radar and unnoticed by the human eye.

There was an even stealthier method of infiltration, but it required the greatest effort for Hitori. He had to let go of his corporeal shape, dispersing it into the air, becoming one with the wind. Transfiguring into a mist felt alien to him, much more than any other aspect of being a vampyr. The first time he attempted it Hitori felt as if he was drifting apart, his consciousness dissolving in the air. The sensation reminded Hitori of dreams he'd had as a boy where his spirit left his body to go flying. It felt unnatural, a dislocation of the soul, if he still had a soul. He hadn't dreamed since becoming a vampyr, and he missed the sensation. Days were for sleep, while his life was a nocturnal one.

Hitori stood outside the navy yard at Pearl Harbour and thought of the breeze, letting himself drift apart, becoming a pale cloud of mist on the air. He floated into the military facility, past unwitting sentries and sailors. His cloud form wafted inside the headquarters of the signal corps, slipping unseen past an armed guard at the night entrance. In the coming hours, information crucial to the success or failure of the coming attack would be channelled through this place. For the Japanese to retain the element of surprise, it was vital that any early warnings of their incoming forces be stopped or stymied here.

The US Army had a mobile radar post at Opana Ridge on the north side of Oahu. That was bound to detect the attack waves of Kates, Vals and Zeros long before they could reach their targets on the island. The longer Hitori could delay news of that detection spreading, the better for the first wave of Japanese planes. No doubt there would be other warning signs, too. It was Hitori's job to delay detection for as long as inhumanly possible.

Having infiltrated the building, Hitori gathered himself back into human form at the end of a darkened corridor. It was Saturday night and the signal corps' headquarters was all but deserted, a skeleton crew keeping watch on Oahu's military communications. Intelligence files at the consulate stated that there was a shift change due before midnight, when staffing levels would fall even further. Hitori waited in the shadows. Long months in Manchuria had taught him the virtue of patience. When fighting an enemy like the Chinese, your goal was not to win the next battle but to achieve a certain, sustainable victory. That took years, even decades. Battles could be won in days, but wars took far longer. Patience was a virtue, even in war.

His patience was soon rewarded. Two men in uniform appeared from opposite directions and greeted each other as friends. Hitori melted into the shadows to observe them, quickly gleaning the fact that one of the pair, Harrison, was due to take over the graveyard shift. "I just got to hit the head before I start," Harrison told his colleague, a wry smile on his face. "I don't know what the cook is putting in his chilli, but it ain't doing me any favours." The two men went their separate ways, the tall, lean figure of Harrison hurrying into a room at the end of the corridor. Hitori waited a minute before following him. Anyone standing outside the bathroom would have heard a low murmur of voices, a scuffle and the sound of bones snapping like twigs.

Hitori emerged six minutes later, dressed in Harrison's pristine uniform. The owner's corpse was hidden above the ceiling titles in the bathroom, his neck broken, his eyes staring into oblivion and his mouth twisted into a silent scream of anguish. Hitori strode into the communications room and smiled at the ensign manning the systems. "Hey, how's it going?" he asked, speaking English with a generic American accent.

The lone ensign frowned at Hitori. "Where's Harrison?"

"He asked me to take his shift."

"Why?"

"He ate some of that chilli they were serving in the mess tonight. I told him not to, but he wouldn't listen to sense. You know what Harrison's like."

The ensign still wasn't convinced. "I'd better call the lieutenant, make sure he's happy about you stepping in. No offence, but I don't recognise you and I thought I knew everybody on the base." He reached for the phone, but Hitori was across the room in a flash, his hand closing over the ensign's.

Hitori pushed his thoughts at the ensign. *Don't call the lieutenant.*

The ensign blinked. "Maybe I don't need to call the lieutenant."

He won't appreciate being disturbed.

"You know what he's like about being disturbed on a Saturday night."

You're feeling tired yourself.

The ensign yawned. "I'm exhausted."

Why don't you go to bed early? Get some sleep.

"Could you cover my last hour on shift? I'm dying for some sack-time."

"Sure, no problems," Hitori replied, removing his hand from the ensign's fist. "You get some shut-eye, I'll fill in for you."

"Thanks, you're a pal." The ensign slipped off his headphones and stood up, yawning once more. "Can't remember the last time I was this tired. See you tomorrow," he called on his way out.

Hitori took the ensign's place at the controls. A pair of clocks opposite him stated the time in Hawaii, Washington and Manila. It was 22.30 hours on Saturday at Pearl Harbour. The capital city of the Philippines was on the other side of the international dateline, but five hours behind. That meant it was 17.30 hours on Sunday in Manila. In Washington, it was already half past one in the morning of December 7th, 1941. War was about to engulf the Pacific.

PART THREE: War

Extracts from a speech delivered
by President Roosevelt to a
joint session of Congress on
December 8, 1941:

"Yesterday, December 7, 1941 - a date
which will live in infamy - the United
States of America was suddenly and
deliberately attacked by naval and air
forces of the Empire of Japan.

"It will be recorded that the distance
of Hawaii from Japan makes it obvious
that the attack was deliberately planned
many days or even weeks ago. During the
intervening time the Japanese Government
has deliberately sought to deceive the
United States by false statements and
expressions of hope for continued peace.

"The facts of yesterday speak for themselves. The people of the United States have already formed their opinions and well understand the implications to the very life and safety of our nation.

"Hostilities exist. There is no blinking at the fact that our people, our territory and our interests are in grave danger."

ONE

IT WAS NOT yet dawn as Marquez, Chuck and Bravo got into their Dauntless bombers on the USS *Enterprise*. The carrier was still some two hundred miles west of Oahu, on its way back home to Pearl Harbour from Wake Island, but it was routine practise to send a scouting mission of SBDs ahead to look for potential enemies. If all went to expectations, they should arrive at Ford Island in the centre of Pearl Harbour in time for breakfast, around 08.00 hours.

It was standard operating procedure for the bombers to patrol in pairs, and Chuck had chosen Marquez as his wingman for this mission. It would be good training for the younger pilot, Chuck believed, and he preferred sharing the morning sky with Marquez to some of the alternatives. Bravo refused to be anybody's wingman and would always usurp the authority of any senior pilot to whom he was assigned. Chuck had seen enough of Bravo's tail on their last pairing and possessed little urge to repeat the experience.

All eighteen SBDs were airborne by 06.30 hours, the air group led by Commander Young. No sooner had Chuck and Marquez started the scouting mission than Bravo flew past, having already broken protocol and abandoned his partner. The cocky voice addressed them through the radio earphones in their flying helmets. "Hey, slowcoaches, last one back to the field at Ford Island has to buy the drinks tonight!" Before Chuck or Marquez could reply, Bravo swept past and flew on towards Oahu.

"Just once I'd like to see him fall on his ass," Marquez muttered, his voice crackling through the static in Chuck's earphones.

"Amen to that," the senior pilot agreed. "His antics are gonna get somebody killed one day. Let's hope it's only him."

HITORI HAD BEEN listening intently throughout the night, scanning the radio frequencies for any hint that the Americans had detected what was coming. He was bemused to hear a Hawaiian radio station playing music long after most people would be in bed. Still, it might prove useful as a homing signal for approaching Japanese aircraft. There was some chatter about the sighting of a submerged submarine approaching Oahu on a westerly course around four in the morning, but the American vessels involved did not seem concerned. To Hitori, it sounded as if similar sightings were not unknown in the waters around Hawaii, another useful piece of happenstance.

When the clock displaying the local time on the island reached half past six, Hitori offered a silent prayer in the name of the emperor that all the planes leaving the Japanese carrier fleet to the north of Oahu would meet with success in their mission. Less than thirty minutes later there was another report of US ships sighting a submarine in the defensive area west of the island. The sub was attacked with shots and depth charges, but subsequently went unseen. The Americans presumed it had been sunk or driven off.

It was past seven o'clock and the sun had risen before Hitori heard any inkling that the Americans were aware of what was coming. The radar operator stationed on Opana Ridge called headquarters to report a blip on his screen, representing a sizeable force of at least fifty unidentified aircraft 100 miles north of Oahu and closing. Hitori responded and told the private all the signal corps personnel had left for breakfast. He knew there was still time for US planes to be scrambled if the alarm went any further up the chain of command, turning the surprise attack into a massive dogfight above the island. By delaying that, Hitori knew he was probably saving hundreds of Japanese lives. The act was not entirely selfless, since the best chance for him and Kimura to escape Oahu depended upon the attack being a success, enabling their getaway plan.

A few minutes later Hitori heard another station contacting the radar operators, telling them not to worry about the blip. A flight of planes from the US mainland was due that morning, explaining the unexpected blip on the radar. Hitori could not help smiling. Even the Americans seemed determined to ensure that the surprise went ahead unhindered and undetected. Still he lingered, waiting for the minute when the first attack wave was due to pass the northern headland of Oahu. Once that happened, there were less than fifteen minutes before the first Japanese bombs fell on US soil.

Hitori used that time to fulfil the final objective of his mission, destroying the communications centre at signal corps headquarters. He picked up the chair on which he'd been sitting for the past nine hours and smashed it into the radio equipment again and again, until all that remained was a smoking, sparking heap of scrap metal. The building had been given as a key target to the incoming bombers, but until they arrived, he didn't want anybody else using the equipment to raise the alarm. Once the job was done, he strode from the communications centre. Now came the hardest part of the mission, getting to his escape route in early morning sunshine without being burned alive. Even if he made it in time, would Kimura?

PAXTON'S HEAD WAS pounding fit to burst, his tongue felt as if someone had swapped it during the night with an overused leather strop from a barber's shop, and every part of his body ached. He had a horrible suspicion it was morning, but for the life of him the marine couldn't remember what had happened the previous night to leave him in such a state. Paxton doubted it was anything to be proud of and certainly nothing good. Having no urge to open his eyes and be blinded by daylight, he delegated the task of discovery to his other senses so that they could assess the situation and report back.

A cool breeze floated over his skin, spreading goose bumps across his body. His body was stark naked, except for a sheet of coarse material gathered around his back and buttocks, and his right hand was lying atop something moist and sticky. Paxton could hear birds calling in the distance, and a car engine roared into life nearby, before rumbling away. Three smells tangled with each other in the air: the sweet and sickly scent of hibiscus flowers, the stale tang of urine and something metallic, yet all too human. It's the smell of blood, Paxton realised. What the hell had he done last night?

The marine opened his eyes, squinting to lessen the shocking glare and brightness of his surroundings. Slowly, gradually, he adjusted to the light and opened his eyes wider. He was on a porch, lying on a day bed. Bamboo blinds hung around the outside of the porch, shielding it from prying eyes. Paxton relaxed a little. Perhaps things weren't so bad after all? Then he turned to his right and saw what was sticking to his hand.

Kissy Nagara's lifeless eyes stared back at him, a mute accusation in her glassy, empty pupils. Her face resembled boiled chicken flesh, white and devoid of colour, drained of all life. But her neck was a rich ruby red, blood still bubbling from two jagged puncture wounds in the skin. Paxton's hand had slid beneath Kissy's neck and gotten sticky in the tacky crimson residue congealing on the sheet. He pulled his hand free and it jerked the material, so the dead woman rolled closer to him, like a sleepy lover seeking an embrace. Paxton instinctively moved further away to escape Kissy's corpse and fell off the bed, landing heavily on the cold wooden floorboards. He hissed an obscenity, cursing himself for having gotten so drunk that... No, I didn't do that to her, Paxton decided, his mind racing in a dozen different directions. I'd remember if I had done something like that, something that depraved... wouldn't I?

The marine noticed his shorts beneath the day bed and pulled them on, grateful that they had not been soaked by the urine leaking through the mattress. He had felt dead drunk while floating back to consciousness, but the sight of Kissy's corpse had sobered him up in record time. Paxton glanced around, searching for the rest of his clothes. They must be here, somewhere.

"Looking for these?" a cold, chilling voice asked.

Paxton twisted around to find the manager from Tokyo Joe's standing at the other end of the porch, holding the marine's discarded clothes out at arm's length. What was the man's name again, Paxton wondered, his memory still an alcohol raddled blur, Kawasaki? No, Kimura. "They're mine," the marine said, his voice hoarse and rough at the edges. Kimura threw Paxton's clothes into the wild, unkempt garden beyond the porch. "Hey! I said those are mine," Paxton protested, getting to his feet. "Be careful with them."

"You're in no position to lecture me about being careful," Kimura sneered, looking down his nose at the marine. "Waking up next to the butchered body of a Japanese spy, today of all days, that won't look good on your file."

"Japanese spy?" Paxton spluttered, his eyes unable to avoid glancing at the cooling corpse on the day bed. "Kissy is a spy?"

"Was a spy, past tense," Kimura observed, his voice dripping with disdain. He opened his lips and ran his tongue around them, cleaning away the last few drops of blood that lingered there. Paxton could see elongated canine teeth jutting down from Kimura's upper jaw. The marine had seen enough horror films at the local picture house in San Diego to recognise fangs, but his mind rebelled at the evidence of his own eyes. This Japanese man couldn't be a vampire, could he? It was impossible! Vampires were make believe, fodder for fright flicks that gave people a cheap thrill and encouraged sweethearts to cuddle closer together in the back row at the movie house.

The marine pushed those thoughts to one side. Something else Kimura had said set alarm bells ringing in Paxton's head. "What did you mean about today of all days? What's so different about today?"

Kimura held up a hand for silence and tilted his head to one side, listening to sounds coming from beyond the porch. Paxton also listened, becoming aware of a low thrumming noise in the distance, getting louder as it was getting closer. The thrumming was similar to the sound of an approaching aircraft, but replicated a dozen times over and then a dozen times more. Thanks to the many months Paxton had spent at Pearl Harbour, he could recognise the engine noises of the different aircraft used by the US Navy and other branches of the armed services. This noise was different from all of those, similar but not the same. He moved to the edge of the porch and pushed aside the nearest bamboo blind to get a good look at the sky.

A low-wing monoplane fighter zoomed over the building, so close Paxton could clearly see a blood-red circle painted on the underside of each wing. As soon as it had passed, two more followed it, then another three at a higher altitude. The marine stared up into the blue, unable to believe what he was seeing. Dozens of Japanese fighters and bombers were swarming across the sky above Oahu, all of them headed in the same direction, south, towards the harbour down below, all flying straight for Pearl.

Paxton staggered away from the side of the porch, letting the bamboo blind fall back into place. "It's an attack," he gasped, his mind still reeling at the reality of what he'd seen. "The Japanese are attacking the navy yard!"

"Consider yourself fortunate that I have fed well in the last few hours," Kimura hissed in the marine's ear, startling Paxton with his proximity. "I haven't yet acquired a taste for American blood, especially when it runs so thick with alcohol. But soon my kind will feast on your soldiers as a farmer eats his own swine. Remember this day well, it's the beginning of the end. Our empire will drive you from the Pacific, my brethren will drain you dry."

Kimura moved so close that the marine could smell Kissy's blood on the vampire's breath. "I need to leave, but I'm going to mark you with a wound that cannot easily be hidden, a sign to all my brethren that you are now my thrall. You promised to protect that woman, to save her, and you failed.

She died because of you, and her blood is on your hands. Every time you see this wound, it will remind you of that failure, that betrayal.

"Some scars never heal," the vampire continued. "This will be one of them. When next we meet, you will be my plaything, my chattel to do with as I wish. Remember this moment well, for it is when your slavery began." Kimura stretched his hand out across Paxton's bare chest, letting the sharp, talon-like fingernails scratch at the skin until they came to rest above his right nipple. *Don't move*, he hissed inside Paxton's thoughts, *or it will be worse for you.*

Kimura ripped his nails downwards, slicing through skin and flesh, a spray of pink droplets clouding the air. A flap of something wet and red fell to the wooden floorboards, and Paxton felt hot moisture running down one side of his chest. He looked down and saw a ragged oval of skin on the porch floor, a nipple in the middle of it, several dark hairs sprouting from the skin. Where that nipple should have been was an absence, a raw slice of his breast exposed to the air, blood running from the wound. The marine clamped a hand over his breast, trying to staunch the bleeding. Then the shock of his injury hit and he sank to his knees, spewing green bile on the floorboards.

Remember this day, Kimura told the marine. *From this day until you die, you are mine, my thrall. I own a piece of your soul.* Kimura reached down and picked up the chunk of skin and flesh with the nipple on it. *I'll take this with me, as a memento. I believe you Americans call it a forget-me-not.*

Paxton watched in horror as Kimura grinned at him one last time before fading away into a mist, vanishing before his eyes. The marine was still kneeling in the same place when a sedan burst out of a garage beneath the house and drove away, hurtling down the hill towards Pearl Harbour, tyres screeching in protest. In the distance Paxton could see that the Japanese fighters and bombers were closing up into formation above the navy yards. A flash of light exploded below them at the harbour, the dull crump of the detonation reaching the wounded marine a moment later. A plume of smoke billowed upwards into the air. The attack on Pearl Harbour had begun.

WALTON HAD BEEN idly looking out of the window of the captain's office, watching a marine colour guard prepare to hoist the stars and stripes, when a wave of airplanes flew in formation towards the navy yards. "That's strange," he said. "I mean, I know some pilots are fond of showing off, but why are they practising fly-pasts first thing on a Sunday morning?" Walton stepped aside to let Maeda see. The other marine had spent the night under guard in the captain's office, waiting to explain what had happened. "Pat, what do you make of it?"

Maeda joined Walton at the window, happy to have something different to look at. He had studied every photo and citation on the office walls a dozen times over and probably knew them better than the captain of B Company. He watched the fighters approaching the base in a V-formation, like birds heading south for winter. "Those aren't our planes," Maeda said.

"They're not?" Walton asked, raising a hand to shield his eyes from the early morning sun. "Well, whose planes are they then?"

An explosion rocked the building, followed closely by one dull crump after another, all on top of each other. Next came the sound of machine guns as the approaching aircraft opened fire. "They're enemy planes," Maeda realised.

"Don't be stupid, Pat. Nobody would attack an American military base."

"Tell that to the pilots of those planes!" Maeda shouted, dropping to the office floor. The young marine beside him remained standing, still gawping out of the window. The sound of machine guns was matched by the roar of the approaching aircraft engines. "Walton, you idiot, get down before you get shot!" Maeda grabbed his comrade and pulled him to the floor moments before the windows were blown apart. Enemy bullets shattered the glass before slamming into the office's walls and floor, broken glass showering the two men like hailstones. Then the fighter planes roared over the building, more than a dozen of them, all still firing their machine guns.

Maeda was first to risk a glimpse out of the window when the wave of enemy aircraft had passed. Down below, half the colour guard was dead or dying, their bodies shredded by the surprise attack. Survivors tended to the wounded as other marines spilled onto the parade ground eager to see what had happened, not realising the danger they were entering. "Get back inside!" Maeda yelled, cupping both hands around his mouth. "We're under attack!"

The men on the ground looked at Maeda as if he was insane. Another attack wave of enemy fighters was already on its approach, coming in low over Pearl, heading directly for the navy yards. Maeda spotted a bugler with flame red hair tending one of the wounded. "Morton, sound general quarters!"

The bugler looked down and realised he was still clutching his instrument in one hand. Morton sprinted to a loudhailer mounted on a stand at the edge of the parade ground and, after spitting on the ground to wet his lips, blew general quarters. Immediately all those outside raced for their appointed defensive positions, everyone running in different directions. But the next wave of enemy fighters was already upon the navy yards. The rat-tat-tat of machine guns cut through the air like some staccato dance of death, its chilling rhythm perforating the quiet Sunday morning with brutal disregard. Those still out on the parade ground threw themselves flat. Some were lucky enough to escape the strafing bullets, but many were not so fortunate.

Maeda peered at the underside of the enemy planes as they flew over. Beneath each wing was a circle of blood red, the symbol of the rising sun. Maeda felt a sickening lurch in his stomach at the significance of this, both for the future and for him personally. "It's the Japanese," he gasped, hardly able to believe he was saying the words. "We're being attacked by the Japanese!"

"But you're Japanese," Walton whispered from beside him.

"I was born in San Francisco; I'm as American as you are!" Maeda snapped before crawling towards the office door. We've got to get out there! We've got to fight back!"

"You can't leave, Pat," the other marine protested, "you're under arrest."

"Don't be ridiculous," Maeda snarled. "The Japanese Empire has just declared war on the United States! For all I know, this aerial attack could be a way of softening us up before they launch a full-scale invasion of the Hawaiian Islands. We've got to get up on the roof!"

"Why the roof?"

"That's the best vantage point to see what's going on, and it's the best place to return fire. We can take a machine gun and use it against the enemy, maybe shoot one or two of them out of the sky!" Maeda had reached the doorway. He looked back across the bullet riddled office at the terrified youth. "I can't operate the machine gun on my own. Are you coming with me?"

Walton bit his bottom lip, terror all too evident in his eyes. Taking a deep breath, he scrambled across the floor towards Maeda. He had almost reached the doorway before the next wave of Japanese fighters swept in over the navy yards, strafing the marine barracks and other buildings with bullets. Walton shoved Maeda to safety before diving on top of him. The pair hugged the floor as the room around them exploded, furniture and fixtures shot to pieces by the passing planes. Once the attack had passed,

Walton retrieved his metal helmet from the floor and patted the other marine on the back. "Pat, you all right?"

"I'm fine, but you're a lot heavier than you look," Maeda complained. "Now, let's find ourselves a machine gun so we can start fighting back!"

MARQUEZ WAS LOOKING forward to getting back on the ground at Ford Island. Life on board the *Enterprise* was fine, but it wasn't home to him yet. Maybe in time he'd become like Chuck, who got antsy when they stayed in one port for more than a few days. For now, the ensign still called dry land his second choice as home, Marquez was always happiest in the sky. As the youngest pilot on the Big E, he took more than his fair share of ribbing from the other fliers, but Marquez liked to think they were learning to respect him. If nothing else, he had the best eyes of any pilot on board, so it came as no surprise when he noticed the approaching aircraft before Chuck.

Bravo had flown ahead in his private race to reach the field at Ford Island before anyone else, no doubt abandoning his wingman in the process, but Chuck and Marquez maintained a two-plane formation. Their SBDs were still west of Pearl when Marquez saw a large formation of planes buzzing around the facility at Ewa Mooring Mast Field, near Barbers Point on the south-west coast of Oahu. Marquez glanced over one shoulder at Mead, his radioman and gunner. "Hey, Sid, you heard anything about US Army pilots being out and about this morning?"

"Nothing yet, why?"

"Looks like a squadron of them are circling Ewa." Marquez radioed Chuck to see if he could explain the cluster of aircraft above Barbers Point, but the lieutenant had no further intelligence to add.

"Skid," Mead cut in, "one of our friends is coming over to say hello."

Marquez twisted around to see a single-engine aircraft approaching, but he couldn't get a good sight of it. "Funny, it doesn't look like any of our planes. What do you think, Sid?" Before Mead could answer, a line of bullets blistered the SBD's skin, scaring the hell out of both pilot and gunner. Marquez jerked his controls to the right as the aircraft swept past, almost colliding with Chuck.

"Skid, what the hell are you doing?" the lieutenant yelled via his radio.

"We're under attack, I repeat, we're under attack!" Marquez shouted back. "Those planes at Ewa aren't ours, I think they're Japanese. We need to take evasive action, now!"

"You're sure?" Chuck replied, his voice tinged with disbelief.

"I'm damned sure, and my fuselage has the bullet holes to prove it!"

"Understood. Okay, break right on my command, but stay in formation!"

"Roger that!"

The enemy plane was coming around for another gunnery pass, slicing a tight arc through the air as it turned back to swoop at the two SBDs. "Break right!" Chuck snarled. Marquez followed the command, swinging his aircraft over in formation with the lieutenant. The two of them slipped beneath the oncoming enemy plane, escaping the hail of bullets spitting from its armaments.

"That's a Japanese Zero!" Chuck exclaimed. "Sweet mercy, this is it! The Japanese are attacking! This means we're at war!"

"What do we do?" Marquez replied, keeping his Dauntless tight to Chuck's wing. "We haven't got enough fuel to get back to the *Enterprise*."

"Just as well," the lieutenant said. "We'd be in danger of leading the Japs straight to the big E if we went back to her. Long as she remains out at sea she'll be almost impossible to find. Be grateful the *Enterprise* wasn't in port when…" Chuck's voice trailed off. Marquez couldn't tell if there was a malfunction with his radio equipment.

"Lieutenant, are you there? Lieutenant?"

"We have to get back to Ford Island as fast as we can," Chuck replied. "If the Japs are attacking Ewa, chances are they'll be attacking Pearl as well. All those battleships and destroyers in the harbour are sitting ducks!"

"Skid!" Mead shouted from behind Marquez. "The Zero's coming around for another pass! Permission to open fire?"

"Lieutenant?" Marquez asked. He'd never been in a real dogfight before and the proper protocols for this situation had vanished from his mind. Having your tutors explaining the correct way to engage an enemy aircraft was one thing, but recalling that while being peppered by live ammunition in the sky was something else.

"Yes, fire at will!" Chuck shouted back.

The gunner in each Dauntless unleashed his M-2 Browning machine gun, blazing away at the Zero as it scudded past. One of the gunners scored a hit on the Japanese plane and a thin plume of black smoke issued from the fighter as it sped away, intent on finding easier prey. "I hit it!" Mead shouted.

"Good shooting," Marquez said, "but don't start celebrating just yet. I've got a feeling there's plenty more where that one came from."

Both SBDs were halfway between Ewa and Ford Island. The sky ahead was alive with small black clouds, evidence of considerable anti-aircraft fire between them and their destination. News of the Japanese attack must have spread and those on the ground were determined to shoot anything that moved out of the sky, regardless of its origins or markings. "Sweet mercy," the lieutenant whispered, shock and awe audible in his voice.

Before Marquez could say anything, his Dauntless came under fire from another Zero. He twisted sideways and saw a trio of Japanese planes on attack vector. "Three enemy bogies closing in, nine o'clock high!"

"Dive!" Chuck commanded. "Get as close to the deck as you dare, Skid, let's find out what these bastards have got!" The two pilots flung their SBDs towards the lush green island below, while both gunners were concentrating their fire on the approaching Zeros. The enemy planes skimmed overhead, undone by the swift reactions of the two navy pilots. But no sooner had Chuck and Marquez escaped one threat than they flew straight into another. The sky around them exploded in a storm of anti-aircraft fire. "Break left!" Chuck yelled. "If we stay on this heading, our own guns will bring us down! Break left!"

Extracts from a speech delivered
by President Roosevelt to a
joint session of Congress on
December 8, 1941:

"The attack yesterday on the Hawaiian
Islands has caused severe damage to
American naval and military forces. Very
many American lives have been lost. As
Commander-in-Chief of the Army and Navy
I have directed that all measures be
taken for our defence. Always will be
remembered   the   character   of   the
onslaught against us.

"No matter how long it may take us to
overcome this ... the American people in
their righteous might will win through to
absolute victory. I believe I interpret

the will of the Congress and of the
people when I assert that we will not
only defend ourselves to the uttermost
but will make very certain that this form
of treachery shall never endanger us
again. With confidence in our armed
forces - with the unbounded determination
of our people - we will gain the
inevitable triumph - so help us God."

TWO

PAXTON KNEW THAT one man could make little difference in a battle, and there was even less a single soldier could do to stop a war. But he was determined to get back to B Company's barracks, if only to right some of the wrongs he'd committed. The marine searched the tumbledown house for bandages to dress his wounded breast. Kissy's home was little more than a shack, with pitifully few possessions to show she had ever lived there. I guess her corpse on the front porch is enough evidence, Paxton thought. He found the cleanest sheet in the house and ripped it into shreds, before using them to bind his wound. He tied them as tight as possible to stem the bleeding.

The marine found the last of his clothes strewn about inside, carelessly cast aside during some drunken moments of passion the previous night. It was almost ironic, he had fantasised for months about getting Kissy into bed. When he did turn fantasy into reality, he'd been too drunk to remember any of it. He got dressed inside, not wanting to spend any more time near her corpse than necessary. Kissy's cold, empty eyes stared at him every time he ventured out on the porch to see how the attack was progressing. Only after he'd pulled on his boots and was ready to leave did Paxton dare return to the dead woman's side. He crouched down on one knee and kissed her cold, waxy forehead. "I'm sorry," he whispered. "I know I promised to protect you, but..." Paxton closed his eyes, overcome by his guilt and shame.

"Spare me your pathetic remorse," a low, sibilant voice hissed at the marine. He opened his eyes to find Kissy sneering at him, hatred in her eyes. "You only cared about yourself, about what you wanted. I was just another whore to you, another notch in your belt, another conquest to brag about!"

Paxton fell over backwards, unable to comprehend what was happening. "But y-you can't... You w-were dead... I saw you!"

Kissy sat bolt upright on the bed, the sudden movement startling him. She lifted a hand to her throat and stroked her fingers across the wound, caressing the twin punctures as a lover would caress a nipple. "I was dead, but my master gave me a better gift than life, he made me an immortal!" Her head twisted around to glare at Paxton and her lips drew back into a sick parody of a smile, revealing the fangs that had grown from her upper jaw.

The marine cursed under his breath, not sure he wasn't still dreaming. This had to be a nightmare, didn't it? Creatures like Kimura and whatever Kissy had become weren't real, were they?

"I'm real enough," she replied, "and I can read every thought in that puny, sick, sordid little mind of yours. Can you read my thoughts? Can you guess what I'm going to do to you, you disgusting worm?"

"Stay back," Paxton warned, scrabbling away across the floor, until his back slammed into the rotten wooden banisters that enclosed the porch.

Kissy was on her feet in the blink of an eye, stretching and flexing her lithe body, the joints and tendons popping as she sloughed off the onset of rigor mortis. "I think I'll start with your eyeballs," Kissy ventured, a playful grin playing about her lips. "They always were your best feature. Would you prefer I plucked them out with a fingernail, or should I suck them from their sockets?"

The marine found himself praying, a long forgotten invocation for god's mercy and protection coming to mind when he most needed its reassurance.

The vampyr laughed at him, mocking his sudden religious fervour. "If you're expecting some deity to rescue you, I fear you're going to be terribly disappointed. Vampyrs are the new gods and we walk the earth. Worship us!" Kissy flung herself at Paxton, the talon-like fingernails of her left hand clawing into his face, shoving it aside to allow better access to his neck. The marine tried to fight back, tried to resist her, but she whispered sweet words of seduction in his ear. Paxton felt his will giving in to her words, his resistance crumbling before the soft, soothing murmurs of her voice.

Kissy licked her lips, ready to plunge her fangs deep into the soldier's throat, to suck the life from him as it had been sucked from her. But a massive explosion nearby threw a concussion wave outwards, rippling the air and blowing the bamboo blinds away from the porch. The rising sun slipped through the gap and set fire to Kissy's face and hair. The vampyr screamed in agony, slapping at her face and scalp, trying to put out the flames.

With the spell broken, Paxton was able to fight back. He swung his legs up into the air, pitching Kissy over the top of the banisters and out into the garden. The moment her body was bathed in sunshine, she burst into flames, becoming an inhuman torch. The marine twisted around, getting ready to repel her next attack, but the vampyr had more pressing problems. She lurched across the garden, every inch of her burning with incandescent radiance while black, greasy fumes rose into the air. Kissy shrieked and screamed, wailing like some demented air raid siren, like a thousand sets of fingernails clawing at a blackboard. Paxton clamped his hands over his ears, but even that wasn't enough to block out her cries. She screamed inside his mind as well, attacking his thoughts with her pain.

Kissy had just set foot on the steps leading up to the porch when her body exploded, one final shriek hanging in the air as a cloud of dust and ashes settled to the ground below. Paxton stayed where he was, gasping for breath, his mind racing at what he had witnessed. The sunlight had killed her, it had burned her alive. She had been killed by a monster and, after dying, had become like that monster. She

had craved his blood and bent his will to her own.
There was no denying it: Kissy Nagara had turned
into a vampyr. The marine shook his head. He never
would have believed it possible if he hadn't seen it.
Hell, he had seen it and still wasn't sure he believed
it. Of course, whether or not he believed didn't
matter; there was no proof, nothing to corroborate
what he had witnessed.

Paxton dissolved into hysterics, tears streaming
down his cheeks. He was laughing so hard he didn't
think he'd ever be able to laugh again. One day earlier he'd been a bored grunt hoping to get lucky with
an Oriental waitress. Now he knew that waitress
had been a spy, he'd encountered two supernatural
monsters, and a few miles away a war had broken
out between America and Japan. The marine kept
laughing, not wanting to imagine what could possibly happen next. That didn't bear thinking about.

It NEEDED BOTH Maeda and Walton to get the heavy,
awkward Browning machine gun up on to the roof
of B Company's barracks. The two marines worked
as fast as they could to get it ready for firing, Maeda
locking the gun into place on its bipod while Walton
checked that the firing mechanism was ready. The
machine gun had been in storage for months and
there was no real guarantee of when it had last been
serviced. The corps had protocols for such things
during wartime, but it had been peace until this
morning.

Maeda's eyes searched the horizon as he worked,
trying to anticipate from where the next attack
might come. It was only a matter of time before the

fighters returned for another strafing run over the navy yards. When the Zeros came back, the two marines knew they would be easy, inviting targets for the enemy pilots. Walton struggled to load a 250-round ammunition belt into position, but his hands were shaking too much, fear getting the better of his training. He could smell burning oil on the air and tasted the tang of adrenaline at the back of his throat, bitter and metallic.

In the distance a massive explosion rocked the harbour, closely followed by a second and then a third. The horizon was spotted with small black puffs of smoke where anti-aircraft fire was detonating in the sky, while huge, dark plumes of smoke billowed from the vessels moored in pairs along battleship row. Walton had always enjoyed walking around the docks, admiring the destroyers and aircraft carriers, wondering which of them might one day transport him to some distant land. *Guess I'll found out soon,* he thought, *assuming any of them are seaworthy after today, and that I'm still alive.*

A fresh explosion, louder and closer than anything so far, rocked the navy yard. Maeda raised a hand to shield his eyes, peering through the pall of smoke that hung over the harbour like a shroud. A fireball was mushrooming into the sky from one of the vessels. "That's the *Arizona,*" he said, his voice sounding thin and weak against the cacophony of noise. "I think it's sinking."

Walton didn't bother to look. Instead he made the sign of the cross and whispered a brief prayer for all those who must still be trapped inside the vessel. "May God have mercy on their souls."

"Amen," Maeda replied, priming the machine gun for firing before sweeping around in search of targets. "Now, let's see if we can even the odds!"

HITORI WATCHED THE carnage enveloping Pearl Harbour and nearby military installations, with quiet satisfaction at his own involvement in events. He and Kimura may have played only a small part in the unfolding events, but the intelligence they had gathered over the previous days and Hitori's intervention at signal corps headquarters had contributed to ensuring the initial attack came as a surprise to the Americans. That had improved the safety of the second wave of dive-bombers and fighters. If the US forces had gotten their planes off the ground, the second attack could have been disastrous for the incoming Japanese. Instead many American aircraft had been destroyed while still on the ground, and the confusion engendered by wave after wave of Zeros making strafing runs at aircrews was keeping most of the other planes grounded. There was still a blizzard of anti-aircraft fire for incoming Japanese aircraft to cope with, but US aerial resistance was negligible.

Hitori had arranged to meet Kimura at Hickam Field by nine that morning. The US Army air base was south of Pearl Harbour, along the coast from the city of Honolulu. It had been pounded repeatedly by Japanese dive bombers because Hickam Field was home to the 18th Bombardment Wing, a potential threat to the Imperial Japanese Navy's fleet. Hitori had assigned himself the task of guiding in the Vals, secreting transmitters in each hangar, all of them broadcasting a homing signal for the dive bombers on a specific frequency. Moving between buildings without attracting attention was not easy, as he had to keep his skin concealed from the sun at all times. Fortunately the field was quiet on a Sunday morning and few paid any attention to an officer going about his business.

The first strike came just before 08.00 hours, eight Vals raining bombs down on Hangars 7 and 11. One American craft being prepared for take-off suffered a direct hit, exploding with devastating effect. When the smoke cleared Hitori could see the shredded corpses of more than a dozen men, while others lay dying on the apron beside the landing strip. Next came the Zeros, sweeping back and forth above the airfield, strafing the hangars and ground crews with merciless ferocity. Planes parked outside were set ablaze by the Zeros, the fighters returning again and again, despite the increasing ferocity of anti-aircraft flak coming from the ground.

Not long after 08.00 a dozen American planes tried to land at the field, but were attacked by their own side as well as the Zeros. Anything moving in the sky was a target for those on the ground, regardless of what markings it bore or whether the planes were making recognition manoeuvres. Eventually eight of the aircraft landed, but from his hiding place in the shadows Hitori could see that all of them had sustained damage to their fuselages. The other four flew off, no doubt trying to find safer landings elsewhere. The vampyr smiled. News of the friendly fire incidents would soon spread among anti-aircraft crews at the airfield. With luck, they would be less likely to shoot down any plane obviously trying to land. That could help when the time came for him and Kimura to be extracted.

"Identify yourself! Who are you and what are you doing in there?" a gruff voice demanded from behind Hitori. He swivelled around to find an American sentry aiming a sub-machine gun at him. The soldier's eyes widened when he realised Hitori was Japanese. "You're one of them!" His gaze darted around, searching for any sign that Hitori was not alone. "Where are the rest of your buddies, Tojo, or don't you understand English?"

"I understand English perfectly well," Hitori replied. He reached inside the sentry's thoughts and pushed. *You needn't be afraid of me.*

The soldier's face twitched, as if someone was stabbing him with a needle. "I needn't be afraid of you," he said, parroting Hitori's commands.

You're perfectly safe, so you can lower your weapon.

Again the sentry flinched before repeating what he was told. "I'm perfectly safe. I can lower my weapon." But his hands did not move.

Lower your weapon, Hitori urged, pushing with everything he had.

The soldier's face was a mass of spasms, tics and twitches, his will battling against the powerful suggestive impulse implanted in his mind by the vampyr's orders. A drop of blood fell from the American's nose, followed by another and another, until blood was pouring freely from both nostrils. Still the sentry would not give in, would not lower his weapon.

Locked in a battle of wills with the soldier, Hitori did not dare attempt to change to another form. Instead he walked towards the sentry, all his power bent against the stubborn American. *You will give in to me or I shall crush your mind*, Hitori snarled. *You will surrender or you will die!*

"Never," the sentry gasped, his finger closing around the sub-machine gun's trigger. Hitori flung himself at the soldier, swatting the barrel aside with ease before closing a fist around the obstinate American's neck, lifting his foe's body clear off the ground. The sentry's feet kicked at thin air.

"You've remarkable willpower," the vampyr hissed, "but it won't save you!" Hitori ripped open the sentry's collar with his spare hand, exposing the throat. But doing this also freed the twin chains hidden inside the soldier's tunic. His dog tags hung from one chain, while the other supported a silver cross. It pressed against Hitori's skin, burning its way into the vampyr's flesh. He cried out, hurt and enraged, before tossing the sentry to one side. The American collided awkwardly with the side of a concrete barracks block, his neck snapping with a dull crack, before the lifeless body slid to the ground.

Hitori was busy staring at the cross burned into the back of his left hand, the skin bubbling and smoking as if acid had been poured over it. The acrid smell of burning flesh rose from the crucifix-shaped wound, insinuating its way into the vampyr's nostrils, making him gag at the stench. He hadn't felt pain or exhaustion once since becoming a vampyr. Yes, he often rested during the hours of daylight, but that was as much about avoiding the sun as anything else. He had forgotten what pain felt like, had begun to believe himself invulnerable like Constanta. Now the simple happenstance of a silver cross falling against his skin had reminded Hitori of his weaknesses. The pain was both exquisite and excruciating.

"Hey, Ronnie, you okay?" a voice called out, just ahead of the sound of hurried footsteps approaching. Hitori realised he had lingered for too long in one place, absorbed in his own thoughts when he should have kept watch for more sentries. Before he could escape half a dozen guards armed with sub-machine guns had surrounded him, while another of them was examining the corpse of their fallen comrade. "Ronnie's dead! His neck's broken!" The blond soldier picked up the metal helmet his dead colleague had been wearing. It had crumpled at the point of impact where Hitori had thrown Ronnie against the concrete wall. "Did you do this to him?"

"In a manner of speaking," the vampyr replied. He studied the faces of those surrounding him. There were too many for him to control all their minds at once, and he could not escape by transforming his shape. Trying to flee as mist, wolf or bat would mean exposing himself to direct sunlight and he would be dead within moments of leaving the shadows.

"You murdered Ronnie!"

"Killing an enemy soldier is not murder in wartime."

The soldier who had been studying the corpse stormed over to the vampyr and dragged him out of the shadows, into the morning air. Fortunately for Hitori he was wearing a peaked cap, gloves and a heavy overcoat with the collar turned up, protecting him from the sunlight, for now. The furious soldier drew a .45 pistol and pressed the barrel against Hitori's forehead. "Give me one good reason why I shouldn't kill you, right here, right now. You said it yourself; our two countries are at war, so killing you wouldn't be murder."

"I am attached to the Japanese consulate here on Oahu. I possess full diplomatic immunity," Hitori replied, staring into his captor's eye. "Shoot me and you will suffer the consequences. Now, take me to your leader."

Maeda pulled on the Browning's trigger, firing swift, deadly bursts at the next wave of Zeros as they scudded low over the navy yard. Walton crouched on the left side of the machine gun, making sure the ammunition belt fed straight into the weapon, keeping it from jamming or misfiring. Try as Maeda might, he couldn't get a bead on the Japanese fighters. They were appearing out of the black fog created by burning ships and buildings, coming in low and fast, moving far quicker than he could react. "Dammit!" he snapped as half a dozen enemy planes shot past his position atop B Company's barracks. His training told him to aim ahead of the target, let them fly into his line of fire, but that was easier said than done with an enemy passing over your head at three hundred miles an hour.

"We're nearly out of ammo," Walton shouted, struggling to be heard above the sound of exploding bombs and anti-aircraft barrages. He glanced around, but Maeda had exhausted all they had brought up in their rush to reach the roof. "I'll have to go back down and find some more."

"Not yet," Maeda replied. "I still need you to feed the ammo belt."

"Here they come again," Walton said, pointing to the east.

Maeda swung the Browning around to face the approaching Zeros. So far they had been concentrating on other parts of Pearl, strafing the navy yards and approach roads. Now they were heading for the barracks blocks, and B Company's home was directly in their path. Walton scrambled to stay alongside the machine gun, his eyes fixed on the incoming fighters. There were three of them, all swooping at the two marines on the roof, guns blazing. "Pat, they're after us!"

"I know," Maeda snarled. "Let's change their minds." He got his eyes down level with the Browning's sights and took aim just ahead of the Zeros. He sensed rather than saw the line of bullets stabbing into the far end of the barracks roof, each round throwing up dust and chunks of cement. Maeda closed his finger around the trigger, let out a breath and opened fire. The Browning spat high velocity death at the Japanese fighters, shooting round after round into their path.

Everything around Maeda seemed to slow down, as if time was coming to a standstill on top of the barracks. Before the Zeros had passed in the blink of an eye, but now it felt as if they were in slow motion. Maeda watched as the line of enemy bullets traced straight lines across the roof towards him and Walton. He saw the propeller on the enemy fighters turning in the air and the muzzle flashes of their machine guns. He felt every tiny movement of the Browning as it fired back at the Zeros, the jerk of the ammunition belt as it fed through the weapon and spilled out on to the cement opposite Walton. A dull pain stabbed into his right shoulder, as if someone had jabbed him with a stick, and he heard Walton cry out.

Then the Zeros were ripping through the air overhead and spluttering away, their engines choking on the fumes clogging the sky. Maeda twisted around and saw black smoke billowing from the lead fighter, accompanied by orange tongues of flame and white sparks. "We got one!" Maeda shouted, his left fist clenched in triumph. "We got one of them!" He turned to Walton, eager to share the moment with his comrade. The young marine's face was ashen, and a stream of blood was pouring from his mouth. "Walton? You okay?"

Walton fell forwards, pitching face-first into the cement. Maeda saw a handful of gaping holes in his comrade's back, tracing a line up Walton's spine. He pressed two fingers to the youth's throat in search of a pulse, but found nothing. Only then did Maeda realise how heavy his own right arm felt. He looked at it and was shocked to see gleaming white bone exposed where an enemy bullet had ripped through his uniform and buried itself in his body.

Pain lanced through his arm and chest, and he was finding it hard to breathe. There was a trickle of blood on the front of his uniform, escaping a small hole over the right breast. Maeda stuck a finger in the hole and found a much bigger hole underneath the fabric, soft and wet and terrifying. He was gasping for air, unable to get enough into his lungs. It felt like when he was a boy and his father had taught him to swim. The first day Maeda had swallowed a mouthful of the sea and had to be pulled from the water, choking and coughing. He had learned his lesson, but now that drowning sensation was back.

Another trio of Zeros was already closing on the barracks building, intent on finishing the job their colleagues had started. Maeda tried pulling the Browning's trigger with his left hand, but it was too weak and he had exhausted the ammunition supply firing at the last attack. He was a sitting duck on the roof, unable to get away and with nothing to take cover behind. The Zeros opened fire, fresh lines of ammunition peppering the roof, tracing a deathly path towards the wounded Maeda. The marine had one option left. "I'm sorry," he whispered before grabbing his comrade's dead body and pulling it over him as a shield. Walton's corpse protected Maeda's head and torso, but his legs remained out in the open and exposed. The marine screamed in pain as the passing pilots found their target with cruel accuracy. He was almost grateful when the darkness took him. Whatever happened next, Maeda didn't want to be conscious for it.

MARQUEZ WAS FIGHTING for his life above Pearl Harbour. He had gotten separated from the lieutenant soon after they broke left to avoid a blizzard of anti-aircraft fire. Chuck took evasive action to avoid a head-on collision with a Japanese bomber, diving beneath the approaching Val. Marquez had continued on his course, not realising where the lieutenant had gone until it was too late. Four Zeros appeared from the clouds and any attempts to get back into formation had to be abandoned. Marquez was flying for survival, plain and simple. Two of the Zeros got in behind him and opened fire, their machine guns shattering the glass at the back of the SBD's canopy.

Marquez heard a cry of pain behind him and felt something wet hit the back of his neck. "Mead, are you okay? Sid? Sid, can you hear me?" The pilot didn't dare look around, all his concentration bent on trying to shake off the pursuing Zeros. He twisted the controls, first to the left, then hard to the right, zigzagging the Dauntless through the bleak sky. "Sid, talk to me! Sid!"

"I'm hit," the gunner replied.

"How bad is it?"

"Bad enough."

"What about the radio? Can you call down to the ground, tell them to stop firing at us, tell them we're on their side?"

"No good... radio's shot to hell."

Marquez muttered a curse. "What about the gun, is that still working?"

"Enough to deal with these bastards," Mead replied, coughing and spitting. "You keep us in the air, Skid, I'll do the rest."

"Thanks. I'll get us down as soon as I-" Marquez's words died in his throat. Another Dauntless had appeared from a cloud of black smoke directly ahead, on a collision course with them. Marquez wrenched his controls left and hoped his counterpart in the oncoming SBD did the same. The two aircraft flashed past each other, coming within a few feet. Marquez glimpsed a crudely painted cartoon of Tojo on the side of the passing plane. It was Bravo's Dauntless, the damned fool had almost killed them with his antics.

Marquez levelled out his wings and found himself directly behind an unfamiliar tail. It was one of the enemy aircraft, a Zero. The SBD pilot urged his plane forward, extracting every last ounce of speed from the bullet-riddled Dauntless. If I'm going to die on the first day of the war, Marquez thought, I want to take at least one of these damned Japs with me. He closed up to the Zero's tail and opened fire with his machine guns, the bullets tearing into the back of the enemy fighter. He kept his finger on the firing button, emptying his magazines into the Zero, ignoring the greasy black smoke pouring out of the rear of the enemy plane. Oil was leaking from the Zero, and it spattered against the front of Marquez's canopy, obscuring his forward view.

He heard Mead coughing behind him, the sound dying away to a sick, empty gurgle until the gunner was making no sound at all. "Mead? Mead, are you okay? Mead, talk to me! Can you hear me back there?" Then there was another chilling noise from up ahead, the sound of an engine dying. All those rounds he had fired into the Zero were doing their job. The clouds of smoke from ahead of the SBD abruptly parted to reveal an empty sky. "We did it,

Mead! We took out our first Zero!" Marquez was grinning from ear to ear until a shadow fell on the top of his canopy. The Zero was directly above him and coming straight down.

The pilot must have pulled the nose up too fast and stalled it, Marquez realised. That sent the Zero into a loop and it was coming down on top of the Dauntless. In the time it took him to think all of that, his pilot's instincts had already taken over. He ripped the SBD's controls to one side, tilting the left wing up to meet the tumbling Zero. A moment later the two planes collided in mid-air, metal screaming in protest against metal. The SBD lost its left wing, sheared clean away by the Zero's impact. That sent the remains of the Dauntless into a spin, cart-wheeling towards whatever lay below it. Feeling as if he was trapped inside an out of control ride at a travelling carnival, Marquez reached up to open the canopy and found it was already missing, torn away by the collision. He undid his safety harness, closed his eyes and let gravity do the rest, tumbling from his aircraft as it tipped over and over in the sky. Marquez counted to ten and tore on the release mechanism for his parachute, hoping and praying that it would open.

Extract from <u>Unsolved Mysteries</u>
<u>of Pearl Harbour</u> [2006]:

Conspiracy theorists have long pro-
pounded a variety of wild notions about
the Japanese surprise attack on Pearl
Harbour. Perhaps the best known of these
is that US President Franklin D Roosevelt had advance warning of the attack
and chose not to alert those in Hawaii
and other American bases in the Pacific
that came under fire that day in
December, 1941. [In Pearl Harbour the
Japanese strike happened on Sunday,
December 7th. On that day, the enemy
also attacked US bases in the Philippines, but because these events happened
on the other side of the International

Date Line, they took place on Monday, December 8th.]

In truth, there is little hard evidence to support the theory that Roosevelt let the attacks happen, believing they would galvanise the American people into joining the war that other nations had already been fighting for two years. It is all too easy to ascribe motivation to ignorance, incompetence or a simple lack of joined-up thinking. There were numerous warning signs of what the Japanese had planned, but the significance of these is only apparent with the benefit of hindsight. More recent attacks on American soil by foreign enemies have shown that all the warning signs in the world can go unheeded or unnoticed.

There is a more obscure branch of Pearl Harbour conspiracy theory that remains largely unexplored, surrounding events at Hickam Field on that fateful day. Several eyewitness accounts exist that suggest an enemy aircraft landed on the airstrip during the Japanese attack. A member of the ground crew working there that Sunday morning even claims to have seen at least one person get into the plane and be flown away from Oahu. Sadly, the crewman died in mysterious circumstances not long after giving his statement, so it cannot be corroborated.

Most of the buildings at Hickam Field suffered sustained attacks by enemy aircraft, destroying any evidence that might confirm or deny any records about this mysterious incident. Furthermore, all official documents relating to these events have remained sealed ever since, due to certain unspecified national security concerns. The Pentagon has refused all applications to open these files under the various freedom of information protocols instituted since the Second World War. Indeed, those in charge of records relating to Hickam Field refuse to confirm or deny such files exist. If there were no files, surely military authorities would be eager to say so and defuse any suspicion? By maintaining their charade of plausible deniability, all they do is heighten suspicion.

There was one survivor from Hickam Field who was willing to talk about his experiences that day, although he requested anonymity in exchange for his testimony. Private X told our researchers that he was standing guard at the perimeter gates when a car driven by a Japanese national approached Hickam Field. Bear in mind, the surprise attack had already been raging for more than an hour by this point. Private X contacted the base commander and was told to admit the Japanese man, despite the fact that the visitor wore no military uniform and had no credentials. Unfortunately, the man known as Private X died before his account could be recorded, denying us another piece of the puzzle.

Despite this loss, it is apparent that something strange was happening at Hickam Field that morning in December 1941. How was an enemy aircraft able to land on an American airstrip in the midst of a surprise attack and, apparently, pick up at least one passenger from the ground? Who was the mysterious Japanese stranger who entered the base, and why was he allowed free access? And why does the Pentagon still refuse to open the files on this incident, more than sixty-five years later?

THREE

HITORI WAS SHOVED into the commander's office at Hickam Field at the end of a sub-machine gun, his wrists bound together behind his back with tight ropes. A grim-faced colonel was sitting behind a desk, talking on a black telephone. His eyes widened at seeing a Japanese man in a signal corps uniform escorted in under guard. The colonel slammed the phone down. "Well, Cochrane? Who the hell is this?" he asked the blond soldier closest to Hitori.

"He won't give his name, rank or serial number, but we found him hiding in the shadows near the landing strip, sir. Says he's attached to the Japanese consulate here on the island and claimed diplomatic immunity."

"Did he now?" The colonel picked up a still smoking pipe from an ashtray on his desk and used a long match to relight it. "If he's got diplomatic immunity, why's he wearing a US signal corps uniform? Did he answer that?"

"No, sir," Cochrane replied. "We only discovered the uniform when he took off his coat and hat outside your office, sir."

"Why the hell did you bring him to me? The man's plainly a spy!"

"Yes, sir. We thought you'd want to question him."

"Did you? And since when did the army pay you to think, Cochrane?"

"If you want to shout at anyone," Hitori interjected, "I suggest you shout at me. I'm the enemy, colonel, not the men of your unit."

The colonel snapped to his feet, anger colouring his features crimson. "Don't you tell me what to do, Mister Tojo!"

"My name is Zenji Hitori. I am an officer in the Imperial Japanese Army. Under the terms of the Geneva Convention, you are required–"

"Don't you dare quote the Geneva Convention to me, you murdering bastard! You and your yellow friends lost any rights to the protection of that agreement when you launched a sneak attack on Pearl Harbour."

"Nevertheless, you will treat me with respect, colonel," Hitori said.

"I don't care if you bring Emperor Hirohito his damned newspaper every morning before breakfast, Hitori. You'll get no damned respect from me!"

"In that case, I wish to make a trade," the vampyr announced.

The colonel glared at him. "What kind of trade?"

"I have information about the Japanese plans for

invasion. I will share that information with you, in exchange for certain... considerations."

"What considerations?"

Hitori tilted his head towards Cochrane and the others. "Perhaps it would be better if we continued this conversation in private. Not all Japanese agents have slanted eyes and olive complexions, if you know what I mean."

The colonel chewed on the end of his pipe, considering the implications of this. "Very well. Cochrane, you and the others stand guard outside."

"But sir, at least one of us should remain in here to protect you from–"

"I don't need your damned protection, soldier! I was fighting my own battles when you were still filling your diapers, Cochrane. Don't you think I can handle myself against an unarmed Japanese spy? I mean, you did search him for weapons before bringing him in here, didn't you?"

"Yes, sir, but–"

"But nothing! Get out and take the others with you. What happens in here could determine the course of the damned war, and I don't want any of you screwing that up for me. Have you got that?"

"Yes, sir!" Cochrane replied. He led the other sentries out, still glaring at the prisoner with deep distrust. The colonel waited until they had gone before speaking, puffing on his pipe while studying Hitori's inscrutable features.

"So, what are these considerations you want?"

Hitori smiled. "A Japanese bomber will attempt to land on your strip at 09.00 hours. You will arrange for nearby anti-aircraft units to stand down or direct their fire elsewhere at that time, until the bomber has safely departed."

The colonel snorted derisively. "What possible reason could I have for letting an enemy plane land safely on my airfield and leave unmolested?"

"That aircraft is coming to extract my colleague and I. In exchange for permitting our escape, I will leave you a complete plan of the Japanese invasion of the Hawaiian Islands, other US military installations across the Pacific and the intended attacks upon Los Angeles and San Francisco."

"You're bluffing," the colonel retorted, jabbing his pipe at Hitori.

"Can you afford to take that risk?" the vampyr countered. "Would you wish history to remember you as the man who could have saved tens of thousands of American lives, all for allowing two Japanese spies to escape?"

"But why would you betray your country's plans to me, to us?"

"The emperor did not want this war. He was bullied into it by the likes of General Tojo and his cronies in the Black Dragons. If Japanese operations over the next few weeks fail, it would give the emperor an excuse to pull back from the war, to save face by using Tojo as a scapegoat for the failure."

"You'd sacrifice thousands of your countrymen to stop a greater war?"

Hitori smiled. "It is the honourable thing to do."

The colonel studied his captive. "Honour means that much to you?"

"More than life itself."

"It's a good deal," the colonel conceded, "but I don't have the authority to make it. I'll have to consult with my superiors, see what they have to say. I'm guessing they'll want to talk with the joint chiefs in Washington, maybe even President Roosevelt. I'm sorry, Hitori, but you won't be getting on any plane at 09.00 hours, not from my field."

"You are making a terrible mistake."

"Maybe, but this is how we operate. Until you understand that—"

You are the one who does not understand, Hitori hissed inside the colonel's mind. *You have no choice in this matter. Do as I say, when I say.*

"I will do what you say, when you say," the colonel repeated, his face devoid of all thoughts or emotion. The telephone on his desk rang, breaking the spell that Hitori had cast over him. The colonel picked up the receiver. "Yes?" He listened for a few seconds. "What? You've got a Japanese civilian in a car at the gatehouse, demanding to be allowed on to the base, and you call me?"

His name is Kimura. Tell your guards to escort him and his vehicle to this building, Hitori urged. *You are personally taking charge of this matter.*

LIEUTENANT RICHARDS KNEW he didn't have enough fuel left in his Dauntless to stay airborne much longer, but he was determined to keep fighting for as long as he could. The skies over Oahu had begun to clear as 09.00 hours approached, the Japanese Kates, Vals and Zeros turning away from their targets. But a second wave of enemy aircraft swept in to take their place, scattering their payloads like so

much deadly, black confetti on the military installations spread around the island. From his vantage
point in the SBD Richards could see how the
Japanese had targeted both the vessels moored in
Pearl Harbour and the surrounding airstrips,
ensuring that airborne retaliation was all but impossible. That left nothing but anti-aircraft fire to resist
the second wave. The element of surprise was long
gone, but the Japanese were still able to attack their
chosen targets with impunity.

The lieutenant's gunner had been fatally
wounded a few minutes after the Dauntless lost
contact with Marquez. Richards hoped the young
wingman had found somewhere safe to set down,
though he was yet to see such a landing place himself. Those on the ground seemed intent on
destroying everything that moved in the sky. The
lieutenant had performed every recognition
manoeuvre in the book, but still the anti-aircraft
units below were doing their best to shoot the SBD
to pieces. He suspected that friendly fire had
claimed his radioman, effectively ending any hope
of contact with the ground crews at Ford Island.

"You still here?" a familiar voice drawled in the
lieutenant's earphones.

"Bravo, is that you? Where the hell did you go?"
He looked around and saw his comrade's SBD
pulling into formation as wingman.

"Been to most places on the island, looking for
somewhere to put her down. Ewa's shot to hell,
same as Wheeler and Hickam. Tried Kaneohe and
Bellows Field, but the Japs beat me to both of
'em."

The lieutenant cursed the enemy's superior tactics. "They've been one step ahead of us all damned day! Somebody should've seen this coming!"

"Maybe they did," Bravo sneered.

"What do you mean?"

"I never did like Roosevelt. How do we know he didn't let this happen?"

"You think the president would let an enemy attack happen on US soil?"

"Give him an excuse to get us into the war, wouldn't it?"

The lieutenant couldn't believe what he was hearing. "I liked you better when you didn't say much of anything to anybody."

"I get that a lot," Bravo conceded. "You got any suggestions what we should do? I'll be flying on fumes soon unless I land this thing."

"It's time we took the fight to our yellow friends," the lieutenant decided. "They've had it easy, blowing seven kinds of hell out of Pearl and every strip on the island. Let's give the Japs a taste of their own medicine."

"Now you're talking," Bravo replied. "I'll see you in hell, Richards." His SBD peeled away in search of a fight, leaving the other lieutenant alone in the sky once more. The lieutenant offered a silent prayer to the heavens before following the other pilot's example. He tipped one wing and went down into a slow spiral towards Pearl, where more than a dozen enemy fighters were tormenting the harbour.

PAXTON HAD BEEN walking for nearly an hour when a jeep of MPs shot past on its way towards the navy yards. It screeched to a halt before reversing back up the hill to him. The jeep had four MPs packed into it, all wearing metal dishpan helmets and clutching rifles. "Where you headed, soldier?" the driver asked, tipping his helmet back to get a good look at Paxton.

"Marine barracks," he said without thinking, "B Company."

"What happened? You on a 48-hour pass when the Japs attacked?"

"Something like that," Paxton replied, not wanting to get into the details.

"Uh-huh," the driver said, looking him up and down. There was a massive explosion down in the harbour, a fireball mushrooming into the sky. Moments later the sound of the blast reached the jeep. All five men were transfixed by the spectacle. Two hours ago it had been a peaceful, unremarkable Sunday morning; now they were witnesses to all hell breaking loose on an island in the middle of the Pacific.

A trio of Japanese fighters roared overhead, pursued by an SBD, the sudden noise startling Paxton and the MPs. "We're headed down to the navy yards, we'll give you a lift," the driver told Paxton, jerking a thumb at the rear of the jeep. "Guys, make some room back there. We've got a marine who's trying to get back to his base. Least we can do is take him where he can do some good, right?"

Paxton clambered into the rear of the jeep, wedging his butt between the two burly MPs already there. He winced as the effort strained the wound where his right nipple had been. "Something wrong?" one of the MPs asked.

"Got into a fight last night," Paxton lied, "nothing serious."

MARQUEZ WAS GRATEFUL his parachute opened after he abandoned the plummeting, broken Dauntless, and even more grateful that none of the wreckage from his plane or the shattered Zero had torn though the fabric canopy. But his gratitude was soon washed away when he splashed down in the harbour, between Ford Island and the navy yards. The parachute sank down into the water, threatening to take Marquez with it to the bottom of the harbour, and the clasp on his harness was jammed. The pilot battled to undo the metal clasp, but his fingers were being numbed by the cold water and the harness had tangled itself around his yellow life-preserver. Eventually he fought his way free by sacrificing both, shrugging the parachute and life-preserver off over his shoulders. That left him without a buoyancy aid to help him stay afloat until a rescue boat could find him.

Marquez turned around in a slow circle, trying to get his bearings. He was used to seeing Pearl from the cockpit of his SBD, everything laid out below him like a vast tablecloth. It all looked so different from the surface of the harbour, choppy water and greasy black fumes obscuring most of the landmarks. Marquez thought he recognised Battleship Row, but instead of half a dozen proud navy vessels moored in pairs, all he could see were burning wrecks, vast clouds of black and grey rising from the ruins. The pall of smoke hid the morning sun, casting a queasy, funereal light across the harbour.

A Japanese bomber screamed over Marquez's head, its air brakes fully extended to slow the plane as it dived towards a nearby battleship. It might be an enemy plane, but Marquez could not help admiring the bravery and skills of its pilot, bringing the bomber in low and fast. The Val released its two bombs and peeled away into the sky, anti-aircraft fire peppering the air around the Japanese plane. Behind it the battleship took a direct hit, flames and debris skyrocketing upwards from the deck. Shrapnel from the blast showered the cold, choppy water around the pilot. He ducked beneath the water, not wanting to be wounded or knocked unconscious by falling debris.

When he resurfaced, the ship was still on fire. Marquez could see a tug coming alongside it, trying to give aid. He watched in horror as men set alight by fires on board the larger vessel dived into the water, trying to put out the flames burning them alive. The young pilot wanted to look away, but his eyes were riveted by the grisly, ghastly spectacle. He swam towards the survivors, determined to do what he could to help them.

As Marquez got closer another Japanese plane swooped down low over the water. His sharp eyes were drawn to three things about the aircraft: It had a longer canopy than the Val, suggesting the plane was a three-seater, probably a Kate; secondly, the bomber was jet black from nose to tail, and from wingtip to wingtip, even the glass canopy was tinted black, something he'd never seen before. The sole distinguishing mark on the aircraft was the emblem beneath its wings: the red circle of the Japanese Empire, clutched in the talons of a bird of some sort. As the Kate got closer, Marquez realised it was not a bird, but an image of a bat with its wings unfurled. He had never seen the insignia before, but it still sent a shudder of fear through his body.

Most important of all, the Kate's pilot had opened fire with his forward machine guns, strafing the harbour as he flew over it. "My god," Marquez whispered, "he's targeting the sailors in the water. That's barbaric!" The young pilot shouted at those nearby to get down, but few heard his cries above the cacophony of explosions and screaming aircraft engines. Bullets from the Kate cut deadly lines across the harbour, maiming and killing men intent on trying to escape the burning ships. Marquez dived back below the surface, bullets zipping past him underwater. He swam on, holding his breath for as long as possible before going back up for air. The water was dark, an oil slick spreading across the surface and blocking the sun.

Marquez saw somebody else ahead, also taking refuge below the surface, facing away from him. He swam towards him, using his best breaststroke to scythe through the murky water. Marquez tugged on his shoulder when he reached him, but got no response. He twisted him around in the water and came face to face with a corpse missing its lower jaw. A swollen, listless tongue licked at the crimson water, stained by blood and viscera. Turning the corpse had given its limbs a grisly momentum, and the arms wrapped themselves around Marquez, as if trying to embrace him. He pushed and kicked the body away, watching it tumble into the depths before swimming up towards fresh air.

The young pilot broke the surface gasping for breath, his mind haunted by the image of that dead sailor, his body still shuddering at the corpse's touch. A dozen more corpses were floating in the water around him, and the burning remnants of the battleship he'd seen explode were close on one side. The underwater currents must have been stronger than they seemed, Marquez realised. He heard the rat-tat-tat of machine guns and twisted around to see the Kate coming directly at him, both barrels spitting bullets, butchering all those still alive in the water. Marquez tried to duck back beneath the surface, but the crush of bodies around him made that impossible. It felt as if the dead were clinging to him, making sure he joined them.

Helpless in the water, Marquez watched as the Kate got closer by the moment, two lines of bullets stabbing into the water ahead, both of them tracing a path directly to his position. He wanted to close his eyes, but the Japanese plane held him mesmerised, like a rabbit in the headlights of a truck. A prayer sprang into his mind, the words of a child, but still they tumbled from his lips, one last invocation before the end. "Now I lay me down to sleep, I pray the lord my soul to keep," Marquez whispered in the water.

An SBD burst from the dark clouds billowing out of the battleship and flew in front of the Kate. The Japanese plane broke left to avoid a collision, its radial engine screaming in protest at the sudden change of trajectory. The two aircraft passed within a few feet of each other, the greasy black air swirling and curling behind them. Marquez cheered as he recognised the markings on the Dauntless that had saved him; it was Lieutenant Richards's plane! Twisting around in the water, the pilot watched as another SBD gave chase to the Kate, driving it away from the harbour, sending the enemy bomber south towards Hickam Field. Marquez smiled. Unless he was mistaken, that was Bravo. As usual, it was Chuck who had come to the aide of those in the water, risking himself to save them, while Bravo went chasing a Japanese kill.

"Is anybody still alive out there?" a gruff voice called. Marquez looked around and saw a tug nosing its way through corpse choked waters. Most of the crew was lining the edge of the tug, seeking survivors among the dead.

"Over here!" the pilot shouted, waving an arm in the air.

A lifebelt splashed into the harbour close by and Marquez swam towards it, grateful to be getting out of the chilling, bloody waters. He might be a navy pilot but any affection he had possessed for the sea had been vanquished today. He wanted revenge against an enemy that had turned Pearl Harbour into a killing ground, and had murdered his radioman, Mead. Now, more than ever, he wanted to be in the sky where he belonged.

SERGEANT DWIGHT COCHRANE was worried about the colonel. He'd worked for the old man at Hickam Field for three years, maintaining security around the army air base. In all that time the colonel had never broken a regulation, ignored an instruction or done anything that went against army procedure or protocol. All that had changed since the discovery of the Japanese spy near Hangar 15. The colonel was acting like some green, first-year rookie, choosing to interrogate the prisoner alone in his office, instead of under armed guard in a holding cell. A few minutes later the colonel called Cochrane and ordered that all the anti-aircraft units stationed around Hickam stand down, despite the fact that the field was still under attack from Japanese planes. Now the colonel had commanded sentries at the outer gate to allow another Oriental on to the base. Deciding that enough was enough, Cochrane knocked on the colonel's door and entered the office without waiting for permission.

"Sir, I've no wish to question your judgement, but I have to say..." The sergeant's words petered out as he took in the scene inside the office. The colonel's body was splayed out across the desk, with only an undershirt and shorts to maintain his dignity. The prisoner was crouching beside the body, his face clamped against the colonel's neck, wet sucking sounds escaping his lips. Worst of all, the colonel was moaning with pleasure, his eyes rolling back into his head as if caught in a moment of utter, overwhelming ecstasy.

Hitori ripped his mouth away from the colonel's throat, crimson droplets spilling down his chin. He hissed at the sergeant, lips drawn back to reveal two long fangs, strained red with fresh blood. Hitori was wearing the colonel's uniform, stolen from the dying man's body. Cochrane reached for his sidearm, fingers fumbling at the flap on his holster. Before he could pull the pistol free Hitori had already vaulted the desk and had a claw-like hand clasped around the sergeant's throat. The sharp, jagged fingernails dug into Cochrane's skin, scrabbling at the arteries carrying their rich red cargo around his body.

"What are you?" Cochrane whispered, his voice hoarse with terror.

"We're the future," Hitori replied, licking his ruby lips. "We're the new world order, the master race that will command humanity after this war."

At last the sergeant got his sidearm free and stabbed the barrel into the prisoner's side. "Yeah? Well, my little friend here says otherwise!" He pulled the trigger and fired six quick shots into the prisoner.

Hitori staggered backwards, screaming in anger, his elongated fingers clutching at the wound, his eyes riveted on the holes made by the bullets. But he did not die, did not collapse, did not succumb as Cochrane expected. Instead the prisoner started laughing, his screaming becoming a mocking cackle of mirth. "You fool! Mere bullets cannot kill my kind!"

The sergeant turned to run, about to shout for help from the other sentries outside, but a single word froze him in his tracks: *Stop*. He felt the beating of his heart decrease, the blood pumping through his body slow like some mighty steam hammer grinding to a halt. Time seemed to slide away from Cochrane until there was only him and

Hitori's voice left alive. The world outside receded to nothing, the sounds of bombs falling, and anti-aircraft guns in the distance, dying away. He was alone with only this fiend for company.

Hitori walked around the sergeant in a circle, his gaze fixed on the frozen soldier's fearful face. "Your mind rebels against the reality of your senses. You saw me feeding on the blood of your commanding officer, but you dare not think of the name your people use for my kind. We have had many names in the history of humanity: vampyr, nosferatu, djavoli, creatures of the night. Why should one word frighten you so? Why should a name terrify?" Hitori reached into the sergeant's mind, giving back to Cochrane the power of speech. "Why?"

"Vampires don't exist," the sergeant said.

"I exist," Hitori replied, pulling back his upper lip to expose his fangs. "I feed, I kill, I hunt, I consume. Would you deny all of that?"

Cochrane shook his head.

"Good. Then you can be my thrall, my escort. The colonel has outlived his usefulness and you will take his place." Hitori snapped his fingers and the spell was broken. Cochrane could hear the bombs falling outside, the anti-aircraft guns blasting at anything that moved across the sky. The sergeant opened his mouth to call for help, but no sound came, no words escaped his lips. "You are mine now, body and soul," Hitori hissed.

A car horn sounded outside the office. Hitori strode over to the window and looked out. What he saw seemed to please him. "Good, Kimura's here, at last. Time we were going." The vampyr marched past Cochrane and out of the office, snapping his fingers like a master summoning his pet. "Come!"

KIMURA SAT IN the battered saloon, watching the black Kate as it circled high above Hickam Field. He thought it fortunate that the surprise attacks on Pearl Harbour and the other military bases on Oahu had been such a success. The carnage and chaos created by the disorganised American response had kept security on the ground to a minimum. The US forces were concentrating all their energies on repelling the waves of Kates, Vals and Zeros. Kimura had been challenged just once as he drove from Kissy's home to Hickam Field.

A checkpoint had been established on the road south that passed the headquarters of Admiral Kimmel, Commander in Chief for the Pacific. Kimura had needed all his powers of persuasion to get past that, *pushing* the sentries at the checkpoint into allowing him through. After that the greatest threat had come from trigger-happy Japanese pilots, intent on machine-gunning anything that moved on the ground below them. The saloon was twice targeted by passing Zeros, its roof and passenger side door punctured repeatedly by bullets. Kimura enjoyed the irony, if not the reality, that his own side was coming closest to destroying him. He had found Hickam Field virtually unguarded, a single sentry stopping traffic at the gate. Another *push* and the soldier called his commander for orders.

Now Kimura was sitting outside the colonel's office in the heart of Hickam Field, surrounded by burning hangars and ancillary buildings. The blazing remnants of US Army bombers littered the apron beside the landing strip, but the runway remained all but untouched by Japanese bombardment. Hitori's orders had been obeyed by both attack waves. Kimura heard a clock tower in the distance, though it was impossible to count the chimes over the noise of war all around him. Nevertheless, he sensed it was 09.00 hours. The Japanese storm had been lashing Oahu for at least sixty minutes. Besides, the black Kate circling overhead was descending towards the airfield. This was the moment of truth.

Two men emerged from the administration block at Hickam, one dressed in the uniform of an American army colonel, the collar of his coat pulled up to shield him from the sun, a peaked cap keeping his features in shadow. Kimura smiled at Hitori's disguise; his old friend had gotten a promotion on Oahu. The other man was a sergeant, his face bearing the blank, passive look that typified thralls. He walked ahead of Hitori, a sub-machine gun in his grasp. Several members of ground crew ran towards the sergeant, shouting and waving their arms, gesticulating at the Kate coming in to land. The soldier flinched, a trickle of blood escaping from one nostril, before opening fire on his fellow Americans. Once they were dead, Hitori signalled Kimura closer.

The Kate made a hurried, ugly landing, its undercarriage skidding and bouncing along the runway. The bomber's brakes eventually took effect, slowing the plane enough for it to manoeuvre past two American B-17s that had touched down earlier. The

Kate circled around them and waited at the far end of the landing strip. While it was doing that, Hitori climbed in beside Kimura. The sergeant trotted after his master and got in the back of the vehicle, hands gripping his weapon so tightly the knuckles were blanched white. Kimura and Hitori exchanged smiles, pleased to see each other again.

"I was worried you wouldn't make it," Hitori said in Japanese.

"I had to eliminate the Nagara woman," Kimura explained, "make sure she couldn't tell anyone about us. Better our presence here remain a secret."

"You succeeded?"

"Of course," Kimura replied, hurt that his friend had even asked. He drove them across the landing strip to the waiting Kate, its tinted glass canopy designed to keep the pilot and passengers safe from sunlight. Hitori muttered instructions to the blank-faced American sitting behind them, commanding the sergeant to keep back anyone on the ground who might attempt to stop their escape. All three men abandoned the saloon beside the runway and headed for the Kate, the two vampyrs taking care to keep themselves shielded from the sun. Kimura clambered up on to the aircraft's wing and slid back the canopy enough to get inside. Hitori hissed one last command at his thrall before joining Kimura inside the Kate and sliding the canopy shut. The menacing black bomber rolled along the landing strip, picking up speed before lifting up into the air.

Inside the cockpit Hitori tapped their pilot on the shoulder once. He nodded and made one last pass over the airfield, dropping his bomb on the block

where the colonel's body lay dying on a wooden
desk. The building exploded in a fireball of destruc-
tion, removing all evidence that the vampyrs had
been at Hickam. As the Kate climbed away into the
sky, four Zeros joined formation with it, one at
either wing as sentry planes, while one took position above the Kate and the other below it as flying
shields. Hitori and Kimura were too valuable for further risks to be taken. Their job on Oahu was over.
The first wave of Japanese aircraft was already on its
way back to the task force, and the second would
soon follow. The attack on Pearl Harbour was all but
over. The Pacific war had just begun.

COCHRANE WATCHED THE Japanese bomber fly away,
his gaze fixed on the plane as it became little more
than a speck in the sky. Ever since that moment in
the colonel's office when he had heard the word
Stop in his mind, the sergeant had been fighting for
control of his actions. Cochrane felt as if he was a
prisoner in his body, a puppet being controlled by
invisible strings. His limbs did the bidding of
another master, no matter how hard he battled to
stop them. His body committed atrocities for which
he could never forgive himself. He had murdered
indiscriminately, gunning down his colleagues in
the hall outside the colonel's office.

After executing the last of them, he stole a sub-
machine gun from the dead hands of his best
friend, Matt Davis. The two of them had grown up
together in Tulsa, they had volunteered together,
and they had gone through basic training side by
side. The army had torn them apart after that, but

chance had brought them back together at Hickam. Now Matt was dead and Cochrane had murdered him. It didn't matter that the slaying was an involuntary act, in fact that made it worse somehow. The two friends had always promised to look out for one another. Instead Cochrane had slaughtered his closest buddy, too weak to resist the urgings of some unholy monster.

Hitori had made Cochrane go first as they stepped outside. When the ground crew came running towards them, the sergeant knew what was going to happen and had closed his eyes, unable to witness the murders he was perpetrating. He felt the sub-machine gun jerking in his grasp, heard the cries and torments of his victims, and tasted the salty tears of grief running down his face, but he couldn't stop himself, couldn't control his own body.

He had stood in the centre of the runway and watched as the Kate took off and witnessed it swoop back to bomb the building housing the colonel's office. Cochrane looked at the burning building where he had butchered Davis and the others. He stared at the corpses of the ground crew, killed by his hand.

All the witnesses to his involuntary treachery were dead, and nobody ever need know it was him who had slain his brothers in arms. But the thought of trying to forget what he'd done, let alone trying to forgive himself for doing it, was too much for the sergeant. Cochrane knew he'd never be able to look in a mirror again. He'd never be able to look himself in the eye without reliving his crimes, without seeing the ghosts of those whose lives he had stolen.

End your misery, a voice whispered in his thoughts. Was it his own mind speaking, or was it one last, lingering command from Hitori? In truth, it did not matter. Cochrane jammed the end of the sub-machine's barrel in his mouth and pulled the trigger.

[Public Law 328 - 77th Congress]
[Chapter 561 - 1st Session)
[S. J. Res. 116]
Joint Resolution

Declaring that a state of war exists between the Imperial Government of Japan and the Government and the people of the United States and making provisions to prosecute the same.

Whereas the Imperial Government of Japan has committed unprovoked acts of war against the Government and the people of the United States of America: Therefore be it resolved by the Senate and House of Representatives of the United States of American in Congress assembled, that the state of war between the United States and the Imperial Government of Japan which has thus been thrust upon the United States is hereby formally declared; and the President is hereby authorized and directed to employ the entire naval and military forces of the United States and the resources of the Government to carry on war against the Imperial Government of Japan; and, to bring the conflict to a successful termination, all of the resources of the country are hereby pledged by the Congress of the United States.

Approved, December 8, 1941, 4:10pm. EST.

FOUR

MARTINEZ ROLLED OVER and smiled when he saw Angela, Mrs Martinez, beside him in bed. Mrs Martinez, that sounds weird, he thought. Mrs Angela Martinez. Well, it would take some getting used to, but what the hell. They'd spent a glorious night together, savouring each moment as if it might be their last. Angela was transferring south to Manila on the midday transport, so who knew when they'd have the chance to spend another uninterrupted night together. Everybody kept talking about war, how it was only a matter of time before the Japanese attacked. Even if it was inevitable, it was still in the future, right? They still had a few hours before Angela had to leave.

Martinez moved nearer to his new wife, intent on giving her an unexpected reason to wake. Her eyes were still closed, but she couldn't help smiling as he got closer. "I never knew you Latin lovers were so insatiable," she murmured. "If somebody had told me, I would have gotten married years ago."

"Yeah, but you only met me in the last couple of months," he replied, grinning at her playfulness. "You might have been disappointed with someone else. And how would you know they were a real Latin lover? Never accept any substitutes, that's my policy when it comes to love."

"You better not," she said, opening her dazzling green eyes. "I hear any rumours you've turned into Don Juan Martinez while I'm stuck down in Manila, I'll be back here faster than you can say unscheduled castration."

"Ouch," Martinez grinned. "Don't even joke about a thing like that."

"Trust me, it's no joke." She slid a hand down his chest until it nestled between his legs. "Now, where did we get to last night?"

"I thought we gave each other a thorough examination."

Angela smirked. "True, but would you value a second opinion?"

"Maybe a third, too."

"Only if we've got time. Come here, lover–" Their flirting was interrupted by hammering on the door.

"Martinez," Buntz shouted from the corridor, "you in there?"

"You better believe it, Arnie."

"Well, finish whatever you're doing and get dressed. The Japs have attacked Pearl Harbour. The sarge wants everybody at their posts, now!"

"What did he say?" Angela whispered.

Martinez jumped out of bed and pulled on his trousers. "Buntz, if this is your idea of a practical joke, I'm gonna rip you a new one!"

"It's no joke. The Japs have been bombing the hell out of Pearl all morning. They hit the *Arizona*, other ships too. Radio says there could be hundreds, maybe thousands dead on Oahu. Word is we're next in the firing line!"

Martinez fastened his trousers and opened the door. Buntz was standing in the corridor, biting his fingernails. "Jesus, you're not kidding."

The other soldier shook his head. "Aimes sent me to find you. Says if you're not back at the battery and ready for action by eight, he'll have your nuts for paperweights." Buntz peeked over Martinez's shoulder and caught a glimpse of Angela pulling on her brassiere. "Trust me, with a woman that good-looking, you don't want to be minus your manhood."

Martinez pushed Buntz away from the door. "Keep stealing a peek at my wife and you'll be the one minus his testicles, Arnie, not me."

"Sure, sure, look, I'm just passing on the message, okay? What you do with it is up to you, but I suggest you stop your grinning and hitch up your linen. Sounds like we're gonna be in for a bumpy ride." With that he was gone, waddling away along the corridor, pausing to hammer on each door as he passed it. "Everybody up! Get moving! The Japs are coming!"

Martinez went back into the bedroom and found that his wife had already finished dressing. "This is it, isn't it? The war, it's really happening."

Angela pulled on her shoes. "Sounds like it. First thing I've gotta do is contact Manila, see if they still want me on that transport. If the Japanese start bombing the Philippines, it's a safe bet Clark Field will be a prime target. Half our planes in the Pacific must be over there. The base hospital's gonna need more nurses, not less." She threw the few personal possessions she'd brought into a canvas bag. "We'll need more blood, too. Once the wounded start coming in, we'll be lucky if our supplies last a day."

Martinez watched her, unable to believe how calm she was, how reasoned and efficient her response to the situation. "You're already planning how to treat the wounded and I haven't got my shirt on yet," he said.

She smiled at him. "Yes, you'd better get dressed. I don't mind looking at my husband whether he's half-naked or not, but Sergeant Aimes might." Angela finished packing her bag and checked under the bed to make sure she was leaving nothing behind. "Well, who knows when either of us will make it back here?"

"Didn't you hear what Arnie said, love? We're going to war."

Angela stopped what she was doing and walked across to him "I know. Five minutes ago we were making love and now..."

"It doesn't seem real, not yet."

"It will when the bombs start falling."

"I know." Martinez touched a hand against her face. "I just wanna remember this moment, savour it. Who knows when we'll see peace again?"

Angela kissed him, her hands in his hair, her body pressed into his. Distant voices were bellowing orders, and heavy feet ran past their room. Finally, Angela broke off the kiss, but she stared into her husband's eyes. "You look after yourself, Mr Martinez. Don't do anything stupid and don't try to be a hero. Nobody wins a war on the first day, but plenty of people get killed trying. Don't you be one of them, okay?"

He nodded, emotion choking him. "You be careful in that hospital. You're supposed to be a nurse, remember, not one of the patients."

Angela smiled as a tear ran down her face. She gave him a quick kiss on the cheek before going, striding away along the corridor, not looking back.

SUZUKI AND HIS cadre of vampyr pilots had been sitting in the black tinted cockpits of their Zeros since before dawn. They had spent so long preparing for war that none of them wanted to miss the first sortie over enemy territory. Now they were taxiing down the airstrip, waiting for the signal to accelerate into the sky. The bombers were first to take off, more than a hundred and eighty Mitsubishis ascending into the clouds before assembling into their flying formation. The Zeros were next, nearly a hundred of them, including Suzuki and his six kyuuketsuki. The fighters' principal task was escorting the bombers to their targets and engaging any enemy combatants in the sky.

Once the aerial bombardment was complete, the Zeros would have an opportunity to strafe the American facilities on the ground, causing as much damage as possible. That was where Suzuki expected his pilots to come into their own. Kyuuketsuki units were still an experiment as far as Tokyo was concerned, just another weapon in the empire's war arsenal. Suzuki knew there were already mutterings among those who controlled the naval aviation programme, complaints about him requisitioning the navy's finest planes and pilots for some ill-defined mission. It was vital that the kyuuketsuki perform well in this attack, proving their worth as pilots and weapons.

Suzuki listened as Otomo contacted the others via radio, confirming that all the vampyrs had gotten off the ground without incident. The seven black Zeros assembled into a flying V formation, with Suzuki at its head and Otomo at his right wingtip. "History awaits us all," Suzuki told his vampyr samurai on the frequency reserved for the kyuuketsuki, the signal transmitted at a pitch too high for most humans to hear.

"Our fellow fliers will be aiming to devastate the American ground facilities, destroying any planes still on the ground when we reach the target and disabling support facilities. I have a different mission in mind, brothers. Our objective is to strike horror and dread into the hearts of the Americans. We shall hunt them down and slaughter them, one by one if necessary. We shall put fear in their hearts and doubt in their souls. We will kill without mercy or remorse. Men, women and children will all die before our machine guns. Let the legend of our black fighters and our savagery begin today. Let them know fear as they've never experienced it before. Let them know terror!"

"WHERE THE HELL have you been?" Aimes folded his arms when Martinez raced across the grass to the anti-aircraft gun. The rest of the unit had been in position and running drills for ten minutes when the private arrived. To make matters worse, Martinez was out of breath and half his shirt was hanging out of his trousers. "You look like you've only just gotten out of bed!"

"That's because he has," one of the other recruits quipped, getting a cheap laugh from the others. A glare from the sergeant silenced them.

"If I wanted any comedians in my unit, I would've become an entertainment officer, not an artillery sergeant!" Aimes bellowed. "The next man who cracks wise near me can do a hundred press-ups with me sitting on his back." None of the soldiers felt the urge to demonstrate their gift for humour after that. Satisfied, Aimes turned back to Martinez. "Well?"

"Sorry, sergeant, I was on my honeymoon."

"Honeymoon's over, loverboy, we decided to have a war instead."

"Yes, sergeant, so I've been told."

"So good of you to join us for it."

"Yes, sergeant."

"Yes, sergeant," Aimes echoed, mimicking Martinez's accent. Several of the other recruits giggled, but quickly stifled their amusement, lest they be next for one of the sergeant's razor sharp tongue lashings. "Now, since Wierzbowski has chosen the most inconvenient possible moment to get hospitalised, we're a man short. But something tells me the Japanese won't pay any attention to that. We've never actually had the chance to test fire our weapons during our many, many drills, because some genius never saw fit to supply us with any ammunition fit for that purpose, but I doubt the Japanese will bother about that, either. What ammunition we do have is no use beyond an altitude of twenty thousand feet, so it'll probably be next to useless against the enemy's bombers. As a result, even if we get one of the Japanese planes in our sights, chances are our shells won't reach them. So, you might well be asking yourself, what the hell are we doing out here?"

Several recruits exchanged worried glances, but Aimes was not asking for their opinion. Instead he thundered on with his speech. "We are here because our gun is a deterrent. I've never been in a Japanese plane, but I'm guessing they won't like the taste of our flak. The more we can do to make their job difficult, the better this battle will go for our side. If we can shoot one or two of them out of the sky, that's a bonus. Our task here is to fight back and to show them we're not afraid of their sorry, yellow asses.

"Make no mistakes, gentlemen, we are at war with the Japanese Empire. The President might not have said so yet, Congress and the Senate might still be arguing in Washington DC about whether or not to declare what everybody knows is a simple fact, but we are at war. No quarter asked and no quarter given. Everything you've ever done has been about preparing you for this day, this battle, this damn war. Prove you've got what it takes by making yourself, your family and your country proud. Chances are, some of you won't be alive by this time tomorrow. Hell, I think it'll be a miracle if any of us are still alive by the time this war is won. We are in harm's way here, and the Japanese are coming to do us that harm. Well, we've got a chance to turn them back, a chance to show them what Americans are made of: grit and determination, hellfire and vengeance. Today's the day you learn what it means to be a soldier. Today's the day you earn that uniform you wear."

THE MPs TRANSPORTING Paxton reached the navy yards at midday. They were forced to stop several times en route by civilian disturbances that threatened to disrupt the rule of law on Oahu. More than a third of Hawaii's population were Americans of Japanese parentage, something that gave the attack by Japanese planes on the American island an extra, unhappy dimension. One intersection was blocked by Japanese residents cheering the enemy aircraft overhead. The MPs felt obliged to put a halt to their demonstration, fearful that it would provoke retaliations by other citizens. Closer to the navy yards the MPs intervened to prevent an angry crowd that was vandalising a store run by a Japanese American family. The owner had been brutally beaten and his wife was in danger of suffering the same rough justice.

Paxton stayed in the jeep both times, not wanting to get involved. His mind was still rebelling at all he had witnessed that morning. He could picture the reaction of people across America, hell, across the whole damned world, upon hearing that Pearl Harbour had been attacked by the Japanese. Folks would be shocked that the US had been caught flat-footed, Paxton thought, stunned that a little nation like Japan could catch America cold.

How would they react if someone told them that the Japs were using vampires as spies on our territory? Nobody would believe it, of course; he could hardly believe it himself and he had seen Kissy transform into one of those monsters, seen her burned alive by exposure to nothing more harmful than sunlight. Try to warn others about this danger and he'd be thought a madman or a malingerer, acting insane to get himself discharged now that war had broken out. No, I must keep what I've seen to myself, Paxton decided. I've got enough guilty secrets, so one more will make little difference.

When the jeep delivered him to the navy yards, Paxton thanked the MPs and waited for them to drive away before approaching the gatehouse. He expected to be arrested at any moment, but was surprised to find that his return made little impact. The sentry at the gate recognised Paxton and ticked his name off a list on a clipboard. "I went absent without leave," Paxton said.

"Then count yourself lucky the Japs attacked this morning," the sentry replied. "Captain's declared a temporary amnesty on all AWOL recruits so long as they report back to barracks before sundown. He said we'd need every man we could get and military justice would have to wait awhile."

"So I'm off the hook?" Paxton asked, unable to believe he'd dodged punishment for his attack on Sergeant Hicks.

"I said a temporary amnesty. Captain's offering suspended sentences for outstanding offences. Keep your sheet clean for a year and then you'll be off the hook, assuming you live that long, of course." The sentry arched an eyebrow at the marine, intrigued by Paxton's obvious relief. "Why d'you ask? What did you do that was so bad you decided to go AWOL?" Once the marine had explained, the sentry gave a low whistle. "You're the one who laid out Hicks? I wouldn't want to be in your boots when he recovers!"

"The sarge is still alive?"

"I'd take more than a skull fracture and concussion to kill that old soldier."

Paxton was relieved to know he hadn't murdered Hicks, but didn't savour the prospect of serving under the sergeant again. "Where is he?"

"How should I know?" the sentry shrugged. "Try one of the field hospital units; they've got them set up all over the base." He walked past the marine, his attention already focused on an approaching truck.

FATHER KELLY DIDN'T hear about the attack on Pearl Harbour until he made his daily visit to the base hospital shortly before noon. He had been praying at the chapel most of the morning, after a sleepless night haunted by a vision of Catherine. The priest knew she was dead, he was the one who had found her body and led her funeral service, but the beautiful young women in his dreams seemed more alive than ever. She spoke to him, asking the same question over and over again, the same question she'd been asking him in his sleep every night since she died: why?

The priest still didn't have an answer, despite spending two hours on his knees in the chapel, praying for guidance or an enlightenment that never came. Father Kelly said five novenas without interruption before giving up for another day. If he kept busy tending to the needs of others, it helped him forget the numbing hollowness in his own soul, if only for a while. That was better than the constant memory of how he'd failed Catherine.

He was surprised to see Wierzbowski in the ward and approached the private, ready to make light of whatever was ailing the soldier. "What's it this time? Another dislocated knee, or did you bruise your knuckles teaching Arnold Buntz a much deserved lesson?" Not that I condone violence, of course."

"Hello, father," Wierzbowski responded, his voice thin and weak. "I'm surprised to see you here. I thought they might have shipped you out."

"Really? Why?"

"You haven't heard? About what's happened at Pearl?"

Father Kelly shook his head. He was soon shaking it in disbelief after Wierzbowski described the reports he'd heard over the armed forces radio. "But that's terrible! And you say the Japanese gave no warning of their attack?"

"Seems they didn't."

"That's appalling," the priest whispered. "Declaring war is bad enough in a world already ravaged by so much fighting, but to attack an island populated by so many innocent women and children..." He thought back to his brief time at Oahu, en route to this posting. "You're sure this isn't some kind of hoax, like when that Welles fellow made his broadcast about Martians?"

"It's no hoax, father." The newly married Nurse Martinez came over to check Wierzbowski's chart and temperature. "Radio says President Roosevelt is expected to declare war in the next day or so, if not sooner."

"My God," Father Kelly said, making the sign of the cross and offering up a silent prayer for all those killed or injured back in Hawaii. As he did so, the priest was all too aware of the inherent contradiction. His own faith might be in question, but the habits of a lifetime died hard. Besides, even if I'm not sure I believe in God, Father Kelly thought, that doesn't mean He's stopped existing. Once his prayer was finished, a new and worrying fact occurred to him. "Pearl Harbour is between here and mainland America, isn't it?"

The nurse nodded, eyes fixed on her watch as she checked the pulse in Wierzbowski's left arm. "And we're between Pearl and Japan."

"Exactly," Father Kelly agreed, "so why did the enemy bypass us to attack Hawaii first? That doesn't make any sense to me."

"The whole Pacific fleet is stationed at Pearl," she replied. "Take that out of action and life gets a lot easier for the Japs. Besides, the sun rises five hours earlier at Oahu, and bombing's probably easier in daylight."

"Then it's only a matter of time before this base is attacked."

"That's what the doctors reckon," Nurse Martinez said. "Wierzbowski, I've got good news and bad news. What do you want first?"

The patient shrugged. "Good news, I guess."

"The treatments have worked, you're getting better."

"And the bad news?"

She grimaced. "Another few days and you can go back to your unit. Right now, I'm not sure that's the safest place to be."

"I'm not sure anywhere's safe now," Father Kelly observed.

The nurse nodded. "You're probably right." She noticed the priest staring at her. "Is there something wrong, father?"

For a moment Father Kelly believed he was looking not at her but at Catherine, as she would have been if still alive. So often she had talked about her dreams of becoming a nurse, helping people by easing their pain, making a difference to their lives. She saw it as a noble calling, a vocation like the priesthood. She saw him as noble, not as a man but as a healer of souls, and he had taken advantage of that naivety, had used his position of trust to–

"Father Kelly, are you all right?"

The priest shook his head, pushing away the images in his mind, the memories of what had happened back in Chicago. "Yes, yes, I'm fine. Sorry, my thoughts wandered there for a minute."

She walked around Wierzbowski's bed to put a comforting hand on Father Kelly's arm. "I know how you feel. Yesterday I was getting married and today we're all standing on the edge of war, with no way of knowing where it will lead us or what effect it'll have on our lives, or the people we love."

"Yes. Yes, you're right. It feels as if events are spiralling out of control. That's a frightening sensation for anyone, let alone those in a war zone." He patted her hand in thanks before walking across to a window that looked out over Clark Field. Dozens of P-40 fighters and B-17s were taking off, no doubt in search of the enemy, trying to head off an attack. "I fear my services could well be needed later, but is there anything I can do right now, my child?"

"We need fresh blood. If the Japanese do come–" The nurse stopped and corrected herself. "When they attack, we'll need all the blood we can get. The other nurses are setting up a donation station downstairs."

"I saw that as I came in and wondered what it was for. I'll go and give blood then. It'll feel good to do something useful. Prayers and comforting are all very well, but they aren't as much use as bullets or blood in a battle."

THE VAST AERIAL armada of Japanese bombers and fighters was approaching the Philippines when Suzuki felt a prickling sensation run up the back of his neck. He shivered, unable to account for his sudden feeling that they were on a collision course with trouble. "Otomo, can you see any sign of the enemy?"

"No, sir," the wingman said. "There's nothing up here except us."

"You're sure of that?"

"Yes, sir," Otomo replied. "Why do you ask?"

Suzuki hesitated before answering. "I can't shake the feeling that we're flying into danger. It's nothing tangible, more like a jangling at the back of my brain."

"Perhaps you're one in a thousand."

"Explain."

"Before he left for his own mission, Commander Hitori arranged a meeting with us while you were busy elsewhere. He said he wanted to see what sort of pilots you had chosen for the first squadron of kyuuketsuki."

"That sounds like Hitori, always wants the last word."

"He told us that one in a thousand vampyrs develops latent abilities they never knew they'd possessed. A sixth sense for danger was one such ability."

Suzuki snorted, his sceptical nature making it difficult for him to believe in such notions. But the uneasy sensation nagging at his brain was getting more insistent by the moment, demanding his attention. Perhaps there was something to what Hitori had told his recruits. Three months ago, Suzuki would never have believed in vampyrs, and now he was one of the undead, drinking the blood of living humans to sustain him. How was the idea of an instinct for imminent danger any more unbelievable than that?

"Kyuuketsuki, we must change course," Suzuki said. "On my mark we break right and fly directly south until I determine otherwise."

"Sir, I don't mean to question your judgement, but are you sure about this?" Otomo asked, doubt all too evident in his voice.

"Yes," Suzuki replied, trying to sound more certain than he was. "Prepare to change course: Five, four, three, two, one, break!"

The seven aircraft tipped up their left wings and headed south, moving away from the rest of the planes. Within a few seconds the Japanese flight commander was on the radio, demanding to know why the kyuuketsuki had broken away from the rest of the aerial armada. "Contact our advance radar stations, they'll have the answer," Suzuki said. He wasn't sure if he believed this himself yet, but it was the only response he had.

A minute later the rest of the Japanese planes changed course too, following the vampyr fliers south. The flight commander called Suzuki in person. "One of our radar stations detected another presence in the sky, at least fifty enemy aircraft moving to intercept our former heading. How did you know? The radar station said the presence was right at the edge of its range."

"How I know is not important," Suzuki maintained, "but remember this in the future. When the kyuuketsuki takes action, you should pay attention."

MARTINEZ WATCHED THE B-17s and P-40 fighters returning to nearby Clark Field, showing no signs of having engaged the enemy while they were away. He and the other artillery gunners had been poised beside their anti-aircraft weapon all morning, waiting for an attack that never materialised. Now the sun was directly overhead, the blistering heat and humidity sapping their strength. The recruits were grumbling about having to stay out in the sun, when there was nothing to shoot at. Aimes sent two of them to fetch water and K-rations from Stores. The artillery teams didn't dare leave their guns in case the Japanese did attack, but they still had to take on liquid and food.

By midday even Martinez was expressing doubts about the radio accounts of a surprise attack at Pearl. "You know what reporters are like, always exaggerating everything to make their stories more exciting. The whole thing probably boils down to two guys in a midget sub popping up in the middle of the harbour and taking pot shots at the battleships," he muttered.

"Stow that garbage, Martinez!" Aimes barked. "We've got our orders and we'll stick to them, until somebody tells us different. If the Pentagon had wanted you to think, they would have made you an officer, not a grunt."

"Yes, sergeant," Martinez responded, "but how do we know that radio broadcast wasn't a hoax? Maybe the brass set it up as a kind of test to see if we're ready for war if it happens."

"There's no if about this, soldier. President Roosevelt, Congress and the Joint Chiefs may not have declared war on the Japs yet, but you can bet your bottom dollar we'll be at war by this time tomorrow. Is that clear?" Martinez didn't respond. He was too busy staring at something over the sergeant's shoulder. "I asked you a question, soldier! Is that clear?"

"Yeah, yeah, whatever you say, sergeant…"

"That's insubordination, Martinez. One more crack like that and you'll be spending the first week of the war on report!"

"I think you'll have to report me later," the private said, pointing at the sky. A black cloud had appeared on the horizon, moving towards Clark Field and its neighbour, Fort Stotsenberg. But the dark mass in the air was moving too fast to be a meteorological phenomenon. "Looks like the war's arriving."

BUNTZ WAS so busy arguing with the two artillery gunners outside the stores building, he didn't notice the dark cloud on the horizon, getting bigger by the minute. "You two clowns go back and tell Sergeant high-and-mighty Aimes that if he wants to requisition K-rations from me, he needs to supply the proper documentation, in triplicate, or else he and his men will go hungry." Buntz jerked a thumb at his office. "See that in there? It's my private domain. Not only do I run Stores for Fort Stotsenberg, as far as you're concerned I am Stores. You want something, you have to go through me, end of story."

But the two recruits had stopped listening to him. The fresh faced pair dropped the supplies they were trying to requisition and dashed away, back towards their anti-aircraft emplacement. "That's right!" Buntz shouted after them. "You better run! I'm the guy in charge around here, not Sergeant Aimes."

He watched the sprinting soldiers and realised his words were falling on deaf ears. Then he noticed the black cloud in the sky and heard the thrum of distant engines, getting louder and nearer with each passing moment. Private Arnold Buntz muttered a profane curse under his breath, all notions of his superiority forgotten in the face of more than two hundred and fifty enemy aircraft. He watched as a shower of black objects tumbled from the cloud, falling towards the US planes parked outside at Clark Field.

The Pacific war had reached the Philippines. The Japanese attack had begun. Buntz did the only thing he could think of at that second, the most historic moment of his greedy, grasping life: he ran for the nearest latrine.

TO: Sister Marie Kelly, Our Lady
of the Sacred Heart Convent,
Chicago

Dear Sis,

I watched people die today. The
Japanese attacked Clark Field and Fort
Stotsenberg with bombs and bullets,
causing God only knows how much damage
and death, and pain and suffering. Now
that we're at war, I know I can't say too
much in my letters to you, in case these
missives should fall into the wrong
hands. I'm sure you'll forgive my vague-
ness about specifics: censors have
better things to do with their time than
worry about a priest telling his sister
the nun any military secrets.

I've seen death before of course, many
times in fact. As a parish priest I sat
with the old and the young alike as they
passed from this life into God's eternal
embrace. I've witnessed people dying so
peacefully you'd think they had merely
fallen asleep, and others who raged
against the end as if it were a foe they
could pummel into submission. I always
thought such experiences would be ample
preparation for life as an army chaplain. Death is death, and there's no
denying it.

But the reality of so much death coming
so quickly to so many, it rocks you back,
it pushes all your certainties aside.
I've never felt so helpless and yet so
needed as I did today. Helpless because
holding a gun is anathema to me, let
alone firing one. The Japanese planes
came and I could do nothing to turn them
away beyond prayer. Invocations to
heaven may be good for the soul, but I've
found they have little effect when your
enemy can neither hear your prayers nor
understand the language in which they
are spoken. So yes, I felt helpless amid
the onslaught.

But I also felt needed. I was in the
base hospital when the attack started,
stacking sandbags in front of windows and
helping to move patients away from vulnerable parts of the building. The

hospital at Fort Stotsenberg is small and primitive by Chicago standards, but it is a solid enough building. That probably saved quite a few lives today. The first casualties reached the hospital not long after the bombing began, men risking their lives to deliver comrades in arms to the care of doctors and nurses. I'd never seen so many broken bones, so much scorched flesh.

The sobbing and wailing and groaning undid me at first, the level of suffering overwhelming me. But my training at the seminary and all my time as a parish priest was better preparation than I ever thought possible for life during wartime. I know that probably sounds amusing, even incongruous, but I believe it to be the truth. As a priest, your actions become ritualised, an automatic response overtaking you in certain situations. So it was for me today. I saw a soldier dying and found myself giving him the last rites, without even thinking. It was simply the right thing to do, the natural response to his suffering.

When I wasn't committing men's souls to the Lord, I was helping to save their lives, in my limited way. I carried stretchers, I put pressure on wounds to stop them bleeding, I even held one man down while his leg was being amputated.

I'd never felt more alive in my life, in the midst of so much death and carnage. I believe I've found my true calling, the reason I took the cloth and became a man of God. But there was one moment from today that will haunt me forever, no matter how much good I do during this war, one loss that I cannot overcome or undo. The look in that person's eyes on facing death...

Forgive me, sister, I am rambling. I have not yet slept and am not sure when I will sleep again. My nerves are still jangling from the day and my heart is overflowing with emotion. Thank you for being there, someone to whom I could pour out my soul, a confessor for my sins.

  All my love,
  Shamus.

FIVE

THE BOMBERS ATTACKED first, unloading their deadly cargos from 23,000 feet. The bombs rained down on Clark Field, sprinkled like explosive confetti from the sky. The blasts walked down the runway where all the B-17s were parked, the aircraft engines still warm from their abortive search for the incoming Mitsubishis and Zeros. The American planes were stripped of their skins, either blown off by the explosions or burnt down to the frame by the scorching fires that followed. Within minutes the US aircraft were little more than twisted hulks, metal skeletons like the bones of some extinct species. Thick black smoke from the fires billowed up into the tropical sky, creating a dark shroud in front of the green mountains around the facility.

The anti-aircraft guns manned by the 200th Coast Artillery peppered the sky with flak, but their powder train fuses were only effective to 20,000 feet

389

and could do no damage to the high altitude bombers. After ten minutes of firing uselessly at the heavens, Sergeant Aimes ordered his unit to stand down. "Stop wasting the damned ammunition!" he bellowed, pulling the recruits away from their guns one by one. "Stand down! You're not hitting anything, you're just blowing holes in the sky."

Martinez was last to abandon the effort, so intent was he upon targeting the enemy aircraft. "But we can get them, sarge! They can't stay up there forever; sooner or later those yellow bastards will run out of bombs. They'll have to come down here to shoot us. That'll be our chance!"

"Exactly," Aimes agreed. "Until they do come down, there's nothing we can do. Be patient, soldier, the war won't be won or lost today."

"But they're kicking the crap out of us!"

"We'll get out turn, don't you worry about that." The sergeant gestured at the remnants of nearby Clark Field. "Count yourselves lucky you didn't enlist with the Air Force, otherwise you might be over there."

No sooner had he finished speaking than a fresh wave of bombs was dropped on the airstrip and its surroundings by Japanese planes, flying over in a V formation. The Clark Field barracks exploded in a fireball, followed seconds later by the PX and two hangars. An air raid siren wailed in protest, its mournful tone underscoring the barrage of explosions rocking the ground.

"Sweet Jesus," Martinez whispered. "What do we do if the Japs start bombing us? We haven't got air raid shelters or any trenches for taking cover."

"We're about to find out," the sergeant said, his face full of grim resolve, one hand pointing at the next wave of bombers. They were flying directly towards Fort Stotsenberg, those at the front of the formation already unloading their bombs. "Everybody, hit the dirt! Get down, now! Do it!"

The men of the anti-aircraft unit flung themselves to the ground, clutching metal helmets close to their heads. Martinez could hear someone praying, reciting the rosary. The young soldier glanced around to see who it was, but couldn't find him. Then he recognised the voice praying, it was his own.

BUNTZ REALISED THAT hiding in the latrine wasn't the safest option when the door disintegrated, blown apart by a nearby explosion. The portly recruit got off the toilet and pulled up his trousers in one, swift movement. Hell, if he was going to die today, he didn't want it to be on the crapper. Talk about your undignified ways to die. Buntz frowned. Was there a dignified way to die in the middle of a war? Probably not, he decided. Buntz waddled to the empty doorway and peered out. He could see a pile of smoking rubble where the entrance to his beloved stores building had been. Those bastards had blown it to pieces.

There was a whistling sound overhead, and Buntz looked up to see a fresh cluster of black shapes tumbling out of the sky, headed directly for the latrine. Grabbing hold of his still unfastened trousers, he started running for what was left of the stores. Somehow his mind had emptied itself and all he could think was how bombs never struck the same thing twice. It was only as Buntz reached the remains of his domain that he remembered it was lightning that was never supposed to strike twice in the same place, and even that wasn't true. His Uncle Bob got hit by lightning twice on the same golf course one summer. Of course, it never happened again, thanks to Uncle Bob being dead and all.

Buntz couldn't resist one last look back as the first bomb hit the latrine. The building exploded in a ball of fire, its detonation showering everything nearby with a torrential downpour of excrement. The blast threw Buntz inside the stores, and flung a wall of human bodily waste in after him. He survived the impact, but nearly choked to death on what he swallowed. The obese private coughed and spat, desperately trying to clear his throat. When he was able to speak at last, two words escaped his lips: "Aw, shit."

"SWEET JESUS, THEY just blew up the latrine," Wierzbowski whispered in disbelief. He'd gotten out of bed and was crouching on one side of a window in the hospital ward. Father Kelly was on the other side of the window, also looking out at the devastation being wrought by the enemy's bombs. "Forgive me, father, I didn't mean to take the Lord's name in vain."

The priest waved away his apology. "Don't worry about it, son. I was thinking much the same myself, although not in those same words."

So far the hospital had escaped the Japanese bombardment, but it was only a matter of time before it too suffered from the onslaught. Nobody had thought to put a Red Cross symbol on the roof, and no one was sure if the enemy would take any notice of such a display. For all those inside the hospital knew, the Japanese might consider that a provocation. Wierzbowski realised he had next to no understanding of the enemy or what it wanted from starting a war. I'm a soldier, he decided, just another grunt on the frontline. I don't need to know the reasons why we're at war; it's enough to know that we are. Enough to know I can kill as many of them as I want, and people will call me a hero instead of a murderer. He smiled, enjoying the realisation.

"What's happening out there?" Wierzbowski turned to see Nurse Baker, no, she was Nurse Martinez now, scuttling towards them, staying down in a low crouch to keep herself out of harm's way.

"They've been bombing Clark Field to bits for half an hour at least, and now the Japs are starting on us," he told her.

"What about our anti-aircraft gunners? Can't they stop them?"

"Not unless the enemy planes come down into range."

The nurse bit her bottom lip. "So Juan and the others are sitting ducks out there, waiting for a chance to fight back."

Father Kelly stretched out a comforting hand. "It'll be all right, Catherine."

She smiled. "Thank you, father, but my first name's Angela."

"Of course it is. Forgive me, my child, I got confused for a moment."

Wierzbowski noticed doubt and distress pass over the priest's face. What was troubling Father Kelly, and who was Catherine?

THE ZEROS HAD been hanging back, watching the Mitsubishis bombarding the American airstrip and base below. The fighters had come on the mission principally as escorts for the bombers, ready to protect them from a counterattack by US planes, but less than a handful of Americans had gotten off the ground as the bombing began, and they were soon driven away. As long as the Zeros stayed above the maximum range of the anti-aircraft guns below, they need not sustain any damage or losses. But where was the satisfaction in flying this far, only to watch the bombers have all the fun?

Otomo was bored. He'd been as patient as he could be, staying out of danger and fulfilling his duties as fighter escort, but his impetuous nature eventually got the better of him. He called Suzuki on the radio, using the special frequency reserved for the kyuuketsuki fliers. "Permission to go down and engage the enemy directly, sir!"

"Not yet, Otomo," his sire replied. "We've been ordered to wait until the bombing runs are complete. Once that happens, you can have all the sport you want with the Americans. Until it does, you'll be putting yourself and your aircraft in danger. You could even jeopardise the mission."

"Please, sir, tell me you don't believe that."

Suzuki hesitated before replying. "In truth, no, I don't, but this is our first mission. We have to prove our worth, both to the doubters among the imperial fliers and to our leader. Hitori expects–"

"Commander Hitori isn't here," Otomo snapped. "I'm going in!"

"Otomo, don't! We need to–"

But Otomo wasn't listening anymore. He removed his flying helmet with the radio earphones inside and put his Zero into a steep dive, savouring the sensation as it accelerated towards the US base below. He would show the Americans why they should fear the kyuuketsuki. He would make them quake in their boots, show them how feeble and weak their forces were, and what a powerful enemy they had made in the empire. He would show them all.

"SARGE! SARGE, HERE they come!" Martinez was looking at the sun, stabbing a finger at the sky. "This is our chance to fight back."

Aimes squinted up into the heavens. It was hard to see anything through the clouds of thick, black smoke floating past, but there was a shape getting bigger as it got closer, and it was no bomb. "Martinez is right! Everybody, get back to the gun, now! Those yellow bastards have been blowing us to pieces. Let's show them we ain't licked yet, not by a long way."

The artillery unit was up off the dirt in seconds, every man running for the anti-aircraft gun nearby. All those months of training and drilling that Aimes had made them do, all those exercises and repetitions they had endured while the sergeant snarled at

them and cursed their efforts had all been leading to
this. While other artillery teams around them were
still hugging the ground, Martinez and his brothers
in arms were loading their weapon and getting ready
to fire. Aimes suppressed a smile of pride at their
precision. There'd be time for that later, so long as
they survived the rest of the day.

"Director team, what's the range?" he barked.

"Damn thing's coming in too fast to get a good
fix."

"Anticipate, man, anticipate! Give us your best
guess."

The soldier manning the director bellowed calcu-
lations to the crew on the gun. They responded
within moments, adjusting the position of their
barrel to take account of the rapidly approaching
Zero's changing position overhead.

"Ready to fire?" Aimes demanded.

"Nearly," Martinez yelled back.

"Nearly's not good enough, damn you! Fire!"

"Fire!" Martinez echoed. The three-inch gun
blasted a hole in the sky, but its projectile exploded
above and beyond the Zero. "Too high!"

"Reload!" Aimes snarled. "Damn it, reload and
fire again."

OTOMO LAUGHED AS the puny Americans below tried
to blow him out of the heavens. The first flak
scudded past him, detonating uselessly where his
Zero had already been. These fools were no match
for his expertise. Vampyr or not, Otomo had always
been the best pilot wherever he was: in training, on
manoeuvres, on board the Akagi. Soon the whole

world would know his name: Otomo, the great flying ace of the Pacific; Otomo, the Japanese pilot who single-handedly changed the course of the war. Otomo–

More American flak shot by his cockpit, fizzing through the air as it passed, but the second attempt was closer, much closer. The Zero jumped and juddered as it accelerated towards the ground, the controls dancing in Otomo's hands. He couldn't understand the sudden change, not until he twisted his head around and saw the flames on his tail through the canopy's tinted glass. The Americans had got lucky and now his Zero was like some crazed creature. Otomo had once watched a film from America about men called cowboys who tamed horses and herded cattle. His plane was like a wild animal, fighting with him for mastery. They did battle as the ground got closer and closer.

Otomo realised how close he was to the deck and wrenched backwards on his controls, determined not to be beaten in his first attack. He saw the anti-aircraft gun emplacement that had humbled him and swore a quiet vengeance against them. Otomo opened fire with his twin 7.7 mm machine guns, savouring the moment as battle was joined. "Fear me," he whispered.

TWO LINES OF bullets strafed the anti-aircraft team as the Zero shot past, pulling up its nose just in time to avoid flying straight into the ground. Martinez heard men cry out in pain, as the enemy's bullets found their targets. Something hot and wet spattered his face on one side, while a pink aerosol choked his breath, making him gasp for air. The recruit looked around to see three corpses on the ground and another man dying beside them: Aimes. Martinez dived across to the sergeant, who was coughing blood, his teeth flecked crimson. An angry red stain was spreading across Aimes's chest. "Medic!" Martinez yelled, straining to be heard over the cacophony of anti-aircraft guns, explosions and men sobbing. "We need a medic over here!"

The sergeant coughed another mouthful of blood, spitting it out to clear his throat. "Did we get him? Did we kill the bastard?"

Martinez had seen the Zero fly past, its tail on fire. "Yeah, we got him, sarge. Don't know if we killed him, but we hit him all right. That's one Zero that won't be making it back to the land of the rising sun."

Grim satisfaction spread across the sergeant's face. "You take over."

"I can't," Martinez protested, "I'm just a grunt."

"You'll do," Aimes replied. He coughed again and was gone.

OTOMO GRIMACED. HE'D wrestled with his Zero and won back sufficient command of the plane to keep both of them in the sky, but little more. The controls were a mess, more flak had blown a hole in his canopy, and shafts of sunlight kept seeping inside, setting his face on fire. The rest of his body was safely covered by the flight suit, but his chin and cheeks were exposed. Otomo screamed in frustration and felt his tongue catch fire, flames licking the inside of his mouth. He'd never make it back to

Taiwan in his shattered, battered Zero, let alone safely land the plane's remains.

The pilot had switched his radio back on and, against the odds, found that it was still working. The earphones in his flying helmet crackled into life, static mixing with Suzuki's voice, the words fading in and out. "Otomo, are you all right? Otomo, can you hear me? Respond!"

"I hear you," he replied, struggling to speak at all.

"Status report, now!"

"Doomed," Omoto said, "but I'm taking them with me."

"No, Otomo, you–" The radio died as electrical explosions danced around the cockpit, incinerating the controls. Otomo tried to slap the fires out with his gloved hands, but there were too many. His Zero was little more than a brick in the sky, searching for a final, fatal resting place.

The pilot punched a hole in the black glass in front of him, squinting to see through the sunshine where he could die. A two-storey building loomed ahead, the largest structure within what few moments he had left. Otomo gave the controls a last, savage jerk and flew his plane at the side of the hospital, emptying the twin machine guns into the windows ahead of him.

FATHER KELLY FLUNG himself out of the way as bullets shattered all the windows on one side of the ward, but Wierzbowski wasn't so fast. Maybe it was curiosity that made him linger on his feet, or maybe the malaria had slowed his reactions. Whatever the cause, the patient was still standing when the suicidal

Zero attacked the hospital. The priest tried to pull Wierzbowski down to the floor, but it was too little, too late. The patient's body jerked and spasmed, spatters of blood bursting from the bullet impacts, before he toppled over like some mighty tree. Wierzbowski smacked face first into the floor, his skull resounding with a dull thud as it hit.

The priest could only watch, fear freezing his limbs and his will. "I need a nurse here," he said, his voice little more than a whisper. Realising that nobody had heard, Father Kelly tried again, louder this time. He saw Nurse Martinez respond, getting up from behind the sandbags where she's taken shelter. He saw the Zero suddenly filling the windows of the hospital. And he saw the screaming face of the Japanese pilot, his features burning with white flames.

Then the plane flung itself into the building.

Suzuki watched Otomo's downfall with mute resignation. The pilot had been his best recruit, the finest flier among them all. But Otomo knew his own strengths all too well and they had made him arrogant. The pilot believed he was invincible before he was made a vampyr. Adding the promise of immortality to his abilities made that arrogance worse, not better.

Suzuki watched as the Zero caught fire, saw it skittering over the anti-aircraft units on the ground, and witnessed the plane's last moments before it flew into the side of a building, blowing like some merciless, divine wind of fury. "Otomo's dead," Suzuki announced to the other kyuuketsuki. "He ignored orders to chase glory and paid with his life. Let that be a lesson to you all."

"What do we do now, sir?" one of the other vampyr pilots asked.

"We avenge him!"

MARTINEZ DIDN'T NOTICE that the hospital was on fire, he was too busy directing the anti-aircraft gun's fire. The lone Zero had been one target, making it much easier to focus. Now half a dozen fights were diving towards the unit, black wraiths against the early afternoon sky, taking up a V formation. Above them he could make out more Zeros turning over, starting their attack runs on the base. There must be nearly a hundred of them, he realised.

"Here they come!" he shouted. "Let's send the bastards straight back to hell where they belong. Fire!" Martinez watched as his men blasted their weapon at the enemy, taking out another Zero with their first shot. But the rest of the black planes were too fast, coming in too steeply for the artillery unit to get a good fix on their trajectory. They swooped down, strafing the artillery battery before scudding past. Martinez watched them go, noticing the tinted black glass of the cockpits and the strange insignia on the side of each Zero, of a bat clutching the rising sun in its talons. Then they were gone, already well past the anti-aircraft gunners, and a fresh wave of Zeros was coming in.

FATHER KELLY OPENED his eyes and saw Catherine standing in front of him. She smiled, that same sweet smile he'd fallen in love with. "Make love to me," she'd once whispered to him, and he had, though it shamed him to admit it. When he had realised his mistake and told her it couldn't happen again, could never happen again, Catherine had come apart. She had threatened to tell her family, tell the archbishop what Father Kelly had done. When that didn't work–

"I'm sorry," the priest told her. "I'm so sorry."

She smiled at him, even as the shrapnel tore through her body. It carried her across the ward, pinning her to the far wall. Even then she didn't scream, didn't cry out. Her lips moved, but only blood came out of them.

Father Kelly blinked and realised that it was Nurse Martinez on the wall, a massive shard of burnt metal protruding from her abdomen. He scrambled across the rubble and chunks of burnt, smouldering flesh to reach her, unsure whose corpse he was stepping on. Something exploded nearby, making him flinch, but the priest kept going. His years of training and routine drove him forward, despite the danger and the carnage, and the howling in his ears.

The priest reached Nurse Martinez and took hold of her hand, touching the wedding ring that had been on her finger for less than a day. "Angela, can you hear me? It's Father Kelly. I'm going to give you the last rites. Give me some sign, so I know you can understand what I'm saying."

The beautiful nurse blinked at him. One of her eyes was filled with blood and the other had something embedded in it, but she still blinked at him.

"Listen to me, my child. God knows your sins, he knows all of our sins, and he knows that we're sorry. He forgives you your sins, Angela. You are free of all your worldly cares and worries. No more tears, no more pain. Go to God now, and be with him in Heaven. Be at peace, my child." Father Kelly made the sign of the cross and mumbled the Latin phrases to commit her soul into God's holy care. "Amen."

She blinked again, a single tear of blood seeping from one eye. The nurse opened her lips and whispered something that Father Kelly couldn't hear. He leaned closer, tilting his head to one side. "Tell... Juan... I love..."

Then she said no more.

To THE EAST, Pearl Harbour was still burning when the Japanese broke off their attack on the Philippines. It was late afternoon on Oahu by the time Marquez found his way to the landing strip on Ford Island. Of the eighteen SBDs that left the *Enterprise* that morning on a routine scouting mission, at least seven had been shot down or had crash landed. Exact numbers were not yet known as communications had broken down with several outlying landing strips on Oahu, including Kaneohe and Haleiwa Field. It was hoped that some of the unaccounted for planes had sought refuge from enemy fighters and friendly fire elsewhere in Hawaii, but nobody knew for sure.

Marquez found Lieutenant Richards being tended by a medic at Ford Island, having suffered burns to his hands and face after his SBD had caught fire. Bravo had already refuelled and taken on board fresh ammunition before flying off in search of any remaining enemy planes still haunting the skies over Oahu. "He's claiming two kills," Chuck said, wincing as more bandages were wrapped around his scorched hands. "Nobody saw them, so I guess we'll have to take his word for it, but I've got my doubts."

Marquez grimaced. "He's determined to grab all the glory, isn't he?"

The lieutenant nodded. "We'll see how glorious Bravo looks after I give evidence about him abandoning his wingman when he left the Big E this morning. Coker got picked off by four Zeros near Barber Point. That wouldn't have happened if Bravo had stayed in formation. Coker was young, he didn't know any better. Bravo's a damned menace to everyone in the air group. But we lost so many good pilots today that they'll probably let him off with a slap on the wrist. As far as Bravo's concerned, that's next door to a commendation."

Marquez nodded. "Look, lieutenant, I wanted to say thanks. You saved my butt after I had to bail out over the harbour." He detailed his narrow escape from the Kate strafing survivors in the water. "I'd be dead if it wasn't for you."

"I'm sure you'll do the same for me one day," Chuck said. He noticed the younger pilot grinning. "What's so damned funny?"

"I was remembering what I said this morning, before we took off from the *Enterprise*, how all the waiting around was driving me crazy."

Chuck nodded. "I also told you there'd be plenty of war to go around."

"You still think we'll crush 'em in weeks?"

The lieutenant frowned. "Not now. From what I've seen today, most of the ships anchored at Pearl got the crap blown out of them by the Japanese. It'll take months to get some of them refitted and ready for action, and too many of the others are nothing but history. We're lucky all the aircraft carriers were out at sea, otherwise the navy would hardly have a fleet in the Pacific still worthy of the name. Coming back from today, it'll take time."

A radio operator ran into the medical bay. "You seen the commander?"

The medic tending Chuck shook his head. "Not since breakfast, why?"

"Admiral Kimmel's called an emergency meeting of all command staff from across Oahu. Pearl's not the only place the Japs have hit. We're getting reports of attacks on the Philippines, Wake Island and Malaya. Word is there are invasion forces moving to occupy Guam and God alone knows where else. They're all in for it." When the radio operator had gone, the three men he left behind looked at each other, absorbing the meaning of his words.

Marquez broke the silence. "I guess you were right, Chuck. There's gonna be plenty of war to go around before this is over."

"God help us all," the lieutenant muttered.

SUZUKI AND HIS kyuuketsuki strafed Fort Stotsenberg again and again, making numerous passes over the base while machine-gunning anything that moved below them. The other Zeros followed their example, seeking to emulate the merciless savagery of the black fighters. The kyuuketsuki peeled away from the target only after exhausting their ammunition, Suzuki leading them back towards Taiwan. But for the loss of Otomo, the mission had been an unqualified success. May all our battles be this simple, Suzuki thought.

PRIVATE MAEDA WOKE in a makeshift bed, surrounded by dozens of other wounded marines. Maeda looked around and realised that they were inside the non-commissioned officer's club near the navy yard at Pearl. He tried to sit up but dizziness forced him back down into bad. A medical orderly noticed that Maeda was conscious and came over to examine him. "How are you feeling?"

"Like someone drop-kicked my butt from here to Honolulu and back again. What the hell happened?" Maeda asked. He glanced at the wounded on either side of him, but did not recognise either man. They must be A Company, he reasoned, otherwise I'd know them. Then again, the bandages covering most of their faces made it hard to tell. Maeda reached a hand up to his own features and was relieved to find no dressings or absences, everything still in its proper place on his face.

"I'm told they found you on the barracks roof, under the body of another marine. The two of you had been manning a machine gun."

"The body of–" Maeda said, before his memory came flooding back in bits and pieces. "Walton, is he all right? Is he here?"

The medic shook his head. "I'm sorry, he... He didn't make it."

Not after I used his body as a human shield, the marine thought, but he kept that to himself. "The Japanese, the attack, what happened?"

"Nobody's too sure yet, but Pearl wasn't the only place they hit."

"San Francisco?" Maeda asked, suddenly worried in case his parents were in harm's way on the mainland.

"No, no, Pearl's as far east as the Japs came. Mostly they've been hitting places like Malaya and the Philippines," the medic reassured him.

The marine breathed a little easier. The rest of the family was safe, for now. But who knew how long the conflict would last, or how far the Japanese would get before somebody stopped them? Another worry hit Maeda. How would people on the mainland react to the surprise attack on Pearl Harbour? How would his parents cope as expatriate Japanese on American soil? He needed to get in touch with them, to find out what was happening back home. But try as he might, his strength had deserted him. "I can't seem to sit up," he told the medic. God, don't let me be paralysed, Maeda thought.

"Better if you don't try for a few days. The doctors managed to get most of the bullets out and re-inflate your lung, but it was touch and go for a while."

"My lung?"

"The right one collapsed after a bullet passed through it. You also suffered wounds to the right shoulder and both your legs."

"My legs..." Maeda realised there was a canopy over the bottom half of his body, shielding his legs from view. "I can't feel my legs!"

"It's okay," the medic reassured him. "Don't worry, they're still there. You're pretty heavily sedated for the pain, so you won't feel much of anything for the next few days. After that... Well, it's a case of wait and see."

"Will I walk again?"

The medic smiled. "You'll be in plaster for a month, and using crutches for a while after that, but the doctors expect you to make a full and complete recovery." Another patient among the wounded nearby cried out, his pain all too audible in the normally cheery clubroom. "Look, I've got other guys I need to check up on," the medic said, already walking away. "I'll come back and see how you're doing later, okay?"

Maeda nodded, a sudden wave of exhaustion washing over him. He had no idea how many hours must have passed since he blacked out on the roof, but it was dark outside the windows. That meant it was night. Maeda brushed a hand across his jaw but found no stubble, so it was probably still Sunday. Twelve, maybe fifteen hours ago he'd been in the captain's office, waiting to face charges for helping Paxton go AWOL. Where was Paxton now? And what had happened to Sergeant Hicks? Maeda cursed himself for not thinking of them sooner, when he could have asked the medic for news.

"Lying down on the job as usual?" a familiar voice asked.

Maeda saw Paxton approaching, picking his way through the rows and rows of cots sprawled around the NCO's club. "That's rich coming from a guy who left me in the lurch to chase a girl called Kissy." The wounded marine waited until Paxton had reached his bed before asking how his comrade had gotten back on base. "Don't tell me, you snuck in while everyone else was busy fighting the Japs, right? Nobody even noticed."

"Not exactly," Paxton replied. He explained about the captain's amnesty and his suspended punishment. "I guess that applies to you, too. The captain said Piper blamed you for helping me get away."

"Piper, that asshole! He'd report his own mother if she broke regs."

"Not now," Paxton said. "Piper got blown up by the Japs in the first attack wave. One of the doctors told me he died an hour ago."

"Oh," Maeda replied, wishing he could take back what he'd said, "sorry."

"Hey, no skin off my chin. Besides, you're right, Piper was an asshole. I'm sorry he's dead and all, but we weren't exactly the best of friends. Way I figure it, there's no point crying over dead people that I never cared about much while they were still alive, right?"

Maeda rolled his eyes at Paxton's attitude. "What about the sarge?"

"Still alive and kicking, unfortunately: large as life, and twice as ugly."

"No change there, then. He's gonna make life hell for us, isn't he?"

"Oh yeah. We're marked men, as far as he's concerned," Paxton agreed.

Maeda could feel his energy seeping away. "You heard about Walton?"

The other marine nodded. "I also heard tell you brought down a Zero."

"We both did. I couldn't have done it without Walton. He was terrified, but he still came with me up onto the barracks' roof. He didn't flinch, not once, not even when..." Maeda's voice faded as tiredness swamped him.

"You look done in," Paxton observed. "I'll go, let you get some rest. Medics say you'll be up and about before you know it."

"Great. I can't wait."

Paxton gave Maeda's left hand a friendly squeeze. "Thanks for saying what you did to Piper. Most people in the unit wouldn't do that for me, and I appreciate it. From now on, I've got your back, come hell or high water."

Maeda couldn't help smiling. "We're marines, remember? Before all of this is over I'm guessing we can expect to see plenty of both." Sleep took him, its black embrace darker than any eclipse. But Maeda's slumber would be restless, haunted by the sounds of Zeros flying by, mingled with Walton's screams.

ONLY AFTER THE final Japanese aircraft had flown away did the survivors at Clark Field and Fort Stotsenberg have a chance to take in the enormity of what had happened. The runways were destroyed, littered with the burning wrecks of broken, blasted B-17s and P-40s. The barracks at Fort Stotsenberg were half a mile away from the airfield, but they had suffered just as badly. Half of Stores was gone, blown apart by enemy bombs, while the base hospital was a mess. The suicidal Zero had devastated the first floor, collapsing part of the roof and smashing in the western wall.

It was Father Kelly who came and found Martinez, and told him about Angela. The priest was covered in grey dust, the only clean areas on his face where tears had washed away the grime. Martinez couldn't stop looking at the priest's hands, stained burgundy by dried blood, as Father Kelly recounted what had happened to Angela. "Her final words were 'Tell Juan I love him'. She died thinking of you. She didn't suffer, I don't think. One of the doctors said the shrapnel severed her spine, she wouldn't have felt a thing after that."

"I want to see her," Martinez muttered.

"Juan, I don't think that's a good idea. Give the other nurses a chance to clean her up. You don't want to remember Angela as she is now."

"I need to see her!" Martinez howled, before collapsing into tears. The priest embraced him, patting the shell-shocked soldier on the back.

"In good time," Father Kelly said. "You'll see her in good time."

WIERZBOWSKI AND BUNTZ were waiting for Martinez when Father Kelly brought him to the hospital. The doctors had patched up Wierzbowski with temporary dressings over his bullet wounds. The bloody bandages reminded Martinez of the bright red poinsettia flowers his mother loved to grow, back home in New Mexico. Buntz had climbed out of the bomb-blasted Stores building after the enemy attack was over, little the worse for his brush with death. He

and Wierzbowski nodded to Martinez, neither of
them finding any words to speak.

"She's through here," Father Kelly said, ushering
Martinez through a door and along a corridor. They
passed a large pile of discarded uniforms covered
with blood and dirt. A soldier's helmet sat to one
side of the debris, the metal crumpled like a discarded love letter. Martinez couldn't help wondering
whose head had been inside that helmet. Was it one
of his unit? They had lost half a dozen good men to
Japanese bullets and bombs, not counting Sergeant
Aimes. It was hard to imagine life without his rat-a-
tat-tat voice barking orders at them, berating their
efforts to match his standards.

The priest stopped outside a closed door and
knocked on the blank wood. It opened and two
nurses emerged, their faces hollow and numb. One
of them was Ruth, who had been Angela's best
friend among all the hospital staff. She looked right
through Martinez, not even recognising him. When
the nurses had gone, Father Kelly patted the young
soldier on the back.

"You can go in now, son."

HITORI STOOD ON the edge of the aircraft carrier,
watching the white caps on the waves below as twilight settled over the Pacific. He wondered how
Suzuki and the other kyuuketsuki fliers had fared on
their mission to the Philippines. No doubt there
would be losses, but he hoped they had acquitted
themselves well against the enemy's guns and
grunts. Kimura had proven himself an able lieutenant on Oahu, though he displayed a sadistic

streak that troubled Hitori. Would each successive generation of vampyrs be more violent, more brutal than the last? If that were so, what future would they have in the Japanese Empire's war with the Americans? Yes, the kyuuketsuki had sacrificed much in the service of the emperor, but did that also mean sacrificing their humanity?

Something else was troubling him, something Constanta had said as they had stood on that balcony in Tokyo, three months ago. Hitori shook his head, unable to believe so little time had passed since he had become a vampyr; it felt more like a lifetime, a lifetime of lifetimes. How long would eternity feel if these three months were anything to go by? But there was no use wondering over such enigmas. He had more urgent issues to address than eternity.

"When the war of the humans is over, the vampyr nation will rise up to start a new war, the war of blood, a crimson conflict to decide the future of the world. We shall take our rightful place as the dominant species. Humans will be to us as cattle are to humans: fodder, nothing more, nothing less." Those had been Constanta's words, and at the time Hitori had not questioned them. Standing in the presence of his sire was intoxicating, like drinking too much warm sake on a hot night. Now he had seen the consequences of his deal with that devil and borne witness to his own animal savagery.

Imagine a world where there are thousands of vampyrs like me, Hitori thought, swarming across cities and continents. It was one thing to use the worst weapons imaginable to win a war, but what about during peacetime? He was building an army of kyuuketsuki, vampyr samurai more brutal than any fighting force seen in history. What happened when the war for the Pacific was over? What would be their next target? Hitori shook his head. As a soldier, he'd learned not to care about faceless civilians, they were the enemy and that was all, but what about his wife, Aiko, and their son Noriyuki? What would happen to them during Constanta's unholy war of blood?

His thoughts were interrupted by the sound of Kimura's footfalls. "Quite a day," his lieutenant commented, joining him at the ship's edge.

"Quite a day," Hitori agreed. "History in the making."

"And we were there! We fought the enemy at Pearl Harbour as our bombs pummelled their navy into submission. According to what I've heard from our pilots, the Americans don't have a fleet anymore; the Pacific is ours for the taking. This war could be over within a few months."

"Don't be so certain, Kimura. The Americans I encountered on Oahu were many things, venal, proud, cowardly, brave, but they weren't very different from our own people. We Japanese believe ourselves superior to them, grandly saying we have an empire. When I looked inside the minds of the Americans, I saw that they believed much the same about themselves. To them, we are little yellow men, a race of tiny and insignificant people."

"But they must know differently after today? We destroyed their navy, and attacked their islands with impunity. We proved our superiority today."

"Perhaps, but I fear we may have merely woken a slumbering giant, forcing it to pay attention to what's happening across the world. Once that giant puts on its armour, America will not be so easily undone again. What we did today was sting a mighty beast. I fear the retribution for hurting its pride will be terrible and relentless."

"But surely–" Kimura protested, before a gesture silenced him.

"Trust me," Hitori said, "the war for the Pacific has only just begun. I'm certain we shall play an important part in the years to come, the battles ahead."

ABOUT THE AUTHOR

Fiends of the Rising Sun is
David Bishop's tenth book for Black
Flame and his eighteenth published novel.
Born and raised in New Zealand, he
worked as a daily newspaper journalist for
five years before moving to the UK. After
a decade editing such acclaimed comics
as *2000 AD* and the *Judge Dredd
Megazine*, he quit to go freelance and
moved even further north to Scotland.
Besides being a prolific scribe of pulp
fiction novels, Bishop also writes scripts
for radio drama, comics, computer games
and articles for magazines.
The long-awaited book of his definitive
2000 AD history, *Thrill-Power Overload*, is
being published during 2007.